T5-CVG-765

Falling Up the Stairs

JAMES LILEKS

Falling Up the Stairs

E. P. DUTTON NEW YORK

Publisher's Note: This novel is a work of fiction.
Names, characters, places, and incidents either are the product
of the author's imagination or are used fictitiously, and any
resemblance to actual persons, living or dead, events,
or locales is entirely coincidental.

Published in the United States by E. P. Dutton,
a division of NAL Penguin Inc.,
2 Park Avenue, New York, N.Y. 10016.

Published simultaneously in Canada by
Fitzhenry and Whiteside, Limited, Toronto.

Library of Congress Cataloging-in-Publication Data

Lileks, James.
Falling up the stairs / James Lileks. — 1st ed
p. cm.
ISBN 0-525-24655-X
I. Title.
PS3562.I4547F3 1988
813'.54—dc19 88-2433
CIP

Designed by Earl Tidwell

1 3 5 7 9 10 8 6 4 2

First Edition

For my parents

I wish to thank Victoria Sloan, Craig Cox, Jonathon and Wendy Lazear, and everyone in Minneapolis–St. Paul whose support and kind attention has kept me writing for the last ten years.

PART I

Purgatorio

1

The last time I tried to quit my job I was turned down—on the grounds that I was incompetent. My resignation letter was returned with editing marks circling the typos, inventive spellings, infinitives split so wide they would never heal. It was all rather embarrassing, considering that I was a writer for a newspaper. Carver, my boss, told me I'd have to try harder if I wanted to quit, and that was the end of my resignation.

I had every reason to quit and leave town. I hated my job. I had no enthusiasm for anything, and consequently laundry was starting to pile up. It wasn't that I was tired of life, really—just my own. Other people's lives seemed perfectly worthwhile, and only the logistical difficulty of assuming them and the likelihood of being caught kept me from concocting some sort of swap. The morning of Trygve's visit, however, I'd had a night of long thick sleep, rocked and cosseted by pleasant dreams of love and success; waking was like being unrolled from a bolt of flannel into a bed of roses and feathers. I opened my eyes and smiled and started looking forward to things. I turned to tell Jane about it.

She didn't respond, which was typical of her in the morning. More so since she had packed and left, seven months before.

I sat up and looked at my clock. Almost eleven. Apparently I had looked so sweet while I slept the alarm hadn't had the heart to wake me. I was late for work, very late.

That was the morning the bee landed on my neck.

There was a hive somewhere in the yard, and its inhabitants generally behaved. But the previous night I had set out a month's accumulation of aluminum cans for recycling, most of them soda cans, quite a few containing a half inch of liquid. The soda attracted the bees. They fed on the artificial sweeteners and mutated into beings of canny and perverse intelligence, the caffeine honing their will to the sharpness of a martyr's. In the dark they stood on one another's shoulders until one of their number could reach the doorknob.

The bee chosen for the mission waited until the next morning to bite me. I was shaving my dimple, which is a little like painting a golf ball after it has rolled into the cup. I felt a tickle on my neck. Then something skewered a pore with what felt like a twenty-gauge auger dipped in sulfuric acid. I shrieked a high C and clawed at my neck, coming away with segments of bee in each hand. The bee buzzed something untranslatable, and I fluttered my hands like a distraught maître d', scattering portions of bee onto the counter. I tried to remember if I was allergic to stings, if the morning would end with me clawing the phone with clammy hands, sliding headfirst into a coma. The bee, meanwhile, with the typical insect nonchalance toward dismemberment, was waving its legs about distractedly, like a man dreaming of flagging down a hotdog vendor at a ball game. I grabbed the nearest can of poison, a can of hair spray, and lacquered the creature to the Formica, and then beat it into bee puree with the butt of a hairbrush.

I turned to the mirror, a feral snarl on my face, only to notice that I had nicked a substantial divot from my cheek when the bee gave me the business. Blood was trickling down my chin and beading on my jaw, and I had to do some work in the stanching department before I became too faint from lack of blood to notice the coma. I groped in the medicine cabinet for a styptic pencil and daubed at the wound, wincing in preparation for the sting. It didn't sting. I looked in the mirror to see an attractive trail of blue-hued blood sliding down my face. I looked at the pencil: one of Jane's eye pencils.

Another item for the museum. She'd also left without her toothbrush. I lay awake nights worrying about her tartar buildup.

I stuck a scrap of tissue on my face. Took a deep breath. Applied antiseptic to my neck and picked up the razor. My hands were shaking, but that was no problem; all I had left to do here was drag sharp metal over crucial veins. Shaving completed, I rubbed moisturizer on my face. It was another of Jane's unguents, this one a substance she had put on her legs after shaving. If my face felt as good as her legs I would be in fine shape. I walked unsteadily to the bedroom and put on a shirt. The top button would not fasten for the welt on my neck. It was now about eleven. I had to get to work. First, however, breakfast.

The kitchen was proof that the universe leans toward disorder. I am as good a cook as I am a housekeeper, which is to say that I spend more on antacids than detergent. Starting every meal is a challenge. First off, there is the matter of finding a clean plate; the sink was choked with settings for fifteen, fusty encrustations on each that would take elbow grease and an hour of sandblasting to remove. The sink itself was lined with what looked like elbow grease. The jumble of dishes looked as though they had dived there in some mad competition to reach the drain. About two dozen cups sat on the rim of the sink, an inch or so of sludge the color of old boots in each, flies strolling around one or two of the more venerable examples. Cutlery jutted up from cloudy glasses, mostly forks and knives. The spoons would be long at the bottom, meals from a bowl being the first recourse of the single man. The sight of this put a boot in my appetite's face.

I opened the fridge to find a carton of instant quiche. I took it out and looked at the expiration date. Yesterday. Eleven hours ago. Unless the thing was quartz-timed I could probably slip under the deadline, but only if I moved fast. Ahh, to hell with it, I decided. There would be a tray of something stale and sweet and fried at the office. I made coffee, standing over the machine until it spat out the last few drops.

I poured a cup, went into the living room, lit a cigarette and coughed bitterly. I had to quit. Every morning I sounded like I had just been pulled from the sea. But thirty more cartons and I'd have enough coupons for the golf clubs, or the iron lung. The last few months had seen some heavy coupon accumulation. When Jane and I had had problems before, I smoked my way to one free cup and matching saucer per spat; but after she left I was soon up to an entire place setting by five P.M. The present cigarette made me feel lousy, and in general I felt as poorly as I ever had. Not death warmed over but cold and coagulating in a broken microwave. Maybe if I didn't show up they would finally fire me. There was hope, after all.

Then the doorbell rang, and I groaned. It was a series of chimes installed by the previous tenants; it played "shave and a haircut" but omitted "two bits." No one ever entered this house without looking slightly ill at ease. I looked through the peephole and saw a man hunched with age, a wisp of gray hair circling his bald head as though he were wearing a smoke ring. His face was sad but used to it, and his eyes looked tired. He looked like a salesman for a long and painless illness. I opened the door.

"Master Jonathan Simpson?" The old man's face sparked to life, and his eyes were those of a child, dazzled by the bauble dangling from the rim of the crib.

"The same."

"I thought you'd be taller." One palm patted his cheek. "You were such a tall boy."

"Do I know you?"

The eyes turned sad. "I had hoped you would remember me. I am Trygve. Your Aunt Marvel's manservant."

I just stared. No words, no thoughts were equal to the event. Trygve. Still alive, and here.

"Do you mind if I come in? There are a lot of bees about out here."

"Trygve. My God. Come in, come in." I waved him inside and he tottered through the door, smiling with a distant look of a pope in a motorcade. He was carrying a hat, which he set on the end table; he made some futile gestures designed to shed his coat, and I helped him take it off. He sat down and patted his knees. I sat down and looked at him, astonished.

"Trygve. God. It's been years."

"It has." He looked around the living room. "Since anything in particular?"

"Since I saw you."

"I know. And you were such a tall boy then."

"Trygve, did, ah, someone drive you here? I mean, did you make it up here alone?"

"No." He looked toward the door. "I'm here on business and if you give me a minute I shall recall just what it is. Could I have a glass of water? My throat is somewhat dry."

I held up a hand and went to the kitchen. I leaned against the door and peered out at Trygve; he was examining his hand as though it were an object he was considering bidding on. I leafed through the catalogue of reasons for Trygve's appearance. I hadn't seen him in years, not since the last time I was at Aunt Marvel's house down in Minneapolis.

House? Hardly. Mad King Ludwig's Bavarian castle was a Levittown tract house compared with this place. Local historical surveys regularly categorized it as one of the "largest" houses in the city, a verdict that tactfully omitted aesthetic judgments. It had been built to the specifications of Billy Marvel, a nineteenth-century timber baron, who had a dream of his own personal Xanadu. Unlike Coleridge, no one had awakened him in the middle of the dream; he slept long enough to imagine every gruesome detail, right down to the cherubims gripped in the rictus of poisoning and holding their stomachs that made for the waterspouts draining the eaves. The house was vaguely Gothic, just as its occupant was vaguely sane; buttresses held up turrets, and gargoyles danced in the tracery of the upper floors. Stained glass panels above the windows in the main living room illustrated scenes in the life of Billy Marvel, including an Annunciation where an angel gestured at a tree with one hand and held out an ax in the other.

I lived there once. A descendant of the primary Marvel had married a Simpson, causing great scandal; she was from the wrong side of the tracks no matter how you gerrymandered the town. She took me in while my parents clawed their way toward a divorce; for while their bitter disputes were over my head, the objects they hurled at one another were not. I spent a year there under her serrating gaze, roaming the clammy halls, shivering in the great vaulted rooms. There was no one with whom to play; for all the phallic totems of the turrets, the Marvel union was childless. Uncle Marvel I recall only as a bleak stumpy figure roaming the house with a snifter in one hand, bashing into the furniture and performing feats highly amusing to an eight-year-old, such as falling into the fireplace. Whenever he used to stroke my head and say he wished I was his child, I had the feeling it was so that he could legally beat me.

My only companion was Trygve, who even then struck me as kind but uncommonly dim. He would tell me stories such as "The Day the Butcher Forgot to Deliver the Roast" that, while lifelike in their excruciating accumulation of detail, lacked dramatic tension and frequently ended in morals such as Always Check Your Monthly Statement. There was also a maid who treated me as though I would steal into her bedroom some night, perch on her chest and steal her breath. And a housekeeper—Grunewald, surely long in the grave by now. When the divorce was settled and my parents, referred to by Aunt Marvel as Gog and Magog, were eternally cloven, I went to live with Ms. Gog and went about bundling the memory of the year into a trunk in the spare mental attic of my childhood.

Now here was Trygve in my living room, twenty-one years later and 120 miles away, older and demonstrably foggier. And thirsty. I pulled a bottle of spring water from the fridge and searched the sink for a glass. They were all opaque with mysterious fluids. I could always fish a Dixie cup from the trash and iron it out. No. I took the bottle out into the living room and handed it to him.

He sipped and beheld the bottle with mild alarm. "Should this have a flavor?"

"No. It's water."

"It behaves like soda."

"It's just springwater."

He sipped. "It's very . . . active. I am used to much calmer water." He took another sip. "Are you certain this isn't champagne?"

I nodded.

"So. Tryg. How's Aunt Marvel."

"She remains dead. That's why we're here. It's about the house." He leaned forward, eyes worried. "You have to come home, Master Simpson. You have to come home and save us."

There was another ring at the door. Trygve looked around the room in confusion, then hummed "two bits" to redress the equilibrium. I got up and looked through the peephole. I saw, distorted through the convex window, a huge cigar with a face hanging on by its teeth at the other end. I opened the door.

"Yeah, you got an old man in there?"

An old vaudeville joke coughed in the wings, and I feared that if I said no he'd offer me one. I answered honestly.

"Well, tell him the meter just hit three bills. If he wants me to wait I'm going to need somethin' up front." I looked over the man's shoulder and saw a taxi sitting at the bottom of the hill.

"Trygve." He tottered over and smiled at the cab driver. "You didn't take a cab up here, did you?"

He nodded. "The car was low on gas, Master Simpson. And I get lost rather easy nowadays. Last week I got lost, where was it I got lost, oh: on the steps. If it weren't for the fact that my feet were pointing to where I was originally bound, I think I should have been completely at sea."

"I was just telling yer friend here," said the cabbie, "that I awready used up the three hunnert you gave me, so I need a, y'know, token of yer goodwill."

"Of course." Trygve pulled out a wallet and leafed through it, producing three bills of generous denomination. He handed these to the cabbie, but I intercepted.

The cabbie beheld me with no great love. "You'll get the money when he gets in the cab," I said.

"Suit yerself. The meter's still running. As long as Pops has the scratch, you guys can start a game of Monopoly for all I care." And he turned and huffed his way down the steps.

I shut the door and helped Trygve back to his chair.

"Trygve, what are you doing here? Why did you take a cab? You could've called."

"Oh, but I did. I kept getting a recording. There have been lawyers writing as well but you haven't written back." I had been receiving letters from a Minneapolis law firm but had ignored them, thinking them dunning letters for old student loans. "I had to come up and talk to you. You heard, of course, about Madame Marvel."

"Did I hear you say she *died*?"

"Yes. She fell up the stairs."

"You mean down."

"Up, I'm afraid. You recall that chair she had on the stairs?" Did I. Aunt Marvel was subject to dizzy spells, and between her twirling theatrically onto the floor and Uncle Marvel thudding drunkenly into the doorframes, I had been given an almost preternatural aversion to the sound of bone striking wood. To make certain she did not bounce down the stairs in the midst of one of these spells, she had installed, at considerable expense, an electric chair that ran along the wall of the great curving staircase in the main hall. The sight of Her Sternness, as my mother called her, sliding slowly down the stairs with her gaze fixed on whoever she was coming down to visit, was my first impression of life at Marvel Manor and a persistent motif of my nightmares.

"It was horrible," said Trygve, looking into his bottle. "She had come down the stairs in the chair and was climbing out when she hit the button that turned the chair on. She got her foot caught somehow and it took her up the stairs. Quite against her will, from the sound of it." He shuddered.

"I hope she, ah, died quickly."

"Not at first. But eventually, yes, she did."

I winced. And then I knew why Trygve was here. "She didn't leave me the house, did she?"

Trygve smiled, his eyes all honey and kindness. "Yes. She always remembered you and the time you spent at the house. She called you 'the little ray of sunshine.' " She had hated sunshine. Said it made her old. Heavy curtains barricaded every window. "And she had no children of her own, you know. Very sad. I think she thought of you as her own son and wanted you to see the house was maintained as she would have liked it."

Not damn likely. Trygve was a little off here. She hated the house and more than likely she'd given it to me out of pure, distilled spite. "What about all her money?" I asked Trygve. Might as well act like a son.

"Here and there. Charities, mostly. Although she did remember me."

"How much did she leave you?"

"Three hundred and seventy-five thousand dollars. I am now rich beyond my wilder dreams, Master Simpson. Which is why"—he held up the water bottle—"I think champagne is utterly appropriate."

All I could do was lean over, grab another cigarette, light it and smile at Tryg, digesting. But there was more.

"The reason I'm here," he said, "is to warn you that you might lose the house. You see, your Cousin Oscar is living there. He says he is entitled to the money and the house since he was closest to your aunt in the months before she left us."

I kneaded my forehead. Not Oscar. Not now. Oscar was what happens when you don't clean the weeds from the gene pool every season. "He's going to contest the will? Argue about it, is that what you mean?"

"Yes. He has a very good lawyer too; I've seen his briefcase and it's quite handsome. I know if he gets the house it will be the end of Grue and myself. We shall be thrown out. And if I also lose my money I don't know what we should do. That's why I'm here. You have to help us, Master Simpson. Please make Oscar go. He makes us wait on his hands and feet; he has parties where the police come and take everyone away. Please. If you have any fondness in your heart for your aunt or the house, I beg you to help us."

And he was doing so well until that last line. Still. Oscar's participation in this matter was enough to tell me there was real evil afoot here, cheaply shod though it may have been. Oscar was, essentially, a one-man Nazi-Soviet pact. Last I'd heard he'd been banned from every hospital in town for selling do-it-yourself will kits in the cancer wards.

"All right. I'll try to come down this week." I smiled a smile borrowed from a game-show host, and Trygve clapped his hands.

"Wonderful, Master Simpson. I shall tell Grue to make your room ready. I think it's just as you left it."

Meaning that the *Playboy* purloined from Uncle Marvel was still under the mattress? We'd see. I handed Trygve his hat and helped him clamber back into his coat. I steered him outside and down the steps to the cab, where he climbed into the backseat with the difficulty of an astronaut fitting himself into a space capsule. The cab drove off, Trygve leaning out the window and waving. I was halfway up the stairs before I remembered I had his three hundred dollars in my pocket. Not a bad start for the day after all.

When I got back inside I heard the phone ringing.

"Simpson? That you?" Carver, my boss. I winced, then drew the receiver an inch from my mouth. "I'm sorry, but I can't come to the phone right now. If you'll leave your name and—"

"Cut it. You're late again. You're so late you're almost early for tomorrow. Get your ass in here so I can kick it out the door." He hung up.

I wondered if I'd kept the letters from the lawyers. After a few minutes digging through the bin where I kept bills, I found the letters, buried at the bottom, all bearing postmarks of the previous month.

I read the last one. It expressed concern that I had not yet contacted the law office about these matters unsettled. As the executors of my late aunt's estate they were obligated to inform me of the possible delinquency of several bills regarding the house. There followed a list of bills—water, gas, phone, a lawyer's bill equal to my gross adjusted annual income, a tax assessment equal to the lawyer's bill and, for the final touch, a copy of a letter from the city inspection office detailing the numerous repairs that had to be done to bring the building up to code. From the list of repairs it was obvious that I'd either have to raze the building or convert it into a monastery for those who had renounced modern convenience.

Where was I going to get this kind of money?

Where was I going to get any kind of money?

I thought of the manor and I shivered. Then I stood and slouched my way to the bedroom. I chose my tie like a man who gets to pick the rope by which he is hung and left home for work.

2

It was a ten-minute drive to work. I thought of that every morning I did it on foot. My car was in the shop for repairs on its air conditioning, and I'd have it back in time for winter, when its heating would abandon me. In the meantime I walked everywhere. This morning I was only a half a mile from the house when a passing old farmer with the word *Zeke* stenciled on the side of his truck took pity on me and gave me a ride. He was a grizzled number with a wen on his nose the size of a medicine ball and a wandering eye that clapped on to me the moment I got in and kept me under observation while the other eye handled the driving. There was a gun rack in the back window stocked with three guns, all of which smelled as though they had been recently used. He talked about farming and the damn Jew bankers and the lying media. He asked where I wanted to be left. I chose the local implement dealer, halfway between the bank and the paper, and thanked him with great politeness.

I was working in Valhalla, a town named for the mythological Norse heaven, located in equally mythological northern Minnesota. For a profession I passed as the social editor of the *Lacs Standard*, a daily paper serving the eight-county area and the nine people who lived there. If "social editor" conjures up notions of black-tie soirees bubbling on til dawn, parties borne along on the spume of limitless champagne, of epigrams batted like shuttlecocks across the dinner table, you've never been to northern Minnesota. Up here etiquette is a matter of knowing where not to scratch yourself when the womenfolk are present; and the parties, far from ending at dawn, usually end in gunplay or slide shows. Most of what I reported concerned the doings of good and pious folk. And you know how lively they can be.

Valhalla sat on the edge of Lake Lelac, sliced in two by Highway 11. The highway had been an old county road until it was paved and numbered in the twenties, when the town anticipated a boom as a way station between Minneapolis to the south and the mining districts up north. The town had leaped to the road's edge with cafés and shops, but business never kicked over, and Valhalla leaned back and dissipated like a crowd told the parade has taken a different route. Nowadays there were about five hundred people in town. No crime and less divorce, few children, a plain brick church with a graveyard stocked with sturdy Scandinavian names. Ten miles to the east was the town of Hardwood, or rather AR WOO —several letters had been blown off the sign in various storms. To the south was the town of Prosper, which never did. Jane had been born there.

Lake Lelac was not entirely weeds, but of the purported ten thousand lakes in the state it was one of the least august examples. Quite a few lakes had been mapped and christened by the French, who had wisely decamped before they could hear their language slaughtered by the thick tongues of the Scandinavian immigrants. Lake Lelac indicated that words failed even the French. Lelac means The Lake, making its appellation—Lake the Lake—sound more like some Mafia nickname than a resort. Its primary export was tourists; it drove them away. The water was filled with bloated, rheumy-eyed bullfish, grumpy and bewhiskered like Victorian plutocrats. They were the sort of fish you hit hard on the edge of the boat before you throw them back, just out of aesthetic principle. In the winter there was ice fishing, mostly for the remains of the people who had fallen through the ice the previous winter.

I had come here five years before, eyes glazed and heart addled over a young woman. Jane. We'd met at college, on the school paper, and had a relationship of such depth and intensity I often had to pinch her to make sure I wasn't dreaming. She was from this area, and wanted to come home to work. We both got jobs at the local paper and set up house at the edge of town. Not that we were married or anything. Not that this wasn't a bone of contention the size of a brontosaurus femur.

One night about a year ago she had leaned back after lovemaking and said there had to be a better way of doing this. I asked her if she wanted me to run down to the Ben Franklin and pick up some handcuffs. She didn't laugh. She explained that she was feeling trapped by the town, stultified, hemmed in. I got the point. I have to get out, she said. So do I, I replied. But something told me the two I's were not shaping up to constitute a we.

Within a month rejection letters from various newspapers were appearing in the mailbox. I was hurt. If it was rejection she wanted, I would have been perfectly willing to *pretend* to be formal and merely polite; she didn't have to go looking for it. Then came the firm offers from prospective employers. Then came the rejection of my own firm offers made in the dark at night. Eventually she left me for a job in New York City, professing undying love, explaining that she was, in essence, leaving me for better dental benefits.

I would have gone with her but for two small things: I was at the time under contract to write a monthly feature on rural life for a magazine catering to urban devotees of the rural ideal. My editor, a college friend, requested something "spare-ish, slice-of-life with undertones of angst and alienation." I obliged with a whopper lie every month. Valhallians didn't know from alienation; it was me who held the corner on the angst market around here. I was an outsider. I dressed wrong and I spoke with an even Midwest accent instead of the chunky lumpy vowels of the region's speech. I was just publishing my diary. I was also paid well to do it, so I couldn't leave, not yet. That plus the fact that she didn't ask me to come with her kept me in town.

She called often, at first. She hated New York. It was dirty and the subways smelled awful; the people were brusque and you could hardly see any sky from her window at work. But the people at the office were okay, and there was this one guy, oh, I'd love him. Turned out that in my absence she did it for me—and nightly, from the sound of the end result. She called me one night to tell me she had a cold and a promotion and a ring on her finger.

It was no flash-in-the-pan affair, she assured me; they'd been seeing one another for months. Took a load off the brain, that one did. I drove down to the Hilltop Tavern and bought a bottle of scotch, Clan

Anderson, a local brand, and drove straight home, there to sleep off this nightmare.

For a month I had been pummeling my liver and my ego: the latter battered down to the size of a small, worn stone; the former damn tired of having to translate all these poisons into benign and friendly fluids. This was the month that began with my unacceptable resignation from the paper.

The *Lacs Standard*, pun unintended but woefully accurate, had its offices in a two-story refurbished hotel on the edge of the lake. The lobby still had the ambience of a hotel, the feeling that there was a bellhop waiting perpetually in the wings. Marge, a wizened matchstick in her seventies with thick cloudy lenses interceding between her and reality, gave me a smile, her face looking like a crumpled piece of paper someone had hastily tried to spread out. I winked, leaned against the counter of the front desk and waited for her to dislodge my mail from its narrow slot. Then I went down the hall to the wire machine, still chattering mindlessly away. I put the mail on the machine and looked at the story coming over: hog market reports, and garbled at that. SOWS5%%% 4WTFEA.JKNS5 UP. I tore off the paper, wound several yards of the world's misdoings around my arm, picked up the mail and went to my office.

In addition to running the social column I also sifted through dispatches from the local and national wires, performing triage on the events of the day to determine which would make the paper. I lit a cigarette, put my feet up on the windowsill and began to read. Nothing had had happened overnight; no wars, no plane crashes, no errant ICBMs arcing over the polar cap. The local news was thin stew as well, but Minneapolis had a curious item.

> BLOOD FOUND IN BREAD (AP) CUSTOMERS AT SEVERAL MINNEAPOLIS SUPERMARKETS REPORTED FINDING A STRANGE DARK SUBSTANCE IN LOAVES OF WHITE BREAD—A SUBSTANCE LATER DETERMINED TO BE BLOOD, PROBABLY OF A COW OR GOAT. POLICE DEPARTMENT SPOKESMAN DET. HARLEY BISHOP SAID THE INCIDENCES WERE ISOLATED AND THAT THE POLICE HAD NO LEADS. POLICE ALSO REFUSED TO SPECULATE ON A MOTIVE.

I looked up and wondered where the prankster had gotten the blood. Perhaps they had a deal with a devil-worshiping organization.

The next item was also from the bread beat.

PROTEST AT GRAIN CO. HQ (LOCAL) THIRTY-THREE PROTESTORS WERE ARRESTED TODAY AT THE HEADQUARTERS OF THE MUNSON GRAIN COMPANY IN A DEMONSTRATION AGAINST ALLEGED PESTICIDE TREATMENT OF GRAIN. PROTESTORS BROKE INTO CORPORATE OFFICES AND SPRAYED MANAGEMENT OFFICIALS WITH COMMON INSECTICIDES BEFORE POLICE ARRIVED TO WQIOWENFNSL QWIW41329NFNS&&&&&

I looked down the page to see if this was a typo or the police had indeed wqiowenfnsled the protestors. There was Det. Harley Bishop again: asked if he thought there was a connection with the bread tampering, he had replied, "Do I look stupid? Of course there's a connection."

I shrugged and stubbed out my cigarette.

The phone buzzed; I swatted a button and picked it up, expecting a quivering voice to impart the particulars of the latest potluck bacchanalia. But it was Carver.

"Well, lucky, lucky, lucky us, you're in. Drop by. Now." And he hung up. I sighed and went down the hall to his office, pausing outside to assume the hunched shoulders and contrite features of the penitent. Then I went in.

Lou Carver was standing at the window looking out over the lake, fat hands clasped behind his broad squat back—his usual posture of the captain watching the water wash over the gunwales. He turned, said I should sit and reinforced the wish with a gesture that said "Heel." He picked up a cigar as thick as a baby's arm and screwed it into the corner of his mouth, then took a rumpled newspaper from his desk and threw it to me. It was the paper from Minneapolis.

"Look at that. Front page under the fold, right side. That's my daughter's doing."

I examined the paper.

It was a version of the story I'd encountered on the wire, the protest at the grain company. 33 ARRESTED AT MUNSON GRAIN HEADQUARTERS was the head.

"Kathy," Carver said, lips tight, "is in the pokey. You understand? My little girl is in jail."

"I'm sorry."

"You're sorry! Smoking Judas on a shingle! Think how I feel! You ever been in jail? No? Well, I have. It's no Sunday social."

"What were you in for?" I said the words with a certain manly satisfaction.

"What? Oh. Being loaded." Carver coughed, touched the knot of his tie, looked away. "Every Carver male's spent a few of his weekends in the tank. A fact of manhood. Detroit bar mitzvah, only the rabbi's got this badge, see. Boy gets born, his parents don't start a college fund, they start salting away bail money. But a daughter. Christ on a crutch. And for what? For breaking into a CEO's office and squirting him with bug killer?" He sat down and stabbed in his shirt pocket, came up with matches and lighted his cigar. The smell that filled the office refuted the notion that the country really needs a five-cent cigar.

"I have to go bail her out. After I let her sit a day in jail and learn a lesson. I want you to look after the place. Now, I oughta kick your ass six ways from Sunday for not coming in on time, 'cause I didn't know if you'd be coming in at all and I had to give today's operations over to Bluchinski. Who, as we know, is as dumb as a bench. But he wants tomorrow off anyway, so you come in bright and early and play me for the day. You oughta know how to do that." He wheeled around in his chair and looked out at the lake again. It was gray and throbbing, like the resting place of departed hangovers.

"Sure I do." I relaxed. Carver had too much on his mind to garrote me. "I come into the office, snap at the help, read the paper, ream someone out for a typo, then spend the afternoon staring out the window."

Carver turned slowly around in his chair. "I'm not that bad."

"You're worse. It's none of my business, but something's bothering you, Mr. Carver."

He just stared at me, no clues on his face. He might as well have been auditioning for a spot on Mount Rushmore. I stood. "Is that all?"

"Yeah." I walked for the door, but Carver called my name, and I turned.

"Listen, Simpson. You're, ah . . . young."

"I suppose."

"You tell me, then. These punks. What are they all about? Drugs? Music? Shacking up?"

"Why?"

"Because my daughter is one of 'em. She has these horns on her head, see. I don't get it."

"It's a phase," I said. "Peer identification. She'll grow out of it."

"She has this tattoo, right here on her head. A spider. And the name of some band. If her mother were around today this would just kill her to death."

"Like I said, a phase. Youth."

"Youth!" Carver raised his hands to the sky. "When I was her age I was in the service, and you want to talk about tattoos?" He tapped a finger hard on his skull. "Did I get one? Do I have Glenn Miller written on my noggin?"

"It's fashion, Mr. Carver. Not particularly good fashion, but—"

"My baby has horns, that's all I know. All right. You're no help." He turned and faced the lake again.

"Is that all?"

"Yeah. Get out of here. And thanks."

I walked back to my office, pitying Carver. I'd met Kathy—or Spanks, as she now wanted to be known—one Christmas a few years back at an office party. She was a mousy little creature with steel ball bearings for eyes, thin prissy lips around small even teeth and a complexion that bespoke a diet of—well, to be honest, of pesticide-laced white bread. She was at the time going through the phase of feminism best described as Angry at Dad. Poor Lou. I scowled at the idea of having to edit the entire paper the next day, but it would pass, and when it did I would not have his troubles. I went back to my office, there to face the depthless strata of social notices piled on my desk.

For the next hour I played archeologist, digging down into the records of the community, finding promotions in companies since gone bankrupt, descriptions of hot-dish dinners held for people long stowed away in the cold earth of the church graveyard. Everything but the topsoil I threw away, and then I scrolled a fresh sheet of paper into the typewriter. I could practically write these things from memory; they were all the same, always had been. Each was a note from some dusty old creature who had gone to the home of some equally frangible creature, there to judge the quick and the freshly dead. The first was typical.

> Mrs. Elijha Gunderwein, Mrs. Elam Anderson, Edna Peterson and Eloise Marston attended a sewing circle at the home of Elma Smith last Monday. Coffee and cupcakes were served. The quilt is to be donated to the Elim Church charity drive.

The sewing circle, I added, *is merely a cover-up for their lesbian cabal*. Next:

> Mr. and Mrs. Jack Peterson unexpectedly visited the home of Mr. and Mrs. Victor Anderson last Tuesday during dinnertime.

That was all. I checked the return address—naturally, the Andersons. *You can bet*, I typed, *that it's the last time the Petersons show up without calling*.

I did this every week. It made me feel better. Next:

> Sonya Salmon met Mrs. May Parker, wife of the Rev. Parker of Elim Lutheran, at the Kopper Kettle Kafe for lunch Wednesday at one o'clock.

Oh, now really. It was common dirt in town that Mrs. Salmon was having an affair with a local pediatrician, and this was a bald attempt to establish an alibi. I typed: *Witnesses will attest to her presence.*

> Mr. and Mrs. Adolf Torgerson were entertained at the home of Mr. and Mrs. Pete Johnson last Tuesday. Roast ham and yams were served.

Yeah, yeah, but what did you do for fun? That's what we all want to know. I thought a second and typed: *After supper Mr. Torgerson bit the head off a parakeet and spat it thirty paces, breaking his previous record, not to mention the living-room window. Mrs. Torgerson played a medley of show tunes on a bagpipe fashioned from her colostomy bag. Mrs. Johnson, clad in a stunning latex interpretation of an SS uniform, administered dessert. The evening concluded with a black mass and a round of bridge.*

I should have stopped there, taken lunch, gone for a walk, done anything but open the next one. But I had no idea.

> Mr. and Mrs. George Samuelson of Prosper take pleasure in announcing the engagement of their daughter Jane Louise to Simon Peter Hoffman of New Haven, Conn. Jane is employed as an editor of an in-house organ of Pulse Tele-

communications, and Mr. Hoffman is a junior executive of the Universal Export company. The wedding, to be held in Prosper, is set for spring.

I read the letter a few times again, wondering what howling harpies were at work here. Time was, I had been the house organ. Then I noticed that the letter was typed on my old Smith-Corona, an ancient contraption Jane had lent her folks a year back. I recognized the leaping *P*, the blotted *L*. This was really too much. Maybe they'd be calling to borrow a few chairs for the reception. I curled the letter into a tube and rolled it between my palms until it was thin and shredded, and then I burned it in the ashtray. I emptied the ashtray in the wastebasket and threw the ashtray away. As I left the office, en route to the dumpster to throw away the wastebasket, I told Marge I had an interview to attend, take my messages. I spent the afternoon at the Hilltop Tavern questioning the Scotsman on the Clan Anderson label. He didn't understand what had happened either.

I was sitting in the living room having the morning's ration of coffee, chewing on a granola bar that cherished a rather obvious ambition to be a candy bar. The news was on, and I paid it half a mind; the previous day's perturbations were still grousing around in the back of my brain. So Jane was getting married. Well, more power to her. In fact, let me tighten those straps. Any word from the governor on the pardon? No? All right, then, more power to her.

I reached for a cigarette, sat back and wondered if I could get away with being late. This was the day I was supposed to play Carver, but if the boss couldn't be late, who could.

There was a thump of the paper against the door, the usual abrupt greeting from the outside world, a sullen dog that didn't care whether or not you let it in. I opened the paper with a little trepidation; while at the bar the previous day, three drinks into my hegira from responsibility, I had regretted leaving without doing my work. I scanned the front page; there were no gaping patches of white space where the wire copy should have been, so someone had covered me. Good. I turned to the social page.

I screamed as loud as a man can scream. Glass exploded for blocks around, dogs knelt and whimpered, deaf folk cocked an ear to the sky. I screamed and shut my eyes tight until I saw colors and fireworks, and then I looked at the paper again. It was all there, every hideous and uncontestably libelous word of it:

Lesbian cabal.

Witnesses will attest.

Black mass.

Good Christ, I'd really slung the mud. I dropped the paper, kicked it back up into the air, plowed my hands through my hair. Someone had just taken the copy out of my typewriter, set it in type and sent it through. Bluchinski. The idiot. Assumed I knew what I was doing. Fool. Why didn't the goddamn copy editor catch it? Because we proofed our own columns, the *Standard* being too cheap to hire a night desk editor. I stood there for a minute, desperately trying to fob the blame off on someone else, every accusation turning into a boomerang that came whistling back to smack me square in the skull.

What to do? I kicked the paper until it carpeted the room, a black-and-white collage of my own idiocy. I knew I was one of the first stops on the paper boy's route. The paper would be all over town within minutes. I could chase him down, knock him over, steal the bag and throw it in the lake. That only left the Hardwood and Prosper editions. Forget it. I yanked the phone plug out of the wall, took the receiver off the hook for good measure. What was I going to do? Go in and take my punishment, of course. Get roasted to the consistency of jerky by Carver when he returned, and take it manfully. That's what I had to do. The only honest, decent thing. That's what I had to do.

Honest and decent men don't call sixty-year-old Norwegian housewives lesbians, I thought, and I went for my suitcase. I was going to get out of town before the locals showed up at the bottom of the hill with torches. Jane, God bless her, had left me this one suitcase.

3

"You got friends down in the cities there?" the trucker hollered.

"No. Maybe. Been a while since I've been there."

"What?"

"No friends," I shouted. As if the din of the diesel weren't enough, there was a tape playing. "I left my baby in 'Bama, my wallet in a bar, I'm back in jail and I got this brand-new scar. I'm jest a good-timin' boah." Weehah. I was papered against the door, as though thrown there by centrifugal force, one foot stabbing an imaginary brake. The trucker, a square-jawed soul wielding an eighteen-wheeler with the jaunty and boastful logo Bob's Independent Meat on the side, had picked me up at the Gas-N-Gullet on Highway 11. The garage where my car was stowed had been closed, and I'd hiked down the road, banging my knees on my suitcase, thumb out like a hook waiting to snag someone. My driver—Bob himself—was evidently starved for human contact and gorged himself on me, embarking on a monologue on the rigors of the road as soon as I was settled in the cab.

He drove with the ease of one long accustomed to the thrust and parry of four-lane traffic. Pity there were only two. The road was pitted with potholes that reshuffled the discs in our spinal cords, and there was a trip down a hill so steep the plunge made me believe oxygen masks would drop from the roof.

All of this was a pleasure cruise on the calm open seas compared with the mess that greeted us in Minneapolis. The Highway Department, evidently overstocked with road repair signs, had decided to close off all the main arteries save one lane. Signs bade us beware of repairs, but there wasn't a construction man to be seen, just acres of pristine concrete marked off by barrels. Motorists looked hungrily at the forbidden lanes like East Germans staring across the Berlin Wall. All the traffic into the city was funneled into one lane. Cars moved faster on the assembly line.

"Well, now what's this there?" Bob muttered. He was prowling up and down the dial for a traffic report. The news was not welcome. A semi hauling industrial waste had overturned several miles down the road, blocking all lanes, as well as nearly dissolving the driver. Bob threw the rig in neutral and stretched.

"Well, ho-de-do. We got a coupla hours of dead-ass time here. You play cards there? I got a deck in the glove box."

We played blackjack. For an hour the conversation consisted of "Hit me" and "I stay." We sounded like two bored Norwegians at an S&M party. After an hour Bob yawned and decided to get some "Z time," laid his head on the chrome stripping along the window and dropped off effortlessly.

I was not tired. Anything but. I was tense and claustrophobic and my skin felt too small. I closed my eyes and listened to my stomach deliberate the stale roll Bob had offered for breakfast, and then I began to examine the landscape outside.

I concentrated, hard, on the surrounding billboards. There was one to the right—one half was a cigarette ad for a roughneck brand, a grim young man buried up to his neck in swamp water, both hands holding his gear above his head, a lit cigarette in his mouth. It was an image meant to be observed in passing at sixty mph, but I had the leisure to reflect on how he could have possibly gotten out a cigarette, let alone have lit the thing, without dumping his baggage in the swamp. The other ad was for a decaffeinated coffee, with a man identified as a neurosurgeon extolling the benefits of a steady hand.

The brand name had been obliterated by black paint, and a black band was sprayed across the doctor's face.

THE DECAF PROCEDURE IS CARCINOGENIC. SAYS THE AIL was sprayed below.

"AIL?" I said.

"Whuzzat there?" said Bob, waking.

"Nothing."

"Mmzzm," he remarked, and went back to dreams of banjos and level highways.

I was still edgy. The traffic showed no signs of loosening. We'd be here for hours—time enough for Oscar to abuse the servantry and the citizens of Valhalla to reach for their lawyers. I gathered my bags, said thanks to slumbering Bob and climbed down from the cab. When he woke he would think I had been a mirage. I made a note to write an article for a trucker's magazine about a phantom hitchhiker seen around northern Minnesota—a young man with a suitcase, seemingly real, but actually dead, his ectoplasm forever roaming the roads. Bob would not sleep for weeks.

I walked along the shoulder. There was an exit a mile down the road and I walked up to the ramp. I stood at the top of the ramp, wondering which way to go next; motorists slowed as they passed, marveling at the sight of a man standing on the freeway exit ramp, apparently stopped for the light. When it changed to green I crossed and stepped into a bus shelter. I set down my bag and examined the map. Primary colors delineated the routes, a Mondrian grid laid over a Jackson Pollock mess of streets. I chose the routes to take me to Marvel Manor—five years I had been absent from this town, but I still knew where my roots, my twisted, gnarled roots, were.

Two hours and three buses later I was deposited on Park Avenue, trying to remember if Marvel Manor lay up or down the street. There was no life around except for an old bundle of fur eking out a path down the sidewalk a block away. She was moving slowly, appearing to come no closer. Perhaps she was losing ground against the earth's rotation. I started walking in her direction and caught up with her in a minute. Her face was a weathered scythe with flinty gray eyes, a grim mouth etched below; she was swaddled in an ancient raccoon coat and wore a beret with a bright yellow tartan plaid. Her walker was brass and a fuzzy cross hung from one of the struts.

"Excuse me," I ventured. She squinted up at me with suspicion. "Do you know which way Marvel Manor is?"

"Eh? What?"

"Marvel Manor. It's the big ugly—"

"Ah." She spat. "Ye'll be goin' that way. Where Ah come from. An' ye can go straight ta hell then while yer at it." And she began to walk away.

"Excuse me?"

She stopped. "If ye have business there ye be goin' where the Auld One goes. A house o' sin, it be. I dinna ken how people can carry on so. Day an' night." Fierce eyes stared at me. "Screams an' crashes we hear, music, if ye can call it that, playin' so loud it looses the mortar from the heavenly vault. The polis comin' every night. It's the ruination of the neighborhood and ye aught to hang yer head in fear of yer Maker for yer soul be lost the moment ye cross the threshold." She stamped her walker in front of her and moved on.

There wasn't much I could add. I turned and started walking, a coil of trepidation unwinding in my stomach. This had Oscar's name on it and it did not augur well.

Two blocks down the street was Marvel Manor. The years had not been kind to the block—indeed, they had operated with considerable malice. The house to the right was now a funeral home, and the house to the left had fallen to a wing of the nearby hospital, which, when I was living there, had been growing through the neighborhood like some untreatable tumor. Now it ran over the property line and stood less than ten feet from the west wing of the manor. Across the street was a pair of billboards. One bore the image of a smirking young man reading a newspaper, with the words THE NEW METROPOLE. READ IT. END OF DISCUSSION written below. The other had a picture of a young couple cooing at their newborn, cans of diet soda in their hands.

SACCHARIN CAUSES UNSIGHTLY TUMORS. SAYS THE AIL was scrawled below in black paint.

The manor itself was miserable. The stone, black to begin with, wore a thick sooty coat of carbon from the exhaust of traffic. The sidewalks were a latticework of cracks, all sprouting with a rich surplus of weeds. The lawn had not been tended to in some time, and the head of a lawn jockey peered out in wide-eyed terror from a thicket of thistleweed and crabgrass. A set of tire tracks ran from the street, over the boulevard, and terminated in an eight-foot-wide indentation in the wrought-iron fence. On the upper floor, toilet paper fluttered from the tracery, and one laughing gargoyle sported a top hat. I had to step over the chalk outline of a body to get to the front door.

I rang the bell. Somewhere deep in the house a slave put the wood to a gong. It was five minutes before the door cracked open.

Trygve had a lei around his neck and the look of a small lapdog made to wear a sweater. His eyes were glassy and there was no recognition for a second. He smiled, folded his hands and stared at me kindly, the lei making it seem as though he were imitating a Hawaiian undertaker. Then sparks flickered; joy flared in his eyes and he looked at me as if upon The One Whose Coming Was Prophesied. He seized my hand and pulled me through the door, down the hallway and into the main room.

There had been a party. You could have said that about Rome after the sack, too. All the furniture in the room had been pushed to the walls, as though someone had complained there was not enough room to swing a giraffe. Plastic cups were scattered everywhere, bloated cigarette butts bobbing in those that remained upright, and the floor had the adhesive property of a movie theater floor. Leis of various colors were scattered around. The remains of what had been a banquet table lay at one end of the room, the tablecloth pulled off and spattered with the detritus of the hors d'oeuvres. A stereo system in the corner was hissing blue smoke, music intermittently crackling on like communiqués from parties on distant planets. One man in a tux lay by the fireplace, a cenotaph of uncles past, and it gave me an unpleasant jolt; another woman lay beneath the staircase, only her legs protruding, and I desired to take off her shoes, see if her feet shriveled and Munchkins emerged to cheer me.

"Master John? Master John?" cried a wavering voice from behind me. "You this truly is?"

I turned to the kitchen door and saw her: Grue, the housekeeper. She came toward me, arms out, threw her arms around me and hugged like a nutcracker working a tough walnut. "Grown you have! And you were such a small boy!"

Grunewald was her name, but her unpronounceable Germanic first name led Aunt Marvel to call her just Grue. The children in the neighborhood regarded her as an extra grandmother life had provided free of charge, and there was something maternal about her: she was a strong woman, hewn of oak but upholstered with kindness. She had shins like fireplugs and hips as wide as an oven door. Her head was stuck directly onto her shoulders with the usual Prussian predilection for omitting the neck, and to watch her turn her head in the direction of Aunt Marvel's yodeling demands for attention was to watch a large and noble owl. Perfunctory to her mistress and protective of Trygve, she was always gentle to the children of the neighborhood, always indulgent, and every week we lined up at the back door to lick the spoon when she made her famous cakes. What this gesture had in friendliness it lacked, of course, in simple public hygiene; childhood diseases romped unchecked through our neighborhood, and that wooden spoon paid many a pediatrician's mortgage. But Grue knew not what she did, and I remembered her fondly. But I had forgotten her mode of speech—the pliant English language contorted into thick chewy pretzels of German sentence construction. Listening to her talk, one's eyes went down to bosom level for subtitles.

"Here to live you are?" she said, eyes shining with hope.

"I think so," I said. "Depends what we can do about your, ah, guest."

She spat. "Into the gutter back will we be throwing him, that's what we can do." Then she patted me on the head, standing on tiptoe to do so. "You make him go away. In you move and I feed you again, eh? Put some meat on." She poked an iron digit in my stomach and smiled. Trygve was standing next to her, beholding me with the same smile of expectation. They were going to be delivered from Oscar.

"Oscar!" I bellowed up the stairs. "Oscar! I know you're up there! Get down here! Now!"

Oscar was my cousin on the Magog side. We grew up together and it's a wonder I grew up at all. He was a year older than I was, which gave him the prerogative of setting the rules of play whenever our families met for social functions. Neither of us enjoyed the other's company, but we went through the motions of play, however joylessly, for more than a decade. His torment of me progressed from simple exploitation of childhood fears, such as locking me in the basement with all the monsters, to truly novel experimentations. He discovered, for example, that a BB gun, pumped up in excess of the manufacturer's parameters, can penetrate both pants and flesh. I still felt that wound on rainy days. It was Oscar who perfected the waterproofing of fireworks, and set off an explosion in my aquarium that left water, broken glass, and dazed fish all over the room. I was always sworn to silence, for he spoke often of a platoon of frozen Nazis he had at home, ready to be resuscitated to do his bidding. We both held tight to these childhood memories, although for different reasons.

"He's still asleep," Trygve explained. "It was quite a party."

"I can see that. Go get him, Tryg. We've got to have a talk."

No need. A toilet flushed upstairs, a door banged open and there was the sound of slippers scraping on the floor.

Oscar came gliding down in the electric chair. A ratty plaid robe was wrapped around his shoulders, his face cradled in one hand, the other hand on the controls of the chair. At the bottom of the steps the chair bumped to a halt and he winced. Then he looked up and saw me.

"Uh-oh." He fumbled with the controls and the chair whirred upwards. I bounded up the stairs three at a time until I caught up with him in the middle of the flight. He reversed direction and started down again.

"That's right," I called. "Run away."

"I'm sick. Go away."

He hadn't changed. Still balding, soft and paunchy. His face was fleshy, spotted with a drinker's blotchy blush, and his skin tone spoke of a diet of poor food, and lots of it. His eyes were remarkably hard and glossy; if he crossed them you'd expect the click of billiard balls. The voice, as ever, had shards of casual malice wrapped in a pasty dough of weary and unconvincing decadence. Cornered, the pretenses were dropped, and he betrayed a prodigious talent for sniveling. I knew this from the day at his house when I opened the freezer and found no frigid Nazis.

"I'm not going, Oscar." I walked down to the bottom of the stairs, and he started sliding up again. "You're going. As soon as you get out of your little deus ex machina there you're going to pack your traps and get your sorry ass out of my house."

"Oh, it's your house now, is it." He was now at the top of the stairs. "And where have you and your deed been hiding yourselves?" he shouted. "Maybe I have squatter's rights, you know."

A remarkably apt image. I started up the stairs as he began sliding down again. As we passed I reached over to haul him off the chair but I got a fistful of robe. It came away in my hands as he glided off, leaving him sitting cold and pitiful in black fishnet underwear.

The woman downstairs began to snore. I trotted down and covered her with the robe, earning me a meaty snort of gratitude. When I turned from this task I saw that Oscar had dismounted and was standing over the man in the tux, wobbling in some unseen wind. "Party's over, friend. Up and at them." He kicked the man gently in the kidney. "Rise and shine." When there was no response he dragged the tux coat off and put it on.

"It's cold in this heap, if you hadn't noticed. You should see the heating bills you get. Ohhhhhh." He put the back of his hand to his forehead. "I shall die of this hangover. I shall die. Trygve!"

Trygve shuffled over, still wearing the lei.

"Ah. The Trygish one. Be a man and bring me an iced coffee. Make it Irish iced coffee." He put his hand to his head again. "Largely Irish." Trygve nodded and departed. Oscar lay down on the steps and stretched out his limbs in a posture of Prometheus bound, waiting for the birds to pluck out his liver. I sent the electric chair humming unladen up to the top of the stairs and sat down next to Oscar.

"Some party. What was the occasion?"

"Tuesday."

"You know there's a chalk outline of a body out on the steps?"

"Really. There wouldn't happen to be a body inside of it, would there?"

"No, but—"

"Good. This is a recycling day, I believe. I hope the poor fellow made it to the curb. Ah well." He sighed. "Let it never be said of me that my parties died before my guests began to do the same. Now, please leave me to perish unmolested, cousin. Whatever you have to talk about can wait."

"Can't. I'm moving in. Today. A precondition of that is your moving out."

He looked at me with a mixture of fear and suspicion. I had seen the expression on the face of a badger cornered in a culvert at Jane's parents' farm. They had blown it out with a shotgun.

Oscar closed his eyes. "So how long has it been since we had the pleasure."

"You usually had the pleasure. I got the tourniquets. And it's been about five years since I left town so—"

"Half a whole decade? Really. Haven't seen you in *all* these years and this is how you treat me. No hallo, how have you been. We're family. You and I were even blood brothers, if I remember."

"Hitting me repeatedly on the nose until you skinned your knuckles doesn't exactly qualify us as blood brothers. And we're not family. My parents divorced, you know."

Trygve had shuffled in with the drink. Oscar took it with both hands and sucked it back, ice cubes clinking against his teeth. He gave a gurgle of pleasure and held the glass out. "Be a manservant and freshen it." He lay down again. "So. What exactly are you here for?"

"How many times do I have to tell you? Do you want me to hammer cuneiforms into a stone tablet and come down the steps dressed like Moses before you believe me? What are *you* doing here, that's the question."

"I was living here before Auntie met her end," he sniffed. "She was a lonely old woman and when I was, ah, forced to leave my dwellings she took me in. Better the company of someone I hate than no company at all, she used to say. Every day she used to say it." He scowled. "Night after night I entertained her. Letting her win at pinochle. Letting her win at Monopoly. You try that sometime. You try playing with someone who insists on buying Jail and Free Parking. You know she used to make me wear Uncle Marvel's clothes? Mm-hmm. I would stand there while she told me all the things she never had the opportunity to tell him while he was alive. She made me follow her around with an inflatable pillow in case she started fainting. And what, what did I get for all this?"

"Nothing, if there's a God in heaven."

"That's right. Not a cent. You got the house and our farina-headed friend gets the cash. It isn't fair, it isn't fair."

"It doesn't get any fairer, Oscar. I wouldn't doubt that Aunt Marvel pegged you for a brownnose and gave me the house because she knew it would give you a stroke. She saw how you used to treat me. What did you have against me anyway?"

"Nothing. You were handy." He yawned. "Ancient history, cuz. What I want to know is why now? Why not a month ago? I've grown used to the place." He pouted.

"I didn't know I even owned this rock. Trygve told me—" Tryg had reappeared, the lei now slung like a strap for a festive gun holster. "Tryg came up to tell me I had the house and that it had a problem with a pest of your general size and behavior." Oscar glared at Trygve, who stuck out his lower lip in defiance.

"It's so hard to get loyal help nowadays," Oscar murmured to the ceiling. "You'll see, Johnny. Wait until you have butlers of your own. So I've misbehaved. That's no reason to kick me out. You could let me stay. There are twenty rooms here. You'd never see me. Trygve could slide all my meals under the door. For you I would live on pancakes and pizza. No?"

I shook my head slowly from side to side and pointed toward the door.

"Oh, well. As you want it." He sat up and took the drink Trygve had been holding out. This one went just as fast as the other. He gave me what would have been a level look if the deck behind his eyes wasn't pitching with drink. "I didn't want to bring this up. I had hoped you would be friendly. But. I am forced to. You see, I, ah, cannot leave."

"Sure you can. Remember how we used to play wheelbarrow? I'd be laying down on the beach and you would grab my legs and start pushing me around? Of course you can leave." I searched my pockets for my cigarettes. "Only question is, how."

"I mean it. You need me here."

"I need a blood clot in my brain too. Every morning I get up and hit myself in the head with a hammer."

"I mean, you need me. I have made certain . . . obligations. On behalf of the house."

"You mortgaged it. You bastard."

Oscar laughed, bitterly. "There's no mortgage. Never was. This place is dripping with equity, and it is all yours, all yours. No. I am talking about renting the place out. Parties, such as the one last night. People pay for venues like this one."

"Not interested. And if I was I still wouldn't need you. Finish your drink and pack, Oscar. I want to stay here tonight and I want you gone. In body and in spirit."

"Tonight?" He winced and looked into his empty glass. "That will be difficult."

"Why."

"It's rented. For a party."

"What party."

"A band in town. Just released a record. They're having a party here tonight."

"What? How? How did they know?"

"I took out some ads, you see. Mansion for private parties. Conventions in an unconventional place. That was my line. Do you like it?"

I knotted my hands, looked down. "Oscar."

"It's a perfect place, cuz. We're between a mortuary and the terminal ward. It's not as though the neighbors are going to complain."

I took a deep breath, counting to five. I got lost after three.

"Call them up. Call it off."

"Can't. They, ah, all paid deposits."

"They all? How many parties have you booked?"

"Thirty-six. Practically booked solid through January." He made a brave attempt at a smile. "We're all the rage."

"Call them up. Now. Cancel the parties. Give them their money back."

"Can't. Money's tied up."

"Untie it."

"Well, it's, ah, locked up in the car."

"I'm confused. Is the money locked up or tied up? Do we need keys or a knife here?"

"Well." He was pale, and looked shrunken in his tux jacket. "We need just three more payments and then the car is all mine."

"You spent the money on a car. Oh, Christ, you are a genius."

"Well, I wasn't about to do anything as déclassé as save it, for heaven's sake." He looked up and smiled. "See? You can't throw me out."

I stood up spluttering random phonemes. Oscar rattled the ice in his glass. "I understand your reaction. But let us be adults now, eh? You need to let go of the past, Johnny. Let go."

I took the past by his lapels and dragged him, flailing and begging, off the stairs and down the hallway. I opened the front door and threw him out of the house. He stumbled back and fell neatly into the chalk outline. I slammed the door and leaned against it.

I was appalled with myself. Pleased, but mainly appalled. My heart banged with adrenaline, the blood was thick in my ears, my veins filled with a hot broth of shame and rage. Here I was, the kid who took pride in his childhood because he had never kicked over an anthill, throwing what one could charitably describe as a fellow human being onto cold hard concrete. Onto bone-breaking brain-bursting concrete. My God. What had I done, could I have—

Fists drummed against the door and a thin sick voice cried *let me in*.

I locked the door.

I went back into the main hall, pulled up a chair and sat down. Trygve was standing in the doorway, the lei now a belt.

"Would you like some nice cookies?"

"No. Thanks."

Oscar hammered on the door. I turned around and saw him glaring through the window. Then, he sank out of sight. The mail flap opened and a pair of lips protruded.

"Trygve. *Trygve.* This is your master's voice. Bring me the keys to my car. Bring me the keys and some pants. Please."

Trygve looked at me, and I nodded. "Just the keys," I said. "Take the house key off." Trygve smiled and leaned toward the mail slot as though about to feed a dangerous animal; he pushed the keys through the slot and sprang back.

From a window I watched Oscar, still in a tux coat and fishnet underwear, get into a black Saab and drive away.

I left instructions with Trygve to gather Oscar's belongings and put them on the porch, and to wake the remaining guests and escort them out as well. I told him I would return that night, and then I left Marvel Manor.

A block down the street the Scottish harridan saw me and began to cross the road, but her pace was such that I was a block past her while she was still in the middle of the street, earning me a curse of new and redoubled vigor. I stood at the bus stop feeling anger simmer in my veins, telling myself that it would all turn out for the better. That "better" was defined as uncontested possession of a gruesome house I couldn't afford to heat was a telling remark on my new station in life.

The bus lumbered up and the doors sighed open. I climbed aboard and rode it until it stopped and turned around and took me back to Park Avenue, during which time I figured out exactly nothing.

4

Nothing bad happened for a week. Not that I gave it much of a chance: I didn't move from the house. I didn't think that hideous ruin would fall on my head if I walked about town, but when you don't feel proud of yourself you don't feel like dancing down the boulevard with a rose between your teeth. I preferred to remain interred in the dark curtained walls of the manor, brooding over what I had done, what I was going to do next.

I certainly wasn't going to answer the door. Every night a crowd appeared around sundown, loud people and plenty of them, all determined to have a party. They pounded on the door and howled for, in order of popularity, admission, their deposit and Oscar's hide. Each night we sat silent in the dark, not moving, waiting for the horde to move along.

Most evenings I spent in bed in my old room, drinking and reading old Tom Swift novels. After two scotches my reading ability sank to a fifth grader's level, and thus assisted I relived my childhood. It was hard to sleep without the liquor's assistance; the hospital next door cast vats of watery light into my room. From my window I had a view of the top half of one floor, the bottom half of another—an unnerving sight that made me pine for a horizontal hold knob. When the picture really started to roll I capped the scotch bottle, dog-eared the book and sank into the thin, guilty sleep of the exile.

After a week in the crypt I decided to go out and rejoin the living. The day began as usual, with Tryg and me struggling through one of Grue's breakfasts. She believed that a good day commenced with some no-nonsense gluttony, and to this end served nothing but potato pancakes and blood sausages. They sat in the stomach like wet newspaper. This morning was no different; I washed the mass down with hogsheads of coffee and juice and staggered away from the table and said I was off to explore the city. I praised breakfast and said I could do with a light supper, something that would silt up my arteries at a slower rate. I asked her when she was going to make her famous cake, and she smote herself on the forehead and said On it she would get right away. I told her not to make any special effort and went out to the garage.

We had an old Pacer, used only for shopping excursions. It was an ugly car, squat and round; it had the wheelbase of Kate Smith, acres of glass and orange paint that recalled a nauseated pumpkin, but there was some hellfire under the hood. I took it out on the highways to limber up the engine, then I drove downtown.

The city had changed. I'd have been disappointed if it hadn't. I drove around for half an hour, finding new skyscrapers where there had been parking lots, parking lots where there had been buildings. I recognized the city, and it recognized me, but like anyplace one has been away from for a while, we kept our distance and treated one another with a measure of formality. I didn't run any yellow lights, the rhythms of the traffic signals having long passed out of memory; the city, on its part, presented me with an occasional landmark from my time. I drove around until the things I remembered roughly equaled the number of things that had vanished.

I parked at the library and went to the periodicals room. It was filled with bums, dozing in the warm carrels on back issues of *Life* and *Time*. I found a stack of recent *Lacs Standards*. They had run the correction to my column on the front page. It was the main story. WE DIDN'T MEAN IT, in ninety-six-point type. The next issue had a story entitled LACS STANDARD COLUMNIST DISAPPEARS. My picture, taken from a job application five years ago, grinned innocently out at the world, happy, young, fresh from a toss with Jane, probably. The police did not suspect foul play; office records showed no money was missing. Carver was quoted as saying that if I had any sense I had joined the navy. There were many letters from those I had slandered. The most typical was from a Zeke Gunderwein; he was stewed that I had called his wife one of them lesbians, and that it was a pity we lived in a society—I'm paraphrasing here—where the only thing a man could do was sue instead of doing the right thing, which, I inferred, involved some rope and a tree. Another writer, again writing on behalf of his wife, wanted to floss my molars with a twenty-gauge shotgun. I put all the papers back. I asked the clerk at circulation how long they kept the papers around; she said they would all be transferred to microfiche, and would be around for all eternity. Thus assured of my immortality I left the library.

I walked around for a while, ending up at a narrow little bar on the north margin of downtown. I took a paper from the counter and sat by a window with a view of a parking lot and a billboard. The sign was for something called Jui-C, which sounded like a kosher sacramental wine fortified with vitamins but was actually a new soda. REFINED SUGAR ROTS YOUR TEETH AND BUMS YOU OUT. SAYS THE AIL was sprayed below. I chuckled.

I was on my fourth coffee, contemplating a scotch, when sparks fell onto the paper and skidded into my lap.

I stood, beating at my groin. I looked up; sparks were dropping from a heating unit above me. The waiter swore and walked over to a switch on the wall, which he struck with the heel of his hand. The heater ceased whirring and the sparks stopped. The waiter apologized, said they'd been having trouble with that thing, could they make it up? A drink? Perhaps a sandwich? This was a better offer than I'd get from Grue's cuisine, so I said yes. I said I had to call my butler but after that, bring a menu, by all means.

Trygve answered on the fifth ring. "Tryg? It's Jonathan. Tell Grue I won't be—"

"Marvel! Hah. Hah! Manor! Hah. Hah. Hah. Hah."

"Tryg? You all right?"

"Hah. Hah. Hahhahhahhah—"

"Trygve! This is Jonathan! Master Jonathan! What's going on?"

"Master hah Jonathan hah! It's Grue! Grue! Hah!"

"What? What? Calm down." Christ. I ran a hand through my hair. "What the hell is—"

"She is not hah! Dead! But she is trying hard!"

A greasy seed of nausea bloomed in my gullet, and I leaned weak against the wall of the booth. "What's wrong?"

"She is not breathing right and her face is gray and her tongue is purple and there is too much of it out of her mouth. Hah hah hah."

"Did you call the doctor? Call the doctor!"

"I looked in the phone book! There are so many!"

"Okay. Call 911. Do you understand? 911."

"911 what? That's only three numbers! I need four more!"

I was going to be a bad parent. "Stay there," I shouted. "Don't do anything. I'll get the doctor." I slammed down the phone, dialed the emergency number and dispatched an ambulance to the manor. Then I stood on the corner, arms waving for a cab; it would take too long to get back to the car. One hewed up to the curb within a minute and we took off.

There was no ambulance outside and the manor looked peaceful. The gargoyle above was still in his top hat, laughing. I bolted through the front door and stood gasping in the entrance hall, yelling Trygve's name. There was a long wail from the kitchen, and that's where I went.

Grue was lying on the floor, wooden spoon in one hand. The other hand had something beige smeared on the fingers. She looked as dead as dead ever gets. But I found a pulse, an act that required I find a neck, and the slight changes in elevation in her prodigious bosom indicating breathing, albeit shallow and irregular. Mute eyes stared up at the ceiling, like someone enduring a commercial until the next act of the show came on. Drops of the beige substance were spattered on her apron and led in a trail across the floor, up the cabinet and onto the counter.

"What happened? Trygve, what happened?"

"I was in the next room, then she was dead! I—I—I—She's—" And he began to blubber. I took him by the shoulders and steered him into the living room, where I pushed him into a chair, with the instructions that he should let the doctor in when the ambulance came.

I was kneeling over her, slapping her palm and feeling utterly futile, when I heard him shout, "Do firemen count?"

I turned to ask what the hell he was talking about and saw two firemen in full regalia step into the kitchen. They looked at Grue, who had now turned the same shade of gray as the linoleum, as though she did not want to clash. One of the firemen sprinted back toward the front door, and the other assured me the ambulance would be present shortly.

"An ambulance is what I called for!" I shouted. "What the hell are you doing here? Do you see a fire? No fire. If my house is burning down are you people going to send over a couple of radiologists?"

"We're trained for most medical emergencies," the fireman said with great solemnity. "We can usually handle things. But this looks bad. My partner is calling on the radio for an ambulance now."

"On the radio? There's a goddamn hospital next door! Shout! Forget the ambulance. Help me get her over to the emergency room."

"We can't move her, son."

"She's not that heavy. We're both men. We can do it. Come on. Here. Help me get this door off the hinges. We can lay her—"

He put a hand on my shoulder. "They'll be here. Don't worry."

Grue was blue, with her extremities tending toward aquamarine, when the ambulance arrived, but she was breathing. Seconds after the siren of the ambulance ceased, two men in white coats entered the kitchen, hauling a stretcher. Both looked at Grue and swore to themselves. One of the paramedics made a brisk evaluation of her vitals, speaking to the other in a tongue made of numbers and odd Latin morphemes. "How is she?" I asked.

The paramedic with *Bob* stitched on his uniform told his comrade to ready the ambulance, then looked at me and asked: "Did you find her here?"

"No. I found her in the cellar and dragged her up here and smeared beige goop on her. Come on, for Christ's sake, how is she?"

"Bad." The other, Pete, was unbuckling the straps on the stretcher. "Bad BP, bad pulse, bad reflex reaction, bad."

"Do you know what happened?" Pete asked. "She pass out, have slurred speech, chest pain, what?"

"I wasn't here. The butler found her there. Trygve, what happened?" Trygve was standing in the doorway with a hand over his mouth, face white, eyes wide and moist. His lips moved but no sound emerged.

The paramedics hoisted Grue onto the stretcher, and the spoon slid from her hand and clattered on the tiling. They began to drag her out of the room, shouting commands to the two firemen, both of whom stood around looking resolute and useless. They slid her in the ambulance, climbed in and went whooping down Park. The firemen climbed into their truck and left quietly.

I went back into the house to tend to Tryg, who was standing by the front window, one hand still in front of his mouth.

"Will Grue be all right?" He was almost crying, and I knew that if he started, I would too.

"I don't know, Tryg. I hope so. They'll take good care of her."

"She's taken such good care of me," he said. "I don't know what I'll do without her."

"I'll be here."

"But you aren't her. You don't smell like she did. She smelled so kind." A tear sprouted from the corner of his eye, found a wrinkle and coursed down its bed. Then he frowned and squared his shoulders. "Well. We all have to go someplace."

"That's sometime." I patted him on the shoulder.

"When?"

"When we all have to go."

"Yes." He stared out the window, then looked at me. "Where are we going?"

I went back to the kitchen. There was the ruins of a cake Grue had been making for me, at my request. Apparently she didn't make them from scratch anymore, for there was a box of mix on the counter. It was a generic brand, a white-and-black box with the words *Bundt Mix* in blunt letters on the front. I checked the ingredients, which, as usual, looked like a bill of lading from a chemical company loading dock. On the back were black letters, written in the style of the lettering on the front.

AIL.

I picked up the box and examined the letters. They had been drawn on with a magic marker. There were no other marks or explanations. I looked inside the box and saw a piece of paper wedged between the box and the waxed bag that held the mix. I pulled it out and read it.

> Don't eat this cake it's poisoned and it's fast death. But if it wasn't poisoned it would be slow death from chemicals. Death to bad food before its death to you. AIL.

My hands started shaking, and I dropped the note, thinking it too was impregnated with poison. I washed my hands, scrubbing them with a handful of sink cleanser that left my cuticles green. I plowed through the cupboards until I found some plastic bags. I wore two as gloves and put the box and the note into bags. Then I sealed the bowl of mix with plastic wrap and carted the whole grisly mess out of the kitchen. I told Trygve not to eat anything in the house, to order Chinese or pizza if he got hungry. I put on a coat and went next door to visit my neighbors, the doctors.

I walked into the emergency room of the hospital and set the bowl down. The receptionist looked at it, then me; I could see a question coalescing behind her eyes, but she thought better of it and asked me what I needed. I asked about Grue, and after a minute of consultation with the computer she told me that Grue was up in intensive care. She gave me directions and I set off down the hall, the lethal bowl held in front of me like a bomb on its way to the disposal squad.

Intensive care was behind a door with a two-foot sign shouting QUIET. Inside was a broad white hallway, the walls decorated with pitiful cardboard cutouts of clowns, cheering no one. I passed doors, some silent, some loud with frantic commands behind the frosted glass. The atmosphere on the floor was that of a moment in a tug-of-war when both parties are exerting equal pull and the rope has frayed to a single strand.

At the reception desk I told the nurse my business and was told to wait for Grue's doctor. I went to the waiting room, which looked down on Marvel Manor. The view from the main hall evidently looked up into the intensive care ward. Cheering.

The air was blue-gray from cigarette smoke, and half a dozen people sat collapsed in the chairs, looking asphyxiated. The doctor arrived after a few minutes and slumped into a chair. His face was drawn and tired, his eyes bloodshot. He looked awful.

"Do you feel all right?" I asked.

"Vitamins," he said. He kneaded the bridge of his nose. "I need to start taking vitamins or something." He sighed. "The nurse said you might have information about Mrs. Grunewald's condition."

"How is she."

"Not very good. What's your information."

I picked the bowl off the floor and held it out to him. "This. It's bad. Not spoiled. Poisoned." He gave me a drawn, tired, bloodshot look. "Look, I'm not making this up. Have you heard of AIL? Seen it on the billboards?" He shrugged, nodded. "Okay, then. I don't know what's going on here, but there was a note in the box from a group, signed AIL, and it says they poisoned the cake. As a protest against additives, I gather. Here." I showed him the note. He read it and closed his eyes. "There's probably enough in here to kill a dozen times over. But she only licked her fingers. That's probably why she's just sick." I took a deep breath. "I'm not making this up. The sooner you find out what's happened to her the better you're going to be able to deal with other cases. Because I think there will be more."

He looked at the bowl and sighed. Delicate fingers worked the base of a cheekbone. "Why not. I can't find anything else wrong with her. Nothing I can explain, anyway. Let me get some of this down to toxicology." He took the bowl and stood up.

"I need the bowl back."

"This isn't a church social."

"I have to take it to the police, that's why."

He nodded and walked out. I followed him and stood looking at a poster that gave hints on how to prevent everything from which the occupants of the wing were probably suffering. He came back with the bowl, gave it to me and rubbed his eyes. "I can't guarantee this'll do it," he said. "She's old. She may not respond. We may not find anything in this bowl."

"Just try. And get some rest," I added.

"I think it's tension," he said. "I need a hobby."

City hall looked like the brother of Marvel Manor, the one in the family of whom the parents are proud and the rest of the siblings regard as a pompous idiot. I had entered with my bowl of poison, explained my case to the information desk and asked to whom I should speak. The woman at the desk couldn't decide if I had a matter for the police or for Public Health, and she spent a full five minutes mulling the matter over before she sent me down to the police with the instructions to see Detective Bishop.

One look at Bishop and you suspected he had been demoted and sent here for some horrendous and unprovable offense. He had a head like a peeled potato and the flabby build of a policeman whose only developed muscles are in the wrist that holds the billy club. His main occupational hazard was probably a crick in the neck from looking the other way. When I came in a smile spread over his face like an oil slick. "You the boy they called up about?"

"Yes. Simpson."

"Bishop. Harley Bishop. Detective."

"Jonathan Simpson. Social editor."

"Park it and tell me what this is all about."

"It's this." I sat the bowl and the box on the desk. "Bundt cake mix. It's tainted. Poisoned."

"Yeah, yeah, poisoned. Well, look here, son, it's generic." He pointed to the box, leaned back. " 'S not poisoned. Stuff's just naturally bad. What, somebody get a tummyache there? That what you—"

"I found my housekeeper collapsed on the floor. She'd taken one taste of the mix. She's in intensive care at St. Luke's. Call them if you doubt me. Point is I wouldn't be suspecting anything if it weren't for this letter." I pulled out the letter and pushed it across the table.

He read the letter. His face drained.

"Holy hell."

"You heard of the AIL?"

"Heard of 'em? Hell, we've been getting letters from this sicko for a month." Bishop leaned back and shouted out of his office. "Nashua! Who's on the AIL letters there? Poison threats?"

"You are," came a voice from the other room.

"I am? The hell I am. Since when?"

"Since yesterday. 'S on the assignment board."

"Aw, hell." Bishop spat into his wastebasket and sat up. "Don't tell me this guy is actually serious."

"I don't think it's one guy," I said. "AIL. Sounds like an acronym. A group. They have a problem with modern nutrition, judging from what I've seen on the billboards. Here—it's on the box too." Bishop examined the box, one hand kneading his jowls. "I don't think they meant to hurt anyone," I said. "I mean, why would they mark the box and put in the letter?"

"Aw hell no, just because they fill a bundt box with poison don't mean they expected anyone to up and die. Now, tell me what happened. The whole business." I told him. He made faces of nausea and displeasure at the work he saw coming. When I finished, he reached for his phone. "Mary, listen sweetheart, I hate to do this to ya, but you gotta call a press conference. . . . Yes. I know . . . I know it's a lot of work. I know we never get on the TV anyway. We will with this one. I promise. So get 'em all down here fast as you can, okay? What? . . . I don't know, they'll probably just film me talking. . . . Well hell no, I ain't gonna let you go home and change. Listen to your pappy now and do as I say." He slammed down the phone, rubbed his head. "Jesis Kee-rist. Somebody want to blow the whistle on me for hirin' my own dotter, they can go right ahead and it won't be too soon." He slammed his hands down on the table. "All right. You leave me be here, now. I gotta call the distributors and get this bundt stuff here pulled off the shelves there."

"Call me if you find anything?"

"What? Yeah, yeah. Gimme your number." I wrote it on a scrap of paper, which he shoved in a shirt pocket already overflowing with pieces of paper. An examination of those scraps would probably clear up half the unsolved crimes during Bishop's tenure. We shook hands and I left, thinking, The AIL has nothing to fear, nothing.

I went back to my car at the library. It would have been there, parked right beneath that sign, if the sign hadn't read NO PARKING 4–6. It had been towed.

I walked back to the café to get my free sandwich but a different waiter was on duty, and he didn't know anything about free food. But sparks fell in my lap, I said. Well, why didn't you say so. I ate my meal, reading the paper I had left, finding crucial quotes in the stories pitted by tiny scorch marks.

Going home was not an appealing option. I went to a bar on Sixth Street, a shiny room full of young men in suits and older women in suits. I sat at the bar feeling naked and jobless, watching a game show, unable to hear the questions, feeling deaf on top of it all. The network news came on, with the usual progression from war to horse-saved-by-young-girl's-love story; then the local news. *Poison Alert*, read words on the screen, followed by a picture of Bishop. I sat up and motioned for the bartender to turn up the sound. He did. I still couldn't hear. Bishop was standing at a lectern, a young woman in a dull black dress standing next to him; Bishop's mouth moved and he held up the box of bundt mix. A lot number appeared at the bottom of the screen. The anchor then handed the story to a woman who stood in front of Marvel Manor. Close-up of Trygve standing at the window, waving, smiling. I put my head in my hands.

I toured five or six bars that night, each a little more deserted than the last. Finally I found one quiet enough so I could hear myself ask Grue for that cake. I had drunk enough scotch by now so that I could hear every damning syllable as though enunciated through a bullhorn held an inch from my ear, see every line in her face crinkle as she smiled up at me and said on it she would get right away.

I finished my scotch and ordered another one.

Around eleven I called the manor to see how Trygve was doing. Instead of Tryg I got some drunken idiot who enjoined me to drop in and kept using *party* as a verb. I finally got through to Trygve. He sounded composed. He said Oscar was there and having a party. Trygve added that he could take no more and was leaving that night for Canada, and if I would excuse him he had to pack. I told him to inform Oscar that the party would be over in an hour or I was calling the police, and not to go to Canada, for God's sake. I hung up and stood in the booth for a minute, breathing deeply. There was steam on the glass when I left it.

I flagged down a cab and flopped into the backseat. "Where to" said the cabbie, and I told him.

"Ahh, yeah. Party Central. Sure. Hang on."

He drove away from downtown, humming what I recognized as a death aria from *Cavalleria Rusticana*. We turned at a corner that brought us onto Park.

"Uh-oh," he said.

It was a good night to rob houses or exceed the posted speed limit or poison food, for a great portion of the city's squad cars were clustered outside of Marvel Manor. Police were standing on the street herding the gawking traffic along while their comrades pulled manacled revelers out of the house and stored them in the waiting paddy wagons. Spotlights were aimed at the front door, giving sudden and unwanted celebrity status to those who staggered out addled and blinded. We pulled up alongside a wagon full of festively dressed arrestees, all of whom had the same woebegone expression of orphans just told that their parents will not be returning, ever again. I didn't see Oscar or Trygve.

"You want out?" said the cabbie. "None of my business but I think the fat lady sang. You know that expression? It ain't over til—"

A policeman was rapping on the window, and the cabbie rolled it down. "Move along. If someone called for a cab here you might as well forget it. Everyone's going downtown."

"Why?" I said, leaning over the front seat. The policeman shone his flashlight on me, and I shrunk back with guilt. "What's going on in there?"

"What *wasn't*. Disorderly house. That plus your basic drugs-and-weapons haul. You want to join this party?" He gestured at the paddy wagon.

"No," I laughed.

"You live here?"

"WellofcourseIdon'twhywouldIlivehere?"

"All right. Then get moving."

The cabbie nodded, rolled up the window and pointed the cab back downtown. "Where to now?"

"I don't know. Downtown."

" 'Kay." We drove on, listening to something twangy and pimply on the radio. The cabbie cleared his throat. "Boy, they finally did something about that house. No offense if you were going there. But some of the stuff I seen just picking up fares there. Make your hair curl." Makes my butt ache, as though someone had shot it with a BB gun. "What did that cop call it, a disorderly house? What's that?"

"Dust under the bed. Carelessly folded towels." I was staring out the window. This entire day, as I used to say in my theater critic period, was straining for effect. I didn't want to get out of the cab. I wondered how much it cost to take this thing to Valhalla. Of course, three hundred dollars.

Then I knew where to go. When I had gone to the university there was an all-night place near campus, the area of town called Dinkytown. Coffee was cheap and they let you sit as long as you liked. I had sat there long enough to know most of the waitresses and even to date a few. Like Sarah. Ach. Sarah. Now bandaging poor folk in New Guinea for the Peace Corps, probably. I had to go back, if only to see if the hole I had punched in the bathroom wall the night we broke up was still there. I gave the cabbie new directions. Twice an ambulance passed us. Maybe I wasn't the only son who'd come home for comfort and cake.

5

I was at low tide when I drifted into the Diner, with enough energy to walk and breathe as long as I didn't attempt both simultaneously. There was a phone near the door, and I dug out a quarter and called home. "Marvel Manor," he said in a grave voice.

"Tryg. It's Jonathan."

"Master Jonathan. Oh. It's been the most horrid night. Most horrid."

"I know. Have the police left."

"No. They're all arresting people and two who are not police are staying here eating buffet food."

"What do you mean, not policemen?"

"They say they are plain clothed men, and I certainly won't dispute that."

Damn. "Are you okay?"

"Peak of health, Master Simpson."

"Fine. Did they arrest Oscar?"

"Master Oscar hasn't been here all night."

"All right. You take care of yourself and I'll be there tomorrow."

"I have to go. A policeman is waving at me." He hung up. I turned around and looked at my home for the night.

It hadn't changed since I'd left five years before. Nor had it been swept. It was the sort of bistro people say reminds them of New York—hot, cramped, with all the grease that never made it into the patrons' arteries congealed on the wall and the fixtures. A single fan on the ceiling sawed through the torpid air, and ghastly fluorescent light made everything stark and unreal, giving it the look of something an alien culture had reconstructed based on observations through a very powerful telescope. There were two patrons. In a refreshing twist I noted that the salad bar had been removed and a lunch counter added.

There were three stools between the two men, and I chose the middle one. Under the pretext of giving my neck a thorough scratching I took a look at my company. Here were two of the breed for whom the world is one long Formica tapestry of spilled coffee, ashes, exhausted packages of sugar, hidden bogs of sticky jam, all coated with a patina of mutterings and solitude. One was gaunt and thin as hay, smoothing back his oily hair with a motion that worked hard to disguise its compulsiveness. The other was fat with a back like a sofa about to launch a few springs. Both wore headphones, music trickling from their ears, wires disappearing into their bodies. I pulled out a cigarette and lit it, and instantly both looked at me with beseeching eyes. I gave them each a cigarette.

Then I saw her. She was fitting an order onto the kitchen wheel. It couldn't be her. Not after all these years. Maybe her kid sister. If she'd had one.

No. I couldn't mistake Sarah from any angle. She was standing on tiptoe, her taut calves the only view her smock permitted. Her hair was, as ever, bound with a simple rubber band, black wire flowering out on both sides of the cinch. She put her hands on her hips, cracked her back, a habit that always made me wince. She bent down to start scrubbing the waitress's station, humming. I would have called out but I was so tired, so drained of pleasure or the hope of it, that I saw not Sarah but her uniform—the promise of coffee, a holy sister out to salve the mendicants—before I saw her.

I put my head down and coughed, and from the edge of my vision I saw her stir and come over to my place at the counter.

"Coffee?"

"Mrgh."

"Cup? Or do you want to visit the trough in the back?"

"Trough." I yawned. "I think I must have picked up narcolepsy from a toilet seat tonight."

She laughed, and I looked up. Shock cut the cables from her jaw and it dropped, hung there; her eyes made such a show of starting from their sockets that I nearly ducked for fear of being beaned by one. Now I gave her a good long examination; she'd grown to look even better. Thick black hair the color of coffee left long on the burner, bushy eyebrows and inky eyes full of brio. Her uniform flattered her figure, which was the sort of arrangement you normally encounter falling lengthwise out of a magazine. She wore no makeup, but her lips were full and vivid. I had the same feeling I had years ago when I'd met her—that she could not possibly belong to this tableau, that this was no real restaurant, but a CIA front or a movie set.

God, she's fetching, I thought—proof we are selective in what we choose to remember. Sarah had not ended her tenure in my life earning the best references. She'd been my first—first love, first tumble, first love lost. It was best that it had ended, I suppose; we were unsuited in ways that don't surface until after you are wholly comfortable with someone. She had a hair-trigger social conscience and was always devoting herself to the cause of the day, whereas I was a flaming moderate. But I could overlook the pillow talks about imperialism for the same reasons she never minded my disinterest: we got along well, made one another laugh, and had some capital thrashings in the sack. In the end she had left me for some unshaven lout who won her heart by dressing up as Trotsky for a Halloween party, ice pick in the skull and all. I had wept gales over that, forgetting as one does the inconsistencies in our coupling and remembering only the talks and frolics. Daft as I thought she sometimes was—smart as they come, but somehow daft—it had taken five months of Jane to cure me of Sarah. But that prescription, we know, had run out.

She put down the coffee, staring at me with amazement suitable for beholding those who had been buried the day before. Then she scooted around the corner and, before I could revolve on my seat, embraced me in a clinch used to immobilize the hands while a comrade removes the weapons.

"I take it this means you missed me," I said.

"Jonathan, my God!"

"Missed, and worshiped too." I smiled and gave her a dry kiss on the lips; she laid a buss pure of passion on my cheek, stood back and beamed. From the man's headphones came a long shmaltzy blast of Harry James.

"Where've you been? How are you? What are you doing here? Don't tell me." She held up a hand, glanced back at the kitchen. "Save it. I have to finish a few things and then I'm off. Can you wait? Are you going anywhere? Are you meeting anyone? No? Good." Something sounding large and hairy shouted "*Sarah*" from the kitchen. "Wait." And she practically danced back to the kitchen.

Sarah got off at one, and we retired to a side booth. A sign said it was reserved for two or more people, and given my physical state we didn't qualify. But she had energy for both of us. "Where have you been? How are you? What are—"

I held up a hand. "I'm fine. Just got back in town. I was working up—"

"Ooh. Wait. *Martha!*" Another waitress looked over at us. "The special goes to Death, all right? I forgot." Then she turned back to me.

"Death?"

"Death. The guy on the right. The thin one. Actually his name is Mort but it's the same thing if you think about it etymologically. See, there's Sin and there's Death—"

"You're telling me."

It wasn't a joke but she laughed. Christ, I had forgotten that laugh—throaty, indulgent. "Sin and Death, silly, over there at the counter. Close personal friends. My companions here every blessed evening. They both have those idiotic headphones on all the time, so I can say what I please about them; they never hear."

"Nicknames, that it?"

"Yup. From *Paradise Lost*. They were the gatekeepers on both sides of the entrance to hell." She jerked a thumb over toward the kitchen, where there hung a haze of smoke and aerated grease. "A place with which I am also familiar. You read *Paradise Lost*?"

"Saw the movie."

"There's no movie, you're just being smart. Although there should be one. Have Capra direct it. *Mr. Smith Goes to the Lake of Eternal Torment.*"

I looked at her for a few seconds. "You're still in school, aren't you."

"Does it show?"

"A little."

"I suppose it would." She sighed. "I'm in grad school now. English. I keep looking through want ads for someone with a knack for classical allusion, which seems to be my only skill. Anyway, don't start giving me trouble about that. You took your time getting out of school."

I grinned. "I got out in one day. It was preceded by seven years of classes, granted. But at least I graduated."

"Hey. I like being a perpetual student."

"It's a living."

"Not exactly. When I fall behind on my loans I'm the only one in the department who gets threatening letters from the IMF. If I default I take three banks and a Latin American country with me. Argh." She tapped the knife on the table. "But I don't want to talk about me. Where have you been? What are you doing?"

Libeling the good countryfolk, killing the servantry. The usual. "Sarah, it's been years. That's like asking me to sum up the weather."

"So? Mostly cloudy, lots of sun, what? Still seeing that blonde with the legs and the big, ah, eyes?"

"I didn't know you ever knew. And no. I'm not. Still seeing Trotsky?"

Pause, recognition. "Mark? Oh, God, no." She laughed. "He got old fast. Insisted that sex in the traditional positions was bourgeois."

"What did he want? Proletarian sex? No, let me guess. He wanted to be across town, press a button, which would give you an orgasm. As long as you were in an airline office."

"Or an embassy. Yeah, that's about it."

She'd changed. All the Midwestern innocence and spun-candy sincerity was gone; time had fired and polished this one. She was still somewhat guileless, but older, and she wore it well. Talking with her was like ending a day of trying on new shoes by slipping back into your own.

"Look." She checked her watch. "I want to talk but I am going to lose steam soon. I've been at this all night and it's time to snooze. You want a ride to your car or something?"

Life was a new shoe again. "No car. No home."

"What?"

"If I go home I'll be arrested, probably. Nothing I did. A little mix-up. Don't look skeptical. You want the truth?"

"Usually."

"It's a long story. I'll tell you sometime. You go on home." My eyes got big and wet and began to sting with hopelessness again. "I'll just stay here tonight. With Sin and Death."

"Nonsense. You'll come home with me."

I really hadn't expected this. I looked at her for signs that she was joking. Like if we kept up this conversation, BURMA SHAVE would be at the end of it. "You're kidding."

"No. Come home and stay with me."

I reached a hand across the table and held hers lightly. "You mean it."

"I do." She smiled. One hand squeezed mine and the other played with the chain on her necklace, making the butterfly bob between her breasts. "I have the most comfortable sofa."

I don't go to bed on the first date. That's just the way I am. How I would be if I ever had the chance I'm rather anxious to find out. Not that I expect every night on the town to end up as a tour of the rim of Krakatoa, mind you, but there are times in your life when you are perfectly willing to ignore the Rod McKuen collected works on the bookshelf and the inevitable print of the sad-faced mime in the bedroom and engage in some mutual exercise. I was not in the mood for this when Sarah invited me over; I had one foot in the grave, like someone testing the waters. I just wanted to sleep, and if she had any ideas of seducing me, I'd gracefully decline. Dredge up a weak smile, the old consumptive Leslie Howard charm, and beg indulgence while I belly-flopped into Lethe for the evening. But she had no plans to seduce me.

"Mac is away for the week," she said as we walked to her car. I shuffled along behind her, exhausted but all too jacked up on coffee, and I felt like a flat tire dancing on the highway as the semis rolled over it. "He has business out in San Francisco."

"Mac?"

"My roommate."

"MacDugal? MacTeagle?" MacLover?

"MacAdam, if you can believe."

"He sounds like a fast-food version of original sin."

"You don't know how right you are, Jonathan." She didn't say much until we got to the car. It was the same old brown Pinto, still held together by paint and bumper stickers.

"I still live over by the university. You know the place. The building's as quiet as ever, except for the Cossacks."

The passenger door was taped shut. I got in on her side and buckled up. "The Cossacks? Mr. and Mrs.?"

"Real Cossacks." She started the engine and prodded the car onto the street. "Actually they're Ukrainian. They drink and dance and argue a lot and have bitter fights about the best way to recapture the homeland, and they get terribly sad and drag out the balalaika and sing songs about bread." Now she was wide awake, eyes bright, driving with casual assurance, one hand hanging out the window, palm raised as though she were giving the wind the high-five. "And then there's the Armenian couple at the end of the hall. Wonderful people, but the spices they use. Sometimes I think they run a mummifying shop out of the living room."

"It was all students living there before."

"And now it's a DP clearing house. And owned by Germans, too." She shook her head. "That's the irony, I suppose. And me. I know what some of them think of me. I'm living in sin."

"Do you own or rent?" I mumbled.

"Rent." Pause. "I'll always rent."

We drove in silence for a while.

"Go ahead, say it," she said. Her voice was tight. "I know you're aching to. Same job. Same apartment. Still in school. Perpetual renting midthesis waitress."

"Did I say a thing?"

"No, which is why I know you're thinking it. Listen, Mr. Simpson, I like stability. I need a little here and there. Half of my friends graduate and leave every year. I don't have any family. Mac is . . . Mac is what he is. The only faces I can ever count on seeing are Sin and Death, neither of which tips. I can't even depend on myself for continuity—even the cells in my body replace themselves every seven years, for God's sake."

"All the cells change every seven years?"

"Mm-hmm." She punched the accelerator to fly through a yellow light.

"That's a day I want to mark on my calendar."

"Not all at once, Jay."

We were silent for a few blocks. I stared out the window, struggling with the notion that I was handed a new set of fleshly raiments every seven years. "That can't be right," I said. "You can't grow new brain cells."

"Well, everything changes but the brain."

"And scars. I still have all my old scars."

"Everything changes but the brain and the scars, then." We both smiled, and she rolled her eyes and said: "Figures."

A few minutes later we scudded into the gravel lot behind her apartment building. "This is it. United Nations West." I stumbled out of the car and yawned my way behind her.

Sarah's apartment was spare, ascetic, nothing like the clutter of five years before; then the apartment had been clotted with emblems of undergraduate enthusiams—ghastly Guatemalan tapestries, pottery not so much hand thrown as hurled, gutted stubs of candles stuck in straw-skirted fiaschi, Picasso's *Blue Guitar*. Now the walls were stark white, the only decoration being an old painting of Dante—or someone with his nose—clutching his chest at the sight of who I presumed to be Beatrice. There was a sofa along one wall, and a bookcase made of bricks and boards jammed solid with paperbacks. Propped up in one corner was a guitar, painted blue.

"Home. Let me get you some blankets, okay?" She left for the bedroom, humming. I sat down on the sofa and, still feeling dispossessed, riffled through the hand of botherations I had been dealt until I found one I could do something about. Grue. I explored the room until I spied a phone in the kitchen, dug the hospital's number out of my pocket and called. Sarah came in, laden with blankets, while I was waiting. "Friend in Tokyo I was supposed to call," I said, and she nodded.

The nurse came on, sent my call down into the cortex of the hospital's phone system until it surfaced in the appropriate ward. The doctor on staff told me there was no change. They hadn't even isolated the poison yet. I thanked him and hung up.

"How's Tokyo?" she called from the living room.

"Rainy. Prosperous."

Sarah came into the kitchen. "You look sad, Jay."

I lit a cigarette and blew a ring up at the fluorescent halo on the ceiling. "It's Grue. My housekeeper. Still out. Comatose."

"What happened?" She sat down and brushed her hair. "She have a stroke?"

"No." I closed my eyes and rubbed my forehead. This was, after all, a dream; none of it had happened. I was back home and was going to wake up any minute now. And be stung by a bee. I opened my eyes. "Heard of the AIL?"

Sarah frowned. "Sounds familiar."

"Billboards? Spray-painted messages?"

"Oh, sure." She smiled. "Those are kind of funny."

"Yeah, well, they or he or she or it poisoned the sweetest old lady I ever met. Hardy har."

Sarah's eyes got big and wide. I explained. I started with the bee and ended with the party.

"You have an interesting life," she finally said.

"It's kept my attention."

"That's so awful. About your grandmother."

"She's not my grandmother. But she fit the mold. I would have adopted her but she beat me to it."

She stared at the floor. "And here I was, cheering those AIL people for having the right attitude. I mean, all that stuff is so bad for you. But poisoning people. My God." She shuddered.

We simply sat for a while. Finally I just felt angry and tired of being alone and I leaned over and gave her a hug. She held it for a second, doubled its intensity for a second and released me. "You okay?" she said. I nodded. "I'm sorry things are what they are." Meaning Mac or Grue or the eternal threat of nuclear annihilation, who knew? She pushed me away and said, "Bed," and got up and left the room. I heard her door click shut.

The sofa was comfortable enough. I had a view of the bedroom door. I lay there for a long while waiting for the light under her door to go off. I was fading into sleep when the phone rang; her door banged open and she came out of her room, dressed in a robe, knotting the cord around her waist. She took the phone and carried it into her room, cradled like an infant squalling for attention. Her end of the conversation was all whispers and hisses; I heard her pace, throw herself on the squeaking bed, get up and pace again. I heard her bang the phone back onto its cradle, only to have it ring again. The light under the door was still burning when I finally fell asleep.

6

"Describe your symptoms," said the doctor. He was a short man, a dinosaur egg in a white smock, with a round smiling face. He had his thin hair plastered down to a point, a spade between the two shiny onions of his eyes. Fat hands rested on his knees.

"Well, I'm tired all the time. Not profoundly but generally tired. I have tightness in the chest and frequent headaches and every so often I see black spots. Should I go on?"

"Mmm. Not should you but will you, is the question. Well." He smiled. "You have a rare and hopeless disease that only strikes people who deserve it. It's a real four-star fatal disease, let me tell you."

"How long have I got?"

"Have you made arrangements for lunch?"

I woke up gagging. I closed my eyes. I heard the sweetest sounds you can wake up to—the gurgle of the coffeepot, the hiss and sizzle of bacon having a spat with the pan, the voice of a beloved humming over the makings of the meal. If only I knew who the voice called its mistress. Then Sarah appeared over me, holding a skillet, ready to beat from my reluctant brain my preference in eggs. "God, I had an awful dream. I was going to die."

"You look like it. And you sound exhumed." She smiled a warm maternal smile. "I woke you up because I have to get to class and I thought I'd wake you and tell you I won't be here to wake you up later. There's espresso on and I made you breakfast. Plenty of bacon with nitrites to give you cancer."

"It's too early in the morning to get cancer," I murmured. I closed my eyes. My brain felt like a bruise on a banana.

"How long are you going to stay here?" she called from the bathroom.

"How long is your lease?" I said.

"You don't sound good, Jonathan, if you don't mind an opinion.

I'm going to lay out some vitamins here for you to take. And take them with the spring water in the fridge, okay? Tap water has fluoride in it."

"I thought fluoride was good for you. Helped your teeth."

"They've been testing it on mice. It causes cancer."

"The mice got more dates, I'll bet."

"Everything is bad for you. The food you eat and the water you drink and the air you breathe or would breathe if you didn't smoke. I can't believe that none of the stuff I taught you about nutrition sunk in."

"I listened. I just didn't believe it. My parents ate what I eat and look where they are now: Arizona. Florida."

"Minus their gall bladders, I'll bet."

"Any organ that can be removed without shortening your lifespan isn't pulling its weight."

"Fine. Be that way. Die of a stroke at age forty if it'll make you happy. I have to leave." She came out of the bedroom, poking arms through the sleeves of her coat. "You can stay tonight if you like. My door is always open. Just lock it on the way out if you leave, okay?" And I heard the door slam. The front door groaned open, the screen banged shut and I heard her whistling down the steps outside the window.

I lay there for a decade. This morning the hangover, ever inventive, had spewed forth a band of Lilliputians who had sewn me to the sofa. Of course I felt awful, but I wasn't going to give the Granola Queen the satisfaction of knowing it. I passed some time examining the ceiling. It was the same old ceiling. The same fault line still ran across it north to southeast. I rolled over on my stomach, an act of some bravery, and looked out the window. There was that old church, a gray weathered ruin. Two banners hung above the portal, Celebrate and New Life, snapping and twisting in the wind.

For entertainment during breakfast I had the paper. And such a pleasure it provided. The main story, of course, was the poisoned mix. Most of it dealt with Bishop's news conference; details about Grue's condition were sparse. There was a picture of bundt mix, and a lot number to avoid on pain of death. Elsewhere, on page one of the metro section: HOUSE RAIDED. I had been in town, what, a week plus change, and my life already filled half the paper.

I smiled at the article next to the piece on my house: GRAIN

PROTESTORS STAGE INCIDENT AT MUNCO HQ. This time they hadn't just occupied the office; they'd dumped fertilizer in the executive suites.

I wondered if Bishop was smart enough to investigate the possibility of links between the protestors and the AIL. I hoped so.

I took a bath, feeling, as is typical when you bathe in other people's bathrooms, more naked than usual. I shaved with one of Mac's razors, the dullness of which suggested he had not grasped the concept of disposability, and then laid an inch of Sunny Farms Natural Toothpaste on my finger and distributed the loam-flavored mixture around my teeth. I had to smoke a cigarette to restore the equilibrium in my mouth. After ablutions were concluded I put on my sweater, which smelled like a deep-fried bar rag. Out of sheer nosiness I decided to see if Mac had anything I could wear.

In the bedroom was a picture of the two of them, Sarah beaming at the camera, Mac glowering at it as though he thought it would steal his soul but had been convinced the cost was negligible. He was a burly one, an ambulatory bank vault. From his posture it looked as though he had to pick the asphalt from his knuckles at the end of every day. I pawed through the closet until I found one of Mac's coats, an item of the color you see when people hit you hard in the head. It was cut loosely, presumably to offer greater freedom of movement as he swung through the trees.

There were no symbols of his presence in the room—or in the entire apartment, for that matter. All the books were Sarah's, the posters were hers—I knew her taste, strictly pre-Raphaelite—all the bric-a-brac from South American countries in need of land reform, hers. Mac's existence here could probably be distilled down to that six-pack of beer in the fridge and the athlete's foot medication in the medicine chest. As far as I could tell, about the only thing he had going for him was an opposable thumb—which, of course, I could easily imagine wrapped around my larynx.

But this was not and would not be any of my business. The last twenty-four hours had taught me once again that Sarah and I liked one another too much to try to get along. I wrote out a note thanking her for the sofa and breakfast and said I would call.

I called the manor but got no answer. I didn't know where Trygve was in the habit of going in the morning besides to sleep, but to assuage my fears about what might have happened I called admissions at the city jail. I was immediately put on hold, and I listened to a recording on how to avoid burglary. An operator came on, and I requested admissions; I was put on hold and dropped in medias res into a disquisition on how to report a burglary, for those who didn't heed the counsel of the previous message. Finally a human being came on, barked, "City jail admissions."

"Yes, I need to know if you've arrested a friend of mine."

"Name."

"Trygve."

"Last name."

The Butler. "I, ah, don't know."

"Sir, I need a last name."

"Listen. Do you have an old white-haired man in a servant's uniform?"

"Kinda nervous and stupid?"

"What's his bail?"

"Hold on." He put me on hold, returning in a minute. "Five hundred."

"Right. Thanks. Listen, do you take personal checks?"

"Checks? Oh, sure. With ID and amount of purchase only. Hell no, we don't take checks."

"Sorry."

Damn. I hung up the phone, thought of Trygve in jail and closed my eyes. I had to get him out, of course. Five hundred dollars. Where was I going to get that kind of scratch?

In the waiting room of the jail there were two long benches, branded by unattended cigarettes and scarred with dates, initials, oaths. They looked like pews from a religion that had gone out of business. The walls, once white, were yellow with nicotine, like an old man's teeth; the floor was gritty under my feet. The room was nearly empty; apparently, people had been behaving lately. There was one man hunched in a pew, hands in his lap, head bowed. Lou Carver.

Instinct had already notified the muscles required to turn around and flee, but I didn't make a move. Carver was as abject a sight as I'd ever seen, a great lumpy dirigible leaking life.

I walked over and sat a few feet from him; he didn't look up. He was muttering things at his groin, scraping his feet back and forth on the floor. I draped an arm over the pew, composing salutations, but nothing came. "Come here often?" was obviously a little too close to the truth, for I guessed this was about his daughter again.

I cleared my throat. "Could be worse," I said. "I could still be working for you."

He jerked up his head. When he saw me his jaw worked from side to side; his eyes clouded and his brow darkened. A growl rose and died in his throat. His fingers unlaced and thickened into fists. It occurred to me that I was about to be beaten. "You," he said. "You—you—you—you. You."

Carver leaned over and patted me on the shoulder and then put his hands back in his lap.

"How in hell did you find me here?"

"I didn't. I'm here to bail someone out."

"Friend?"

"Butler."

Carver nodded. He was silent for a while. Then he looked at me. "Judas, boy, I don't know what to say to you. You are one stupid son of a bitch for doing what you did." He rubbed a hand on his cheek. "And smart for taking to the hills. I guess."

"I hope you didn't get in much trouble."

"Enough. I blamed you, mostly."

"Anybody sue us?"

"Everybody sued. When the cases are over we're going to have to drop our libel insurance. Can't afford the premiums." He stared ahead, numb.

"Hit me."

"What?"

"Punch me. Come on." I stood up. I meant it. "I deserve it. Deck me. Here, right on the button."

"Go to hell."

"Come on. Please. Nail me one. I'll feel better."

"You're out of your goddamn brain, Simpson. Siddown." I sat. "Yeah, it was your fault. But someone shoulda caught it. Bluchinksi." He snarled, shook his head. "You shoulda told me about Jane anyway."

"Told you what? You knew."

"I knew she'd gone, and I was surprised she took as long to get her tail out there as she did. As much as I liked you kids, I wondered what the hell you were doing up in Valhalla anyway. Or why you didn't go with her. So I read your, ah, parting column, see she's getting loved up by some other guy, right, and I figured it out. I don't blame you for wanting out. I wasn't always a slow slab of guts like I am today, you know. I was young. I know what it's like."

"You do?"

"I do. Being horny as a two-dicked billy goat all the time. It's awful. Women." He sighed, then his eyes narrowed. "Daughters."

"If you didn't know why I was there, how come you kept turning down my resignations?"

He smiled. "Didn't want you to go. You weren't ready. She was. More's the pity. But you, you don't know how to do things practical, son. No offense."

"Mr. Carver?" This from a matron at the doorway, file in hand. "Your daughter is coming out now." Carver got to his feet.

Spanks shuffled out, dealing sullen looks right and left. Her hair was glued into three sharp stalagmites, and she wore a leather jacket festooned with buttons. An enormous crucifix, rendered nearly to scale, hung from her neck. Her eyes were flat and bored, her mouth a thin grim line of disapproval. She looked at Carver and looked away; she looked at me, tilted her head back and gave me a standard-issue sneer.

"Hi," I said, hand outstretched. "We met once. Jonathan Simpson, tool of the bourgeoisie?" But she was looking at her father, forming her features into a mask of repentance.

"Thanks, Dad." She had a manila envelope in one hand; she pulled a rusty bicycle chain out and attached it around her neck. "Jail's a bitch."

Carver turned to me. "You gonna be around? I want to talk to you. First I have to take my daughter to the woodshed and beat some love of society into her." Spanks fingered her bicycle chain.

"There's a café across the street."

"One hour." And he grabbed Spanks by the arm and hauled her out of the room. I didn't doubt he'd have his belt loosened by the time they were out of the building.

Presently the matron came to tell me I could go down to the holding tank. This was a small lobby painted the color of an upset stomach with a Plexiglas window at one end of the room. I told them who I wanted to see and was escorted into another waiting room, this one with a mesh grid between my side of the room and that of the lawbreakers. I described Trygve to the guard and was told to take a seat and wait.

The guard brought Trygve into the room. He was still wearing his butler's tux, with several scuff marks. His hair was disordered, fashioned into a dozen little gray horns, and he looked sad but as eternally patient and addled as ever. He sat down and folded his hands on the table.

"I want to go home, Master Simpson."

"I know. We'll get you out."

"There are big and sweaty men in there. They are all calling me James and saying 'Home' and laughing. I don't know what they're talking about."

"Don't worry. You'll be okay."

"Are we going now?"

"We can't go yet. I need to pay your bail and I don't have the money. You command quite a price."

Trygve smiled with pride. "Do you want some money to buy me, then? I have quite a lot in my wallet."

"You—why didn't you pay your own bail?"

"They took my wallet when I came in."

"Okay. I'll get the money. Don't worry. You'll be out in a minute." And I went back into the adjoining room. It took some stupendous haggling to get the wallet. Tryg was being held as an accessory to the more grievous offenses leavened by Oscar's party, which was why everyone else was tagged and released while he languished in jail. I told the jailers I was a friend, and I gave a Valhalla address, which my driver's license corroborated. After a consultation with Trygve they gave me the wallet. There was around two thousand dollars inside, fifties and hundreds. We both signed a dozen forms for the wallet, and then I went upstairs to pay the cashier. When I brought the receipt back to the office they gave me a happy butler in return and wished us both a good day and a fine trial. Outside I put Trygve in a cab, paid the driver a healthy advance and kept one thousand for myself, lest Trygve get generous with the gratuity or hire the rig to tour Canada. Then I went across the street to wait for Carver.

The cafeteria was in the basement of the Hennepin County Center, walled with windows, looking out onto a well into which a waterfall thundered in the temperate months. It was empty now, with a few scraps of rubbish chasing each other around in the wind. I bought a cup of coffee and took a seat by the window. There wasn't much to do but drink it and wait.

Carver came by in an hour and a half, muttering, the usual stomp in his walk making the cup of coffee in one hand slosh into the saucer. He sat down, poured the saucer into the cup, took half the cup in one gulp and leaned back in his chair. He made a sound like a whale spouting, and closed his eyes. One hand reached into a pocket and came out with a pack of Luckies—cigars, pipes, cigarettes, Carver was indiscriminate and omnivorous when it came to tobacco. He lit the cigarette, looked at me and threw the match into the ashtray as though it was a glove and he was challenging me to a duel.

"How'd it go?" I asked.

"Ten pounds of lawn fertilizer."

"That bad."

"That's what this is about, son: ten pounds of chemical lawn fertilizer. Security caught my daughter dumping Lawn-B-Green into a strange man's desk. Had a scoop and was just measuring it out, calm as a judge. When the police came they were going to handcuff her, and she said, 'Here, I have handcuffs, let me put mine on.' They said no. Know why? Because hers weren't regulation. Hers were jewelry handcuffs. You get the picture? My daughter has handcuffs for jewelry."

The woodshed session had evidently gone poorly. Spanks was unrepentant, regarding the legal system as a lackey of capitalism and refusing to acknowledge its jurisdiction. Seeing as she had told her arresting officers as much and still had spent a day in the tank, I wondered if anything short of a few minutes strapped in the electric chair would convince her that the muscle lay on the other side of the balance sheet.

I wondered if they'd questioned her about the AIL. And what she'd said.

"You just have one daughter, don't you?" I asked.

"Yeah." He loosened his tie. "No sons. Probably a coupla two-tones in Okinawa that have the Carver nose but no one I can stick in my will, if that's what you mean." He smiled.

I had to marvel at this guy. Carver was from the last age of Men—from what he'd told me before, by the time he was my age he'd already brought one person into the world and taken a few dozen out. He had a world war to help him, but still. He needed male bonding to forget about Spanks's misdeeds. And mine. I tilted my chair on two legs and slung an arm over the back. "So. Enough of all this. You following the Vikings this year? Two and oh, with the starting QB out, yet."

"Don't snow me," Carver said. "We can talk about the Vikes if you want, but I'm still going to chew your ass out."

"I don't know anything about football," I said. I dropped my chair back to four legs.

"You know how to run," Carver said. "That's a start. Put the ball in your hands, dress the other team up like the Elim Sewing Circle, you'd set rushing records." He paused. "I'm pretty disappointed in you."

"I'm sorry, Mr. Carver." I looked down at my empty cup. "But only because it's going to make things hard for you."

"You're not sorry you left?"

"No." I looked up. "I couldn't stand it up there anymore. All that peace and quiet and blond hair and polka music. I should have picked a better way to leave. . . ."

"I think you picked a fine way. I gotta give you severance pay now. What are you going to do now, huh?"

"Try to get a job, I suppose."

"With what references? You expect me to tell anyone to hire you?"

I looked down, glared at the table. "No."

"You wouldn't be wanting to come back up, or anything."

"You'd take me?"

He nodded.

"I won't. I can't."

Carver sighed. "Ah, Jesus. Listen to me. I start chewing you out and I end up offering you your job back. Something wrong with me. Went soft somewhere along the line."

"You were always soft on Jane," I said. "She thought you were just a big sweet bear."

"Really?" He smiled, lit another Lucky. "Jane was almost like a daughter. And you were sort of a son. Not enough for me to be able to beat you for running away, but, you know."

"That made us brother and sister," I said. "No wonder she got funny about having sex."

"What?"

"Never mind. You want more coffee?"

Carver was looking into the barren waterfall, eyes distant and thoughtful. "Nah," he said. Then he looked at me. "You know, it's funny this way, but a man who doesn't have sons, he tends to adopt them as he goes along." Carver probed his cheek with his tongue. "You never had a dad, did you?"

"Sure I did. How do you think I got on this earth? Spontaneous generation?"

"I mean a dad. Come on."

I looked away. "Well, not to speak of. Although I do. Speak of him, I mean. And not with a smile on my face."

"He ever do any of that stuff you're supposed to do? Play catch? Teach you how to shoot, take you to ball games?"

"I grew up in a suburb, Mr. Carver. There's not a lot to practice shooting on except burglars. So if you're asking if Dad and me sat up nights in the living room with the lights off and guns across our laps, no. And I hate guns. Hate hunting. I came from the generation that grew up with Bambi, remember. Bambi, and Vietnam. I'm not all that well disposed to firearms. As for playing catch, he took me out once, because he thought that was what fathers and sons did. He hit me in the head with the first pitch."

"It shows."

"Thanks."

"I mean, it shows that you didn't have a real dad. My daughter, she's gotta rebel. Fine. She gets horns on her head and acts like she just don't care if she puts her dad in the box with a stroke, I understand. But you never rebel. You don't have anything to rebel against. You want parents."

"That's brilliant." I gave him a dead look. "The money you've just saved me on analysis."

"Not really." He leaned back and patted his stomach. "That's what you told me at the Christmas party when you were three sheets. Bitching about your parents' divorce. It took a healthy dose of liquor to get you to talk man to man, too. You don't know how to act around a man the age of your father."

"I do so."

"Ahh, no you don't. We worked together five years and you still call me mister. Never Lou."

"You're my boss."

"I was your boss." He hitched up his pants, spouted again. "Don't know what I am now. Some old fart you'll tell stories about to your kids, probably. Old Carver. By the time you tell them about me I'll be eight feet tall and breathing fire and lunching on the legs of reporters I've had killed for getting quotes wrong." He laughed. "Or you could really scare them, and tell the truth."

"I'll try the truth, Lou." There. I said it.

We looked at each other for a while.

"Still doesn't sound right, does it?" he said. I shook my head.

"All right." He put his hands on the table. "Enough of this. We got things to do. You want a job?"

"What?"

He sipped the last of his coffee. "You still want to work on a paper? Down here, I mean?"

"Who'll take me? Hire Simpson and watch the lawyers line up."

"But you still want to work on a paper." I nodded. "Good enough. Let's get you a job down here. I know people. Lots of 'em. I can get you work by this afternoon if you want. Sound all right?"

Father. Pater. Dad.

7

The Sandusky Building was an old restored edifice in the old restored warehouse district. In its new incarnation it was known as Sandusky Place, and had been renovated out of its mean station: the brick had been sandblasted, the windows replaced with mirrored glass. The building wore its modernization well, as most do, looking somehow pleased that it was getting all the attention. Its humble roots, however, were evident over the front door. A bas-relief of a buxom woman who strained the definition of bas-relief stood above the portico, one hand holding a torch aloft, the other holding a pig of noble countenance. The words *Pork Exchange* were carved for all eternity below.

On our way there Carver had explained that an old buddy of his was the publisher of a little paper, or at least had been, the last time they'd talked. He'd be sure to give me a job, if only to make the lawyers he had on retainer work for their money. I wondered why Carver would dump on a buddy someone who'd brought the collective spittle of northern Minnesota on his head, but I did not bring the matter up. A job was a job. And anything would be better than the *Lacs Standard.*

Although the *Standard* soon looked a great deal better.

"*Metropole,*" Carver said, his finger resting on an entry in the Sandusky Place directory. "That sound like a newspaper to you?"

"That's where you're going to get me a job?"

"I'll try."

"Is this revenge? The *Metropole* isn't a paper. It's a shopper. One of those what-to-wear-while-you-shop-before-you-go-eat rags."

"It's a paper."

"Any paper that would fold for lack of ads if tanning parlors were banned is not a paper."

Carver glowered at me. "What do you expect? I got to be the last guy on the block to remind you what you've been doing for the last five years. Maybe this shopper rag won't even take you. So shut up and get ready to be grateful. I'm gonna use up a lot of favors here."

The *Metropole* newspaper was on the eighth floor, begging the question of how many floors the business of swapping sows really took. A rickety elevator took us up, swaying in the shaft, and opened its doors a few inches shy of the floor. Behind a door marked METROPOLE we met a receptionist, a young person of bristling hair and indeterminate sex. It raised plucked eyebrows at us and asked in a neutral voice if it could help us. It could; Carver here for Dickerson. Mr. Dickerson was paged, and we were bade to wait.

Mr. Dickerson soon emerged, wearing first the businessman's mask of feigned sincerity and then, upon seeing Carver, breaking into a leer. They shook and called each other sons of bitches and nogoodlousybastards and hit each other. Dickerson began to drag Carver toward his office but Carver stopped and gestured for me, callow youth of promise, to step forward and meet the great potentate.

"This is Jonathan," he said, a curious note of pride in his voice. "Jonathan Simpson."

"Wha—? Lou, you never told me you had a son."

"He's the old bastard," I said. "I'm the young one."

"Oh, I musta told you about him. He was one of our reporters up in Valhalla there. Far too good to stay up there, though. You wouldn't believe the imagination in this kid's work." He grinned and cuffed me on the ear. "I dragged him down here for you to give him a job. Give him a job, Dick."

"What does he do? You in ads, son?"

"I criticize," I said, unwisely.

"Well, you sure as hell aren't in ads, then. What, you write? Yeah? Okay. I'll give you to Fikes, and don't take it personally. Daphne?" This was to the receptionist. "Call Fikes, see if he's in. Then tell him I have someone for him to interview."

A few minutes later, Carver having disappeared down the hall, laughing with Dickerson, I was wandering around the newsroom, looking for Fikes.

The newsroom was split into a warren of cubicles, clothed in material the color of fluorescent mustard. A few heads bobbed in various cubicles and ducked down, only to have other heads pop up in other cubicles. I had this toy as a child—you bang one figure back in its box with a mallet, another springs up elsewhere. Oh, I felt at ease here.

The *Metropole* was not a large operation, but it was made to seem even smaller by the squalor of the office. In one corner sat a mountain of old newspapers, the most recent of which looked as though it might contain an interview with Dreyfus; another corner was occupied by a stack of typewriters, their ribbons hanging slack with exhaustion, presumably replaced by the computers that sat on each desk. One side of the room was full of old gray desks pushed together like tired beasts clumped around dry water holes; dim thin light struggled through grimy grids of opaque glass along the wall. The carpet was pitted with holes, evidence of carelessness with cigarettes or a small meteor shower. On every level surface stood six or more coffee cups, all with dark brown circles inside.

At the first desk was a weary young man with dark brown circles around his eyes. Made me want to watch him drink a cup of coffee. I stepped up, cleared my throat and asked where I might find Mr. Fikes.

"Where you might or where you will?" said the young man, not looking up from his papers.

"Cut the impertinent bullshit, Solly," came a weary voice from one of the cubicles. The one named Solly shrugged and gestured in the direction of the southern hemisphere. "You'll find the pertinent bullshit sitting over there." Inside the first cubicle behind me I found a man leaning back into his chair, feet up on his desk, studying a copy of the *Metropole.*

"Mr. Fikes?"

"Mmrggh?" He looked up at me. He had a round face with a few strands of hair plastered into a point aimed at his nose. He wore a suit of brown polyester with white stitching, the lapels a palimpsest of past meals, and the width of his tie was dictated not by fashion but by the regulation size for a soccer field. His eyes looked as though he marinated them nightly in tomato broth. "Mmrggh?" he repeated.

"Hi. My name is, ah, Jonathan Simpson? Mr. Dickerson sent me in here to talk to you about working on the paper."

"He did, did he. Mrrgh. Yes. Well. Right. Sit down." He picked a stack of newspapers off a chair and dropped them on the floor, loosing a swarm of yellow dust. "Why did he send you? He said something about work? Doing?"

"Well, whatever you have open."

"Mmr. Mm. You have written before?"

"Yes. I worked over at the, ah, *Daily* for several years, mostly in the arts department. I wrote a column. Criticism. For the last five years I've been employed at a paper up north."

"Doing?"

"Sort of a Talk of the Town feature. Running commentary on the life of the city."

"What did you say the paper was?"

"The, ah, *Lacs Standard.*"

"Plugh." This was a laugh, a mirthless plosive shot from his mouth, the recoil rippling through his jowls.

"I know. Unfortunate name. The editor is a friend of Mr. Dickerson."

"Who?"

"Dickerson? Your publisher."

"Ah. Him. Right."

This was getting tiresome. "Is this a bad time? I can leave and never come back if you like." Fikes's phone buzzed, and he reached over and swatted a button, putting the receiver to his ear, keeping bleary eyes on me. "Mrrghm? Yes. Right in front of me. Mrgh. Hardly. Mrrh? I shouldn't guess it. No. Eeeyessss. Anything? But . . . mrrghm. Right." He hung up the phone and folded his hands over his lap. "You're hired."

"Really."

He nodded but his eyes said mrrrgh.

"What will I be doing?"

"I've no idea."

"When do I start?"

"Immediately."

We sat looking at one another until Fikes coughed and began to tap a pencil on the table.

"I'll put it to you briefly. Mr. Dickerson has told me to hire you, period. Now, he is the owner and his word is gold around here. I should also remind you that America has been off the gold standard for more than a few decades, hence his word may not be the currency which we on the editorial side of things use to transact our opinions. Am I clear, mrgh?"

"Yes."

"Good." He rubbed his hands over his face, tilted back and addressed the ceiling. "I'm in a bind, Mr. Simpson. Our food reviewer is incapacitated. Poisoned. Third time in as many months. Mrrgh. Man has a knack for finding restaurants run by latter-day Borgias." He leveled his eyes at me. "I don't suppose you know anything about food."

Well, he'd never know that I sliced my pizzas with a scissors. "I know enough," I said, looking away with modesty.

"Any experience writing about it?"

"I've been writing for a decade and eating for nearly three. That makes about four decades of experience."

Fikes gave me a dim smile.

"Right. Well. Mrgh." He ran a finger across the point of his hair, looked at his finger as though there were an ADD line across the digit. "I need someone to fill in. I'm not saying this is something I want you to do on a regular basis. I don't even know if you can write. What I want from you is simple. I don't want the vitae of every damn dish. Just describe the menu, the decor, the composition and palatability of each item. Whether or not the waiter serves the stuff with his fingers in the food. Here—" He scrawled a number on a piece of paper and handed it to me. "Our late and lamented reviewer, Martin. Call him before he dies entirely, mrrgh? He'll give you hints and ideas where to go. Have the piece by tomorrow."

"Tomorrow?"

"The day which follows this one and precedes the day after it." He sat up. "And bring me clips. I shall want to see some of those Talk of the Town pieces tomorrow."

"It wasn't called Talk of the Town."

"I don't care. Semaphore Flags of the Fucking Hamlet, whatever it was. Humor me by showing me just what I have been dragooned into employing, would you?"

"Well. That's a problem. I left in a slight haste and I didn't have time to assemble a portfolio of recent work. I can get you something from the *Daily*, though."

"Do so."

"Right. Tomorrow. And, ah, thank you."

"Mrrgh." He looked down at his desk to indicate that our merry colloquy was over. I got up and went back to Solly's desk, asked if I could use his phone; Solly said, "Dial nine to get out" without looking up. I called the hospital to check on Grue; nothing. I called Detective Bishop just to see what was going on; he wasn't in. I left a message. I was halfway through the number of Martin the Dying Reviewer when Solly put a hand on the hook of the phone. I glanced over and frowned at him; he kept his hand on the phone. I looked at him. He needed a shave and a clean shirt and another shave. He would have been handsome, but his eyes had a rabid cast and his teeth looked as though he removed recalcitrant food particles with an ax.

"Grunewald. That's the old lady that almost bought it from the cake mix. And Bishop is the cop in charge."

"The old lady is my housekeeper, and what's it to you."

His eyes widened. "You know her?"

"I'm the lucky soul she was making the cake for. Do you mind if I make my call?"

"Holy mother. I got to talk to you." He put his other hand over the phone. "I'm doing a story on this thing. This AIL business."

"You don't need me. What you need is in the papers and if it's not there, you don't need it."

"You don't understand."

I hung up the phone. He still had his hands on the hook. "Of course I understand. Everyone wants to know how gray the old lady got when she took a swan dive onto the linoleum. Everyone wants the details of what just might happen again, if we're lucky and another stranger gets it. Sorry. This is a private matter."

Solly stared at me. "And you call yourself a journalist?"

I picked up the receiver, looked at the numbers on the phone. "I'm not a journalist at all. I'm a critic." Food critic. I had to be insane. Maybe when I went deaf I could turn to judging opera.

"Well, I am a journalist, mister. And I—"

"You call this journalism?" I pointed to a copy of the *Metropole* on his desk. DISEASE-FREE DATING IDEAS was the head. "From the issue I read, I gather that the only angle this paper would have on the AIL is how dying of poison spoils your complexion. Ten easy makeovers your mortician can do in minutes."

"Don't think I like doing it. I'm so used to the garbage I can write it with one eye shut."

"Judging from the lack of perceived depth I've seen in the paper, I'd say that's just what you've been doing."

"That's going to change. Mr. Boiled in Oil over there"—he jerked a thumb toward Fikes—"is trying to make us competitive with the rest of the alternatives. Make us legitimate. From now on we do covers on big local issues. And this is the biggest. It's also mine." He scowled. "Got it?"

"Fine." I put the receiver back to my ear, looked at the number Fikes had given me.

Solly grabbed my wrist. "Maybe you didn't hear me. I said this story is mine. It's time for Old Lardhead to sit on someone else's copy. I'm going to do the hard pieces from now on. This. Is. One of them. Don't get any ideas of coming in here and taking this one just because it was your maid that bought it."

I looked at the hand around my wrist. "You're a charming man, Solly," I said. "Yet so hard to read." I shook my hand free. "You can have the story. It's not my type of piece. I'm not a journalist. I don't have an objective bone in my body. There are injunctions against me in eight states that keep me from writing anything but reviews of shows that have already closed. All right?"

Solly gave me the look of a dog that has been indiscriminately beaten since whelphood, and nodded.

I went to another phone to call Martin. A thin gray voice answered on the eighth ring.

"What."

"Martin? This is Jonathan Simpson at the *Metropole*. I'm going to be standing in on your food—"

"Ohh, Gaaaaawd." There was a desperate vertiginous croak on the other end. "Don't say that word. The F one."

"Sorry. Ah, Fikes gave me your number, said you'd know of some restau—places that serve—I'm sorry, I have to. Places where I can, you know. Chow down. Judge the sustenance."

"Hold on." I held. There was a groan in decrescendo, the rustle of papers and the shuffle of slippered feet back to the phone. "Okay. Chi . . . blurg. China Diner. I was going to do it next. Just opened. Here's the address." I took it down.

"Thanks. I hope you get better."

"I want to die."

"Well, you know best. Talk to you later."

"Only if you have a Ouija board." The line went dead.

I gave Solly a smile and a wave and went back to find Carver. Behind Dickerson's door I heard the sound of laughter or a cockfight. I knocked and entered. Carver and Dickerson were sitting at a table, faces flushed, the last gusts of laughter playing out on their features. There was a bottle in the middle of the table, no glasses. Either they had dispensed with them or had swallowed them at the sound of my knock. Both relaxed when they saw me.

"Fikes set you up all right?" Dickerson said. He wiped a tear from the corner of his eye.

"Everything's fine," I said. "Friendly group you have in your employ."

"Buncha assholes. But they do the job, and they do it for what I pay them. Listen to Fikes. He's got a turret up his ass but he knows what he's talking about."

"I have to go to the *Daily*," I said to Carver. "Get some clips. Are you leaving town tonight?"

"Nope. Dick and I have some old times to live up to. Where you staying nowadays? I'll give you a call in the morning." I gave him the number. "That a rooming house?"

"It's a twenty-room mansion on Park Avenue."

"Right." He laughed, punched Dickerson in the arm. "What'd I say about this guy?"

Dickerson grinned. "I like this kid, Lou."

"So do I. Always did." He winked. "Hey. Here." And he flung something at me. My hands flew up by instinct, caught it: keys. I had the odd feeling that I should have mowed the lawn to earn them. "That's to the Buick," he said. "It's out back. I don't need it tonight. Go ahead. Take it. Have some fun."

I tossed the keys back to Carver. "Thanks," I said, "but I've got to get my Pacer back from the towing lot before the storage fees exceed its retail value."

Daphne was closing up the shop as I left. She had her coat on and was pulling on her boots. The lights on the switchboard indicated half a dozen incoming calls. She looked up and saw me staring at the phone. "Someone will get them," she said in a monotone. "They pay me to work until five and that's what I do." She went back to her boots. "You want a brownie?"

"What?"

"Over there. Take one." There was a full pan, untouched, sitting on the table by the door.

"They have nuts in them?"

"Could be. It's an uncertain world." She finished lacing her boots and started to get into her jacket. I took a brownie out of the pan, folded it in a handkerchief and put it in my pocket for later. "Thanks," I said. "Daphne?"

She looked up at me as though I were about to announce that two and two equal four. "Is everyone around here always sour?" I said.

"Like what."

"Like Solly. Like Fikes. I didn't get the warmest welcome."

"Fikes is a pain. Solly is a pain but he's my boyfriend so I overlook it. See ya." And she left the office.

Outside I looked around, reorienting myself. Five years ago this had been the unrenovated warehouse district, and, not finding the need to buy bulk, I'd no occasion to visit it. I stood for a moment watching workmen strip a billboard atop a building across from Sandusky Place; there was just the face of a man remaining, beaming teeth a yard high, the reason for his pleasure already scraps of paper at the workmen's feet. When they began to peel off his forehead I started north to the towing lot and then headed for the university.

The *Daily* was tucked in the basement of the journalism building. I parked behind the student union and started walking. Everyone I passed on campus looked young—the women had that fresh sexuality that you find in today's twelve-year-olds, and the men walked with a cocky spring, full of Sartre and fashionable politics. I felt old. But a sweet wave of nostalgia lapped at me as I went down the stairs to the basement of Murphy Hall—the smell of the building was the same. The brew of chemicals from the photo lab, the acrid stink of old coffee grousing around the hallway. And I knew that behind the door marked

Daily would be the same anarchic ruin I had left behind at the *Metropole*, but far livelier: phones jangling from all corners, the receptionist yelling names across the office; the metered click of manual typewriters banging out a story. There'd be the AP wire machine, chattering in the corner and spitting copy from the wire. A haze of gray smoke and blue language. A bunch of greenhorns, kids putting out one of the largest daily papers in the state. Where I made my name. I hadn't even opened the door and I was home again.

I opened the door. Silence. A receptionist sat behind a console two feet across, purring into a headset, pushing buttons. Behind her, where the word *Daily* had been painted in vast black letters, each staff member's autograph signed in White-out, there was now cool neon tubing spelling out *Daily* in flowing script. To the left was the newsroom, gray tables with charcoal dividers, gray computers tilted up like the empty heads of marveling newborns. There were No Smoking signs everywhere. The tapping of keyboards, steady, muted, as if synaptic activity were mere falling dominoes, drifted from the newsroom. The receptionist looked at me and asked, with proprietary intonation, if she could help me. I requested an audience with the librarian. She asked that I take a seat. God help me, it was even comfortable.

Presently the librarian came out. True to the stereotype, she looked like a member of Future Spinsters of America: a pinched mouth sewn into a pucker of disapproval, and a gaze of iron diffused by thick spectacles. She nodded when I told her I wanted copies of my old clips, and waved for me to follow her. Her sanctorum was the former staff lounge. I sat on the couch where Jane and I had rolled around a few times in the middle of the night, with only the police scanner and the AP machine for company.

"Material five years or older is microfilmed and sent to the university archives," she said. "But there should be something in the bound files there." She gestured at a shelf. "You can get it out of there and get copies. There's a machine up front."

I hauled down a few volumes, dusty with sediment of disinterest. Lousy ahistorical punks. I read a few pages at random, feeling vaguely like a man rotting with syphilis looking at his baby pictures. I remembered the stories, the bylines. I saw Jane's byline, which through some byzantine route of the libido, gave me the faint stirrings of an erection.

After an hour I had sufficient evidence to let Fikes sleep easy, and I lugged the volumes back to the copying machine. I placed a book on the glass and began to set the margins.

"Whoa there, buddy." This from a suit and tie with a young man inside. "That's ten cents per copy there."

This was enough. "Look," I said. "I used to work here. I used to live here, for that matter. Back when it was one big happy sty. And in our day we gave the alumni certain privileges."

"What's your name?"

"J. A. Simpson. I wrote a column called Digressions."

"Well. Boy." He stuck out a hand. "Glad to meet you. Your name came up in the edit meeting last week, and here you are. Well."

"My, ah, name came up?"

"Yeah. One of our reporters just got hired as an editorial assistant at the *New York Post*, and that got us thinking about the people who'd left here and made it big, and we were wondering what had happened to you."

I became a lying sack of failed ambition, friend. Let me demonstrate. "I, ah, well—odd you should bring that up, and talk about your coincidences. I've been working out in New York myself." I adjusted the book on the copying machine.

"Doing?"

"Same thing. Editorial assistant." Improvisation of the most desperate kind here. "But at the *Times*." I pushed the Copy button.

Awe. Naked, prostrate awe. "You worked at *The New York Times*? You still there?"

"Nah. You . . . you wouldn't believe the atmosphere there. So petty, so personal." I sighed. "If you're not from the East Coast you might as well be from Peoria, you know, and when they spiked a piece I did on, ah, drug abuse down in the, ah, Upper West Side of the South Bronx, well, I figured it was time to go elsewhere. You know how it is," I added, dearly hoping he didn't. I put another book on the glass.

"You quit the *Times*."

I shrugged and pushed the button again. I changed the subject to the *Daily* and asked when the changes had come about. The suit, who turned out to be the current editor, waxed long about the new computer system, talking for ten minutes without ever getting around to the subject of journalism. I finished my copying and stuffed the papers in my jacket. I looked at my watch and began to excuse myself, but he begged a few seconds more and said he'd like me to meet someone who'd just got an internship at the *Times*, and maybe I could give her some advice?

Around the corner at a desk sat a young woman. She turned around, cigarette in one hand in a posture that begged for a holder and a feather boa, pencil in the other hand poised over a yard of pink paper. She had wide green eyes, glittering like a kitten's, a soft round face with a button nose. Her red hair was unruly, scraps of apple peels rolled in rust and cinnamon, and it fell to her shoulders in wavy hanks, a few strands falling over one eye. She clapped those eyes on me for a second, let them wander diffidently to the editor and then back to me, where they browsed at leisure around my face. She leaned back, squaring her shoulders with the languor of Hayworth settling back into satin sheets. Her sweater tried hard to disguise the features and benefits of her body but was not equal to the task. Her legs, long in comparison with her torso, were wrapped to the knee in boots and swaddled with dark red leg warmers. She drew on her cigarette and let a loose braid of smoke curl from the eave of her upper lip.

"Hi," she chirped.

"Marya, this is John Simpson. He used to work here. This is the guy who wrote Digressions."

"Sure. I've read you. I had a teacher who used your stuff as examples. 'Course, I dropped that class." She took a drag from her cigarette. "I thought you'd be taller."

"He's just back from *The New York Times*. He quit." He shuddered with excitement. "Maybe he can give you some pointers on the place."

"You'll be in news," I said. She was giving me a frank stare, pulling on her cigarette. "I was in edit. Different world. Different values. Different lunchroom, even."

"I'm sure I'll want to hear all about it anyway."

"I'll let you two talk about the *Times*." The editor looked at me in wonder again. "You quit the *Times*."

I shrugged, dark man of principle. Marya's eyes were giving me an indifferent massage, like someone testing a mattress they might buy, if they were in the market.

The editor cocked an ear and said he had to attend to his phone, and left. "So." I lit a cigarette. "How old are you?"

"Twenty-two. Just a kid." She crossed her legs. "Why?"

"Big city, New York. Ages you fast. People there your age are already trying to give up vices you haven't even heard about."

"I don't know. I have big ears."

"You have a place to stay?"

"Mm-hmm. They're going to put me up at some hotel. My parents, of course, think there's going to be like addicts in the lobby."

"Where is the hotel?"

"West Fifty-third? Is that bad?"

"Not really. The addicts will be wearing suits."

"Is it a scary place to be?" She spoke the word *scary* like someone telling a fairy story to a child. Delightful.

"Not when you're twenty-two. It's pretty exciting. It'll make you hard and cynical before your time, of course." I smiled. "Depending on where you stay it'll make you hard and cynical before lunch."

"Oh, I'm already hard and cynical." She puffed on her cigarette and I noticed she wasn't inhaling. Ash fell on her lap and she batted it off. She ran a hand through her hair, knocked some of it back over her eyes and, looking back at her desk, said: "You want to go have some coffee? I have a few minutes."

"I'd like to," I heard myself say, "but I have things to do." Like call the *Times* and ask them to cover for me. My God, she was cute.

"Cool. I'm sure I'll live." She was scribbling on a piece of paper; she ripped off the corner and handed it to me. "My card. Call me. I do want to hear all about the *Times* and the big evil city."

"I really don't have that much to tell you about the *Times*."

"Surprise me."

Would I. I smiled, squared my shoulders and said good-bye. She had turned around before I left the cubicle. I walked out thinking, Twenty-two. As was Jane when we first met. I stopped, then I walked back to her cubicle.

"Marya." She turned around, smiling.

"Yeah?"

"When are you going to New York?"

"Six months."

I nodded and walked away.

Forget it.

I was still at the student union an hour later, playing pinball. My game was off. I kept changing dollar bills for quarters until I had one quarter and no more dollar bills. I had a choice. I could convert one of Tryg's fifties. I could play this machine, again. There was a Cyclops on the backplate with blood dripping from his mouth. Or I could call Marya.

"*Daily*canyouhold," said the receptionist. She gave me no choice but dropped me straight into Muzak, 101 strings all ganged up on one cowering melody. The receptionist came back and asked who I wanted, and I said, "Well, Marya." Back to Muzak. Marya was mercifully prompt.

"Thompson. Yeah?"

"Marya. It's Jonathan. Simpson."

"Of course." I heard gum pop.

"How are you?"

"Been better. My sources won't talk. They never do. I'm taking it personally." I could see the pout.

"What's the story?"

"Football player accused of rape. By a hockey player. Whew. There's something kinda gay about all sports anyway, but this is weird."

We were getting off the desired topic. "I never thought about that."

"I do. Polo? All those men on panting horses flinging long sticks and a loose ball. It has to do with some really deep fear. I know it."

"Would you care to not discuss this over dinner?"

"Pardon?"

"I have to review a restaurant tonight and I wondered if you'd like to—"

"I'd love to. We eat free, is that it?"

"That's about it. Chinese food."

"All I have to do here is get a few more no comments and then I have to break a date and I'll be ready. You want me to meet you there?" I told her where it was. "Okay. Groovy."

Groovy. Jesus. "Keen. Fab. See you at eight, okay?"

I hung up and smiled. This was the first date I'd made in over half a decade. I felt altogether fine about it, as well as about everything else in the world. I stopped smiling when, passing up the staircase, I spied a piece of graffiti. LOVE IS A LIE. SEX IS A LIE, some sad, disaffected soul had written. Beneath, in another hand: TRY LYING MORE OFTEN.

8

China Diner had been a gas station. On the corner across the street was a dry cleaner's that had been a gas station; on another corner a photo developer that had been a gas station. The fourth corner held a gas station, winner and still champion. China Diner had tried to obliterate traces of the previous incarnation, but had not applied a great deal of imagination to the effort. Plastic versions of paper lanterns bobbed from the eaves. The lights over the islands remained, but the pumps had been replaced with uncommonly jocose Buddhas. I wondered if the fuel tanks below were filled with soy sauce. Near the door there was a poster for the Canton Ladies, appearing that weekend. One was named Doo and the other Dah.

Inside I was greeted, or rather noticed, by a man auditioning for the role of a shifty butler in a 1930s murder mystery. He asked my preference for smoking or not smoking; I replied, "Smoking," not bothering to remove my cigarette from my mouth to speak. He nodded gravely and took me into the service bays, where raised platforms on the old hydraulic lifts provided the seating. There was a bar at the end of the building, populated by a man in green overalls slouched miserably over his drink, and a bartender in starched whites staring straight ahead.

From my view through the bays I saw Marya arrive. She got out of a car and blew a kiss, her expression indicating that she would rather have put it on a postcard and mailed it without a stamp. She stopped, leaned into the car, and was pulled through the window, feet lifted off the ground, hands flailing for something to hold on to. Her hands found her scarf and drew it over her head; she pulled out of the window and began to reel in her scarf. The car jumped forward a few feet, dragging her with it, but then she snapped the scarf free and stomped off toward the front door, mouth moving in what I could guess was not a novena.

But she was smiling when she arrived. She said hello and my name in a voice like someone naming what they wanted for Christmas and sat down. She struggled out of her coat, reached for her back and kneaded a spot on her spine, writhing until there was a long and agonizing crack. Then she stretched her arms over her head and gave a long, low moan.

"You look like a cheerleader for a chiropractor school."

"I'll be all right." She leaned back again and twisted at the waist, face strained as though she were passing a stone. "Ooh. Ooh. Ah. There. God. It's this sitting down all day. Murders my little back." She looked up at me, eyes bright. "Have you seen the dishes here yet? I decided since I'm never going to get married I can get my china whenever I want."

"It looked like your ride turned into a masher."

A brief look of incomprehension, followed by a headshake. "No. He was just getting fresh. That was Bill, the editor. You met him. I asked for a ride here. He doesn't like that I'm seeing you, okay. All the way here he doesn't say a word. He's always talking and I know whenever I get the Mount Rushmore treatment I have sinned, so I just shut up too. Then I try getting out and all of a sudden he wants a kiss, okay fine, but this is a kiss *à la français*, and here I am going from being in the doghouse to getting my tonsils cleaned."

"I take it you're close."

"We've been going out for two years. With minor time-outs for Marya's indiscretions." She made a small grimace. "But it's time we saw other people and he knows it. At least he knows I think I should see other people. Do they give us menus here or is it all buffet?"

"Buffet. As much as you like of whatever you want."

Magic words for this one. She got up, straightened her skirt and marched down the steps to the buffet. There was a tray of rice and a dozen bins of fried items distinguishable primarily by their shape. At the end of the table was dessert: Jell-O, wiggling in sympathy with the refrigeration motor, and a pair of crusty squares with the sign DEEP FRIED JELL-O. We loaded our plates and headed back to the table.

"The AIL probably disapproves of all of this," she said. "Take down my last words for posterity if anything happens, okay?" She began to eat.

"So," I said after a while. "You're tired of your boyfriend."

"Mmm?" She held up a fork, swallowed. "I don't know. Yes."

She shooed rice onto her fork with a knife. "He's just incredibly possessive. Has a fit if I so much as sleep with another man." I looked up, cocked an eyebrow. "Just testing. But he is the most utterly jealous man on the planet. Ucch." She fluttered her hands. "Let's just pretend he's dead tonight."

"If you insist."

"Shouldn't you be taking notes on this, Jonathan?"

I stared at her. "No, I have a friend who dated you last quarter. I'll get the answers from him. What are you talking about?"

"The food. Which you said you were reviewing."

"You're right." I took out a notebook and glanced at the putative food. "Do you know what any of this stuff is supposed to be?" She shook her head no. "Try that triangular thing there."

She tasted it, made a moue of contemplation and shook her head. "I think it's fish. No, I think it just sat next to the fish in the fridge." She poked at her food with a miserable expression, like a child who sees acres of spinach between itself and dessert. I found one item that was palatable and ate a great deal of it, nodding while Marya drank scotch and told me of her life up to that point. She'd been born in Fargo, North Dakota. I'd been there. Miles of suburbs around a withered downtown, a shrunken tract of banks and old bars. Her life had proceeded according to formula—indifferent schools, shopping malls, parks after dark, girlfriends' houses, boyfriends' cars. Marya cast herself as one of the Popular Girls in high school. Most of the women I had dated then were from the neurotic-artistic axis of the social constellation. "You should be glad you didn't know me," she said after describing her high school.

"Why?"

"Don't talk with your mouth full, John."

"Jonathan. And why shouldn't I have known you?"

"Because I used to be a brat."

"Used to be."

"I was popular, why I don't know, I was such a snot. Maybe because I had boobs in the seventh grade, I don't know. Didn't you have some stuck-up girl in your high school that all the guys were just drooling over?"

"I can't remember. Too long ago."

"How old are you?"

"Twenty-nine."

"My God."

"I know. Ancient. I'm surprised I still have control of my bowels."

"Let's see." She closed her eyes. "You were the same age when JFK was shot that I was when Robert Kennedy was shot."

I did some quick figuring, and discovered Marya was either poor in history or math. In any case, I had all my teeth when she was but a zygote. I felt old again. "Well, you still have a certain amount of, ah, bratitude."

"It's not easy being spoiled, you know. You have to be cheerful all the time or you're petulant, and petulance gives you wrinkles. Here." She put her fingertips on the corners of my mouth. "But. Enough about me." She was looking at me straight and unblinking now, an unlit cigarette dangling in the flame of the candle. "Tell me about *The New York Times*."

The host appeared and cleared his throat. "Is everything all right for you here? Why do you not finish?" He pointed to Marya's plate.

"I couldn't finish my sixth trip," she said. She distended her belly to a parody of gluttony and patted it.

"Who does the cooking?" I said.

"It is my wife." He pointed to a frail woman standing in a corner of the restaurant, wearing an apron that said For This I Went to College. "Will dessert be surely following?" he said, bowing.

"Only if we can check the lot numbers of your mixes," Marya said. She lit a cigarette. "Otherwise, just drinks would be fine. Jonathan?" I didn't know what was required of me here, so I just shrugged. The host nodded, snapped his fingers. A young man, bearded and thin, bounded up the platform to our table, and the host retired.

"Hello, hello. I'm Eric." He smiled with unnatural gaiety; he was either a displaced actor or a full-blown psychopath. "I'm going to be your dessert man tonight, and as for what I shall be in the future, que sera? Now. Let me just tell you what the chef has prepared. We have a flourless chocolate cake, practically a battleship anchor. We have a lemon tart we are particularly proud of, cheesecake with a raspberry glaze, and also vanilla ice cream if we're feeling a tad plebeian. I'd like to also call your attention to the coffee drink menu on the table there, please take a moment to examine it; I make them at your table and they are all on fire. Quite a sight, rather cocktails à la Belasco. Well? Any word, or shall I announce my retirement now and stage a triumphant return in a few minutes?"

We ordered two pieces of the flourless cake and two flaming coffee drinks, just to get rid of him. Eric had never in his life been more delighted, and he bowed and left. He returned with two slices of cake and a tray of liqueurs with two glasses. We nibbled on the cake and watched Eric incinerate our drinks. Marya's was an Irish whiskey coffee drink, and Eric assumed a brogue. "Oi, and 'tis a sin to waste foin whiskey in this way," he said, pouring the liquor from the bottle into the glass. He touched a lighter to the stream and it leapt to flame; he held the bottle high and the flame stretched the length of the column. He poured a dash of brandy along the rim of the glass, and the glass caught fire.

"Pretty," said Marya. "But you're burning all the liquor. Why don't you just pour it on the floor and give me a cup of coffee?"

"Hush!" he said. "For here be magic!" And he tossed a pinch of powder into the flames. It sparked, crackled and vanished. "Cinnamon. All right, all right then, cinnamon and gunpowder, you dragged it out of me." He put before Marya a napkin folded into the shape of a mitt. "Use that to hold the drink, for it's going to be hot."

"Most things on fire are," she said.

"And for the sir?" said Eric, hands folded. "The same?"

"Give me the Mexican coffee."

"Sí," he said in a nasal voice. "Mehican caffee por the señor con la putana."

"Hey," I said, rising in my chair.

"Yust checking, señor. Hokay. Theese geeve you siesta feeling, no?" A healthy shot of something with Spanish on the label went into my glass. "And now, fuego, sí?" He snapped his lighter to light the liquor, but only sparks came. He tried it a dozen times. "All good theengs come to an end," he said, pocketing the lighter. He looked around. I held up a book of matches but Eric made a show of horror. "Please but there ees sulfur in the machez. I don't haf to use your steenking machez." He fumbled in his pocket and came up with another disposable, still in its wrapper.

I had read about this happening; apparently there are lawsuits. People buy an innocent lighter and find it adjusting on the setting appropriate for crowd control. Eric lit the column of liquor with the lighter, and the flame that came from the thing was about three feet in length. When he stepped back startled, he bumped the tray on which my drink sat, knocking it over and spilling its contents onto the table, splashing into my lap. The liquor had caught fire and rode the fumes across the table, down the tablecloth and onto the paper napkin across my lap. All in the space of two, three seconds. Every trace of Iberian languor fled from Eric's voice. "Jesus!" he cried. "Jesus Christ!" I stood, knocking back my chair, beating at my lap—sweet Lord, my pants were on fire. The one day in my life I do not wear all-natural fibers and it's the day flames land on the nexus of any future sexual excitation and God damn it! I could feel the pants adhere to my skin, my skin—

Someone was screaming, Eric or me I cannot say. The only clear image is Marya, jaw set and eyes clear, throwing her drink at my lap. The coffee put out the fire and, might I add, the coffee was hot. I howled again, looked up to see the manager hastening up the stairs, and I howled at him. Eric made tentative daubs at my groin with a towel but backed off when I snarled. Marya, I saw, was about to burst both eardrums trying not to laugh.

The manager could not apologize enough but was trying. I held up a hand, magnanimous, and said it wasn't his fault.

He gave us promises of everything as we put on our coats. Free food. Partnership in the business. Passage to the homeland and accommodations with relatives. Any of his progeny in perpetual servitude. Marya and I assured him it was all right, neither of us was hurt, most unfortunate, yes, never mind, no, we won't sue, yes, we'll come back and we'll be sure to tell all our friends, no, for Chrissakes already, we won't sue.

He looked at me and his face suddenly split into a laugh. "You could be a restaurant critic! Our very first!"

"Oh, I am!" I said, laughing.

"You hear that?" he shouted to the bartender, laughing. "He's a critic!"

"Everyone is a critic," said the bartender, stoic.

"Oh, yes," he said, laughing, "he is a critic." His face went quiet, and he began to cry. We slid out the door and closed it gently behind us.

Marya walked ahead of me to one of the abandoned islands, sat down and started howling with laughter. She leaned up against a Buddha, beat her fists on her knees, laughing. Then she froze, her eyes squinting shut. "Ouch. Ouch. Back. Damn." She got to her feet, wincing. "Get up," she said, her voice tight. "Please." I stood. "Crack my back."

"What do you want me to do? Dash you against a lightpost or something?"

"Don't make me laugh. Just grab me and pull. Hard." She turned her face up to the moon, closed her eyes and made a face of hideous pain.

I put my arms around her and clasped my hands at the small of her back. "Jerk. Up. Hard." I did. "Harder."

Marya was soft and warm and she smelled healthy and sweet. The second I took her in my arms, ancient instincts born of a need to propagate the species gave swift rise to the most inappropriate erection I had ever had in my life. The word was made flesh and the word was one my parents had washed out my mouth for saying.

"Well?" Marya said. "Do it."

I did it. I pulled her close and hugged her tight, lifting her off her feet. When I let her down she looked me full in the face with wide, surprised eyes.

"Is this something you'd like to share with the rest of the class?" she said.

I dropped her and turned away, face stinging with embarrassment.

"Well." She stretched, looked around the intersection. "What shall it be? Want to do some dry cleaning? Got any photos to develop? Wanna get gas? The night's ours, man."

"I have to go home," I said, speaking into my coat. "I have to write this review."

"That's cool."

We drove home. We did not talk about *The New York Times*, the Big Bang, the Crucifixion of Christ or anything else of which I did not have firsthand knowledge. We talked about the *Daily* and the *Metropole*. She was appalled to hear I was working for the latter; I explained that they were trying to do harder pieces, and cited the AIL case. She was still skeptical. She had been assigned the AIL stories and was curious to see to what degree her work would surpass that of the *Metropole*.

I dropped her off at a house in southeast Minneapolis. "Want to come in? My roommates are out. I make real mean cocoa."

Roommates. How long had it been since I'd gone out with a woman who had roommates. "I can't. I'd like to."

"Just as well. Bill will probably be coming by at midnight to shoot me on general principle. Anyway, so, thanks. Call me?"

"I'll call you."

"Good. I'll make sure my back hurts a lot next time too." She laughed and shut the door.

I drove around the block a couple of times, taking a few looks at her house, wondering how much I wanted that cocoa. Lots. Then I shook my head and drove away.

There was no action at the manor tonight. I let myself in and called for Trygve; there was no reply. I flicked the switches on the wall and the lights came on in the main hall, popping and flickering, as though stretching and yawning after a nap. I found Trygve in the library, asleep in front of the television. The remote control was wedged between his leg and the arm of the chair, apparently depressing the channel-selector button; the stations were revolving in a square kaleidoscope of the modern world—cowboys whooping, guitarists clutching their generative organs, bombers swooping low over Germany, stock market quotations running on the bottom of the screen below a stern man in a suit, a beauty queen striding a runway. I jostled Tryg to wake him.

"Grue?" he said.

"No, Tryg. It's me. Master Jonathan."

"Ohh." He put a shaky hand to his head. "I've had the most unusual dreams."

"Color or black-and-white?"

"In living color," he said, staring at the TV. Then he waved his hands in front of him to dispel his dreams and started to struggle to his feet. I helped him up and walked him to the stairs. He wanted to make me a drink but I said no, I had work to do, he should go to bed. I put him in the chair and he hummed up the stairs, waving like a beauty queen in a convertible. I went to the sidebar and made myself a drink.

There was a typewriter in the library. I lugged it out to the dining hall and scrolled paper in the platen. The ribbon had been used to type first drafts of the Declaration of Independence, but it would have to do. I thought for a minute, then began to lay down the road on which China Diner would hobble to bankruptcy court.

> When I was growing up there was a café downtown called Chow Main, run by former drunks for current drunks. Since the area had the cachet of being the local skid row, my five-year-old brain linked the grimy façade and shabby clientele with Chinese food. Even after I knew better I avoided Oriental cuisine; as practiced by my mother's painfully Occidental hand, it was nothing more than water chestnuts

> lurking like albino beetles in a swampy lair of crunchy and truncated spaghetti noodles. I was introduced to the real thing by a young woman, and I loved it; then again, I loved her, and would have pronounced cold tapioca pudding to be rich and delightful if spun by her hand. Nowadays, grown, I eat Chinese food without too many memories swaying my palate. Or did, until I went to China Diner. Here I found the design panache of Chow Main, the gustatory incompetence of my mother, and food whose shortcomings could not be overlooked were my love for the chef equal to that God had for mankind when He sent His only son to die for our misdoings. It doesn't take much to bury this place; one taste of their offerings is the nudge that sends it sliding into the vast pit its cook has dug.

Et cetera. When finished I read it through, frowning. It was true, all of it, but it did not so much beat a dead horse as call in an air strike. In the old days I'd have nailed 30 to the bottom, unfurled my byline above and handed it in with pleasure. Right now all I saw was the earnest face of the owner. I felt a little like a heel. I felt like something you scrape off your heel. But this was no time to go soft.

It was, instead, time to go to bed. Only eleven, but the day had been long. I wanted to pull the stopper and let it all go gurgling down. I turned off the lights and had begun to pull the drapes shut when the phone rang.

"Simpson. You're there." Someone shouting over music and laughter.

"I'm here. Where are you and who are you?"

"This is Carver. That's Mr. Lou to you." He laughed. He sounded very drunk. "What're you doing, you little bastard?"

"I'm about to go to bed. It's been a long day."

"Make it longer. Meet me downtown at Jolly's."

"Jolly's? Is that where you are?"

"I'm at the Lead Nail now and they're about to kick me out."

"Have you been fighting, Mr. Carver?"

"Went three rounds with the part of myself that oughta keep me out of strip joints, but that's about it. Jolly's. I got something to tell you, you just won't believe it. See you there." The line went dead.

"*I want to go to sleep!*" I yelled at the receiver. "*Everybody just leave me be for a decent interval, all right? Just leave me alone!*"

I hung up and punched my way into my coat. I turned to the windows to close the drapes and saw a man in a white gown standing in the hospital, in the floor above intensive care, the terminal wing. He was looking down at the manor, probably contemplating the stained glass panel of the angel handing Sire Marvel the ax. He waved a slow good-bye as I drew the drapes shut.

9

The man at the bar sold shoes. A samples grip the size of a steamer trunk sat at his feet like a loyal dog. He was a small weed of a man, perhaps forty, with a nose that had taken a cucumber for a role model. One of his front teeth was chipped, a souvenir of a customer dissatisfaction, perhaps. It was a face that had seen it all, liked little of it and probably understood even less. But his eyes were bright and shining. He had taken a seat next to me an hour ago and had begun his oration on his life of sorrows, gesturing only to wave my smoke away from him.

"It's no living, no living at all," he said. "What use in hell do people have for a stranger who shows up at the door and proposes to sell them footwear? They're doing the dishes. They're watching the TV. They're changin' the baby or boffing the farmhand and shoes are not on their mind. Now, what do you do for a living?"

It was nearly midnight, and Carver had not yet shown. I'd been here for an hour, dispensing attention to this dullard in tightly metered doses. I was preoccupied by a vision of Carver facedown in the gutter. In my vision he was snoring, so at least he wasn't dead.

The place was nearly empty. There was a stripper on the runway, her hips playing hide-and-seek with the beat; she had the expression normally found on driver's licenses. A miserable collection of slack-jawed shades sat at the runway, appraising her with rapt indifference. The bar at which I sat with the shoe salesman was empty, save for a bartender with a nose so florid he probably had to squeeze it to get blood down to his feet. Dammit. If I was going to be awake this late I might as well be with Marya having mean cocoa.

"I said what do you do for a living?"

"I'm an atomic theorist," I said.

"Fine. You wouldn't want someone standing on your doorstep trying to sell you atomic theories, would you? If you wanted them you'd go down to the goddamn store and buy them yourself, am I right?"

"You're certainly right there."

"Plus, and this is the kicker, friend, I represent a shoddy line. Known nationally as a maker of cheap, lousy shoes. We advertise in the back of mercenary magazines. The ads call us nationally known. Shit. Joe Stalin was nationally known." A scrawny hand scrabbled into a package of nuts and came up with husks. "Two pair, nineteen ninety-five. Extra laces included. Ten bucks a pair? Five bucks a shoe? Wear 'em once in the rain and you come home wearing soppin' cardboard, dye running down your feet and turning your toes black. Comfortable? Like sticking your feet in coon traps. I have to wear them. I can't even walk in 'em. It looks real good to say you're selling shoes and then limp into the house."

"Why don't you quit?"

"I did." The man looked around the bar. "I ran away. Last week I just didn't check in. Kept my samples case and didn't look back. Now I'm trying to sell off these goddamned shoes, make myself a stake and get on to some other line of work. But even that ain't working. I've got fifty pair of shoes in there, every man jack of 'em hideous. If by the grace of God I make it through the door, I never have the size or style or color they want. And it's hard explaining why I can't order them from the home office. Because I'm on the lam, ma'am. Yeah, that goes down good. It's hopeless." He drained his glass, the ice rattling like dice. The shoeman cleared his throat. "You, ah, don't know of any openings in the atomic theory business, do you?"

"Wanna be a society editor?" I heard a voice behind me say. "Job's open."

I turned around, grinned; there stood Carver, face flushed with liquor and goodwill.

"Are you serious?" said the shoe salesman. His hand tightened around his drink.

"Not at all. Come on, Johnny. Let's take a table where we can see the action." Carver waved a bill at the bartender, exchanged it for a drink the size of a small aquarium and tottered unsteadily to a table near the stage. He draped one hand around the back of the chair, put two fingers to his mouth and let fly a shrill piercing whistle. Then he hooted, clapped and turned back to me.

"To Minneapolis." He raised his glass. "I've had more fun in this town today, the felon who is the fruit of my loins notwithstanding, than I have in a year in Valhalla." He was, I saw, very drunk.

"You and Dickerson go out?"

"Dick. That pansy. Went home. Says drink puts him to sleep. Used to put him in jail. But you're a drinking man, if I remember, right? I'm hungry, *God* I'm hungry. You hungry?"

I nodded. "Starved, but they don't have anything here. We can go somewhere and get a bite and some coffee—"

"Only if the waitresses are nekkid." He was squinting up at the stage. "There's one who oughtn't be nekkid."

"Where have you been all night?"

"Don't know, I really don't. This is Dick's town. Your town. But." He raised his glass again. "About to be my town too."

"What do you mean?"

"I mean I'm moving here. T'stay. T'hell with Valhalla."

"You're not serious."

"T'hell with Valhalla! I'm so bored there I'm about one inch from walking down Main with a machine gun, and shootin' out all the streetlights just so I can have something to put on the goddamn front page besides crop forecasts. Judas." He slurped a healthy fraction of his drink. "There ain't a thing up there for me, son. Wife's gone. Kid's down here. Hanging around with Dick just brought it all back, you know, the old life, times when you were living. I miss it. So." He grinned. "Wanna put me up for a coupla days when I get back?"

"Sure." I smiled. Then I had a new vision—Carver sitting in front of the TV with Trygve, every night, waiting up for me. Carver stalking the halls of the manor as I had, getting jumpy and morose. "Are you going to get a job down here?"

"Got one already. You're looking at your new editor."

"No."

"You bet. Fikes is in for a little demotion. See, I told Dick what you thought of his little journal."

"Oh, you didn't."

"Hell, he agrees. He knows the thing floats away in your hands. He's trying to put some beef in it, and I convinced him to make it a real live newspaper. And who better to do it than me?" Carver coughed, grimaced and held his stomach. "Is there someplace where we can get pancakes or something? I gotta have something to soak up the booze."

I wanted to go home. My head already felt like a balloon, my neck a child two miles below on the ground, crying. I groped in my jacket pocket for cigarettes to keep me going, and my hand encountered a thick lump, like a small animal that had crawled in my pocket to slumber. I took it out. It was the brownie I had liberated at the office, now battered and misshapen. This would garrote his appetite and keep him quiet until he fell asleep. I pushed it across the table; he said thanks. I ordered more drinks and asked Carver what exactly he planned to do with the paper.

"Make it hard." He picked up the brownie and pointed it at me. "Make it look under every rock and dig ten feet. Also, comics. You want some of this? Here." He ripped the brownie in half and pushed it across the table. "We're going to hire new reporters for investigative beats. Make the *Metropole* a name to be feared. And, naturally, I'll want a society editor."

"No."

Carver leaned back and roared. "Just pulling your leg. For you I got a very, very special proposition." He ate his half of the brownie, dragged a paw across his mouth, picked up his drink and raised it in another toast.

"To the *Metropole*'s newest—"

He stopped, stiffened. His eyes bulged as though they were being poked from behind. The hand with the glass lowered, shaking, then fell from his grasp, bounced off the table, rolled off the edge and crashed to the floor. One hand went to his neck, yanking with desperation at his tie as he bolted up. He banged a fist on his chest, grabbed his shirt and tried to rip it open, his Adam's apple making a desperate, panicked dash up and down his throat, the muscles in his jaw throbbing with effort. Then his hands sagged; a thin gurgle trickled from his lips and he fell, his body thudding into the chair and bouncing to the floor like a sack of spuds falling off a truck.

A man at the adjacent table looked over, expressionless. "Ain't we theatrical," he said. There was laughter and some murmurs of worry. I was down on the floor beside Carver. His eyes were open, his skin flickering with the colors of the spotlights. I stuck my ear to his mouth and heard nothing; his chest neither rose nor fell. I felt for a pulse. There was none. I screamed for a doctor, stood up and screamed it again. There was silence; then, laughter, nervous words and whispers. I got down on my knees, praying and cursing, and ripped open Carver's shirt. I had no idea what to do, but one was supposed to hit the victim in the chest, jumpstart the heart. I wedded my hands together and brought them down hard on his chest, again and again, over and over until someone pulled me up by my arms and held me tight. But he wasn't moving. He lay on the floor, one hand open in a pool of beer, the shards of his broken glass around his head winking in the spotlights.

Five minutes or an hour, I'd no idea; all of a sudden there was some unappeasable demon shrieking outside, then there were paramedics swarming around the body. One of them stood up from the body and said something to the others; they all relaxed. I shook free from whoever was holding me and went over to the man who'd examined Carver, grabbed him by the shoulder and demanded to be told whatever he had said to the others.

"Are you a friend? relative?"

A man picks up sons as he goes along. "I'm a friend. What's happening? Why aren't you—"

The paramedic looked down at Carver, then turned to me. "Look. I'm sorry. He's, ah, dead."

"No."

"Maybe you better sit." I sat. "He was dead before we got here. I'm sorry. There's no way we could have brought him back. Do you know what happened?"

I gulped hard and tried to order my thoughts. "He was just sitting there. Having a drink. He ate a brownie and then—"

The paramedics exchanged glances. One of them swore softly.

"It looked like he couldn't breathe but he didn't make any choking sounds. He was grabbing his chest. Here. Like this. He—he—" I felt faint. "He died too fast to be choking."

"Right. We'll find out down at the hospital what happened. You can come if you want."

I nodded. By now the paramedics were hoisting Carver onto the stretcher. This time a sheet went over the body. I closed my eyes, had a vision of Grue being carted off; I heard that spoon clatter to the floor, the hollow sound of life dropping out of a body. The legs of the stretcher snapped into place, and I opened my eyes.

The paramedic with whom I'd been speaking tapped me on the

shoulder and motioned me to accompany him. Everyone stared at me as I walked out, bestowing celebrity on me through the side doors of blame and proximity to the victim. At the door stood the shoe salesman. His eyes had a mad cast to them, and he looked at me in fear. I walked past but he grabbed my arm.

"Jared," he said. "This is Jared's work." I stopped, stared. The paramedic whistled from the ambulance, and I walked out, still looking at the little man. "Jared," he hissed from the doorway.

"Jared who?" I said, but he had melted back into the bar. I started to follow him, and the paramedic shouted after me to come on. "Hold it," I shouted. "Just hold it." And I pushed my way back inside. I looked around for the little man; nowhere. There was a door swinging toward the back, an Exit sign above it. I ran across the bar crashing into tables and knocking over chairs, and fell through the door into cold sharp night air. An alley. Open on either end. No little man.

"*Jared who?*" I screamed. "*God damn it, Jared who?*"

No answer. I walked out to the ambulance. I sat in the back with my knees drawn up to my chest, seated next to Carver's body. The ambulance pulled away from Jolly's All-Nude Bar with no great urgency and rolled down Hennepin, pausing at red lights, observing the speed limit. The radio crackled with messages of new calamities across the city. The paramedics in the front seat were talking about maybe getting something to eat; the one in the back with me was reading a magazine, flipping through the pages, not pausing long at anything. I put my head in my hands and let out the tears. When I was finished the body under the sheet was as still as it had been before.

Louis Aloysius Carver had a liver that looked like a sponge left out in the sun (or so the doctor said; I took his word for it), lungs well paved by years of smoking, and a heart marred by the scars of two heart attacks. There were hints of phlebitis in the legs, evidence of severe arthritis in the hands. His appendix was long gone, and an accompanying scar showed the route by which his gall bladder had exited. He had an ulcer in his stomach and a prostate the size of a tennis ball. Cause of death: cyanide.

It hadn't fit together at first, and for this I can be excused. When you are run through by a sword you do not notice the pattern etched on the blade. But sitting in the ambulance, looking at Carver's body, the fact of his death was gradually supplanted by the reason for it.

There was a reason one of the paramedics had taken the uneaten half of the brownie—my half—and put it in a plastic bag. It was poisoned, of course. And I'd given it to Carver.

It had seemed wrong to bring Carver to the hospital; it would have seemed just as wrong to drop him off at a mortuary. He was beyond the help of medicine but not ready for the ground, just yet. The paramedics explained that an autopsy had to be performed. They handed me his wallet and told me to go to the front desk and help them with the necessary forms. The wallet was an inch thick, stuffed with cards, scraps of paper, receipts. There was picture of Carver in the navy, leaning up against the railing, the ocean a flat gray plain behind him; Carver with his wife, a sober, homely woman with her arm around her husband, staring at the camera as though defying it to guess some secret. There was a photo of his daughter Spanks as a baby, face crumpled with a baby's inscrutable glee. There was an insurance card, which is what the people at the front desk were interested in.

I sat and waited for the results of the autopsy. I sat numb in an empty waiting room and worked hard pretending none of the evening's events had happened. Carver would walk out any minute now, buttoning his shirt, banging his chest and proclaiming himself sound as a dollar, horny as a buck.

I watched TV, a sitcom; I was in no mood to laugh but the soundtrack did it for me, as usual. At the end of the show everyone hugged, and the names of the confectioners to be held responsible for the show appeared. After a few commercials for ice cream, beer, soap and an exercise machine, a repeat of the local evening news came on. Strings simulated the rhythms of typing, bold proud french horns swelled with civic pride. The anchorman appeared, grim and resolute; to his left were the words *Poisonous Scare*. As opposed to poisonous reassurance, I thought. Wait a minute, wait—

". . . and tonight, a bizarre tale of poisoned food and a mysterious organization that claimed responsibility for a terrorist act, only to try to keep it from happening. Marsha Simons has this report." Cut to Marsha, a looker and then some, standing in front of the Pork Exchange. I sat up.

"Mr. Simpson?" I turned and looked toward the door; a policeman stood there. I looked at the TV, back at him.

"Mr. Simpson? Would you come with me for a moment, please?" His voice was deep, the tones flat, like unvarnished oak.

"Wait. I have to see this." The TV was filled with a picture of Daphne; below her name were the words *Thought Nothing of It.* "I didn't think anything of it," I heard her say.

The policeman looked at the TV. "That's what we'd like to talk to you about, sir. If you'd just come along. We'll explain everything."

I got up and followed him to a small room the police had commandeered in another wing. There was another policeman on the phone; files were spread out on the examining table. There was a chart on the wall explaining how to examine one's breasts for abnormalities; it went along with the stirrups that projected from the end of the table. The policeman leaned up against one of the stirrups, motioned me to sit and lit a cigarette. He smoked in silence while his partner talked on the phone. Then the man hung up the phone and turned; he looked at me and his face went blank.

"Bishop," I said.

"I know what my name is," he said. "What I don't know is what the hell you are doing here."

"This is the guy who was with the deceased," said the other policeman.

"No kidding."

I looked down, ashamed. "We are definitely going to want a statement," Bishop said. "Most definitely."

"What do you mean, statement? You don't think I had anything to do with this?"

Bishop gave me the smile you would expect to see if you ripped off the executioner's mask. I was terrified: my heart was a tight fist thrusting up my throat, and my stomach felt full of sluicing mercury. I had the feeling that I was one step away from rubber hoses and phone books—or, given the decor of the room, a speculum thrust into my mouth with the comment that maybe now I'd talk. I opened my mouth and let out a blurt of undifferentiated syllables; I shut it, gulped and tried again.

"He was poisoned, wasn't he?" Bishop and the policeman, whose nameplate said *Sgt. Place,* looked at each other. "Come on. I know it was poison. That goddamn brownie."

Neither said a word. I shook my head, then started talking: about Carver, his phone call, the brownie, his death.

"So you gave him the brownie," Bishop said.

"I gave him the brownie. But I didn't know it was poisoned. It came from the AIL, didn't it? What was that on TV about a poison scare?"

Place had finished his cigarette and was holding the dead butt in his hand; there was no place to put it, and given the healthy purity of the room he had the look of someone standing in a chapel holding a spent condom. He put the butt in his pocket.

There was a knock, and another policeman stuck his head in the door. "We got the TV people here. Christ if I know how they found out."

"Oh, God damn it. All right. I'll help." Sergeant Place fitted his cap on his head and walked out of the room; when the door swung open I heard voices in competition—the tones of voice you associate with a microphone in an outstretched hand. I looked at Bishop. "Am I a suspect? Is he out there telling them you have someone in custody?"

"Everyone," he said, "who breathes is a suspect, as far as I'm concerned. But you are the one who just happens to be there when these folks get poisoned. Now, why do you think I'm interested in you?"

"Because you're an idiot." My eyes started to sting. "If you think I had anything to do with this, you just aren't paying attention. Carver was like a father to me, and I'm not going to sit here and be accused of patricide by someone who can't even spell it."

"Now hold on."

"I've been holding on since I got in here." My eyes dried, and I felt hot, full of nasty, dangerous energy. "You want to suspect me of this stuff? Go right ahead. But take a look at those letters you said you got from that AIL jackass and check the postmarks. Were they mailed in town? Yes? Fine. I've been up in Valhalla for the past five years. And if you can explain how I'm smart enough to be mailing a letter in the Twin Cities the same day I'm putting in a twelve-hour shift 250 miles north, then explain why I'm stupid enough to be on the scene when two people get it from the poison. Huh? I brought this stuff to your attention, Bishop. I've lost one and maybe two people to this thing. And you're sitting here being coy with me when you should be out finding Jared."

Bishop stiffened. "Jared."

"Jared. Don't ask me who he is."

"Jared," Bishop said, "is the name of the guy who signs all the letters. That information has not been made public."

Oh, good God, right back in the soup. I explained about the little shoe salesman. "Ask the bartender. Ask the ambulance drivers. He was there." Bishop gave me a long, hard stare. Then he leaned over to the desk and pulled out a folder. He handed me a picture of a pan of brownies.

"That is one of five pans that were sent by courier to local newspapers, addressed to the editor. Each one was chock-full o' cyanide. Now." He opened his notebook, ran a finger down a page. "The editor of one paper was out all afternoon, didn't get the package. One was on a diet, thought it was from friends trying to tempt him, threw it away. One is diabetic. Another was out of town. Editor of the *Metropole*—where you say you were—he just put it out in the reception room. Said he did not personally care for brownies as they usually have nuts in them, and he doesn't care for nuts." Bishop looked up. "Me, I'm the same way."

He sighed, closed his book. "About half an hour after the packages arrived at the papers, each paper got a call from someone claiming to be from an organization called the AIL. The guy said they had sent the brownies as a protest against preservatives in food or something like that. Said they had meant to include a note with the stuff warning people not to eat them. Said they meant to make a point, not kill anyone."

"Considerate guys."

"Yeah, well, really stupid ones. They got to get someone to handle their PR if they want to get anywhere. This is bush-league. Forgetting the note." He shook his head.

"So how'd you find out about Carver? The ambulance drivers acted like they'd been forewarned about someone dying from poison."

"We knew that someone had taken a brownie from the *Metropole*. Only one missing. A man named"—he checked his notebook again—"Solly Gardner took a call at five twenty-four, impounded the brownie pan, called the police. He's been most helpful." Carver and Dickerson must have left before Solly got the call. "We told the hospitals to alert us if they got any cyanide poisoning. Put the story on the news to alert whoever took that one brownie there. But." He shrugged, palms up, a gesture that stood for Carver's death. I felt my face go hot.

We spent half an hour on details—my life in Valhalla, reasons for moving here, my relationship with Carver. Bishop tried inexpertly to trip me up, but his attempts were as subtle as logs in the road. I just slowed down and climbed over them. It was two-thirty in the morning when we finished.

"You can go. But be available. I'm going to want to talk with you more."

Outside the room stood Sergeant Place and half a dozen people sitting on the floor, cameras and other pieces of equipment lying beside them. The minute I stepped outside of the room people began to struggle up from the floor, hoisting cameras onto shoulders, plugging in the mikes and patting them to test the levels. Hurried hushed commands, then full-throated requests for me to talk. Bishop stepped out of the room behind me and raised his hand. "We'll have no comment at this time," he said.

"Is this man a suspect?" called one of the reporters.

"No comment."

"Bishop!" I hissed.

"He is not a suspect at this time."

"Bish-op."

"He is not a suspect, period."

The reporters turned to me, loosing a flurry of questions about my relationship to Carver, the tableau of his death. I started walking. The reporters wheeled en masse and followed, the thin shrieking light of the cameras spilling on the floor, splashing on the wall; I was split into a dozen shadows, all joined at the feet. I stared at the elevator ahead and kept moving, but they were beside me, mikes outstretched like beggars demanding alms. How did you know the deceased? Do you know why he died? Could you describe the death? The questions pecked at my ears like birds and I said nothing, kept my head down, kept moving for the elevator. I pushed the button and prayed for the damn thing to appear. When it came I stepped in, put my hands on the doors to keep them from closing and faced the crowd, the doors straining against my hands like a dumb beast trying to push an obstacle out of the way. They were still, God help them, hurling questions. "*How do you feel?*" I heard.

"It's none of your business what I feel like!" I shouted. "And nobody needs to know anything other than he died! He was a friend. He was a good man. That's it. That's enough. It's not my story. It's yours now. You want to know who killed him? Okay. Go find Jared. And when you find him bring him to me and then I'll show you how I feel. All right?" I stepped back and raised my arms and the doors closed, the light from the cameras narrowed down to a line between the doors. The car dropped and the light seemed to ascend until it was just a point, then nothing. Your story now, I'd said. I knew better.

10

"I had a roommate who was totally macro. She didn't believe in cancer." Marya was looking at the menu with a Cagney-esque sneer.

"Doesn't matter; it believes in us."

"What?" She looked up. "I wasn't listening."

I repeated what I had said. "You can't will something out of existence. If everyone decided God didn't exist it wouldn't mean that He didn't."

"Oh, I don't know. We created Him that way."

"You don't believe in God."

"Not now. But I will. When I get cancer; then I'll pray like crazy. Got a light?"

We were at a restaurant by the university, a place called the Ansonia. It did not belong near a college. The decor was muted and breakable, and the bar scotch was as old as most of the people who lived around here. The Ansonia, like a member of the peerage cast among commoners, proudly refused to cater to the college crowd. The sentiment was repaid with a complete absence of business. We were alone in the dining room. The waitress sat at the bar reading Kafka—apparently to no effect, for she was all cheer when she visited our table.

I felt odd being out in the world. Something told me I should be home in a hair shirt, or at least something gone to nubs worn inside out. Carver's departure was four days gone, and while I had punished myself enough, my liver bravely standing up for the bullet each night, I still didn't feel at ease allowing myself any pleasure. Especially the pleasure that was sitting across the table reading the menu.

I had called Sarah first. She had insisted that none of this was my fault, and had been successful enough so that I saw that I might, one day, believe her. She had refused my offers to meet and talk—Mac had returned, and they had had a colossal spat. He had left again on business and she was in no mood to see anyone. But I was always welcome to call.

I needed to see a face. Marya was perfect. Or had been, until she started talking about God and judgment.

"What I want to know is, God is all-powerful, right? Okay. Let's say He's, like, all energy. I mean when I was a kid I bought the idea of a big dad, with the beard and the sandals, pointing down and blasting sinners and like that but now I think, if He exists, He must be all energy. So I wonder, if He thinks of something, it just happens, *voilà*."

"Thought contemporaneous with action." God and drunks.

"That's what I said. Okay. So what if God thinks sometime that maybe He shouldn't exist, that this deity gig is getting old?" She laughed. "I mean, zap! That's it! He's outta here! So maybe He never thinks about it, because He knows it'll be the end of the party. But if He knows not to think about it, then the thought has to have occurred to Him, in which case He's been history for a long time. And if the thought hasn't occurred to Him, then what's this all-knowing stuff?"

"Well, that's the trick of being a deity." I sipped my wine. Theology. The way to a woman's heart. "You or me, we can't intercede between origination of thought and realization of thought. That make sense? St. Augustine had a hell of a time with this. He couldn't reconcile free will and omnipotence. If God knows ahead of time what we're going to do tonight"—there was some wishful thinking, hoping for an evening that would put me in dutch with God—"then how can our actions be truly self-determined."

"Oh, that's easy. He knows that He knows it but He makes Himself forget it. Until it happens. Then He says, 'Oh, yeah, I knew that was going to happen.' Perpetual *déjà vu*."

"That's right. You've studied Augustine?"

"No."

I stared at Marya. "You just came up with that on your own?"

"Well, yeah. I mean, that's, like, basic behavior. I do something that's going to piss off the boyfriend but I forget it's going to piss him off until he gets steamed. But enough about God. What about me? I could use some of that omnipotence stuff."

"And if you had it?"

"First, I'd cure world hunger. I think it's really sad that people go to bed hungry."

"I've been doing it for months."

"Second, I'd make my boyfriend disappear. Not die. Just make him wake up in, say, Tanganyika."

"Tanzania. Tanganyika doesn't exist anymore."

"All the better."

"Why don't you just leave this guy and get it over with? You—"

"I don't want to talk about it."

"You brought it up, I thought—"

"So I can put it back down again."

Marya looked away, her eyes slipping in a second from anger to her usual attentive, uncritical expression. I lowered my eyes to my wine, smiling.

"So Jonathan. Tell me what you want."

I sighed. "A place to live that doesn't have twenty rooms and cold floors. A respectable place to work. A housekeeper who is not in a coma. Most of all, a clean conscience."

"I mean, what do you want to eat? I don't know what to get. It all looks delish."

I looked at her for a few seconds; her eyes were bright and friendly. She hadn't heard a word. "Halibut looks good," I said.

"I want a steak."

The waitress came to get our order, which was halibut and a steak. I ordered another glass of wine. This would be the one that made the shade of Carver slap me on the back and retire for the night.

"What did you say about a house?" Marya said after the waitress had left.

"I have this house. A place I lived in when I was growing up. It's an old mansion, really; twenty rooms. Butler, even."

"You have a butler?"

I nodded. "Who is richer than I am. And a housekeeper—"

"I heard about her."

"I'll show you the place if you like." I raised my glass to sip but stopped. "What do you mean, you heard about my housekeeper?"

"She's in the hospital? Right? First victim of the AIL?"

"That's right, but how did you know that woman was my housekeeper?"

"Oh." She stubbed out her cigarette. "Well. They gave her address in the paper. Now, when I wanted to call you a few days ago I tried the *Metropole*, and they wouldn't give me your home phone. So I ran a search on your license plate."

I looked at her for a few seconds. "Do I owe you money?"

"No, silly. It's not drastic. The Department of Motor Vehicles has records of where people live, phone numbers, stuff like that. I was in the building anyway and decided to check it out, no big deal, don't go getting a big head about it. I see the address for the license plate—and the car isn't yours, I noticed—the address is the same as the woman who got sick. So you had to know her or be the guy who tried to do her in, which I know you aren't."

"You just happened to have my license number handy."

"What, B3A 350?" She looked down and smiled. "Remind me to tell you about my memory." She leaned forward. "Your plates are expired, incidentally. I won't tell anyone."

"You like your guys to live on the edge of the law, don't you?"

"Actually, sort of. I'm a sucker for the dangerous unshaven types. I end up bored with the safe nice variety." I visualized a neon sign over my head, alternately blinking SAFE and NICE. I grinned. All enthusiasm for the rest of the evening ran out a pipe in my leg into a grate beneath the table. It made a loud, gurgling noise Marya seemed not to notice. "My boyfriend's idea of being dangerous," she continued, "is to eat mayo that's been out of the fridge for an hour."

"Do I look dangerous?"

"You? No. But let's say I won't take any brownies from you. Oh God." She put her hand to her mouth. "Oh God, oh God, I'm sorry."

I had taken a breath at the word *brownie* and had no intention of relinquishing it. Marya took my hand and squeezed it and whispered, "Sorry, sorry, sorry."

"There are a few things I don't want to talk about," I said in a monotone. "Painful things. That is one of them." God strike me dead for this, but it was too handy. "The *Times* is another."

We didn't speak until the waitress brought supper.

Neither of us was hungry. My meal was a sad halibut decapitated and filleted right in front of me. It was full of bones, and I ate it like a blind man tapping his way through a minefield. Marya's steak had one bone. You couldn't miss it. We ate in silence for a while until I put down my utensils and told her it was okay, that she shouldn't worry about what she'd said. She smiled and nodded and said all right. We continued in uncomfortable silence for another ten minutes. We tried conversation, but nothing took root. Finally I pretended to choke on a bone. I did not drag it out, and she only had to pound on my back two or three times before I raised a hand signaling life would go on. She put her hands on my shoulders and squeezed, sat back down. We tried talking again and it worked.

"I don't know why I ordered that," I said, pushing my plate away. "I hate food that makes me careful." The fish head, staring into the distance with glassy eyes, concurred.

"I'm—" She stopped, shook her head.

"Go ahead."

"No. It's about . . . you know."

"That's all right. I don't mind talking about the AIL, if that's what you mean. It's just Carver that I don't want to discuss right now."

She put her napkin on her plate and drew a cigarette from my pack. "It's just that the more I study these guys, the more nervous I get about eating anything. They're really sick."

"These guys? The police think it could be just one."

She shook her head. "I've read the letters. Sounds like a group."

"You've read the letters? How?"

"Anyone can, if you're a journalist. I had to talk to this gross cop. Bishop or something. Said he'd let me read them because I was such a cute little thing." She stuck out her tongue and made a gagging sound.

I held up a hand. "Before you go farther. I am also doing the AIL story. For the *Metropole*. So we are, technically, in competition."

"Oh, I figured you were doing the story. And no, I'm not going to tell you anything I had to sweat and smile to get."

"He probably won't let me read the letters. He halfway thinks I'm one of them." My shoulders sagged. "I'm going to do a lousy job on this piece. I don't even know what AIL means."

"Nobody did until their last letter. Which I happened to read today when no one was looking."

She paused to give me ample room to grovel. I counted to ten and said: "Are you going to tell me or do I have to go slay a Hydra for you or something?"

"I'll tell you, you needn't be harsh. It stands for Alimentary Instruction League."

I had to put a hand in front of my mouth to keep from spewing my drink out. "You're joking."

"Nope. Clever guys, huh? Alimentary, as in canal, where your food goes down. An acronym that means sickness. Gets the point across."

"So did the brownies. What else do you know?"

Marya smiled. "Lots. Buy me a drink and crack my back and maybe I'll save you some research."

The bill arrived; Marya picked it up. She read it, handed it back to me and said, "You must be rich." I pulled a hundred from my wallet, money left over from ransoming Trygve. Marya looked at it, then up at me. "I'll tell you this," she said. "Money does not impress me." She thought for a second. "But spending it. That impresses me."

We were halfway home when Marya decided she wanted to take a walk downtown, stop in someplace for a drink. I parked the Pacer, got out and shivered; the air had that forlorn November cold that holds the world until snow gives it something new to think about. This was not weather for a walk, unless it was a stroll to the wall to turn up the thermostat. But Marya had already sprinted across the street to Orchestra Hall, earning honks and imprecations from oncoming cars. When I started to cross she turned and ran toward the plaza in front of the hall.

In the summer the square had a small lake in the middle, trees, fountains; now the grass was dead, the fountains and lake dry and dusty, littered with leaves, papers, scraps. Marya jumped down into the cement lake bed, turned around. "Come on. Pretend it's the Red Sea. I'll be the Israelites and you be the pharaoh and his troops." But I was in no mood to pretend and walked twenty paces behind her. She reached the other end, sat on the bank and made gestures calling for the water to rush in on me. I strolled on unsoaked and sat down beside her.

"That's where we're going to go. I just wanted to sit outside for a while." She pointed to a bar across the street called the Times, the name written in the same Gothic script the paper uses. I had a vision of finding the place full of the editorial staff of *The New York Times*, arms folded across their chests, ready to excoriate the pretender. I shook my head and said no.

"Oh, come on. It's your kind of place."

"It's just a bar, Marya. It has nothing to do with the *Times*, although I'm sure it's a perfectly nice bar anyway, but—"

"That's what I mean. You're perfectly nice and you don't have anything to do with the *Times* either." She smiled.

"I don't? I mean you know?"

"Sure." She looked away. "God, I could tell you were making it up when we were talking about it."

"And you still wanted to go out with me?"

"Yeah. You're kinda cute. And I always wanted to meet you anyway."

I didn't say anything for a while. "I'm sorry I lied. I usually don't."

"I don't care. Everyone lies. The test of character is how they react when they get caught. You didn't even try to save your butt. That's impressive." She smiled. "Jeez, if I worked for the *Lacs Standard* I'd lie too." She bundled her coat around her. "That wasn't easy to do, you know. Had to call the business office at the *Daily* to find the change of address from five years back. Then I looked in the Valhalla phone book at the library to get the name of the paper in the area, and I called to see if you worked there. Boy did I get an earful, or what."

"I left under a sort of cloud."

"You're telling me. I got out some back issues of the *Standard* at the journalism library and read your column. I can see why you left." She closed her eyes and repeated, without a missed word, my entire last column. Until I stopped her.

"My God, how did you memorize that?"

She shrugged. "I can memorize anything. Sort of like a photographic memory except I can remember what I hear, too. It's really neat." She looked me in the eyes and repeated the entire wine list from the Ansonia. I had no choice but to assume it was in the right order. "My folks wanted me to go into music, piano and stuff. They thought I'd be this prodigy? But I wasn't into it. Which I regret, because I'd give anything to play piano or something. But this comes in handy in interviews."

"No notes."

"Right. Except that I still have to use a tape recorder or something. My editors wig out if they see me doing something from memory. Never mind that it's always right."

"You're going to make a good reporter."

"I am a good reporter, and I'll make a great one. If I don't go into the Peace Corps."

"You want to go lay pipe in Somalia, you mean?"

"No. I want to fix fishnets on a beach in the Caribbean. Someplace where they need help but not too much of it." She looked into the empty pool. "I don't know what I want to do."

"You don't want to be a journalist?"

"I suppose I do. I like to write. I'd like to write, say, stories.

Except that I don't have any ideas." She put a foot in the pool and kicked some leaves. "Journalism is neat because you get all the plots and characters handed to you. I'm good at it. I'm good at anything, if I put my little mind to it, 'cause I have to do well at it. I just . . . have to. But I don't have any passion for anything. I mean, like, for a job or a concept or idea, you know?" She looked at me and laughed. "You know, I went back to the old issues and read all your stuff. I got jealous. Because you knew what you believed in. I thought, He's going to get big and famous and tell everyone off."

I looked up; the moon was an indecisive sliver, indistinct behind a veil of ice crystals in the air. "I don't know, Marya. Right now I'm just medium-size and mildly infamous."

"What do you mean, medium-size?"

"Medium weight, medium height, that's what."

"Don't kid yourself. Five eight is average. You can't be more than five six. I'm five two and you're no more than four inches taller."

"Wrong, kid." I stood. She hopped to her feet, the promise of a challenge shining in her eyes. We stood toe to toe, arms akimbo, eyes scanning the top of each other's heads. My eyes lowered and found hers, and for a second hers lost their sharp glitter. Then she looked away and put her hands in her coat. "Cold," she murmured. She turned to me with eyes as wide and soft as egg yolks. I took her face in my hands and kissed her. Her hands covered mine, and it was as though her entire body swept up and surged into her palms, her mouth, and kissing her I felt as if I were draining some ichor from her veins. But this one had ichor to spare. My hands slid into her open coat and down her neck, under her arms, along the round flesh of her breasts, down to her back, her backbone, resting with both hands around the curve of her buttocks, pressing all of her up and toward my mouth.

We did this for a long time.

After a while we pulled apart. I looked at her and smiled. I couldn't feel my feet, and my eyes refused to focus, but I smiled. I felt as if Marya had unstuck a valve inside of me, that everything that had made the bolts groan and the needles on the gauge dance in the red was gone, evaporated, leaving me clean and calm. I brushed the hair from her eyes and watched it fall back. "You take a long time to kiss a girl," she said. She looked addled and happy. "Then again, you have the decency to kiss a girl for a long time." She hugged me tight, her lips grazing my neck, then she looked up at me. "Can we go back and play in your big house?"

I parked in front of the manor, walked around the car and opened her door. She stepped out and looked at the house, eyes round with awe and head tilted back, like someone sitting in the front row of a movie theater. "This is yours?"

"Every damn stone."

"It's your folks' place, you mean."

"They got the châteaus. I was left with the chattel. Come on."

It was dark inside, with a sliver of light from the kitchen slicing across the floor. Light from the hospital flowed through the stained-glass windows, casting hazy visions of the Marvel story onto the carpet. Marya gave a gasp. I patted the walls for the bank of light switches and turned them all on one at a time, feeling a little like a mad scientist bringing his monster to life.

"Turn the lights off," she said. Her voice was low and husky. I snapped the lights off. "God, Jonathan, this is incredible." She turned to me, her face lit by the light from the window in the door, the down on her cheek catching the light.

"How many bathrooms?"

"Five."

"Five. Wow. Come on. Show me around." She took me by the hand and led me down my hallway.

The manor had its moments; this was one of them. In the dark with only the stained glass for illumination, it had a certain ruined charm. You couldn't see the roof or the mezzanine, and the ceiling might as well have been the sky on a night with no stars. The great staircase poured down like a stone river, its source uncertain. The acoustics, if you spoke at full voice, were usually atrocious—the words would come clanging back at you like a handful of hurled cutlery. But in the dark, with only the muted thrum of the furnace laboring in the depths, you held your voice down, and whispers seemed to hang in the air, collect, drift up and dissipate.

Marya was standing silent in front of the windows, examining the Marvel Annunciation. The angel held the ax so that it seemed to grow from Billy Marvel's groin, a grim priapic cleaver; the light from the hospital laid the blade of the ax across Marya's face. She shifted her weight to one side and her face was feathered with the angel's wings.

"What are these about?"

"Scenes from the life of the Marvel scion, William Marvel. My great-great-uncle."

"Great-great-uncle, and you got this? What did the son get, Manitoba?"

"I'm the only male relative. Only deserving male relative," I added, recalling Oscar. "What's so funny?"

"You have an ax on your face."

She now had the angel's face superimposed on hers. She brought her fingers to her lips, touched the tip of each with her tongue; then she reached over and rubbed my nose. "All gone." She smiled.

She wanted a tour, and I obliged. It took her fifteen minutes to exhaust the novelty of the staircase. First she had to walk down it like something from a movie, face all regal hauteur, hips swaying like a harlot's, tossing an imaginary stole over her shoulder. She rode the chair up and down twice, the first time in a slow-motion parody of someone careening down a roller coaster, the second time with legs up and over the handlebar, head laid back, arms back with the wrists limp. Her legs were clenched together, the cuffs of her jeans tight at midcalf; her stockings were white numbers with a sprig of lace at the top. One heel had slipped from her shoe, and she dangled the shoe from her toes, the only motion in her entire body being the bobbing shoe. I stood at the foot of the stairs watching her play, hands in my pockets to camouflage the change in my own topography. I was telling myself I was too old for cotton candy; its gets in your teeth, hurts like hell when it hits a cavity, has no nutritional value. Unlike Sarah, vegetables-and-vitamins Sarah.

"I'm moving in." Marya was dismounting. "Hope you don't mind."

"There are five bedrooms," I said. "Take your pick."

"Good. I always have to have a room of my own."

"Really? What happens when you get married?"

She laughed. "Who says I'm going to get married?"

"Oh, everyone does, eventually."

"Not me, Jonathan. Just show me to the bedrooms."

"What?"

"You said there's five. Come on."

The first was a guest room, shrouds covering the furniture; the second was the same, except that the mattress was missing from the bed. The third was mine; Marya sat on the bed and bounced a few times, said "eh" and made a seesaw gesture with her hand. I took it personally. The fourth room was empty. The wallpaper was a cream field on which rabbits followed one another around on an endless gambol. It had evidently been a child's room, decades ago; it was cold, and we left without saying a word. The last room at the end of the hall was the master bedroom. The door wouldn't open.

"Stuck?" she said.

"Locked. I think."

"Why would it be locked?"

"This was the main bedroom. Aunt and Uncle Marvel slept here. It's probably blasphemous to go inside."

"Let's do it." She tried the knob. "It's not the lock. The door's just stuck." She stepped back a few paces, then threw her weight into the door. It flew open. "After you," she said. When I entered the room she kicked the door shut and kissed me. The lights were off. Somehow we found the bed anyway.

We spent some time just necking, that sweet innocent stuff you never do with such contentment after you've slept together. For an hour it was all blindness and laughter, tongues like wet velvet sliding in and out of one another's mouths, hands on random cartography expeditions over each other's bodies. Eventually we broke for air and cigarettes, and Marya, spying a pile of logs by the fireplace, asked me to build a fire. "I mean another one," she added, kissing me. All right, corny stuff. But I hadn't heard happier words in years.

She went downstairs to get some liqueur while I coaxed a fire out of the logs. She came back into the room with a bottle and glasses. She sat them on the nightstand and dropped onto the bed. "There are people at your front door," she said.

"What? Who? Reporters?" I stood up. "Police?"

"I don't know. People. About fifty of them."

I heard the doorbell and faint cries of "Pawty! C'mon, pawty."

"Oscar." Another one of the rental groups. Damn, damn, damn. I told Marya to wait; I'd be a minute. I had to get to the door before Trygve woke; he'd let the whole mangy lot in.

I could see hands pummeling the bars of the door window as I strode down the hall, heads bobbing in the light from outside. I opened the door a crack and found it thrust back by a man in leather with a T-shirt reading Question Authority Then Kill It. I pushed him, which he wasn't expecting; he fell back and gave me a look of bewilderment. There were, true to Marya's estimation, about fifty people milling around, with more pouring in from the sidewalks.

"No party," I said in as level a voice as I could manage. "No. Party. Go away."

A chorus of obscenities rose from the rabble around the door, and someone shouted that they'd paid good money for this place, whodafuck was I to say no pawty, man. I shouted that I was the owner and that they had been bilked by an alcoholic bastard who had no right to rent the place. But I barely had the end of the statement out before the rear of the mob surged toward the door; I stepped back and slammed it shut, bolting it with palsied hands. Furious blows thundered at the door, voices promising dire harm to my person if I didn't let them in and facilitate the progress of their pawty, man. I backed away from the door, panic scrabbling up my throat; I turned on all the lights, made for the phone. To do what—call the police? And own up to owning the joint, which I somehow had neglected to do?

I was standing alone in the main hall, waiting for bricks to be hurled through the window, when I spied a ceremonial shield and crossed swords hanging on the wall—standard issue for manors, apparently. I had never been so happy to see a cliché in my life. I got up on a chair and pulled the shield down; the swords fell to the floor with a dead dull clang. I picked up one of the swords, shouldered the shield—the damn thing was heavy—and marched off to the front door, heart banging away in a tempo to match those of the fists on the door. I unbolted the door and flung it open.

There is nothing like a broadsword to restore public order. Everyone fell silent, fell back. I raised the shield, feeling my muscles give me a preview of the misery they would express in detail the next day, and I shook the sword. "Get out!" I bellowed. "Get out or I'll run you through, understand?" They did. The crowd shrank back a step, muttering; emboldened, I stepped forward, banged the sword against the shield.

It took maybe a minute for everyone to go. I stood on the porch with the point of the sword scraping on the steps. When the last of them had faded off into the dark, I went inside and bolted the door, laughing out loud. I stuck the sword through my belt and walked up the stairs, smiling to myself.

I could feel the heat of the fire at the top of the stairs. I walked into the master bedroom and stood in the doorway. Marya stared at me, mouth open, then she started to laugh. I pulled out the sword, tossed it to my right, dropped my shield and I had most of my clothes off by the time I reached the bed.

11

The road to Valhalla was narrow and winding, as though the pioneers who first carved it through the countryside had no enthusiasm for their destination and wanted to take as much time getting there as possible. Between punching the accelerator to capitalize on the straightaway and riding the brake around curves, my miles-to-the-gallon were barely in the plural; the Pacer drank what I gave it only to demand more an hour down the road.

Around five I pulled over for a fill-up at a gas station in Princeton. I stuck the nozzle into the car, and looked off into the west. The sun was the color of a frozen orange, sliding down between two hills like a coin through a slot, setting off the machinery of night. There was an uneven coat of snow on the ground, which I'd noticed for the past fifty miles. I was driving north into winter; I was driving to a funeral.

I also felt happier than I had in a long time.

After half an hour on the road the light was just a messy smear on the horizon; within the hour, dusk and darkness. The road wove and wound through the countryside, road signs springing up into my headlights like shooting gallery signs. There was no other traffic coming or going, and I couldn't raise anything on the radio but fierce static and the occasional polka station, fading in and out, a message from a distant planet of fat happy Germans. The road made a swing around Mille Lacs, the water thick and black; I watched the reflection of the moon parallel my car, tearing a jagged gash of light in the dark, churning water. When the road pulled away and shot into landlocked darkness, I knew I was about an hour from Valhalla.

Carver was going to be buried in Valhalla the next day. I wasn't thinking of the funeral, however; that was just a shadow in my head. And I had the spotlights turned on the previous evening. After I had dispatched the partygoers with my berserk Norseman routine, Marya and I had broken some records, if not some springs, making sport for hours.

She'd been dressed when I returned, and I helped her take off her clothes. The sweater was easy enough; her jeans I unzipped and slid off with a motion more fluid than I was used to executing—instead of the usual struggling each partner pretends is erotic, taking her jeans off was as easy as sliding your hands along a porpoise. I undid the clasp from her bra, a model that snapped in the front; she arched her back and wriggled out of it, her breasts spilling out, spattered with freckles, gleaming in the light of the fire. She sat in my lap, laced her arms around my back and kissed me, her legs scissored around my waist. She kept her stockings on, and for a moment I knew that this particular detail would be something I would request of my partners the rest of my life.

It would be accurate to say Marya had one orgasm. Accurate if an encyclopedia of thirty volumes were considered one book. She climaxed with frequency and rapidity, and it was a little like going to bed with a Gatling gun. Some, to gauge from her expression and the depth to which she embedded her fingers in my back, were sharp and exacting, a flat sword scattering her coals; some bubbled up like a spring of effervescent honey, and during these she held my face in her hands, her head tilted back, eyelids trembling, her lips parted a fraction as though there were a genie in her she didn't want to escape but that she didn't want to suffocate either. She took delight in everything I did. I could do no wrong except to not do it again. When I took my own pleasure she set a new rhythm, taking my orgasm to the edge of the precipice, cocking it back like a discus hurler and flinging it off the cliff. I fell for a day, landing in a pool of sweat and syrup, and lay there panting.

We spent the rest of the night talking—that long, lazy talk where you pull open the strange doors in yourself—doors you didn't know were locked, doors you'd seen as brick walls. She talked about her boyfriend, referring to their relationship in an emphatic past tense; since she had brought her diaphragm along for our dinner date—as well as a condom for me, in case I was low on stock—I had assumed this was premeditated. I gave her the condensed version of my life story—growing up in the manor, in other relatives' homes, with my mother. I told Marya a little about Jane and a lot about what had been happening the last few days, about Grue, about Lou Carver, about being there the night he died. She listened in silence, holding me tight. I told her a lot about Carver. I hadn't known just how much I wanted to talk about it.

Driving alone, with just the static of the radio for company, I almost hugged myself to remind me what she had felt like. But I caught sight of the sign that said VALHALLA 4 PROSPER 8, the sign that had always made me wonder, What inning? That had been when Jane was around and Lou was alive, and I fell with a thunk back into the reason I was coming here.

Carver was a Lutheran, and Lutherans are brisk about burying their dead. No masses, no swinging censers cloaking the air with perfume, no endless petitions for the departed's soul. A song, a sermon, and downstairs for ham on buns.

The church was a brick box off Maple Street in Valhalla. It was notable for having burned down three times, each time the congregation vowing to rebuild to further God's word, never stopping to consider that perhaps God was suggesting something here—like moving to a part of town closer to the fire station, for example. The most recent incarnation was flat-roofed, a warehouse for souls that was modeled on bank branch offices. The cross looked like a corporate logo.

I sat in the back pew in a corner thick with shadows. I arrived just as a young woman finished warbling a hymn. The minister, a jolly burgher who always had looked as though he were suppressing a smile, stepped up to the pulpit, fighting back the expression of a boy who has just made a naughty noise among elders. He cast a look over the assembled multitude. There were perhaps fifty people there—everyone from the *Standard*, a few locals, some sniffling figures draped in black I figured for Carver's sisters, and, in the front row, Spanks, Carver's daughter, properly dressed in black, albeit leather. The minister began a description of heaven, that Arizona in the Sky, a retirement home for worthy souls. He wound up praising the righteousness of the man we were here to bid farewell. The man who met his end in a strip joint, I said to myself, and I smiled.

We sang a hymn that proclaimed there was no such thing as death. Carver did not join in. We bowed for the Lord's Prayer, the words coming easily from the vault of rote memorization, still poetic in their plain humble piety. The pallbearers filed from the front row and left, hoisting the casket outside where it would be interred. Everyone shuffled out to the accompaniment of reedy organ music; I bent down in the posture of prayer, obscuring my features until everyone was out. Then I put on my hat and my dark glasses and left for the graveyard.

A halfhearted coat of snow lay over the graveyard, dusting the tops of tombstones, collecting on the arms of stone crosses, the upturned palms of wailing angels. An unenthusiastic sun sat high above us, watching, not warming. I followed the tracks to a grave far in the back of the cemetery, a grove of trees empty of leaves, Lake Lelac sawing and muttering beyond. The minister was saying the last formal farewells over the coffin, and everyone's eyes were cast to the ground, shoulders shivering beneath coats. I walked up and stood at the perimeter of the gathering, and when the minister closed his books, etched a cross in the cold thin air and gestured to the attendants to lower the casket, I stepped forward and tossed the bouquet I'd bought that morning.

There was a clicking sound, the noise of a motor-driven camera. I looked up to see a scraggly young man pointing a camera with a telephoto lens straight at me, firing away. Heads turned to him, then to his target. I watched the photographer lope off toward the parking lot. He took a few shots of the church, aimed the camera in the direction of the burial, then got in his car and left spitting gravel. That would be the new photographer the *Standard* had been talking of hiring. He knew how to ruin an event in order to capture it; he would go far.

Someone worked a winch, and the casket began to descend until the shadows of the pit swallowed it up. The mourners dispersed, scurrying back to the church to blunt the notion of mortality with a full stomach. A few from the *Standard* gave me hard looks when they passed; a few patted me on the shoulder. Marge, the *Standard*'s receptionist, painfully frail in a thin black coat, gave me a hug, sobbing into my lapels, and left without a word. When Spanks walked by I called her name. She still had her spikes, but her face was desolate and innocent. She looked like someone who had failed the audition for cheerleading at a black mass.

"I need to talk to you," I said.

" 'Bout what?"

"I just need to."

She looked around, down at the ground. " 'Kay. Later. I gotta go to the reception. Meet me at the Kopper Kettle later."

"When?"

"I don't know, later." She turned and plowed her way back to the church, shoulders hunched, her spikes looking like lightning rods for whatever misery God could throw down her way. I wondered what she'd tell me. I turned back to the grave, knelt at the edge and peered down. My flowers had come to rest right where Carver's hands would be crossed, over the scarred and silted heart it had taken poison to stop. "Good-bye, you old bastard," I said, and I immediately felt ashamed of myself. "Sorry," I whispered. "Sorry."

I stood up, took a handful of dirt, tossed it down into the pit and walked away, eyes tearing from the cold.

"Zeke! You said potato salad or slaw? I forget."

"Said slaw."

I looked up from a copy of the *Standard* and saw a familiar figure sitting at the counter—the old farmer who'd given me a ride to work the day I'd written my last column. I retreated back behind my paper. No one had noticed me and that was just as I would have it. I'd been waiting at the Kopper Kettle for an hour and a half, waiting for Spanks to show, and I didn't want the meeting spoiled by an impromptu lynching. Earlier Sonya Salmon, the woman I had identified as having an affair with the local pediatrician, had stumbled in, red-eyed, taken a booth with a woman and made a soft sobbing speech into a handkerchief. My testicles spent a full hour in my throat.

But the Kettle was empty now, with only Zeke at the counter, muttering over his coffee, pausing between slurps to move a lump of chaw around the gutter of his lower lip. When the bell tinkled he didn't look up. I peeked around my corner and saw Spanks. She sat down across from me, shook a clove cigarette from its pack and said: "So?"

I put my paper down. "So. How are you, uh, holding up?"

" 'Kay. I guess."

"How was the reception?"

"A lot of old farts coming up and saying it was too bad." She blinked, looked away. "Like, I don't know." She was silent for a moment.

Zeke said, "This is pertater salad, Mabel. I asked you for the slaw."

"Gimme a light." I did, with matches that said *Jolly Tyme*, summoned out of some black hole in my pocket. "So. You were with my dad when he . . . when he."

"I was."

"I read about that in the paper. It sounded like he didn't . . ." Spanks put her face in her hands, an act that made me lean back for fear of being impaled by her coiffure.

"Don't think about it now. We can talk about it later if you want. I want to talk about the people who killed him." I patted her on the shoulder, but she drew back.

She blotted her eyes with a napkin. "What do you mean, 'who killed him.' "

"The AIL. Whoever they are."

"Okay, talk."

Damn. "I was hoping you'd know something about them."

"Me? Why?"

"Don't take this wrong, but it seems you and them are in the same line of work. You and your friends go to jail for protesting pesticides in grain, and that sounds a lot like what this AIL is concerned with. Big difference in forms of expression, but it's still the same beef."

The waitress came by and asked if Spanks would like anything; Spanks requested decaffeinated coffee, water process. The waitress nodded and walked away.

"So? Anybody in your group know any of these people?"

"Don't know nothing."

I sighed and leaned back. The waitress came back and deposited a mug of hot water and a packet of Sanka.

"Hey. I said water process."

"There's your water," said Mabel, pointing to the mug. "There's your Sanka. Pour the water over the Sanka. That's the process."

Spanks made the Sanka, chastened, and sipped it before she looked at me again. She raised tired, hollow eyes to mine. "Look. The group I belong to is the Progressive Students Front. We're antinuke. Antitoxic waste, antipornography. Antiracist, -sexist, -imperialist. Antianything that's antilife. Death is not our gig. Whoever killed my dad"—she paused, put down her cup, swallowed—"was as far from us as you can get, so forget about getting anything out of me. Just forget it." She pushed her cup away. "Pay for this, will you? I gotta get out of here."

"I'll call you down in the cities in a few days."

"Why? I don't have anything to tell you."

"Maybe I can talk to your friends. Other people in the Front."

"Just forget it." She started to button her coat. "Anyway, I thought you were like a social writer. This is cop stuff. This isn't your work."

This is Jared's work, the little man had said. I decided on one blind feint.

"It's not my work. It's Jared's."

Spanks blanched—no small trick for someone wearing an inch of pancake makeup. But her face sagged and her eyes went dead as marbles. "Who's Jared?"

"I think you know. He knows about you."

This time she stopped dead and looked at me, her face pale and frightened. Her lower lip quivered. I felt really good about this. Afterward I would go out and kick the first dog to lick my hand. "He knows me? What did he say? Did he write something? A letter, mention my name, what?"

"What do you think he said?"

"Anything. Lies. Mean stuff. He's crazy. Nobody wants to have anything to do with him."

"So you do know him."

"No I don't."

"People in your group know him."

"No one knows him."

"Come on, Spanks."

"Look. I don't know him. No one I know knows him. He just sent letters to us. Scary things. Like that he knew where we lived and where we went and what he would do if we didn't join him."

"Why didn't any of you join him?"

"He does violence. And what does he have to do with this anyway?"

"Pretty obvious. He wrote letters to the police, too." I paused. "He sent the brownies. This hasn't been made public, but he's the one behind this AIL."

"Oh God." She put a hand to her mouth. Then she bolted from the booth and left the restaurant. I threw a couple of dollars on the table and went after her.

Spanks was striding down the street, gusts of exhaust coming from her mouth. I fell alongside and told her that I was just trying to find out who was responsible for the funeral we'd just attended.

"Get away from me. Just get away. I read the papers. You were with Dad. You could have done something. If it hadn't been for you he wouldn't have been at that place anyway and he wouldn't be dead. So don't talk to me about doing something now. And just don't talk to me about Jared."

"It's not my fault your father died!" I shouted. "All right, it is my fault! Okay! But I didn't know. It was a goddamn brownie, for Chrissakes. How was I supposed to know it was poisoned? There was nothing I could have done, Spanks. I'm trying to do something now."

"Then start by staying away from me. You got a lot of balls to do this. My dad was a wonderful man. He gave me so much and he gets killed by people who know people I know. How do you think that makes me feel?"

"There was nothing you could have done either."

"Which makes me as good as you. And if that's so, then what good am I?"

She stamped away, and this time I let her go.

Jared. I was thinking of the name all the way out of town, repeating it like a mantra. I knew it would behoove me to talk to some of the fine fellows of the Progressive Students Front. Maybe they could make sense of this. I'd look them up as soon as I got home.

If I got home. The storm I had seen predicted on TV was stomping its way north, and the farther south I drove the more I drove into trouble. There had been freezing drizzle earlier, so the road was paved with a sheet of ice—with a layer of fresh snow on top of that. The wind was whipping the snow in all directions, and it darted left and right like startled schools of fish, dashing against my windshield in terror. There was nothing to be seen but the absolute and claustrophobic darkness of the countryside, nothing to be heard but the silent scherzo of the snow and the brusque metronome of the wipers.

One hour out of Valhalla I was driving with one hand, wiping the condensation from my oaths and prayers off the window with the other, when I felt the ground change elevation and the Pacer strain. I eased the car over the lip of a hill. I knew this hill. Mexican cliff divers could practice from this hill. I slowed to five mph and began to descend, one foot kissing the brake, the other depressing the gas by millimeters.

All of which was a twine leash on a rutting bull. The Pacer flew down the hill. Screaming would only fog the window again, so I concentrated on braking, keeping the car from spinning off into the ditch. I did such a splendid job that I had no power to get up the other side of the next hill. I was halfway up, wheels whining on the ice, when I began to slide backward. In the rearview mirror I saw the lights of another car probing the top of the hill I'd just left. Sweet Christ enthroned in glory, this was it. Then I hit upon the notion of letting the car slide backward and steering it into the other lane. I let gravity take me down, steering to turn the car around. It turned. It liked turning so much it kept spinning around and around. I held on for dear and presumably truncated life; then the Pacer spun off the highway and thudded into a snowbank. My head cracked against the door and a stitch of pain sliced up my back.

I sat there for a second, afraid to pose questions to my extremities. I wiggled my fingers and toes, moved my legs. I was all right. I flailed at my seat belt to get out. Cars blew up after crashing; I'd seen the movies. The door was stuck against the snow, so I rolled down the window and wriggled out. I staggered around in the snow, wondering what the hell I was going to do now, when I saw the car that had been heading down the hill—it had stopped, perhaps to see what other acrobatics I was going to execute. I waved my arms; it blinked its lights. The driver rolled down the window, asked if I was all right and if I needed a ride. I shouted that a ride was just jack dandy with me, rescued my luggage and typewriter and sprinted across the road to his car.

My driver was, literally, the Good Samaritan. Hussif Al-Abul, from Samaria. "To say the Good Samaritan," he said as he gunned his four-wheel drive over the hill, "is to spit on my people, yes?"

You try answering that one. I cleared my throat.

"Samaritans had a—what is the phrase—bad rep, in the area. So when one of them did something decent he was called the Good Samaritan. To distinguish him from all the others." He shook his head at the folly of the world. "You never even hear about the halfway decent Samaritan."

Hussif was a moderate sort of fellow, as am I, and we had solved the Palestinian question before we were thirty miles down the road. He let me off at the Lac-Vu Motel on the shore of Mille Lacs, wished me a long life, praised my acumen and requested that I name my children after him, and then he sped off.

The manager of the Lac-Vu, less a human than an ambulatory duffel bag of organs with a face, tore himself away from the television set with the effort of someone pulling a bandage off a wound and informed me that no, there was no tow available tonight, nosirree, and yeah, I could have a room, thirty dollar cash, sign here. I struggled through the snow to cabin 13 and clicked on the lights. A bed, a desk. Perfect. Maybe this was a godsend. Here was where I'd write my story on Carver.

I took a glass clad in a polyurethane negligee, undressed it, rummaged in my suitcase for the bottle of Clan Anderson I'd taken from the house and glugged out a couple fingers. I toasted myself in the mirror, lit a cigarette and dialed Marya's number; no answer. I hung up and set up the typewriter. There were a few sheets of Lac-Vu stationery in the drawer. I typed:

> Lou Carver was the kind of man that other men call a man's man.

No, no. There were enough men in that sentence to invade Normandy.

> Lou Carver had a heart as big as all outdoors, although with far less property taxes.

That's right. Cheap laughs at the expense of the dead. God should strike me where I sit. I got up, paced, rolled scotch around in my mouth, sat down, started again.

> You've read the papers; you know that a passel of bastards known as the AIL killed a man with poisoned confection, and you wonder who they are. Better you should know Lou. Lou Carver was an old-school journalist—meaning a sworn enemy of his heart, liver, lungs and decent, pious speech. By the time I met him he had already oldschooled himself into an ulcer and a heart condition and a liver so large it could have applied for statehood. But he never got the chance to have a death of his own devising—a death I imagine he would have faced with courage. What killed him was cowardice. The anonymous cowardice of the terrorist.

I stopped, kneaded my temples. And then I kept writing, writing all night. The manager was far from happy when I woke him up at two for more stationery. I heard a note of anger in his voice when I called at three to place a wake-up call.

The call came an hour early, and the phone rang every five minutes until I took it off the hook. I slept past check-out time, and the manager charged me for an extra day, with pleasure.

"Mrrgh."

"Oh, don't mrrgh me, Fikes."

He looked up from my manuscript with tired eyes. His hair was pushed back, making oily peaks like a freshly whipped pudding. "It's not complete, I know. But it's good. And I have another day. And by then I should know something more about the AIL. I have a lead."

"Really."

I crossed my legs, lit a cigarette. "Yeah. No one's investigated the connection between the AIL and this group of protestors at the U. Why, I don't know. It can't be any more obvious. I was talking to one of their number—Carver's daughter, in fact—up in Valhalla. They've had contact with this Jared I talk about in the piece there. It wouldn't surprise me if someone in the organization knows what's going on here." I tapped my ash in the wastebasket. "Anything happen while I was gone? Any manifestos? Incidents?"

"Mrrgh." Fikes flattened his nose with his index finger, staring at me with baleful eyes. "Well." He looked at my story. "Carver seems to have been a, urrngh, colorful man. I especially enjoyed hearing how he used to shoot ducks from his office window."

I shrugged. "He loved to hunt, and he didn't have the time." Wait a minute. "I put that in the story? I don't remember that."

Fikes rummaged through a pile of newspapers on his desk, pulled one out and threw it across the desk at me. I picked it up: the previous day's *Minnesota Daily*. BROWNIE POISON VICTIM A MAN OF GREAT APPETITES, SAYS FRIEND. It was copyrighted, and it was written by one Marya Thompson. There was a photograph of me tossing a bouquet onto Carver's grave.

Fikes pinched his nose, rubbed it. "I met Miss Thompson once. She was taken to court by the university for printing a story, refused to tell how she got the story. She spent a night in jail. Much pluck. Much of a lot of things." He pushed the end of his snout up with the end of a pencil. "I don't like being caught with our pants down, Simpson. I like it less when we take our pants down of our own volition. Like I say, I have met Miss Thompson."

Fikes ceased to exist at that moment, as did the rest of the physical world between myself and Marya. I got up, left the office, got in my car and made hell for the *Daily*. I turned off Washington Avenue onto a street reserved for buses, drove my car up onto the sidewalk and left it there. I was smart enough to make for the doors of the journalism school instead of taking on the walls, although the walls would have lost. The receptionist at the *Daily* gave me the look that presages calling security, but I strode past her, around the corner to Marya's cubicle. She was on the phone. I reached over and depressed the hook, took the phone from her ear and hung it up. She gave me a look that wild beasts use to convince hunters to let them out of the trap.

"Hi," she said. I could see marbles rattling in her head, but she kept a tight grip on her composure. "Have a nice time at the funeral?"

To my amazement I still had the copy of the *Daily* in my hand. I brought it up, waved it, slammed it down on her desk.

"This, sweetheart, is the quickest way of being nominated for bimbohood that I have ever seen in my life. What the hell is the matter with you? I gave you one fabulous night, the promise of several dozen more and threw in six hundred million genetic replicants of myself free of charge in case you had a use for them and you do this to me?" She gave me the oh-my-aching-paw look again. "That what that was all about, huh? Getting a story?"

She shook her head no.

"I had a wonderful time, Jonathan. Listen to me—"

"What is this doing in the paper?"

She looked down, eyes fixed on some spot fifty stories below sea level. "I have this great memory."

"So get amnesia! You're telling me that just because you—"

"What's going on here?" The young man in the suit, Marya's ex, or probably partner in this episode, had stepped over to her cubicle and was regarding me like a dead fish washed up by the tide. "What do you want here?"

"Far less than I used to, I'll tell you that." I snatched the *Daily* from Marya's desk and waved it in his face. "It's about this. And the means by which your staff gets its stories."

He grinned, displaying perfect teeth, and I wanted to belt him so hard I would be picking teeth from my knuckles with tweezers and a magnifying glass. "You shouldn't have consented to the interview, if that's the problem. Come on. You used to work here. You oughta be the last one to complain. Nothing she wrote was inaccurate."

"Interview? Is that what she called it?" Marya turned white and looked at me like the fox in the trap that knows compassion has just lost out to the going bounty. "If this was an interview, I'd like to see the notes."

The editor shrugged. "Sure. Mar? You got the notes?" She began to fumble through her note pads, hands shaking.

"Notes she reconstructed after the fact," I said. "And let me tell you just what the fact was, laddy buck. I told this woman my life story, abridged version, after a class-A roll in the hay. Understand?"

Now the editor's face went white. I felt like a carrier for albinoism, but I also felt flushed and furious and knew I had color for all three. The editor looked at Marya, who was still staring into some distant basement.

"So next time you roll over and feel like a postcoital chat with this one here, make sure your lawyer's present. And speaking of lawyers, get yours on the phone. Because you're going to have a fun time explaining this story. You're either going to have to stick by the story and produce proof I spoke willingly or admit that Lois Lane here took a source to bed to crowbar a few secrets out of him. And *The New York Times* is going to love those ethics." I added that for spite. I couldn't sue. I knew the business. But I could air the situation in a voice loud enough to require FCC licensing. There was by now a crowd around Marya's cubicle.

"You know the real pity?" I said to Marya. "I'm so stupid I actually wanted to do it again. Give me a call when another of my friends dies and you're on deadline with nothing to write about. And remember: you're always supposed to have two sources for a story. In other words, go fuck yourself."

I rolled the *Daily* into a bat, thwapped it a few times on my thigh and bumped my way through the crowd to the door. I had said just what I wanted to say. My brain felt like a lobster's guts the moment it's thrown in hot water—partly from fury over what she'd done, partly out of anger toward myself. Because I knew there would be a day when she'd call to apologize and I would actually listen. No: to hell with her. I wanted a drink. No, coffee. With sugar. Lots of sugar. And cream. Poured by the friendliest face I knew in the world.

"Since when do you take sugar?" said Sarah.

"I mean it figuratively. I want some sugar. I feel as though I have been licking a barber's strop for the last few weeks."

"I read the papers. Saw your picture. Lousy picture, Jonathan." She put a hand over mine. Sin and Death both looked at her, at me, then frowned into their coffee. "Where have you been, anyway? You didn't leave your number, or call me, or—"

"I've been guesting on 'Romper Room,' " I said. "I want to talk to you. When do you get off?"

"Later. Depends. You have something to do?" I shook my head no. "Okay. You want to go meet at your place? I'd like to see that castle you mentioned."

No, not that. The bed on which Marya and I had tussled would still be unmade, the fireplace full of ash, the shield and broadsword still lying on the floor. "I don't want to go home," I said.

"You want to meet back here later?"

I shook my head no, looking down. Sarah reached into her pocket and pulled out her keys, took one off and handed it to me. "Go to my place. I'll be there. I'll call before I come, and maybe you can have something to eat ready?" She kissed me on the cheek and turned toward the kitchen.

I didn't go straight to Sarah's. I spent an hour in a beer joint that had been one of my college haunts, drinking coffee and shoving a pinball machine around. It was a talking machine, greeting every quarter with a throaty "Bango beat you." Stand in line, fella. I racked up a high score, tilted off three games and felt no better for it.

At Sarah's I sat on the sofa feeling as though the marrow had been siphoned from my bones. I put on a record of some howling late Romantic composer and lay down on the sofa, imagining Marya as Salome drawn by Beardsley, dancing with my head on a platter. I felt foul and sweaty, the cheap deodorant of the Lac-Vu's soap wafting from my body. I needed a bath.

I drew hot water and dumped in a packet of bath crystals made with kelp ("Nonviolently harvested. No plankton were killed.") only to have the bathwater turn the murky green of spinach puree. I checked the package and found it was good for one hundred baths. The water was slow in draining and gurgled out with the sound of a very fat man clearing his throat in displeasure. I drew another bath, omitting the flora, and, as was my habit, brought a TV into the bathroom. Sarah's TV, not surprisingly, was the midget size preferred by people who say they don't watch TV. I turned it on and eased into the tub.

The news was on. The Dow Jones index was up on a late rally, and I felt the usual meaningless relief. The local news returned: a fire in an abandoned warehouse, film of flames snapping at the cold night air, pan shots of the spectators, one of whom undoubtedly set it and had his VCR whirring away at home. Weather. Sports. Nothing on the AIL or Marya throwing herself into the Mississippi in remorse. I started to doze.

Sleeping in the tub is hard to do, surrounded as you are by a familiar but essentially foreign medium. I woke up once when an old war movie blared on and a chorus singing of Johnny, Johnny Jingo fought its way out of the tiny speaker. I went back to sleep and woke up when Sarah put the key in the front door. When the door slammed shut I woke and called out, “Sarah? I'm in the tub here and I'm pretty much naked.”

To my curiosity the bathroom door inched open. Mac was behind it.

Mac in the flesh had a build like the dogs named Spike in old cartoons—little waist, stumpy legs, and shoulders you could drive across and only stop once for refueling. I was staring at him, one hand doing figleaf duty, the other available for gestures, pleading or otherwise, when his expression shifted from neutral to one of broken glass sauteed in lead and sulfur. He said not a word but went straight to work. He picked up the TV set and held it over the tub.

I looked up and saw John Wayne, scowling down on me. In a voice akin to a small bird being stepped on in an adjacent room, I said, “I hope you're kidding.”

He gave me a look bleached of all humanity. “I hope you're grounded” was all he said.

12

Years had passed. Nations and hemlines had risen and fallen. I opened my eyes. Mac still had the TV over me.

“Put it down,” I said. “Let me explain and then you can kill me if you like, but for God's sake drop that TV! I mean, put it down over there and drop it, please. Please.”

Mac was looking at me, his head tilting from side to side in a manner reminiscent of Kong examining the squirming native in its grasp. Then he said "Okay," and put the TV down on the floor. He sat on the toilet, took out a cigarette and lit it. He pointed to the TV and said, "Good movie, dude?"

Dude. Sarah slept with a man who called fellow members of his species "dude."

"Get out of the tub and let's have a talk," he said. He stood and walked out of the bathroom.

I had one foot out of the tub and was about to step onto the tile when I noticed I had already deposited a substantial quantity of water on the floor. And the TV was on the floor, plugged in, war still raging across its six-inch screen. I was able to step onto the adjacent toilet without touching the floor. From there I got the towel, crouching on the bowl like some gargoyle come to terrorize the incontinent. Then I unplugged the set, dressed and went into the living room.

Mac was reading a sports magazine. There was a cigarette hanging out of his mouth. One hand was absently scrabbling into a bag of potato chips. He didn't look up. "Sit down. Sit down and tell me all about it."

I sat. "You're Mac," I said. He nodded. "Sarah's told me a lot about you. I bet she's even told you a lot about me."

"Tell me? About the guy she's shtupping on the sly?" He laughed without mirth. "Oh, that is happening."

"No it isn't. Nothing's happening. We're not shtupping. I mean, we shtupped but that was half a decade ago. I'm Jonathan Simpson. She must have mentioned me."

He looked at me, studying my face. He shoved a handful of potato chips in his mouth and said, "You before or after Mark?"

Mark? Trotsky. "Before."

"You're the critic."

He watched me in silence for a few more minutes. Then he went back to his magazine. I coughed and said it was nice meeting him, perhaps another day the three of us could lunch.

"Sit down," he said, looking at his magazine.

"I am sitting."

"Then stop talking like you're going to get up, dude. We're waiting for Sarah to come home."

We sat. Time passed with a club-footed gait. Mac read his magazine, turning each page with a wetted finger. I sat with my hands in my lap, a bad child waiting for the principal, ignored, full of dread.

Around seven there was the sound of a key in the lock. I made a silent prayer to every god ever devised by man that Sarah should enter and call out Mac's name.

"Jay?"

Mac stood and walked to where I was sitting. He grabbed me by my collar and hoisted me a few inches off my chair. I dangled in his grasp, wondering what the names were of the veins he was cutting off. Sarah came into the room, laden with grocery sacks. Her eyes opened wide and she said, "Mac!"

"Hey, sport," he said.

"What are you doing here?"

"My key still fits. I figured I was still welcome."

I made windmilling gestures with one arm and pointed up at Mac with the other.

"Let him down."

"Oh, so you're sticking up for him."

"Let him down."

Mac dropped me to my chair. "You want to tell me why this joe was buck jaybird naked in our tub? Huh? This another of your friends from the dance studio?"

"No. He's a friend."

"A friend. That's what I told you Kathy was. Just a friend. And hell if you believed me."

"Jay is a friend. There is nothing between us. You think I'd go to bed with him?"

"Hey," I said, coughing.

"You didn't believe me, why should I believe you?"

"I caught you in bed with her!"

"So? This dick's in the tub calling out your name when I come in! And I was just giving her a back rub, for Chrissakes! She was tense! People get tense!"

"Tense? *Tense?* People don't lay on their back with their legs open when they're tense!"

"I'm parked in someone's spot," I said. "I'm sure I'm going to get towed." I stood.

"Sit down," said Mac and Sarah.

"No. If you two want to eviscerate one another you are welcome to do just that. This isn't any of my business and I'm sorry I walked into the middle of this. Now, if you'll excuse me."

Mac looked at me. "You finished?"

"Yes."

"Then sit down." And he shoved me back in my chair.

"Where have you been?" said Sarah. "The three minutes a day I spend not hating your guts I actually worry where you are. But I'm getting tired of coming home and finding you on my sofa with no explanation. Kathy kick you out?"

"I wasn't with her, for Chrissakes. I was out of town again for the company. I told you that. We got clients in Fargo I gotta go nursemaid every week. And I came back because I want to try this again. And what do I find soaking? A critic."

"Can I say something here?" I said. "I've had a bad day. It shows every sign of turning into a bad life. I went to see Sarah at work for a little kindness and a cup of coffee. I didn't want to go home and she said I should come here, which, Buster, is a place that I called home a long time before you knew this woman. What did I say when you came in? 'Don't come in the bathroom, I'm naked.' That sound suspicious to you? If I'd been prancing around the house wearing nothing but a crown of laurel leaves and tooting on a Pan flute, I think you'd have a case. I thought this was a safe harbor and I was wrong. Now I'm leaving." I stood and Mac put a hand on my shoulder. "Get your goddamn paws off me!" I shouted, shaking free.

Mac picked me up and placed me against the wall. "Nobody," he said. "Nobody tells me what to do in my house."

"You pay rent here?" I said.

"Half."

"So maybe I'm standing in the part Sarah rents."

"You're not standing anywhere. You're hanging on the wall in case you haven't noticed."

"Let him down, Mac," said Sarah, her voice tired. She began to take the groceries out of the bag.

Mac let me down. He pointed a finger at me. "Take off, dude. And if I catch you hanging around my bathtub again I'm going to lay a world of hurt on your head."

"Make a reservation first," I said. "Space is limited." I walked out, stopped at the door. Sarah was looking at the cans she had put on the counter. "Thanks for all your help," I said. She gave me a look both accusing and beseeching, as if there was something I knew that I was choosing to ignore. I slammed the door behind me and walked out. Each door in the hallway was open an inch, and each door shut as I walked toward it.

There were fifteen minutes of visiting hours left at the hospital. Grue was at the end of the hall in a private room. Trygve sat in a chair next to her bed, holding her hand, sprawled across her body, snoring. I shook him gently by the shoulder.

"Trees!" he cried. He sprang awake, looked around the room. "Trees." Then he saw me, frowned; his shoulders sagged. He folded his hands in his lap.

"Master Simpson. Good evening."

"What was that about trees?"

"Trees? It was . . . a dream. With bad trees in it."

"Did these trees have faces on them?" He nodded, eyes wide. "And hands? Mean voices? They threw fruit at you?" *The Wizard of Oz* had been on the previous night.

"Yes! You've seen them too?" I nodded. "Then it wasn't a dream. I'm so relieved."

"How's Grue?"

"The same. Although the doctor says there's been no change."

Grue looked too much at ease. Seeing her face without an expression was disconcerting, as though she weren't really inside her body anymore. She should have had a sign on her chest reading WILL RETURN AT with a clockface below. They'd isolated the poison—something with a long name that sounded as if it should be in diet soda—but since they didn't know how Grue was reacting to the stuff, no one knew if she would ever come out of the coma.

I sat with Trygve in the dim room until the nurse came and asked us to leave. I bought Tryg a candy bar in the lobby and helped him out of the hospital. He marveled again at my ability to find the exit of any place with such ease, and we walked, shivering, around the corner to the manor.

When I got home there was a small figure sitting on the steps, the porch light shining on her red hair. I couldn't believe it. Apologies somehow didn't seem her style. I told Tryg to head inside and stood on the walk, wondering what to do. I could be a jerk and turn her away. Or be a gentleman and invite her in, serve her a beverage, hear her out and then feed her to the boiler.

I went up the walk, feigning a cough. She looked up, and I saw she'd been crying. All my anger faded. Well, enough of it faded. I smiled and said hi.

"You bastard!" She leapt to her feet and stomped down the walk.

"Hi," she said to Tryg as she passed him, eyes locked on mine. Marya plowed dead into me and started beating my chest with her fists. I caught them both, which gave her feet the cue to start fracturing my shins. I put one leg between hers, grabbed her around the upper back and started to lower her to the ground in the hopes of pinning her; we both fell over, and I felt my brain bang against my skull.

"You bastard. You son of a bitch."

"I think you have the issue"—I spat, coughed—"of culpability a little reversed here, Marya."

"You didn't have to tell him how I got the story. That was cheap cheap cheap. Do you know what he does when he's jealous? Do you?"

"I don't care if he turns eight shades of green and clashes with the carpet," I said, panting. "I didn't owe you a thing. If you're going to pull that kind of—"

"He's going to call *The New York Times*. Uh-huh. Tell them all about it. Get my internship pulled and they'll give it to the runner-up at the paper and it's all your fault."

I laughed. I just sat there and laughed.

"That's right. Act like it's funny."

"Well, it is. We're even."

"Intentions matter here, Mr. Simpson." She was on her knees, hands on hips. "Intentions. You deliberately did what you did. If you would have listened or given me a chance to talk, you wouldn't have done it, because I did not put that story in the paper! I did not do it!"

I looked at her for a few seconds. "There was another reporter under the bed, is that what you're saying?"

"I'm saying that I wrote what I wrote because everything you said was so sad and so sweet, and since I can remember everything, well, I figured I'd type it up and give it to you and—and—" She was nearly hyperventilating with anger. "And I put it in the computer and ran off a copy. I left the office. Someone on the news desk called up the piece, read it and showed it to the editor. He thought it was notes for a story, and since I hadn't said anything about it he figured I was going to give it to another paper, so he ran it. Which makes him a bastard equal to you. You get it now? Huh?"

"You're kidding me."

"Oh, yeah, right." She stood. "I came here to lie about why I hate your guts in the hope that you'll forgive me." She stamped off down the walk, turned at the gate. "One thing: I didn't have a hundred and thirty-two orgasms like I said. Only had sixty-six and they were short. You and your ego." She walked away, hands in her pockets, shoulders hunched forward.

I sat on the cold lawn for a long time. When it became obvious I was not going to be swallowed by the earth and buried right then and there, I got up and brushed the leaves off my pants. Trygve opened the door an inch and asked if that woman was gone. Assured that she was, he opened the door and let me inside.

The phone was ringing. I went into the main hall, picked it up and shouted "What!" into the receiver.

"Jonathan Simpson?" The voice was muffled.

"Yeah."

"Finally got you at home. You've been out."

"Who is this?"

"Just wanted to say I read your interview in the *Daily*. Hard on the heart to read, my friend. Awfully rough on the AIL, I also noted. And I note with interest that you're a food writer now."

"Who is—"

"Careful what you say, all right? And be careful what you write." Pause; crackle and static. "Mighty big house for the three of you, isn't it? Forgive me—for the two of you."

"God damn it, I have had a day like—" Then I stopped. "This isn't, this isn't."

A chuckle. "It might be. Guess."

"Jared."

"Exactly. Bon appetit!" and the line went dead.

PART II

Inferno

1

The meteor landed right over my bed. Or something as heavy as a meteor. I had been sleeping the sleep of the just, which goes to show how freely they hand that stuff out, when there was a thump on the roof above me. I sat up in bed, heart racing as though from a dream of falling, and stared at the ceiling. No smoking hole, no crater in the floor. I rubbed my face and tried to reconstitute my dream.

Then I heard the thump again, and a scuttling sound. Mice. I'd last heard them that night Marya was by, what, almost a month ago. Marya.

I lay back down and closed my eyes.

There was the chill of a November morning in the house. I got back in bed, pulled the covers up to my neck and rang the buzzer for Trygve. He finally shuffled in, wearing his perpetual expression of a patient waiting to hear if his surgery is elective, mandatory or pointless. I asked for coffee, toast, two eggs, scrambled, and the papers. He nodded and tottered out, banging a shoulder on the doorjamb, making the rest of the distance down the hall and out of sight walking at an angle. It would be interesting to see what my request would metamorphize into by the time he reached the kitchen. The morning before, the same menu had arrived as iced tea, saltines, poached eggs that looked like a bowl of pureed canaries, and, in place of the newspapers, several sheets of stationery.

I would be glad when Grue came back, a blessed event only a few days away. She'd come to a few days before, looked around her hospital room and shrieked that there were chores to be done and here she should not be. Dispute that no one could. I missed her.

Tryg, evidently firing with all cylinders this morning, brought the paper. The front page was a light serving of atrocities, with photographs of the usual suspects smiling and shaking hands. I grazed the editorial page to see which fence the writers would be straddling that day, and then turned to the metro section for news of the latest AIL action.

There was nothing. In the three weeks since Carver had died the AIL had been silent. The billboards had been cleaned, and there were no new defacings. The AIL slipped from the front page, flowered briefly in the letters column, languished in the metro section and died an unheralded death.

I had certainly learned nothing. A call to the Progressive Students Front had evoked a rather glacial reaction; they acknowledged that Jared had made offers, then threats to the PSF, but they knew nothing of the AIL. I hadn't been able to reach Spanks, who'd left her home with no forwarding address.

God, I was a lousy journalist. I had had no idea how to go about this. Lucky for me, no one else knew anything either, so I was able to get away with writing about Carver, pouring large ladles of sentiment over the meager facts like gravy over the heel of a dry loaf of bread. No one had called to volunteer information; no assignations were made in dark alleys. Nobody, after three weeks, cared. Thanksgiving was coming up, after all. Then Christmas. But I couldn't hear about decking the halls without recalling that holly was poisonous, too.

Elsewhere, though, ah, life was better. I had got things square with the gendarmes. I had managed to get the charges against poor Trygve dropped. I had owned up to my possession of the manor, and had the charges transferred to dear Oscar, wherever he was. I had started the applications for a mortgage, to be paid off by a second, but no one would know that for a while. I was even enjoying reviewing food. The mail on my pieces was enthusiastic, and I didn't get poisoned.

Professionally, in other words, things were fine. That I slept alone every night and had heard nothing from Jane, Sarah or Marya should have spoiled little; of course, it had a way of spoiling absolutely everything.

After breakfast I spent a merry minute in the bathroom prying a sliver of shell from my gums. I showered, dressed and drove to the office. It was on the way downtown, listening to the news, that I heard it.

". . . And finally, from Orono: Mr. Bob Ballantine, a local turkey farmer, called police to report that pranksters had broken into his turkey pens and opened up all thirty-five gates. And what did the freed fowls do? That's right—nothing. Mr. Ballantine said he went out to the pens in the morning, saw the gates wide open with all the birds still inside. Asked why they didn't leave, Mr. Ballantine said, 'Because they're dumb and don't know a good deal when they got it.' Police chalked it up to vandals, but me I think it was someone who just wanted a pet. Boy, I'll bet the birds are gonna feel real stupid come Thanksgiving. So if you're putting the turkey in the oven for that Thanksgiving dinner and one of the drumsticks, like, moves, don't worry—it's just kicking itself for not getting away when the getting was good. I'm Doug Gordon with the news. Bruce?"

I didn't even bother to call the office. In ten minutes I was on Highway 12, off to Orono.

"Say it again? You're a what?"

"A restaurant critic." I was addressing the narrow and suspicious eye of Mrs. Bob Ballantine.

"Let me see your badge."

"Badge? I don't have a badge. I'm a critic. We have press IDs."

"Let me see that."

"Well, I don't have one. Wait! Don't shut the door. Please. I want to talk about your turkeys. You can call my boss if you doubt I'm on the level."

"I will. What's his name?"

"Call the *Metropole*. It's in the phone book. Ask for Fikes, and ask him about Simpson."

"Fikes. Simpson. All right. You wait." I did. I stood outside, smoking a cigarette, trying not to breathe too deeply. The scent of the turkey barn indicated there were billions of the things out here, and none of them cursed with irregularity, either. After my third cigarette Mrs. Ballantine's eye reappeared in the crack of the door.

"This Fikes wants to know what you're doing out in Orono."

"Doing a piece on your turkeys. I heard about the vandalism on my radio."

The door opened, and what I presumed to be Bob Ballantine himself filled the frame. His wife, who I now saw was the size of an object you find on a charm bracelet, was standing at his side. Ballantine looked like a stern customer. I gave my best idiot grin, a leftover skill from defusing drunks in Valhalla bars, and told him, in a cap-in-hand voice, why I was here. He nodded, pushed open the door and waved me inside.

The kitchen was warm, bright; it smelled of coffee and bacon. A radio played on the counter. There was a handmade sign over the stove, macaroni letters pasted on a plaque: A HOU IS NOT HOME WIT LOV AND

Ballantine swung his lanky body into a chair and motioned for me to sit. His wife gave me a look of no uncertain disapproval and left the room. I began to crowbar some facts out of Ballantine. Yep, someone opened all the doors on the turkey pens. Nope, din't see no one. Din't hear nothing. He came to life only when I asked about the feed he was using.

"Now, why you go on about the feed? Jist grain. Special turkey grain, not what you use in bread, but nothing special."

"You use Munson's?"

"Never heard of it. You said you wanted to go look at the turkeys." He got up, put on his coat, and we set off across the yard.

"This Munson's," I said, "has all the right additives, they say."

Another frown. "You one of those ecologists?"

"Not at all. I'll litter here if you want me to prove it."

"Hmr." Ballantine pulled an Old Gold out of his pocket, stopped and lit it. "People want plump juicy birds, that's what I give 'em. You raise a bird on plain grain and get yourself a sparrow. All that stuff I use is gummint approved." We were about fifty feet from the pens. "Okay, you see there's about thirty-five doors here. Woke up and found them all wide open. One set of footprints in the snow to all the doors, buncha footprints over by the main door down there. I figure there were a couple of the kids, three at most."

"Kids?"

"High school boys, probly. Happened before."

"Mr. Ballantine, have you ever heard of the AIL?"

There was a silence you could fold up and put in your pocket.

"I shouldn't even try to convince you this was kids that did this, should I?"

I shook my head.

He looked at his fingernails, then squinted toward the horizon. "A couple of months ago I got this crank letter telling me to stop using feed with what you call additives. Told me I was poisoning people. Other friends of mine raising birds, they got one too. Hell." He started walking again. "Birds are good for you. I figured it was nonsense and threw the letter away, din't think any more of it. Then that stuff happened over in the cities."

He trudged ahead, pulled back one of the doors. An idiotic squawking poured out as Ballantine made his way into the pens, kicking turkeys out of the way.

"Did you tell this to the police?"

Ballantine glared at me. It would have been a daunting sight had he not been up to his knees in milling turkeys. "No. And neither are you. Don't make me regret talking to you, son. I don't want nothing to do with this poison trouble." He waded through the turkeys to a pile of burlap bags on the other side of the pen, where he hauled a bag off the top, shouldered it and began to kick his way back across the room.

Feed was pouring out of the bag. I was about to point this out when Ballantine noticed the shift in weight and swung the bag to look at it. He swore, dropped it and went back for another. It, too, gushed seed from the bottom of the bag.

Ballantine stood silent before the pile of bags, not moving. I made my way through the turkeys to his side, and saw that each of the bags had been slashed. Ballantine began to pull the bags to the floor. The bags were piled against a window; as the pile diminished, the letters painted in reverse on the other side of the window took shape.

AIL.

Ballantine stared at the window, not saying a word. Then he turned to me.

"You know, son, you tell anyone about this and no one'll buy my turkeys. I won't make a cent unless every one of these birds is dead and dressed." I nodded. He squinted at me, locking my eyes in a gaze that made me blink with guilt. He nodded, pursed his lips and looked down the turkey pens, over the jostling crowd of birds. "Sweethearts," he called, "kid here has a big mouth. You all going to die in bed this time."

2

AIL RAIDS TURKEY FARM, said the papers the next day. Tests had been made on the slashed bags of grain, and cyanide was found in each of them. The papers had a photo of Mr. Ballantine standing alongside a turkey; given Ballantine's stiff and formal posture, it looked like a wedding photo. The local TV stations all led with the story. The channel I watched showed Bob in the barn, turkeys milling around his ankles, with the words *60,000 Useless Turkeys* under his name. It was obviously later in the day, for he looked tired, peeved, and expressed an intention to shoot every turkey in its bobbing little brain.

The police told everyone there was no reason to worry. It was pointed out that most birds on the market had been fed and killed long before this business started, and besides, most of the turkeys sold here came from out of state. Everyone was told to relax, and, pending an investigation, to go about life as usual.

This promptly led to a run on supermarkets. People picked the markets clean, thinking that if the bird was already dead, trussed and slumbering in its refrigerated crypt, it was safe, and anything that might come along tomorrow or the next day doubtlessly carried holiday greetings from the AIL. There were frantic negotiations at the checkout line; six cornish game hens was the standard exchange rate for one substantial roaster. Trygve hobbled back from the store on market day clutching a turkey to his chest, his pants scuffed and his hair disordered.

The story died down, as they all do, and was replaced by the dream of all the newspeople in town—a taped message from the AIL.

I was at home, still in my robe at noon, reading the paper, when Fikes called. He wanted me down at the office immediately. The police had called, asking if the *Metropole* had received a video cassette; both major papers and the other alternative papers had received one, and they wanted to know who had gotten it. About the tape they would say nothing, other than it was evidence and that they would send an officer to collect it. Fikes had found the tape in my mail slot, opened it, saw the first five seconds and called me down to see it before the police came. I jumped into clothes and sped down to the office.

Fikes steered me by the arm into the conference room, fed the tape into the VCR and turned it on.

The screen went from snow to streaks of static, settling on black. Then a wobbly shot, out of focus, tightening to reveal a sheet of paper and the words *AIL Manifesto #1*.

"Collect them all," I murmured.

The camera made a vertiginous pass across the floor, panned up to a desk. Behind it sat a figure, dressed in black, wearing a black ski mask. Behind him, a sheet with the words *Eat Right or Die*. I stiffened.

"My name is Sinclair," said the man in black. "I am speaking on behalf of the Pure Food League, a nonimperialist, nonsexist, nonracist, pronutrition radical cell dedicated to the struggle of changing America's eating habits by whatever means necessary." The voice was hollow, warped. "We wish to claim responsibility for the following blows against the Merchants of Death: the tampering of the cake mix—"

"Bundt mix."

"Shut up," hissed Fikes.

"But it was bundt mix."

"—the adulteration of Pep 'n' Go cola, available at metro-area U-Shop-Rite stores, the defacement of all billboards that have borne the letters *AIL*, and the recent incident at the Ballantine turkey farm. All acts were done with the guidance and approval of the AIL steering committee.

"We are not responsible for the death of Louis Carver, journalist, and we regret his passing." I sat up. The voice had changed, become faster, as though reading by rote, not conviction. "His death was unintentional, the unfortunate result of incompetence of a member, since discharged. We take, I repeat, take no responsibility for his death."

The voice gained strength again. "This is only the beginning. We will strike until people are afraid to buy that which is bad for them.

We will strike until merchants pull the poisons off their shelves." He held up a newspaper. "We will strike until the media ceases to portray this food as pleasurable and enjoyable."

"Stop," said Fikes, and he leaned forward and froze the picture. "Look at that paper."

I got close to the screen, looked.

It was my most recent review, "In Praise of the Hot Dog."

Fikes let the tape go.

"Consumer, merchant, journalist. None should rest, for none are safe. Do not blame us. Capitalism is the disease. We are the painful and necessary treatment." He paused. "Fruits, vegetables and pure juices with no sugar added are hereby declared tamper-free foods. Juices made from concentrate are still under consideration. A full list of approved foods will follow shortly. You may eat them in peace. Or continue to eat garbage and rest in peace. Farewell." The camera wobbled, and went to static.

Fikes turned off the VCR, looked at me.

"I'm flattered," I said. "I'm also a little scared."

"Mrrgh. I should think so. They don't like you much."

"At least we know there's a they."

"What do you mean?"

"I mean, until now we had no idea if this was one crackpot or a dozen. At least we know there are two. Probably three. Sinclair, Jared and whoever was running the camera." I sighed. "Eat right or die, for Chrissakes. Do they honestly believe this stuff?"

"People believe all sorts of nonsense," Fikes said. He took the tape out of the machine. "I, for one, believe I am about to temporarily become a vegetarian."

I sat there, hands in my lap, cigarette in my mouth. This didn't sound right. Naturally, when you are dealing with people who bring a Leninist perspective to eating habits, a lot is not going to sound right. But there was something I had heard before.

I asked Fikes to rewind the tape. He did.

". . . a nonimperialist, nonsexist, nonracist, pro . . ."

"Stop." I thought for a minute. "That's what Spanks said to me in Valhalla."

"Spanks."

"Uh-huh. Little punker. Carver's daughter. Belongs to a radical group at the university. Jared was trying to recruit from that group about a year ago."

"Mrrgh. Well. Mrg. Sounds tidy. But no one exactly has a monopoly on those sentiments nowadays, you know. Did you say Carver's daughter?"

I nodded.

"Then I don't expect she's with these people. People do a lot out of extreme conviction, but rarely do they participate in the deaths of their fathers."

There was a knock on the door, and Daphne came in. "A large policeman is here for the tape," she said.

Fikes took the tape out. "We'll get it back. I expect they want to look for fingerprints, or handwriting, or something. In the meantime I want another story. Not like the last. No personal angle. Do it in third person, if you are capable of that demanding and obscure little stylistic trick. Just do an overview of the case so far, that sort of thing."

"When?"

"Wednesday."

I nodded.

"And incidentally." He looked at the floor. "Good instincts on that turkey-farm story. If this were a daily we'd have beaten everyone."

"Is that why you look so upset? That we're not a daily?"

"It's having to compliment someone around here," he said. "Goes against my experience. You will disappoint me at some point, I suppose."

"Probably. Sleep with a source or lose my notes."

"See that you do."

3

It was after five when I left the office. I got in my car and drove down to the university, thinking about Spanks. Fikes was correct; being party to one's father's death was in excess of standard youthful rebellion. But there was something not quite right about Carver's daughter—her automatic and baseless distrust of me, for example. Granted, I had led her father by the hand to the grave, but still. There was something edgy and frightened about her, the sort of feeling you get from someone who always takes a seat facing the door.

I had spent the afternoon calling the video camera rental stores in town. There were a dozen. None had recently rented a camera to a Katherine Carver, a Sinclair or Jared. That was no surprise, really. The surprise came when I looked up Spanks in the U's student directory. Her majors were listed as poly sci and performing arts. Which could or could not mean video.

There had been no video department when I'd attended the U, back in the dark ages of the printed word; now it took up the entire fifth floor of the hulking Ellenwood Performing Arts Center. A radio at one end of the floor's corridor boomed something loud, tuneless and popular; laughter cackled from the student lounge, to my right. I went down the hall to the department office.

Behind the desk sat a secretary perfect for the role of the Woman Who Loved Her Boss in Silence for Thirty Years. Her brown hair was done up in a loose bun, and jeweled glasses on a string rested against a pink sweater. She looked up and asked, in a voice of dust and weak tea, if she could help me.

"Sure. I'm looking for a friend, and I think she just had a class in this department and I wonder if you could tell me which."

"I'm sorry, sir, but we cannot give out that information."

"Come on. Make an exception."

She would do no such thing. I understood. The same policy had, years ago, kept two bill collectors from bursting into my English class and hauling me off in the middle of the "Wife of Bath's Tale." I thanked her and left.

They were still dying of laughter in the lounge. I thought a second, then went in, bought a cup of coffee from the machine and took out a cigarette. There were five of them: all young, unshaven, rude and brutishly good-looking, all smoking from a common pack of Gitanes. Two were guffawing, pounding the table; two were smirking, too cool to give themselves over to something as transient as mirth, and the fifth was the storyteller, reining back the attention of the group with "Wait, wait, listen. She not only had the dog—she had the beer, and it was in the trunk."

And they were off again. I stood there with a stupid smile on my face, wondering what kind of story had that as its punch line, waiting for them to stop hyperventilating so I could ask a question or two.

"Any you guys got a light?"

"Yeah." The one telling the story held up a Zippo and lit my cigarette.

"Thanks. Listen, any of you guys seen Spanks?"

"Spanks?" He clicked his Zippo shut and looked around the table. "Anybody seen her today?"

"She left."

"With the dog," said one, and there was laughter again. I waited.

"Damn. When did you see her?"

"I had her in 3001 this morning."

"What's that?"

"Editing lab."

"You had her in the editing lab?" said one of the two who had been smirking.

"So have half the guys in the department."

Groans all around the table. "Sorry," said the storyteller to me. "Guys, have some tact, at least."

"He's not her boyfriend," said one, still wiping tears of laughter from his eyes. "You've seen her boyfriend. Big scary punky mother." He hunched up his shoulders and darted his eyes back and forth.

"Her boyfriend, eh?"

"He likes the horns," said another. "Good for, you know, gripping." He made bump-and-grind motions with his hips.

"If she comes back," I told the smirkers, "tell her her brother was around." Death fell on the table. I left. When I was a safe distance down the hall the laughter began again, as I knew it would.

I was waiting for the elevator when a young man, one of the two who had not been amused, came running down the hall. He waved at me. The elevator opened and I put a hand on the door to hold it. "I'm going down," I said.

He walked up to me shaking his head. "I just wanted to apologize for those guys." He shook his head. "Artists. You understand."

"I understand." Said the critic. I got into the elevator and pushed my floor. "Thanks."

"I also know Spanks, so if there's something you wanted to know —" I punched the Door Open button and got out.

"Yeah." I looked from side to side, assembling a good lie; I hadn't thought this far in advance. "Um, she was supposed to get a camera, you know, one of those videocamera things, for Thanksgiving? Take family pictures. Probably against the rules. But if she didn't get one I was going to go rent one, and I can't get in touch with her to find out."

He nodded. "She has one."

"You're certain."

"Well, yeah. I'm in her unit. See, we rotate, one person does video, one does sound, the other the interviews or whatever. Spanks is on video this quarter so she has the camera."

"Can she take it home?"

"You're not supposed to, but everyone does."

"Okay. Thanks." I regretted posing as her brother; now I couldn't ask him where Spanks was. I thanked him and stepped back into the elevator.

"Hey?" he said. "I'm, ah, sorry. About your dad there."

"What?"

"I heard about your father. I'm sorry. Our class sent some flowers. The roses?"

"The roses." The doors started to close. "Thank you," I said. He stood with his hands in his pockets, nodding, embarrassed.

Jolly's All-Nude Lounge was on Hennepin Avenue, the local sink of iniquity. More like a pothole, really. Compared with the red-light districts of most cities, this was the Vatican. There were three strip joints, six bars filled with bikers, grifters, prostitutes and bewattled old men; two hotels so deficient in modernity that "fireproof" was the only amenity they could offer. To someone from a small town it looked like a dangerous and exciting part of the city; the longtime resident was vaguely ashamed that it was empty by eleven at night.

I had been dropping into Jolly's off and on for the last month, hoping to see the shoe salesman, or talk to someone who knew him. I learned quickly that a strip joint is not a place to approach strangers and say "I'm looking for a guy." Tonight I decided to just sit at the bar.

There was nothing erotic about the place. The decor hailed from the era when a man in a quilted velvet smoking jacket with pomade in his hair was the dominant image of the gentleman at leisure. The tables were all of blond wood, with so many cigarette burns it looked as if the roots were showing; the walls were covered either in red velvet wallpaper or a particularly stubborn crimson mold. I took a seat at the bar and did not look at the stripper. After a while I looked to see just what I should not be looking at. The dancer was someone Rubens would have called Rubenesque. I turned back to my scotch and drained it, ordered another. An equally miserly portion was set before me. Apparently we were at war and liquor was to be rationed. No one had told me.

It was a bar designed to make one depressed and feel alone, and I obliged. I had a fear of ending up in these places, old, gummy-eyed, drooling with lechery. When I was younger, full of sap that was not so much rising as it was constantly on the point of effervescence, I had engaged in all sorts of romantic assignations with no thought to permanence; I was not so much driven by the need for sex as I was towed. But here I was, an ancient twenty-nine. All the cylinders were running, and I had a good ten years of charging up the hill before I began to consider myself over it. But I wanted to be married. If I had kids within the next ten years, they would be teen-agers about the time that my teen years would be in nostalgic resurgence, and I would understand them perfectly.

Mostly, though, I wanted a companion. Someone with whom to grow old, someone to assure me I still looked as young as ever. Jane had been that. Jane was that, at present, to someone else. At least she was consistent. Sarah had been a companion; pity we would have murdered one another eventually, probably over an interpretation of the Constitution. Marya? Who knows. In her view men like me were probably like the bumps they install in parking lots to prevent you from going ninety miles an hour. I had to meet someone sane, happy, appreciative and knowledgeable about twenty centuries of Western culture, with a good streak of weltschmerz, and also my height.

"Gin," said the voice of the shoe salesman. I turned.

He looked ten years younger. He wore a blazer with a crest on the pocket and checked pants that imitated a poor TV signal. His eyes were wide and full of energy; when he blinked it looked like flint striking stone. One corner of his mouth was drawn up in a merry sneer. The same steamer trunk sat at his feet.

"Hi," I said.

"Hey," he replied, looking around. "How's it hanging?"

"Can't complain."

"But I'll bet you try!" He looked at me, then went back to scanning the room, head bobbing like a bird's, bright eyes poking into every pocket of the bar.

This wasn't the same guy. There weren't enough antidepressants in the known world to transform the morose little lemur I had met into this leering knave. But the face was the same, the trunk the same. Was it the same trunk?

"Going to sea?" I said, pointing at the trunk.

"What's that? This?" He grinned. Same chipped tooth as the shoe salesman. But on the same side of the mouth? "Old lady kicked me out tonight. Sent old Jacky packing. Came home to find all my earthly possessions sitting in the trunk on the stoop. Women." He made what was, in his vocabulary of facial language, an expression intended to connote the onset of philosophical pronouncements. But nothing followed.

I stared at him for a few moments, trying to figure this out. Might as well take the direct approach.

"So." I cleared my throat. "You have, ah, shoes in that trunk?"

"Shoes? Couple three pair, sure. Why?"

"Just wondering if you had any for sale, that's all."

"Ohhhh." He looked into his drink. "You're confusing me with someone else."

"I bet I am."

"He looks like me, walks like me, hell, some say he is me." He slapped me on the shoulder. "But he isn't me. Well." He drained his gin and put the glass on the bar, pushed it away. "Gotta go."

"I'll say hello to Jared for you," I said.

"Jared?" He frowned, then leaned close to me. "You know something I don't, friend? This who the old lady tossed me out for?"

"I don't know anything."

"I'll bet you don't," he said, scowling. "You can tell her we'll be just fine without her. Just fine."

"We?"

"Figure of speech." Then he grinned. "Me and my twin brother." He laughed. "I want to meet this guy someday." Then his face darkened again. "Maybe that's who's making time with Margaret."

The dancer had finished to a meek round of applause. The man at the bar bowed to the crowd, then bent over and picked up his trunk. He waved a good-bye to the bartender and tipped an imaginary hat to me and left. I gave him a few seconds before I ducked out to follow him.

I slid out the door, looked up and down the street. There was no one with a trunk anywhere in sight.

4

"Dog meat." Fikes shook his head.

"I didn't explicitly say they used dog meat. If you'll read the piece—"

"I did read the piece! That's the problem! If you had knocked me unconscious and forced the typists at gunpoint to set the thing, I wouldn't be facing the rack! Mrrrr." Fikes dropped into his chair and mashed his face with his hands. "You don't know what it's like to be surrounded by incompetents and still have yourself to blame."

I sat at the far end of the conference room, staring at the floor, my life over. Fikes had called me at home and screamed at a volume that made me wonder why he had chosen the telephone instead of just raising a window and hollering in my direction. He demanded that I come to the office now. He had hustled me into the conference room and slapped a folded sheaf of papers in my hand. There was a man at the end of the table, young, well dressed, tanned. He was tapping a pencil on the table. I recognized him as Barry, the *Metropole*'s lawyer, and I felt the sharp tines of dread poke my stomach. I opened the papers and read them.

Libel. I had done it again. China Diner had sued for $300,000, alleging that I had said they used dog flesh for meat. I had written that the food was so bad that hounds knew better than to scrounge in the garbage pails out back. That wasn't bad. Then I had to go and say that as long as we were discussing hounds, several of the entrees had a taste that suggested they were capable of hearing sounds outside of the range of human hearing. I suggested they rename one of the dishes Sweet 'n' Sour Schnauzer. Innocuous enough.

"Will you guys stop it?" Barry threw his pencil down on the table. "This isn't the end of the world. It isn't even close. This stuff happens all the time with criticism. I don't know why you guys even run it."

"Glad to have you in my corner," I said.

"Are you familiar with libel law?" said Fikes, glaring at Barry. He put his head in his hands again and spoke through his fingers. "Recall, counselor, the sections on reckless disregard for the truth and presence of malice. Consider that Mr. Magic Palate here tossed out the merry implication that dog meat is being served to the customers under the guise of beef. Can you forsee what this is going to look like on the stand?"

"I have to go on the stand?"

"Go on it?" Fikes bellowed. "You'll be there long enough to have your mail forwarded!"

"Jesus," said Barry. He looked up at the ceiling. "You guys."

"Oh, I can hear the questions. 'Mr. Simpson. Could you tell the jury the most delectable varieties of hound it has been your pleasure to consume? Dachshund on a spit? Pan-blackened whippet?' "

"He'll say none of that." Barry ran his tie between his thumb and forefinger. "Nobody will say anything. We'll settle out of court."

"Why didn't you say they used too much MSG?" Fikes wailed. "That we could have tested for."

"Wait a minute. That's an idea," said Barry. "Test their food. Send someone to get everything from the buffet and run an analysis on it. Places uses some funky meats nowadays. Kangaroo meat is big. Maybe they use substandard beef." He sat up, made some jottings on his legal pad. "We'll subpoena them for their records, see what grades of beef they use."

"Now you're talking justice," I said. "So what if they do use kangaroo meat, though? I said they used dog meat."

Fikes snapped his fingers. "You said, 'Speaking of hounds, the food, et cetera, et cetera, could hear above the range of human hearing, et cetera.' Which does not necessarily mean it was dog meat. See what I mean?"

"Not exactly."

"I do," said Barry. " 'Speaking of hounds.' That could be the phrase that saves your ass. Signals that you are using a metaphor."

"Actually, it's setting up an analogy," I said.

"Really?" said Barry. "Damn. Metaphors are defensible. Analogies are tough. We have to get into your head to find out your state of mind. What you were thinking of at the time."

"I was thinking about going to bed with my dinner companion. And that I couldn't because I had to write the review."

"Urgh. That's not good. A good prosecutor will make it look like you took out your frustrations on the restaurant. That's malice."

"Kangaroos." Fikes snapped his fingers again. "Can they hear sounds humans can't?"

"I had one of those silent dog whistles when I was a kid," I said. "No kangaroos ever came running."

"If they use kangaroo meat and we can prove kangaroos hear sounds above the range of human hearing, we might have them."

"Good point," said the lawyer. Fikes pushed a button on the intercom phone and called Solly to the conference room. Solly shuffled in a minute later, scratched his head and said, "What?"

"Find out if kangaroos can hear things people can't," Fikes commanded.

Solly looked around the room at each of us. "I understand completely," he said, and he left.

"Well." Barry put his palms on the table, pushed himself up. "I'll arrange for the subpoenas. Fikes, you oughta find someone to get samples of their buffet."

"Bring asbestos undergarments," I said.

Fikes and Barry gave me a look.

"China Diner has this Irish pyromaniac who serves coffee drinks. Lights them on fire, does patter and fancy tricks. He poured one of the drinks in my lap and set my napkin on fire."

Barry sat down. "Explain this all to me again. Slowly."

I did. At the end of the story he looked at me and said, "You've had nightmares about this."

"No."

"You don't understand. I'm telling you you've had nightmares about this. You have suffered mental anguish."

"Really, I feel fine."

Barry looked at the ceiling and then looked back to me. "Read my lips. You've been under duress."

"A countersuit," said Fikes.

"Bingo. What you have described is grounds for a suit in itself. It'll make a dandy countersuit. They drop theirs and we drop ours and everyone's happy. Kangaroos need never enter into it. *Capisce?*"

I smiled and nodded and started to take my first calm breaths in an hour.

"All we got to do is get corroborating testimony. I'll need a deposition from your dinner partner and that ought to do it. Jesus, guys, why didn't this come up before?" Barry grinned. "We're safe. We're home. We've won. Those guys are dog meat."

A deposition from my dinner partner. Marya would be happy to oblige, of course. Only if she could demonstrate what had happened for the court. "We beat the fire out with a towel, but I think a frying pan will suffice for this reconstruction." I smiled at Fikes and Barry and crossed my legs.

5

"I know what I am thankfully giving for," said Grue. "I am happy that I am not in a box with worms in my dead self, I tell you that." She whacked the edge of the pot with a ladle, sending a shower of gravy into the air. "You promise me that when I die, Gott be forbidding, that in the box you not put me."

"Promise." I was leaning against the doorframe in the kitchen. The room was warm with the smell and sizzle of turkey, bread, stuffings, sauce.

"I want to go with the flame. You make them burn me up. Foosh! Flames. Worms in me I will not have. Burn my dead self and put the ashes in a vase and put that on the mantel there."

"They have places for urns, Grue."

"I know this. But every day I dust around things on mantel. Fifty years, dust, dust, dust. My turn to make someone dust around me."

Grue bent over the stove, opened the door and peered inside. A rich tangy cloud of spices flowed out, and I could hear the busy sizzle of the bird. "All right. Soon. Go, go sit down. Shoo." She swatted me on the back with one hand; Tryg she gestured toward the refrigerator. "Open the champagne," she said.

I went to the dining room. The drapes were drawn. Earlier in the evening I had seen the nurses in the adjacent hospital serving Thanksgiving supper, dressed up as Pilgrim maids, the doctors making their rounds in Miles Standish outfits. I had observed a commotion on the second floor, with three grim Pilgrims working intently on an unmoving body. They had applied a cardiofibrillator; the body had leapt in the air as though bouncing from a fall that had taken seventy years. The doctor had taken the pulse, then turned away, ripped off his buckled hat and kicked it into the corner.

There was a pop from the kitchen, a scream of terror and the shattering of glass. Grue began to shout in anger. I winced, smiled and moved into the study.

It had been snowing since sundown. The sky had been gray all day, a translucent cloth pulled tight over the world. I stood at the window watching the snow gather on the leading. I felt old and lost. Just last year I had been at Jane's parents'. They'd had a bird the size of a zeppelin, and dozens of relatives to help whittle it down to bone. Stuffing. Wassail. Yams. I hated yams. They had teased me about hating yams. Jane's betrothed probably loved yams. Smacked his lips, said, "Fabulous yams, ma'am. Here, let me take another helping, just to reaffirm how glad you are that I'm sleeping with your daughter and not that yam-hating—"

"Turkey is ready! Get here to be eating it!"

I walked back to the dining room, sat at the head of the table. There was a menorah in the middle of the setting, something Aunt Marvel had picked up at a garage sale, thinking it a candelabra. Tryg sat to my left, examining his fork like an archeologist convinced that diligent study will yield its intended purpose. The setting on my right was for Grue. The end of the long table disappeared into the darkness. Grue came in with the turkey, the usual bloated and glistening football. She sat it down, adjusted a sprig of garnish, and stood arms akimbo. "There. You carve." She handed me an electric knife.

I was hunting along the wainscoting for an outlet and had just plugged the thing in when we heard the doorbell. All three of us stiffened. Tryg stood up like a mummy and tottered to the door. I heard a jumble of competing voices, Tryg's fluttering protests mixed with a low purr of assurance. I looked up and saw Oscar walk in, pulling off his gloves by the fingertips.

He glanced at the menorah, then at the carving knife.

"I hope I'm not interrupting any ritual circumcision," he said. I gave a few warning whirrrs on the knife.

"Hey, hey. Hey. Peace. Okay? I don't have anywhere else to go. It's Thanksgiving. I brought you some wine." He pulled a bottle from his coat. "From my private stock. Liberated, if you will, from an appallingly public liquor store." He smiled, hands oustretched. "Not even a hello?"

"Good-bye," I said.

"Come on. You're the only family I have. Granted, you hate me. You're all still the only family I have."

There was silence. Trygve looked blankly at me; Grue was scowling, and I could see her hands clenching and unclenching in her apron. Well, he was family. And there are rules to that sort of thing.

"Sit down."

"Don't mind if I do." Oscar sat down at the head of the table, and set the bottle down. "Have this chilled, will you, cousin? Slightly under fifty degrees ought to do." He picked up the turkey and drew the entire plate under his nose, inhaling deeply. "Well, Grue, what unusual stuffing is it this year? It was cereal last year, right? I remember I got a prize with one of my helpings." He cocked his head to one side and gave Grue what he probably took to be a winning smile.

"Oh, dear Grunewald. Do I smell yams?"

"Shouldn't we say grace?" said Trygve.

We all exchanged glances, and since no one jumped up and declared that God was a fiction, we all bowed our heads.

"Dear God," said Trygve. His eyes were closed, head down, hands clasped. "We appreciate this. Amen."

"That's not enough," Grue hissed. "Tell Him what we are thanking Him for."

"Is this a test?" said Tryg in a quavering voice. We all mumbled No. Tryg knotted his hands together and began to struggle over a prayer. He named every dish on the table, the silverware, the dishes, the table itself, the utensils in the kitchen and was starting on the rooms of the house when Grue cut in with "Amen" and put the inventory to an end.

"And may God grant that the AIL is not about to make examples of us all," said Oscar. "At least before dessert." He clapped his hands. "Let's dig in."

"So. Where have you been holed up? Flophouses? Jail? Bus station lockers?" I shaved off a piece of white meat no thicker than airmail stationery and laid it on Oscar's plate.

"I have been staying with friends. Mmm. Cooked to sheer perfection, Grue."

"You have friends?"

"Mm-hmm. Salt? Have we any Tabasco?" Grue glared at him. "No offense, Grunewald. Yes, Johnny, friends, folks kind enough to take me in. A rude pallet in the back of a Korean restaurant has been my home for, what, six weeks now since you came by?"

"Oh, come on."

"Verity, every syllable, cousin. I was there one night after a week on the streets, as they say, and the management took pity on me. Offered me a job and place to stay. It was getting a little cold to sleep in the car, and the dog with which I share my quarters makes it altogether cozy."

"Car? You still have the Saab?"

"Well, yes." He coughed. "The repossession people don't know exactly where to find me. Stuffing, please?"

"You have a turbocharged sports car and you sleep in the back of an Oriental restaurant. I hope you're not asking me for pity."

"I'm asking for stuffing, as I recall."

I handed him the stuffing.

"You can't stay there," I said.

"I don't know why not. The dog is not a fitful sleeper, and you get quite used to the smell of fish and soy sauce." He smiled. "I ran my garments through the dishwasher before I came, so if I smell like commercial detergent, apologies."

"Well, don't get any thoughts of moving back here," I said.

"Cousin." He looked up, eyes wide, lips curled in a smile. "Did I say anything about that?"

We ate in silence for a while. Grue never took her eyes off Oscar.

"You're certainly making headlines," Oscar said after a while. He wiped his lips. "Just back in town and something of a celebrity. Photo on the front page. Articles all over that paper, what is it called, *Metropole*? Impressive. I read your piece on the death of your friend."

I cut a few more slices with the carving knife, sawing until I hit bone. I handed out slices; Trygve bowed his head and said a quick prayer of thanks. Oscar poured himself another glass of wine, his third, grabbed a roll with shaky aim and trowled an inch of butter on it. He shook the knife at me, still chewing.

"Your last article. On the turkey-feed poisoning. Little extreme, don't you think?"

"What are they going to do, sue me for libel?"

"Well, I don't expect legal action, but then again who ever does? Still, cousin. I would watch your step. You have made yourself the sworn enemy of these people. If they ever want to make an example of someone in particular, they won't have to think too hard."

The phone rang in the study.

Trygve got up and hobbled to answer it.

"I'll make you a deal," Oscar said. "Let me stay here and when they come for you—hic!"—he smiled—"I'll say I'm you."

"Master Jonathan? It's for you."

"He never called me master," Oscar said to his glass. I got up and went to the study, trading stares with Oscar as I left.

I expected one of my parents, a few quick strokes of conversation to whittle on the stick of guilt; maybe it would be the Dead One. Her betrothed had asked her to do something unspeakable with a drumstick, and she was leaving him. Perhaps Marya, heading over for some wrestling and gouging.

"Mr. Simpson?" The voice was muffled, hollow, like a man with a cold speaking through a pillow.

"Yes. Who's this?"

"My name doesn't matter. Just say I'm a friend."

"I insist on my friends having names. Helps me to tell them apart."

"I can't tell you my name. They can't know I'm calling you."

"Who can't?" But I knew.

"You know. Those crazy sons of bitches in the AIL. I gotta talk to you about them. But no one can know. You got that? No one."

Suddenly I didn't feel as though I'd eaten a thing. My body went lean with adrenaline. "I got it. When do you want to meet?"

"Tonight. You know the uptown library? Lagoon and Hennepin? Okay. Half an hour."

"Wait a minute, I'm not sure—"

"I'm leaving town, all right? I gotta get out of here already. You want to talk, come. I won't wait more'n five minutes." The line went dead.

I went upstairs and got the tape recorder I used for interviews, loaded it with a fresh cassette, checked the batteries. A weak red light flickered, the recorder's equivalent of a gas gauge fluttering above E. It would have to do. I stuffed the recorder in the top inside pocket of my trenchcoat, tested the levels, rewound, listened. Then I went back downstairs. Trygve was working a toothpick between two teeth I knew to be dentures. Oscar was swirling brandy in a snifter, holding it to the light. Grue was staring hot holes into Oscar.

"I have to go. Work. Sorry. I'll be back soon."

"Go?" Grue cried. "And leave me with this thing in the black clothes here? Nononononono." She beat her fists on the table.

"Grue." I said it softly. "This is about the people who put you in the hospital. I think I can find out who they are."

"Then go," she said, nodding, satisfied. "Give them something to not be thankful for. And come back soon. I have made dessert special. Pumpkin strudel." I leaned over and kissed her on her cheek. She smelled like flour, like an old soft chair, like an old toiling woman.

Oscar chuckled. "Don't hurry back," he said. "The party will still be going on. We'll all be here."

"Not you," I said. "At midnight my holiday munificence runs out and you are once again a sorry dead-ass trespasser. Got it?"

He smiled and sipped his brandy.

I drove slowly. The snow was thick and wet, and the clouds couldn't get rid of it fast enough. I was hunched over the wheel, guessing the road from the furrows plowed by whatever other idiots were also out on the streets, one hand taking the cigarette from my mouth and tapping it where it guessed the ashtray to be.

Uptown was a neighborhood south of downtown. No, I had never figured that one out either. I parked behind the library and stood outside the car for a minute, looking around. No cars, no people. A neon beer sign glowed from a bar across the street. Next to the bar, under a bower of trees with boughs bending under a leaden coat of snow, was the old Carnegie Library, the usual mass-produced little chapel of erudition. I had checked out Tom Swift books there as a kid; it was now a bar. The new library across the street was almost entirely underground, pulling a shawl of concrete and sod over its head to shield it from the traffic and noise. The entrance was at the bottom of a flight of steps. I checked my watch; I was on time. I turned on my tape recorder and headed down the steps.

The necks of two wine bottles and a bag from a takeout chicken restaurant lay in a corner of the entrance. There was a bench on each of three sides of the landing, and the doorway, shielded from the elements with a slab of concrete. There was something black and big there. Light from a streetlamp above illuminated it below the knee; light from inside the library outlined its body against the glass.

"Simpson?"

"Yeah. You picked a cold—"

A steel beam or a fist shot out and hit me on the jaw. Silent fireworks bloomed in the corners of my eyes and I felt my mouth flood with blood. I staggered back, hit a bench, skidded, fell on the small of my back. Pain made a swift arc up my spine. Something stepped out of the shadows and kicked me between my splayed legs in the soft spot south of the tailbone, and it felt as if I had been dropped from a thousand feet onto a bicycle seat. I heard myself howl and I did not sound as though I was having much in the way of holiday fun.

The figure stood over me. "Knock it off," it said.

"I—I—I—Who—who are—"

The boot came out again and gave instructions to my right kidney that I should cease this line of inquiry. I screamed in one long red peal of pain, breathless and terrified.

"Just. Knock. It. Off."

"Knock what. Off."

The figure bent over me; hot breath, a gross smell of alcohol under a threadbare shirt of mouthwash, poured over my face. "You know the stuff you do? Don't do it anymore." I nodded. I would have assented to the repealing of the Constitution, *just don't kick me again.* Naturally, the figure hauled me up by the collar of my coat, turned me over and kicked me in the tailbone. It was like inserting a sword up my spine and giving it a twist. When he dropped me I didn't move. I played dead. I was made for the role.

Feet shuffled up the stairs. I lay in the snow, bleeding and sniffling. *I am giving thanks that I am not dead.* After a while I sat up; the world pitched, its gyroscope gone. I threw up: long gasping orations into the snow, heaving and swearing, punctuating it all with exclamation points of spitting. All of Grue's labor gone to waste. My jaw was still howling pain where I had been hit; I rubbed snow into the wound, licked some and rolled it around in my mouth to absorb the wretched rank yellow taste. I spit this out. There was a regular catalogue of bodily effluents on the landing by now, but the snow was still falling, covering it all up. I staggered up the stairs.

I leaned against the Pacer. My jaw felt like a ripe split tomato, and two of those kicks had left me feeling as if I'd been given a size-eight suppository with wing tips. The world continued to yaw and tack. I dug in my pocket for a quarter and tottered to the phone booth on the corner. I dialed a number, stood there on *al dente* legs. The phone was answered and I prayed it wasn't him.

"Hello," said Sarah.

"Hlo. Srah. Jnthn."

"Jonathan! What's the matter?"

"Been beaten."

"Oh my God, where?"

"Mouth. Butt."

"No no, where are you?"

"Uptn. Libr. Library."

"Stay there, I'll be right there," she said.

I slid to the floor of the phone booth, looking up at the light six feet above me. It looked like a halo unsure whether or not it belonged to me. I took out the tape player and, with fingers that felt as thick and sensate as drumsticks, rewound the tape, heard the sound of fist hitting flesh. I was still playing it over and over when something smelling of flowers, impossibly beautiful flowers, leaned over me and gave out a cry of distress. There were warm lips on my jaw.

"Don't kiss me. Threw up."

Lips touched the tip of my nose. I was helped up, steered along on legs too indifferent to really be mine and deposited in the seat of someplace warm. The door slammed. I heard a heater working with industrious fury, a radio playing thin tinny Bach. Then Sarah got in the car and eased it into the street. My tape player had run past the incident and had reverted to its previous recording, an interview with an artist. *I get my inspiration from life itself*, came from inside my coat.

"Do you want a doctor?"

"I'll live. Just want to be cleaned up. And then shot."

"Oh God, Jonathan, oh, oh." I looked at her; she was biting her lip, staring at the difficult road ahead. *Being alive, you know, is a form of artwork in itself.* I made a few numb fumbles inside my jacket to turn the player off, but couldn't find the switch.

"Do you want to go home?"

"No. Oscar there."

"My place?" Said with a high pitch, the words snagging on the roof of her mouth.

"Mac there."

"Oh, no." Her mouth was grim. "Mac is a thing of the past. Emphasis on 'thing.' "

It's hard to live in a commercial world, the artist sighed. I leaned back and let him drone on. *But compromise is an art form in itself.* Sarah took my hand and held it tight.

6

The bath felt good. It was the same tub where I had met Mac and almost met my Maker, but now I was safe beneath a mountain range of suds. Sarah sat on the edge of the toilet, leaning over to put a cigarette into my mouth and give me a drag. I had a cup of coffee on one side of the tub and a tumbler of scotch on the other. Gershwin played from the stereo in the other room, exuberant but distant, like noise spilling through the peephole of a speakeasy. I slid down a little in the tub and closed my eyes.

Sarah conducted a few bars with my cigarette. Then: "I'm sorry you were beaten up."

I couldn't help but agree. There was a brief sentence from a french horn in the next room, a declaration made on bended knee. Then a mocking figure on the piano, taking it all back. "Who did it?" Sarah asked. "Did you know them?"

"No," I said. "Probably a stranger. Someone in introductory existentialism at the U. Had to commit a nonfatal *acte gratuite* for the midquarter. I'm just lucky it's not finals time."

"Be serious, Jay."

"I'd rather not." I shifted in the tub, winced. "Serious was what that little assignation was all about and it hurt."

"Do you know anyone who wants to hit you like that?"

"You're a better judge of that than I am."

"Now, what's that supposed to mean?"

"I mean Mac. I doubt he's the one who put the boot into me, but really, Sarah. If I hadn't lipped off in print about the AIL he'd be the first I'd suspect."

"Mac is a pussycat." She dipped the cigarette in the bathwater and it hissed out. "And you're talking casuistry again."

"Casuistry?" I sunk lower in the tub. "I haven't heard that word since we used to argue. You deserve your Ph.D., sweetheart. All three letters of it. You're too smart to defend him."

"I'm not. Since I have, say, yoked my life to his, by defending him I'm defending myself. That's basic psych 1001."

I looked at her. "Could you be any more self-aware? It's like you carry a three-way dressing mirror around in front of you."

"I know." She slumped a little. "I'm just making excuses. I know he's a jerk. I always choose jerks—"

"Thanks."

"You were an anomaly. Everyone else turns into a cad and I never have the guts to break it off. Can we talk about something else?"

"Sure."

"Good. How do you feel?"

"Actually, not bad." My jaw was hurting, but it was a dull throb now, not the loud ah-oogah it had been, and the hot water and scotch were fine therapy. "This all feels wonderful, Sarah." I slid back down into the water again, closed my eyes. "I could stay here all night."

"You'd get lonely."

"What?"

"You'd get lonely." Sarah stood up. "Do you, um, maybe want some company?"

This certainly was the tub of surprises. I smiled and nodded and said yes.

She turned off the lights. I heard a zipper, the squeak of new denim peeled off skin, the scrape of a button being pushed across the tile. I heard something click, drop to the ground. There was an unrecognizable sound, like flannel polishing silk, and then something entered the water between my legs. I looked up and saw her put a hand against the wall and steady herself, and then the other leg came into the water. She shuddered and then knelt down. She brought her body close against mine, gentle as one leaf falling on another; one hand cupped the bruised side of my mouth without pressure, the other went to the back of my head. She lowered herself into the water, onto me, and she kissed me. The water from the bath overflowed and poured out onto the tiles.

Compared with a bonbon like Marya, Sarah was the whole damn sampler. Or at least she had been years ago when we had been lovers. That we were about to climb into the common bed after half a decade apart I somehow accepted as natural.

But this time she was subdued, hesitant, almost sad in a way that was hard to define. Maybe it was all in deference to my wounds. She was still a woman of infinite skill and variety. Wherever she chose to touch me—and I'll admit she had some favorites—she bestowed a rarefied sense of perception to that place. For five minutes, for example, she had me convinced that all my pleasure centers were clustered in an inch-square patch on my sternum.

I lay there and took it. There wasn't much giving on my part, since whenever I moved too quickly my kidney had the sensation of being attacked by dozens of little plastic cocktail swords. She floated over me, administering soft agonizing bites, tracing rivers and tributaries down my chest. Her head buried itself in a place I had not been kicked, two fingers idly dipping in and out of my lips; I didn't feel any pain then. Nor when she climbed on top and began to move in the rhythm of a lullaby, so soft and insistent I felt like a beach lapped by waves of warm water. She stiffened and shuddered; I soon did the same. She sighed and lay down on top of me, her arms lacing around my neck, and she sighed again. I lay there, my body ebbing inside of hers, my mind full of the absolute darkness of the room.

Sarah rolled over and put her arms around my chest. She was quiet for a long time. After a while I started to say something along the lines of approval and gratitude; she put a finger to my lips and said shhh. I didn't say anything. I felt her grip relax and her breathing slacken. She was asleep.

I lay there for, oh, half an hour. Several loud and clamorous aches were staving off sleep at knifepoint, and I stared into the dark, worrying: about being hit again, for whatever reason; about being sued; about waking up to pee blood and having to spend my life on dialysis; about Oscar being home when I returned; about where Mac was now; about Christmas alone. When my jaw started wailing pain again, I decided the aspirin had worn off and more were needed. I slid Sarah's arms from around me and hobbled, wincing and mouthing curses, into the bathroom. I took five aspirin. I looked in the mirror and saw what I expected: the face of a man who had been beaten and had love made to him. The face of a man sure about the first but ambivalent about the latter. I am sick, I thought.

I went into the living room, sat on the sofa and looked out the window. The snow was still falling down, dancing in the streetlight. The sidewalks were snowed solid and the steps of the building had vanished under drifts. I watched the snow fall until the aspirin set in and my jaw quietened.

The caffeine in five aspirin is enough to jumpstart Lazarus without benefit of divine intervention, so I found myself wide-eyed and jumpy. I turned on a light and looked for something to read. The books were an earnest lot of modern philosophy, or what passes for it. Far too many with *holistic* in the title. A few on massage, nutrition. It seemed to be Sarah's collection. The only book Mac picked up was probably the phone book, and only then to prove he could tear it in half. There were a few magazines around, most of which rubbed the reader's nose in the rich topsoil of American misbehavior. I picked up one that had come by subscription; it was addressed to one Jim Robert MacAdam. Jim Bob. It fit. Another was sent to Robert Edward MacAdam, another to Ed MacAdam, another to James MacAdam. I smiled. I had done the same thing, years ago. Send different names to different publications, so you can judge from your junk mail to whom the magazine is selling their subscriptions list.

There was a scream from the bedroom, a thump, the sound of thrashing sheets.

I got up, stopped, waited for the sword to pull out of my kidney, then hobbled into the bedroom. Sarah was sitting up in bed, hand on her heart, panting. She looked up at me as though I had walked out of her nightmare, and pulled the sheets up to her neck. I crawled back into bed and put my arms around her; she held herself away from my embrace, holding her arms around her breasts.

"Nightmare."

"Somebody force you to eat a hamburger, or what?" I brushed her hair out of her eyes.

"No. Just. Something I. Dream about."

"Tell me."

She pursed her lips and shook her head from side to side. And then her body relaxed and she leaned into me. After a while she fell asleep again, and I sat up against the headboard, lights on all over the apartment, holding her until dawn came up. Sometime in the night the snow stopped.

"James Robert Edward MacAdam? That's his given name? He didn't win any of those names at the fair or something?"

"Nope. His full given name." Sarah was at the stove making

breakfast, frying some tofu and soy patties. They smelled like an electrical fire. There was none of last night's sadness or drama, nor a word spoken about what had happened. For all the affection I was getting, I might as well have slept on the sofa. I might as well have been the sofa. As it was I had hardly slept at all, and was slurping down bitter drafts of black Cuban sludge to keep myself from nodding off. My kidney didn't hurt and my jaw ached only a lot. I was talking about her lover to complete the little picture of joy and bliss. "He's Scottish," Sarah said. "But why are we talking about him?"

"Because I want to know what's going on."

Sarah flipped one of the patties over. "He's gone away."

"That's what they said about Halley's Comet."

"He left. Go check the closets. He's gone."

"Who ended it, if I can ask?"

"He was leaving me, so I threw him out. It was time anyway. We had been together, what, oh, three years, seven months, six days and assorted hours and minutes, and I needed, as much a cliché as this is, some time to myself. Plus we had developed some serious philosophical differences."

"Such as."

"He took up with a fast crowd of phenomenologists. Thrill seekers. He got bored with old, drab, empirical me." She turned around and grinned. It was the grin I had fallen in love with, years and years and assorted minutes and seconds ago. "No. Really. He was getting like men get when they get a job and money and responsibility. All these halberds poking him into the middle class."

"The guy who subscribes to these magazines? Middle class?"

"Hard to believe, I know. He doesn't fit the mold. I think that's what first attracted me to him in the first place. Here. Breakfast is ready." She deposited a charred lozenge on my plate, took away my coffee cup and refilled my juice glass. "I'd eat with you but I have to run for class. I'm going to take a bath. There's the paper out in the hall if you want it."

She put the frying pan into the sink, ran water over it. She was standing in the kitchen, fiddling with the strings that tied her robe around her neck, her breasts full against the fabric, and I sighed long and deep inside.

Sarah laughed. She put one hand over her mouth and laughed.

"What."

"You. You look funny. I forgot how you look in the morning.

Your hair. People spend lots of money nowadays to make their hair look that awful and you just have it naturally."

"Thanks."

"Ohhh." She came over and hugged me tight. "I am a shrew, I know. And you have been wonderful to me for no reason at all and here I am, Mouthy Sarah." She got down on her haunches. "Thank you for being here. Have I made that clear? No, I haven't, have I. Well, thanks." I was about to point out that I had called her to bind my various wounds but she was kissing me, by God.

"What did you say?"

"I said I love you. And this used to make me late for class back then, too."

After she left I lay in bed smoking a cigarette, feeling, for a change, like the happiest fool on the planet. Then I decided to go get the paper in the hall. Nothing ever happened on Thanksgiving anyway, as most world misbehavior seems to be planned to avoid American holidays, when no one would be paying attention.

But, well, leave it to our friends in the Alimentary Instruction League to break the mold.

7

HUNDREDS JAM AREA HOSPITALS
IN THANKSGIVING POISONING SCARE
by Catherine Murdoch

At least 600 people were checked into Twin City metro area hospitals during the night, complaining of stomach cramps and nausea—symptoms doctors attributed to bleach ingested in the form of the traditional Thanksgiving turkey. No deaths have been reported, and hospital officials say only ten of the cases required hospitalization.

Speculation was raised that the poisoning was the act of

the Alimentary Instruction League, the terrorist organization that has claimed responsibility for seven food-tampering incidents in the last two months. Police refused comment on the AIL, although Det. Harley Bishop, head of the police unit formed to investigate the shadowy organization, said he was ruling nothing out. "I'd say it might be a copycat thing," he remarked at a press conference held this morning, "but you're talking at least a hundred birds here. That takes organization."

There has been no word from any organization claiming responsibility.

The news reports had doubled the crowds at the hospital. I had to park six blocks from Hennepin General and walk. There were police directing the traffic around the building, cars double-parked for blocks in all directions. Another policeman at the door was holding back half the people who came walking up, letting in only those visibly green. I thought hard about yams and was able to feign a stomachache, walking slightly bent over, hand on my stomach, the other wiping itself on my pant leg. I swayed slightly. They not only let me through but stepped back. The Method Acting School of Investigative Reporting.

Inside the hospital there was the wet, beige stench of cold turkey, so thick you could scoop the scent from the air. Perhaps a hundred people were in the hospital's emergency room, sitting, standing, crouched on the floor. Everyone seemed to have a bowl or bag or box with grease stains on it, all no doubt containing guilty turkey. Nurses, their uniforms dark with sweat, were taking temperatures, fighting off the supplicants who clutched at the hems of their garments. There were wailing housewives and stoic husbands, their lean, edgy sons leaning against the wall, rubbing their stomachs. There were the poor, sitting through one more indignity. I leaned up against the wall, took out my note pad and began to describe the tableau, ask questions. Everyone seemed too full of bleach to chat, but when they learned I was with the media they sighed and did their duty.

They were moving them in and out fast. Some people went through the door to the examining area and were out in five minutes. It was an hour and a half before I was examined. A nurse had come by to ask "Turkey?" just in case I was really suffering from a sprain or a spurting aorta. My bruised face got no comment. Eventually I was taken back to a long, wide room made of curtained partitions. I was bade to sit and wait for the doctor. I heard children crying, muffled moans, a dozen different human sounds floating like dank perfume among the scents of antiseptic.

I felt a little guilty, taking time from someone who might be genuinely ill. But I had suspicions that not everyone out there had ordered the poulet de bleach. When the doctor arrived he confirmed this suspicion with his first question.

"Okay. You feel sick before or after you heard the story in the news?"

"After."

"Really." He looked at me through wan, bleary eyes. "This is the most amazing disease. Seems to be transmitted primarily through the media. Okay. When was the last time you had turkey?"

"Last night."

"You're fine."

"I don't feel fine."

"Nerves. You're fine. Eat some antacids. Take the whole roll. You can go."

"You don't think I ate bleach?"

"I think you think you ate bleach. But if you had, you would have been here last night. You can go."

I left the room but lingered outside; everyone was far too preoccupied to pay attention to me. I wandered back into a room behind the examining station and found a nurse sitting in a corner sipping coffee. I approached her with a big smile, banging a fist on my stomach to show I wasn't ill and had no intentions of becoming so. I told her I was a reporter, and asked if a large number of cases had been feigned. She nodded. But not last night, she said; that had been disastrous. Dozens. Whole families full of bleach. I asked her if there was anyone with bleach poisoning they were about to release.

"Everyone who has it is too busy being sick to see anyone," she replied. "No, wait a minute. There's one. Mr. Perlstein down in 236. First case we got. Came in last night and told us he'd eaten turkey with bleach in it."

"Hadn't he?"

"Well, no. We pumped his stomach and there wasn't any turkey down there. But while he was under observation we got hit with all these other people with stomachaches, and when we pumped them we got plenty of Thanksgiving dinner, so we figured Mr. Perlstein was maybe on the level. He's down the hall if you want to talk to him."

"Thanks." I went through a door, pausing at the nurse's station to ask for directions to Mr. Perlstein's room. The nurse, a sturdy drum of a woman who could be Grue's younger sister, asked if I was a relation; when told I wasn't, she rolled her eyes and muttered that I was lucky.

"Lucky?"

"I'm sorry. He a friend?"

"No. I'm with the *Metropole*, doing a story on the victims."

"Do one on the hypochondriacs, if you're talking to Mr.—"

"*Nurse!*" someone shouted down the hall. "I'm dyin' in here!"

She shook her head, lips tight. "Come on," she sighed. "Follow me."

IRVING PERLSTEIN was written on his door. She told me to wait, and went inside; I heard her ask him if he wanted to talk to a reporter. "I'm dyin'," he said. "Won't last the day. I'm too sick to talk."

I looked through a crack in the doorway; I couldn't see Perlstein. But I did see a large samples case the size of a steamer trunk.

This was my shoe salesman.

I was about to go in when the nurse came out, told me he didn't want to see anyone.

"No, I have to see him. I—"

"Sorry. I have to respect his wishes. It's about the only thing I have left to respect."

"Please."

"Sorry. There's another man down the hall in the lounge, just released. A bona fide turkey case, too. There's some Lois Lane in there with him now, but when she's done you'll get more than you would from the grand faker here."

I thanked her, and she went back into the room. I tried to look through the door to see his face, but saw only the curtain surrounding his bed. I wrote down the room number on a scrap of paper; I would return later. Then I went down to the staff lounge, knocked, walked in.

"Oh no. No. This is my story."

Marya stood up and shoved her chair back. There was a worn and tired man sitting at a table, sad red eyes stuck in a face that looked like a peeled potato. He stared at her, at me, like a dog wondering just who is going to beat him.

"No hello?" I said to Marya. Oh, she looked exceptionally sweet. She wore a green sweater, a thick black skirt; her arms were full of bracelets halfway up to the elbow, and there was a cigarette stuck behind her ear.

"All right, hello. Now out. Go. Please. I've been here all morning waiting for this."

"Are you from a paper too?" said the man. I nodded. "Well, I want to talk to him too," he said to Marya. "I'd like maximum media exposure." She glared at him, poked a hand in her hair for the cigarette and stuck it in her mouth.

I shrugged. "I can wait until you're done," I said.

"Fine. Fine. Take my exclusive. I don't care. Take my shot at a real story. Go right ahead." She thrust her hands in her skirt pockets and came up with a lighter. "He's boring anyway. Go on, interview him. See if I care."

A couple of doctors in the corner of the lounge were looking at us, and I felt my face flush. "Come on," I said sotto voce. "Let's go somewhere else and not yell about this, okay?"

I steered her out into the hall. She walked ahead of me, arms crossed over her chest. She stopped in front of a door marked RADIOLOGY, dropped her cigarette and ground it out with her boot. "Okay, talk."

"How are you?"

"I found that guy, Jonathan. No one else has interviewed him. If I—"

"All right, skip the pleasantries."

"What do you want me to say? You're going to ruin it for me. Why don't you just go in there and get it done with?"

"You're a daily paper, Marya. I'm a weekly. I'm not going to have a piece out on this for two weeks. By which time your article will be bound, yellowed, filed and forgotten."

"That's not the issue. The issue is that you're mad at me and you're trying to get back."

Christ! "Where did that come from? Didn't you even hear me when I apologized? No."

"I was too mad to listen to you."

"And when I called the next day? And the next?"

"I stay mad."

"No kidding. Look, I *am* sorry, Marya. For getting you bounced off the *Times*. For not listening." I felt myself getting angry over how angry she was with me. "For not ending my mortal existence when I had the gall to cross your path."

"At least you're sincere." Her eyes met mine and looked away.

"Well, it's not like I don't have anything to be angry about, young lady. You—"

"Argh!" She turned and walked down the hall. "Don't ever call me that ever. Ever. My dad calls me that when he's about to tell me to get off my high horse and I absolutely hate those words. You might as well just scrape a blackboard across my teeth."

I'd hit a nerve. More like taken hold of it with a pliers. Her eyes were black and nasty now. "Do you know the kind of reputation you got me? You come charging down there like hell on fire and tell everyone I slept with you to get a story! Do you know what that makes me look like?"

"Your boyfriend is the editor! You're already sleeping with the boss! What more can I tell anyone?"

"You—you—"

"And hell is already on fire."

The door between us opened, and an unshaven med tech, white smock over a faded flannel shirt, stepped out. "Do you mind? I'm developing pictures of some serious patients in here. Have some respect." He shut the door.

We stood about twenty feet apart, looking at each other.

"Truce," I finally said. "Ding. Go to your corner. Now, let's think. We're both adults, both of voting age. We're old enough to get legally drunk in any bar in the nation, so I suggest we start acting like it. We're probably going to be running into each other a lot on this story. It's pointless to argue—"

"I think it's sort of fun."

"I'm not saying we have to love each other, although there's ample precedent for that." She looked away. Wrong tack, Jonathan. "I'm just saying let's be civil, that's all. We obviously found something worthwhile in each other before."

"That was sex. This is personal."

That hurt. "That hurt," I said.

"I'm doing my best."

"Is there something I'm not getting here? We're even. There are no balances to redress. You lost your internship. I lost an exclusive. We both got in trouble with our bosses. We should be sitting somewhere with a drink laughing about it."

"I'll have coffee with you in a crowded room where no one will hear me shoot you if I want to. Anything other than that, forget it."

"I'll call you."

"I might answer." She turned away. "Wouldn't that be a statement."

The deposition. Christ in a Buick, the deposition. I called her name and she stopped. "Marya. Please. Don't go. There's something I need you for."

"I'll bet. I'll just bet."

"Would you knock it off? This is serious. Real serious. There are even lawyers involved. This could kill my career."

"Why didn't you bring it up before?"

"I forgot. Don't go—don't—will you just hold on?" She stopped. "It's about China Diner."

"You got sued for libel, didn't you."

"How did you know?"

"I read the review. You ought to know better. Dog meat. If I could have made a citizen's arrest for libel I'd have sued you."

"Well, they beat you to it. And I need a statement from you about the part where I caught fire." And how your back was sore and I fixed it. Put that in writing, please. "We're going to countersue."

"I'll consider it."

"What's to consider? I'll be fired if you don't! I'll spend the rest of my life in penury!"

"Oh, no one goes to jail for libel, Jonathan."

"Not the pen, penury! Poorness! Constricted income! Marya. Please."

"I'll think about it. And what the hell happened to your face?"

"I was kissing your picture. It's in this metal frame. I got too enthusiastic."

I watched her stamp off, shoulders hunched and arms swinging, graceless in her anger. There was no retrieving anything now, I knew. But why was she so intransigent, so hostile? She hadn't, I realized, said for certain that she had lost that internship. Something was not right here.

I also realized that I would have rather spent the morning with Marya instead of Sarah. Something was not right there, either.

8

Minneapolis didn't have just maniacs. We had bashful maniacs. That was what the AIL seemed to be—modest, retiring, shrugging off the limelight for the quiet satisfaction of a job well done. Three days had passed after the adulteration of the birds, and there'd been not a tape, a note, nor a phone call. It was hard not to feel insulted. Terrorists, after all, were supposed to call the paper or wire services, hiss an admission of culpability, and let the media spread the mulch around. Without any word from the AIL, people felt as though they had been left at the altar, poisoned for no reason at all.

When I thought about it, the AIL was playing this with unusual skill. The less said, the more people speculated, the more they talked. They knew that when they finally spoke up, their next manifesto would be greeted like a lost paragraph of Salinger; in the meantime, the television stations played selections from the videotape over and over, repeating the vague demand that we stop with the hot dogs and canned chili, and eat some greens. It was hard to argue with that.

I spent my time at home writing. The *Metropole* had loaned me a computer, complete with a device that let me send my story through the telephone wires if I chose, so my words needed never touch human hands. I intended to use it only in emergencies; until they gave me a desk and a phone and put me on staff, going to the office made me feel connected to something. That the something was run by a bilious sack of margarine was a fact I preferred to ignore. After the lawsuit I had brought on the paper, it was my AIL connection, however unintended and dubious, that kept me working there at all. I knew it.

The AIL seemed to know it, too; when they broke silence, it was me they chose to get the message out.

I had gone downtown to review a new Italian place. I was the only patron. The waiter, when he finally blessed me with his presence, read off the evening's specials like a list of names of those lost at sea. Nothing sounded good. Nothing, to complete the experience, tasted good. I went home to a quiet house, Grue and Tryg were both asleep. I took a shower, dressed in an old robe and went downstairs to brew some coffee. I read the day's mail, limbering up for another evening of procrastinating. Bills, circulars, bills, a plain white envelope with no return address. I opened it; it was a letter, two pages, neatly typed. I read:

> AIL COMMUNIQUÉ #3
>
> SIMPSON:
>
> THE ALIMENTARY INSTRUCTION LEAGUE HEREBY TAKES ALL RESPONSIBILITY FOR THE RECENT INTRODUCTION OF TOXIC MATERIALS INTO TURKEYS, THEMSELVES ALREADY FULL OF TOXIC ALBEIT "LEGAL" CHEMICALS.
>
> THESE REVOLUTIONARY STRIKES WILL CONTINUE AS LONG AS ADDITIVES POLLUTE OUR FOODS AND OUR BODIES AND ROT THE FIBER OF THE PEOPLE.
>
> YOU WILL ASSIST US IN OUR STRUGGLE BY PUBLISHING THE LIST OF APPROVED FOODS CONTAINED ON THE SUBSEQUENT PAGE.

"The hell I will," I yelled. I looked at the other page; fruits and vegetables, brand names of canned goods and juices. I read on.

> OUR CHOICE OF YOU AS OUR VEHICLE FOR DISSEMINATION HAS PURPOSE. YOU, SO VOCAL IN CRITICISM, NOW HAVE THE CHOICE BETWEEN ASSISTING US AND SUPPRESSING THIS LIST, IN WHICH CASE THE SAFETY OF PEOPLE RESTS IN YOUR HANDS. WE TRUST YOUR CHOICE WILL BE CORRECT. IN ADDITION LET US NOTE: IF YOU DO NOT—

The doorbell rang. I put the letter down and stood, heart suddenly thudding with effort. If the AIL sent this to me then they knew where I lived, which meant the person at the door was—

The doorbell rang again.

There's never a semi-automatic pistol around when you really need one, I thought, looking around the room. There was the shield and sword, back up on the wall; there were knives in the kitchen; there was Grue's wooden spoon. Wonderful. Wave the spoon at them and give them mumps.

I took the shield and a sword off the wall, strapped the shield around an arm, hoisted the sword over my head and went down the hall, back to the hallway. When I got to the door I paused, listened; I heard a cough. The bell rang again and I cast a fast glance through the window—

Solly. My dear colleague from the *Metropole* whose beat I had jumped. He was looking unhappy and unshaven, with the posture of a throw rug given life and condemned to wander the world. I opened the door.

He looked me up and down. "Expecting Zulus?"

"I didn't know who was at the door." I leaned the sword against the wall. "I'm a little jumpy. Sorry." Then I looked at him. "What are you doing here?"

"I gotta talk." He swayed slightly, a sapling with bad roots. "I gotta talk to you and it's not because I've been drinking. Although don't think I haven't."

I waved him in and he followed me to the dining room. He stood in the middle of the room; the light from the window ended at his shoulders and his head was wrapped in the gloom. It made him look decapitated.

"I'm almost very drunk," he said.

"That's fine. Hold on. I have to finish this letter."

> . . . IF YOU DO NOT CEASE YOUR PROPAGANDISTIC ATTACKS ON OUR ORGANIZATION WE WILL TAKE THE MEANS NECESSARY TO NULLIFY YOUR VITUPERATIVE PEN.
>
> SINCERELY JARED
> CENTRAL COMM. AIL

"Whozit from? Daphne?"

"It's from the AIL." I stared at the note, hands shaking. "They want to kill me."

"Awww." He sat down with a grunt onto the floor. "You get all the goddamn breaks."

"Read this." I gave him the letter. He read it over and looked up at me: "You write with a pen?"

"No." So I was to do their business now. Bastards. I took a sip of coffee; it was tepid, and I drained the cup. I felt on the brink of rattling off about this matter, yammering with fury and fear—then I stopped and stared at Solly. "What was that about the letter being from Daphne?"

"You steal my story, you can steal my girl."

Jesus. "I'm not interested in Daphne, and I didn't steal your story."

"Daphne thinks you're cute."

"Well, that's nice."

He lay down on the floor and pointed a finger up at the darkness, as though cloud watching on a sunny day. "I can help you on the story. There are things I can tell you even if Daphne thinks you're cute."

"Like what?"

"Like an address. Of someone you want to find. I'll tell it to you. If."

"If what?"

He sat up. "If you let me help you write the next story."

"Maybe." I looked into my empty cup. "If I write another piece." If you do not cease your propagandistic attacks. "And if your information isn't any good, no deal. Don't make me angry, Solly. Since the day I started at the paper you've—"

"I'll tell you just to shut you up." He lay back on the floor. "2802 Hulsey Street."

"What about it?"

"That's where Spanks lives. I was out with her tonight." He closed his eyes. "Daphne finds out, she's going to kill me." And he went to sleep.

Tailing someone is not easy in a Pacer, a car that makes people pull off the road, walk up to you and ask what was going wrong in your life the day you bought it. But I was tailing a bus, where you have a good chance of not being spotted. And it wasn't as though I could lose my quarry, either. It was thirty feet long, and red.

When I had gotten up that morning Solly was still asleep on the floor. I tried to wake him; he groaned and turned to the wall. I thought of smearing a knife with ketchup and putting it in his hand, dousing ketchup on my shirt, sprawling in a chair at the table and waiting. But instead I hauled him up, leaned him against the wall and gently slapped him awake.

He had wanted to come along for the stakeout, and I agreed. Only fair. We were sitting in front of Spanks's house, slunk low in the seat and slurping off cups of gas-station coffee, waiting for her to come out. When Solly's hangover lifted enough to permit speech, he explained how he had known her address. He had been at a club called the Bowhouse, and he had met Spanks. They had talked and danced, and after they had spent some time in the rest room kissing, they had gone so far as to exchange names, phone numbers and addresses. When he had heard her name bells had rung dimly; he recalled the edit meeting where I had mentioned her.

"She kisses weird," he said. "You know how wood gets when it's soaked in water?" I nodded. "That's what her lips are like."

Spanks lived in south Minneapolis, in a ramshackle old house that had seen better days and promptly forgotten them. She came out at eight thirty, a stride to her walk, books pressed to her chest, the picture of a modern coed, if you could airbrush out the horns. Since I had last seen her she had painted the tips of the horns various colors suitable for neckties from the fifties. We both sat up, and I started the car, waited until she was down the street a block and then pulled out of the parking spot. She paused at a bus shelter. I drove by, looking the other way as though rummaging through my glove compartment, and pulled over and parked. I waited, I saw a bus rumble by, and looked in the rearview mirror to check the shelter. She wasn't there, which meant she was on the bus. I pulled behind the bus and followed it at a discreet distance down Como.

The bus made two stops on First Avenue, but Spanks didn't get off. She appeared after the third stop, in front of Butler Square, a renovated warehouse much like Sandusky Place. Spanks bounced up the steps and disappeared inside. I realized the flaw in my plan—it would be hard to take the car into, say, the elevator. I parked, put on the flashers, told Solly to argue the police out of any ticket and ran inside.

She wasn't around. There was a flower cart by the entrance, and I asked the vendor if she'd seen a little punker pass through. "Sure. Bought a rose from me, went that way, to the elevators in the atrium." I thanked her and sprinted over to the atrium; the doors to one of the elevators were closing. I remembered that the other side of the elevator shafts in Butler were glassed, so I went around to see where the car stopped. Sixth floor. When the car returned I took it up.

There was a rest room by the elevator bank, and I was able to stand behind the door, look through a crack and see which of the two hallways she came down. I waited fifteen minutes. No one had yet to void their morning coffee, so I was left in undisturbed quiet. I was ready to give it up when Spanks came down the far hallway, five feet two of spikes and jangling chains. And smiling. When the elevator dinged and closed its doors I made for the stairwell and raced down, taking the steps three at a time. I was outside in time to see her cross the street, walking south. I shot a quick look at the Pacer—Solly was there, head against the door, mouth open in bliss and slumber. Spanks headed into the Multifoods Building—a mere fifty floors, that one, with an adjacent shopping center and skyway connections to the rest of downtown. There was no way I would find her. I stood on the corner, balling my fists, feeling extraordinarily stupid.

And hungry. I went to a Donut Boy shop on Sixth, had something filled with sugar and coated with the same, and washed it down with a cup of coffee, extra sugar. The sugar and caffeine made the world seem to be about two inches from my face, and I walked with brisk and clipped step back to Butler Square. Solly was still asleep. There was a ticket on my car.

Hell with it. I went back up to the sixth floor, looked at the names on the doors of the hallway down which she'd come. Lawyers, commodity brokerage firm, We-B-People, lawyers, lawyers. I didn't expect that Spanks was playing the market; Lou might have left her a packet but I didn't figure her for the investing type. That left lawyers—never a loose-lipped crew when it came to giving out names of clients.

But I could try. I went to the first lawyer's office in the hallway, stepped in and smiled at the receptionist. She gave me the smile she offered to anything with two legs and asked how she could help me. I said I wanted to see the man in charge who represented the young woman with the spikes in her hair. It was a matter of urgency. She got the expression of a beauty contestant asked to sum up the Boer War and said she didn't know what I was talking about. I tried the same line at three other offices, earning me looks of honey and incomprehension.

At the end of the hall was We-B-People, a temporary-help firm. A dark-haired young man, somewhat handsome but looking on the wrong side of his luck, sat at the receptionist's desk, scowling into a headset. "I don't know if she's in," he snarled. "I don't work here. I'm on loan from another temp agency and I don't know anyone here. Right. Bye." He hung up and turned around. I stiffened.

But I didn't know why. I didn't recognize him. But I knew him, from somewhere, and he was not a pleasant memory. "What's your name?" I said, curious.

"Lewis. What can I do for you?"

"I'm looking for one of your temps. Short girl, none too cute, really, hair in spikes. Named Katherine."

He gave me a hard look. "Who wants to know?"

"Well, me."

"She doesn't work here. Why do you want to see her?"

"That's personal."

"Can't help." The phone buzzed, and he reached to press the line, never taking his eyes off me. I looked away, uncomfortable—and spotted a single red rose sitting on a vase on his desk.

Ohhhh. Spanks had a boyfriend. And a fairly proprietal one, too. I backed out of the office and slunk down the hall to the elevator.

So she was up to legitimate matters. The gall. What did I have on Spanks so far. She had a videocamera in her possession at the same time the AIL made their tape. She belonged to an organization from which the AIL had attempted to recruit. Naturally she was involved in her father's death. I shook my head at my idiocy. I had nothing, nothing. Except a parking ticket.

But when I got to the office I had more than that. There was a phone message from an unexpected source. I didn't know he even knew how to use a phone.

9

"Yeah, she's quite the woman. Whew. Here's to her, eh?" Mac lifted his scotch in a toast and sipped. Only a little sloshed out onto his pants.

I held up my scotch.

Mac had called me at work and said he owed me a drink and an apology, dude. I said okay; I needed to be assured that he truly was the blunt-brained idiot I thought he was, that Sarah was better off with someone else. We were sitting in a singles bar on the ground floor of

Butler Square. I'd been here before. No one who frequented it ever seemed to have much to say, and the band played loud enough to spare them the effort of trying. The crowd was mostly venal-faced young men in suits, and secretaries, makeup faded and faces fried from eight hours of fluorescent light. There were mirrors all around, so that when closing time came and you were still alone you'd have someone to blame.

Mac was home here. The bartender knew him by name, greeting him with a reserve that spoke a vast and silent judgment. Half the suits at the bar knew him as well; there was a lot of handshaking, backslapping, faked punches. I was introduced around, greeted with hearty insincerity. We took a seat; the band stopped, and taped music thumped from the speakers.

"I don't know," Mac said, when the waitress had left with our drink order. "I'm way empty. You wouldn't want to go in on a 'za? They got primo 'za. Cooked in a stone oven."

"I'll stick with the drink."

"You want to go with nachos? Wicked nachos."

"That's okay. I ate before I came here. Had a bite at the office."

"Yeah, that's right, you're the food critic."

The waitress returned with our drinks. I dug for my wallet, but the waitress held up a hand. "This one is on me," she said, smiling. "I really like your stuff."

"My stuff?"

"That which you gots," said Mac, leering at me.

"Your writing in the *Metropole*," she said, shooting Mac a brief scowl intended, probably, to refer him to previous dismissals. "It's about the only thing I read in there. Are you reviewing us tonight?"

"No. Left my critical faculties in another suit, I'm afraid."

"Ohhh. Well, the drink's still free." She turned to Mac. "That's two fifty, Mac. As you must know by now." He gave her money and what was supposed to be a winning smile; she gave him standard issue in return and turned to the next table. I wondered how she had known who I was. Had she seen me in the paper, filed my scowling mug in her brain? Restaurant critics are supposed to be anonymous figures. If I was going to be recognized in other places they would be sending the waiter out to stall while they flew a chef in from France.

"So. You poke her yet?"

"Eh?"

Mac grinned. He held out his glass and made the toast to Sarah.

"C'mon. I don't care anymore. Tell me. Are we talking major big-time shtupping action, or what?"

"What exactly do you do for a living, Mac?"

He draped one arm around the back of the chair and laughed. "Bashful? I tell you I don't care. Christ awmighty, I called you up to apologize. I don't care if you poke her. That doesn't mean I don't care for Sarah. She's quite the woman." The glass went up again, as did mine, and this time I recalled a few things that made my loins slacken. "But it just got outta hand. I mean I love her—" But you're not in love with her, I thought. "But I'm not in love with her anymore, you know? There's a difference." But you'll always love her as a friend. "But. Well. I'll always love her."

"As a friend."

"Hell no, as one of the best jumps I ever got my hands around. Being a friend to that lady is what drove me nuts. But. Hey." He put his hands out, palms facing me, backing off. "That's not to say you and her aren't tuned to the same station."

"And which station is that?" I sipped my drink.

"Left end of the dial, I mean. You met her, what, end of college? What was she like then?"

I shrugged. "Like now, only more so. Artsy-folksy-Trotsky. Freeze the bomb for a meatless world. Politics, she lived and breathed the stuff. But she's gotten better."

"Says you. Sure you're not hungry?" Mac snagged the waitress as she came by. "Another for my friend and me. And bring me some nachos, lots of guac, extra 'mentos, two plates."

"Mac. I don't get this. I was at Sarah's place and I saw all these magazines with your names on them. Your many names. All magazines from the left."

He laughed, no pleasure in it. "Dues, dudeski. You hang around with Sarah, you got to buy into that stuff. I met her at this rally of the Progressive Students Front. Now, between you and me and the ferns here, I went to meet women, because I don't know if you've noticed, but the more whacked out their politics, the wilder they bounce, okay? Unless they're dykes. So, I met Sarah at some meeting on something or other. We showed up at this factory that makes, I don't know, warheads, something. I see her and think, Hey, this is all right. I mean I already don't like the bomb, who does, so this is like the premium. We show up and walk around with signs and all the time

I'm walking next to her talking about how bad the world is, thinking that I want to jump her bones, when someone gets the idea that we should go sit in the lobby. So we do. The cops show up. I hid in a restroom. I may have wanted to get laid, but I also wanted a job someday. Didn't want no police record."

"How long were you with the PSF?"

"Quit right after the arrest. So did she. She's not stupid. Those people are real head-in-the-clouds material. Bake sales to raise funds to visit Russia. Sarah hates Russia. You picked that up yet? You want to get on her bad side, start defending Russia."

I was silent for a while, not thinking of anything; as is usual when I drink, the scotches had taken my attention span and hidden it, and I was looking around the bar, trying to find it. When I looked back to the table the food had arrived.

"What's the matter?" Mac said, pulling a hunk of green viscera from the plate. "You shut up."

"Nothing. I just find it strange that a few weeks ago you were holding a TV over my nuts and now you're giving me advice on Sarah."

"Yeah, well, new prospects, bud, new territory."

"Seeing anybody else?"

"Nah." He drew another triangle from the heap, tentacles of cheese clinging to its kin. "I need space." I was about to suggest he draw from the ample reserves between his ears, but he continued: "So, tell me. This going to poison me here?"

"Probably. I can't imagine any of it is good for you."

"I mean, the AIL going to go after appetizers? You seem to know this stuff."

"Would you believe me if I said I had a list at home of all the things they had approved?"

"It wouldn't surprise me if you were behind it. I mean, what a way to get readership up."

"Funny. Listen, Mac. When you were with the PSF—" I stopped. Talking to Mac about his days with the PSF was like asking a stripper about her time in the convent. "Did you have contact with anyone named Jared?"

"Sure you don't want any of this? Max tasty, I'm telling you. No? Okay. No, I didn't know any Jared. That's the guy who's pulling down these poison gigs, right? He wasn't around when I was. But like I say, been three years. You're asking me about this guy? You must not have anything on him, or what?" Mac dipped a wedge into sour cream, offered it to me. I shook my head no. He crammed it into his mouth and reached for a drink. Then his face froze, and his eyes widened. He grabbed his throat. "Shit," he said in a small, choked voice. He began to hack. People at adjoining tables looked over, frowning. I felt panic take the steps in my throat three at a time—not again, not again, no, not again. I sat stunned, pressed back into my chair with horror; I saw Mac, who maybe didn't deserve this, and I saw Lou, who hadn't, Lou, God damn it, my fault, my fault, my—

One of Mac's friends from the bar had vaulted over to our table and was hauling Mac out of his chair. He laced his fingers under his sternum, pulled up in a linebacker's hug, relaxed, did it again. A small gray lump of food shot from Mac's mouth and landed on the table. Mac hacked and swore and spit and sunk back into his chair. His face was mottled and a vein beat madly in his temple. "Dmn." He hacked and coughed again. "Gddmn."

"His throat," his friend said to me. "Size of a dime. Stuff gets caught in there all the time. You okay?" he said to Mac. Mac nodded, clasped his hand and waved him away. The friend left. The waitress brought a glass of water and, in an exceptionally inappropriate move, the bill. Mac drained the glass of water, banged it down on the table.

People had begun to return to their conversations; I caught fragments: Ay Eye Ell; Jared; you never know, you just don't know; a person's afraid to eat anything.

"This shit happens," Mac finally said. "I'll say this for Sarah. She knew where to nail me." He coughed. The band had returned to exact additional punishment and was playing random notes. "We had these fights, she'd . . . I'd be sitting down afterwards, eating something, do the gag routine, and she'd take the whole fight out on my back." Mac slumped back in his seat and loosened his tie; he let his gaze drift over to the band. As if on command the racket resumed.

10

I entered the elevator at the Sandusky Building and tried not to look as if I were in a hurry. Just as dogs can smell fear and the opposite sex can smell desperation, mechanical objects can scent haste, and it is then they choose to show you how much you take their compliance for granted. This elevator would have made a Luddite out of Buckminster Fuller. It jammed at least once a day; it was bound to jam today: I had to get my copy in within the hour or the front page would be vacant. The elevator knew it.

When Fikes had heard I had gotten not only a personal communiqué but the list of approved foods he nearly danced a jig. He had not only scrapped the lead piece to give play to my article, he assigned me a weekly AIL update feature to keep the public apprised, as well as the advertiser rates high. I worried that this would cement whatever tenebrous relationship I had with the AIL, whoever they were; I didn't want to be their spokesman. I did, however, need all the goodwill at the paper I could get. So shaky was my position there that I had willingly kept the letter and list to myself instead of going to Detective Bishop and the other papers. The more publicity the list got, the better for everyone, of course. And once we published it, everyone would run it, as it was not the sort of thing you would copyright. That would be a little like personally hearing from God the date and time of the end of the world and then shopping around for book and film rights. When Bishop saw the list in the *Metropole* he would scream hard enough to strip wood down to the grain for blocks around, but I would deal with that later.

Solly was hunched over his machine, one finger embedded in his mouth up to the knuckle, one finger tapping a button on the computer keyboard. I stopped by and asked how he was doing, testing to see if the previous night's sodality had taken hold.

"I'm cross-eyed from this garbage." He gestured at the screen.

"Annual Christmas gift guide. Buncha stuff no one is ever going to buy. Fur-covered pens that tell time. Umbrellas that beep if you walk away from them, so you don't leave them on the bus. What are you here for?"

"Late entry for the gift guide. Home trepanning kit."

"Really." And Solly actually smiled. He had such bad teeth I sometimes thought he built a world view around them so he wouldn't find things to smile about.

"Ancient health tips of the Aztecs revealed. Drill a hole in your skull and let the evil spirits out. Cures all ills."

"Uh-uh. Not all." He gestured to Fikes's cubicle. "Some ills don't know cures. I could take off the top of my head with a circular saw and that fat ass would still be there."

"Is he in now?"

"The fat ass is in," called Fikes from his cubicle. Solly pantomimed shouldering a bazooka, fired and shot back into his seat from the recoil. I waved farewell and went into Fikes's little kingdom.

Fikes was sitting in his chair, hands laced over his belly, looking up at me like a headmaster regarding a student caught behind the chapel sodomizing the school mascot. One hand made a generous gesture toward the chair where I was to sit. I sat. I looked at him, thinking, Whatever other disasters I have called down on my head these past weeks, I have slept with two beautiful women, and he hasn't. If there is a God in heaven that has to count for something.

"Three things. One, your food-review work." Fikes grimaced. "It has been acceptable. No one has written in to express disgust, so it must be finding the right audience. With one exception, which brings us to two. The lawsuit." I had hoped he wouldn't. "I would like to expedite this countersuit, mrrgh? I wish this had not come to pass, but. We have been sued before and I have learned to expect this." He gave a long, expansive shrug. I began to wonder if perhaps he had slept with three beautiful women lately. "The offending item in your column was perhaps the most egregious item I have let pass, but I did let it pass. Mrrgh. Therefore blame rests with me. Your name is in the suit because that is simply how things are done. Don't let it worry you. Say what you feel. I will dilute your more enthusiastic judgments if need be. Just don't let this keep you from speaking your mind."

He was in love, that was it.

"What's her name?"

"Mrrgh. Who."

"Your lady friend. The one you called 'honey' on the phone the other day."

Fikes blushed ocher. "It shows, does it?"

"Yeah, it shows. Come on. Her name."

"Betty. Now. As to point number three. I assume you have the story, the letter, the list."

"What's she like."

"She's perfectly nice. How long is the piece?"

"Brown hair? Blond?"

"I'd say sandy. She gets angry if anyone calls it dishwater blond. As anyone would. Can I have the list?"

"How does she laugh?"

"Laugh? Wonderfully. Often, yet with just cause. Do you—"

"Smart? Witty? Come on."

"She's a database organizer." Fikes gave a wistful smile. "Tremendous sense of spatial arrangement."

"I'll bet." I winked. "So here's the piece." I handed it to him and stood. "Call me if there are the usual problems."

"Mrrgh." Fikes was paging through the copy. "Where's this list, then?"

"Should be right after the letter."

"It's not."

I saw panic capering in the wings, pointing and laughing. I closed my eyes and saw the letter and list sitting on the dining-room table, right by the computer. "Don't tell me I left it at home."

All sanguinity fled from his face. "For Christ's sake! Simpson! The list is our front page! Without it I'll have to run everything else in thirty-six-point type and pass it off as an edition for the nearsighted! Go! Go get me that list!"

I nodded, sighed and left.

Solly was gone. Daphne was away from her desk. I rode down in the elevator with a tall young woman who had teased and tortured hair, a pouty face and long legs in black lace stockings. She was carrying a portfolio the size of a movie screen. I called her Betty to see if she answered; she didn't. I would have wept if she had.

"News director. That's right. Simpson. No, it's—please. Please. All right. Of course I'll hold. People will die if I don't."

I was walking around the dining room, phone in one hand, receiver cradled against my shoulder, the other hand responsible for the traffic of cigarettes in and out of my mouth.

I had lost the list of approved foods. In the middle of the night it had stood up on edge, trembled and passed into the dimension of misplaced objects. Fifty years from now a couple would attend an estate sale, buy a bureau from one of the upstairs bedrooms, open a drawer and find it.

Fikes had not been happy. Tongues of fire had sprouted from the phone when he issued his opinion on my stewardship of important matters. I went through the garbage one more time, and then I called the highest-rated TV station in town.

I was going to have to ask the AIL to send me another list. If the paper came out without it, they might assume I was thumbing my nose at them, and I had to demonstrate my goodwill.

The news director of the station finally came on the line and asked what I wanted. I explained—who I was, the variety of soup into which I had gotten myself this time. He recognized my name and knew my work.

"You had the list," he said.

"That's right."

"You lost the list."

"That's also right."

"Okay. Let me think. We go on for the noon news in, ah, half an hour. Can you be down here by then? We'll put you on live."

"That's fine. I'll be there in—No. No." What was I thinking? I couldn't go on. "I can't. I can't show up on TV."

"There's no need to get nervous. We can—"

"I mean, I can't. I'm a restaurant reviewer. I shouldn't show my face. I'm supposed to be anonymous."

The man sighed. "All right. How about a phone link? Any problem with them recognizing your voice?"

"No."

"You're sure? All right. Give me your number. We'll call you around noon and we'll talk to you then."

I gave him my number and hung up. I paced and smoked and swore for half an hour.

At noon the phone rang. It was the news director. He gave me a few suggestions—keep it short, clean, and be prepared for questions.

He put me on hold and told me it would be five minutes or so. There had been a plane crash and a bombing in Pakistan that were in line ahead of me.

I had lit another cigarette, feeling a headache start to mass above my eyes, when the front door opened and Trygve tottered down the hall. He had a bag of groceries in each arm. I looked at my watch—I still had a few minutes. I laid the phone down and took the bags from Trygve's arms. He thanked me, daubed at the sweat on his brow and headed back down the hall and out the door. I picked up the phone and heard the newscast proceeding; many people were dead in the worst aircrash since the last one. After a minute Tryg came in with another bag of groceries. He set it down on the table and went back outside. A spokesman for the airline said it was a tragic day for all of us.

When Tryg came back with two more bags I asked him if he had been shopping at the Build Your Own F-16 shop. What was all this stuff? "Today is shopping day," he replied gravely. "You ought to know there'd be a lot; you made the list." I nodded and turned my attention back to the phone. You made the list. I heard my name, and then the anchorman was right in my ear, saying, "Hello!"

"Hi," I said. I was digging through the sacks, pulling out broccoli, carrots, spinach—canned, fresh, chopped, frozen. Everything that was on the list was here. "How's it going?"

"As we were saying, you're with the *Metropole* newspaper—the restaurant reviewer. If I understand this right, you have a special relationship with the AIL, and a message you'd like to send to them. Could you explain?"

Oranges, apples, kiwi fruit, bananas. Damn. Tryg came in with another bag and dropped it on the table.

"That's right." I clapped a hand over the phone. "Tryg!" I hissed. "The shopping list! Did you get it off the table this morning?" He nodded. "Do you still have it?" He began to pat his clothes down, poke through his pockets. He shook his head.

". . . is that right?" said the voice in my ear.

"What? I'm sorry. I wasn't paying attention."

"I said you have a matter of life and death to discuss today."

"No." Pineapples, kumquats, alfalfa sprouts.

There was a moment of silence. The anchor came back on the line and said, in a voice that had the rhythm of a razor slapped on a strop: "Maybe you could explain just what you're talking about."

"I mean, it was a mistake. I thought I had lost the list but my butler took it."

"The butler took it."

"I have to go now. He was . . . he was shopping. I have to go, good-bye." I hung up. I sprinted into the library, turned on the TV and saw the anchor smiling hideously into the camera, a graphic saying *AIL* hovering over his shoulder. The graphic dissolved; his eyes looked left and right. There was a wide-shot of the news desk and a commercial came on.

The phone was ringing in the dining room. I made it in time to take it out of Trygve's hands, hang it up and take the cord out of the back of the phone. Then I upended every bag on the dining table. It looked like everything on the list, all right. I plugged the phone back in; it began to ring immediately. I hung up, then dialed the *Metropole*, asked for Fikes. He started to shout but I told him to shut up and start taking notes. I read off the name of every item on the table.

". . . kohlrabi, fresh . . ." I said, about half an hour later. "Ginger root, looks like it's fresh too . . . blueberry Popsicles . . ."

"Blueberry Popsicles?" he yelled. "What are they doing on the list?"

I held the box up and waved them at Tryg.

"Grue said I can buy a treat each week," he said. "With this much broccoli about, I thought it was a good week for Popsicles."

We finished reconstructing the list. Fikes hung up without saying good-bye.

I sat in the kitchen and had a Popsicle with Tryg. He announced that they didn't taste at all like blueberries, yet they were good. Why was that?

"Artificial flavor," I said, numb.

"I thought so." Trygve smiled. "That's my favorite."

11

"You look wonderful."

"I look like Medusa."

"Well, I love what you've done with your snakes."

Sarah was smoking a cigarette. This was equal to Mahatma Gandhi firing off a few rounds at the target range. But she was nervous, and when she was nervous, all notions about the horrors of smoking were replaced by the greater horrors of biting her nails.

We were at the Café Macro, a new restaurant in the warehouse district. It was spare and noisy; high white walls, high wide windows, white tablecloths, pasty and indifferent help. The place was macro, aggressively so. There wasn't a dish on the menu I recognized as edible; they all had names that sounded like South Pacific words for minor deities.

Sarah did look lovely. Her hair was swept to one side, clasped with an austere band of gold and draped over her shoulder. She wore a dark blue blouse with padded shoulders and a paisley design, great oversized swirling figures that reminded me of paramecia dipped in styling gel. She wore a faint blue lipstick. And she had the nerve to say she looked awful.

"So what's wrong?"

"Wrong?"

"Wrong. On the way over you didn't say a thing about my driving. We get here and you ask the waiter for coffee. With sugar. Refined sugar. Then you smoke. I don't know why we're here instead of Perky Louie's Rib Shack."

She looked up from her menu, eyes two black points with no goodwill for the person sitting in my chair. "I'm going to have the Miso Medley."

I found the item, which was described as a delicate polyphony of fruits and sauces. I rubbed my eyes. "Delicate polyphony. Who they got cooking back there, Erik Satie?"

"Be nice."

"Ahh, it's not their fault, I know. This stupid job is making me unable to think of food without attaching adjectives. I buy a candy bar and I find myself thinking about the rich and congenial argument between the nuts and the nougat. Then I write about the AIL, where food is no longer good or bad but approved or lethal."

The waitress came over, took our orders and reached for the menu. I put a hand over it; I hadn't had the chance to copy down the items and prices yet. I said I'd like to keep mine for a while, look at some of the dessert items.

She looked at me, squinted, then smiled. "Now I get it. I knew I'd seen you somewhere. You're the food critic. Okay, keep the menu. I'll even ask the manager if you can take it home." She made a note on the check and walked away.

I stared after her in astonishment. "That's the second time I've been recognized. What is going on here? Did everybody decipher that photo?"

"It's something of a shock to see you striving for anonymity," Sarah said. "After all those years of trying to be famous."

"In this line of work, anonymity is indispensable. Anonymity and an iron gut. I'm amazed I haven't been poisoned yet."

"So am I," she said. "I've been reading what you write about the AIL. I worry for you, Jay."

I shrugged, the fearless critic. "It's kind of fun, staring death in the teeth."

"You'd lip-off to death and tell it to fix its bridgework."

"You think I'm that brave?"

"I think you're that much of a big mouth, is what I think."

I coughed. "So, tell me about your day. I haven't seen you in a while."

"I know." She reached for my pack and drew out another cigarette. I lit it; she puffed on it inexpertly. "You've been busy," she said.

"With all sorts of disasters." I leaned back. "Some of my own devising. But mostly these bastards in the AIL. Half the city is scared and no one knows anything. Did you read that poll in the paper? Something like eighty-six percent has heard of the AIL and the food tamperings. About ten percent knows what they want. Fifteen percent thought they were for the establishment of a Palestinian state."

"I'm not scared. I eat right."

"Well, you ought to be scared. Once they have everyone eating fresh vegetables they'll decide that only ones washed in spring water from wells in Soviet Uzbek are acceptable. These people are not on the beam. Killing people? Over dietary habits?"

"Ever think that they might have another reason?"

"Like what? They were all fired by hot-dog manufacturers and are just working this out of their system? No."

"What about that girl you mentioned—Sparks."

"Spanks. The more I thought about it I'd have to be God's own idiot to think she was in this. I was just desperate. What the hell business do I have smoking these jackanapes out anyway? This is police stuff. But the AIL drops two of my near and dear, sends me a letter and a list—you saw that story? Right. Well, now everyone expects me, me, the guy who was hired to write about whether or not the forks are spotted, to find out where these bozos are plotting world domination."

"So you've been busy."

"Yes, I've been busy."

"That's why you left my apartment after Thanksgiving and didn't call, eh? Two weeks. Fourteen days. Either way that's a long time, Jay."

I shifted from the political to the personal and ground all the gears in the process. "I've called! You're never home."

"You certainly tried. Sure rang the damn thing off the hook."

"I've stopped by the Diner. Haven't seen you there."

"I've been there, all right? You want me to take off my shoes and show you my bunions?" Her voice rose. "Is that what you want? For me to take off my shoes in a public place?"

I looked around. People were looking at me as though I had just requested some unspeakable perversity.

"Sarah, is something wrong? Something happen? Did you hear from Mac?"

"No." Her jaw tightened.

"I did."

"What?"

"We had a drink together. Shared war stories."

"I suppose you talked about me."

"The subject came up. He asked if we had . . . had."

"Had what?"

"Seen each other. Lately. Then he told me how you two met. That's all."

"Really? The whole story? How he escaped from the police and everything?"

"Mm. Yes."

She smiled, her eyes downcast and dreaming. "Life always has romance when you're young and the government is bad."

The waitress came by with a straw basket covered with cloth. I opened it up, half expecting to see a slumbering foundling within, but there was only bread. I looked back to Sarah, who still wore her faraway expression. Had she always been this odd? Had I forgotten something?

"You miss him, don't you."

"No. I miss what he was but not what he became."

"What exactly was he?"

She sighed. "Big, articulate. Politically correct and handsome."

"Articulate? That bruiser? He has the verbal skills of Java Man. I'm surprised he knows the words for 'fire' and 'wheel.' "

"Not the Mac I know. He could charm the birds out of the trees."

"All the better to put them in cages. Look, I think you're blinding yourself to a few things about this man. Which is normal, but—"

"Ugh."

"What's the matter with normal?"

"No, no, it's not that. I don't feel well. I feel . . . hottish. Flushed." She took a sip of water. "It's the cigarettes. And the sugar, and the tension." She took another cigarette.

"You want me to take you home?"

"No. Let's eat. I need to eat."

"Haven't you been eating? Sarah."

"I've been too nauseous. And tense. As you can tell. I get up in the morning and I just feel blah and it stays with me all day."

Cold hands laced fingers around my throat. "You're sick in the morning."

"Yes. Oh, oh, that's what you're thinking? Don't worry. I can't be pregnant. No, no, no. Certainly not. I took my temperature that morning and it was just what it was supposed to be."

"What do you mean, took your temperature?"

"Rhythm method. One of the ways you determine whether it's safe to have sex is by taking your temperature."

"Determine it's safe by taking your temperature? You might as well base it on whether or not the car needs waxing. That's ridiculous."

"That's Catholicism."

"Well, I'm not Catholic. I'm Lutheran. We don't have rhythm. Weren't you on the Pill?"

"All those chemicals? Feed a few more bucks into the pharmaceutical companies and have my hormones screwed up while *they* make a profit? No thanks. But don't worry. I'm not pregnant. I just got a bug or something. I haven't eaten and I'm overworked. If I was pregnant I would be throwing up more than I am."

"Supper!" sang the waitress, and she deposited two plates on the table.

Neither of us ate much, and not a lot was said, either.

We paid and left. Outside we stood on the corner, a sharp spiteful wind pecking our faces as we tried to decide what to do next. Going home meant trouble; splitting up for the night meant acknowledging it; and going elsewhere just meant delaying it.

"What do you say, the Room?" I said through chattering teeth. Sarah nodded and we hurried down the street.

The Room was the bar I'd been at when I'd phoned Tryg and learned of Grue's poisoning. I'd since learned that it was the latest place to be seen. Which did not explain why it was always pitch-dark in there. The Room was loud, smoky, hot and frequented entirely by artists.

It was busier than usual for a weekday; patrons had spilled out into the hallway that connected the Room to an adjoining restaurant. We walked a gauntlet of thirty feet, cutting between a dozen conversations, dodging gestures, bottles making a fast arc from waist-level to mouth. There was a massive biped standing in front of the door, facing inside; the top of his head bristled in an elaborate fantail, hued in primary colors. Here was something to which Spanks would bend in prayer. I stood on tiptoe to tap him on the shoulder and he stepped to one side, almost like a door swinging open. We pushed our way past him into the Room.

"This is nonsense," I heard Sarah shout behind me. "We'll never get a seat, let alone a drink. Let's go."

What, I thought, and go somewhere where we can talk? I pretended I hadn't heard and kept pushing through the crowd. It was like boxing underwater. The Room, after all, was less a room than a hallway with an exaggerated sense of self. Halfway through the mess we got stalled by someone rooted in the narrow gutter between bar and tables. He was big, flanked by two people bigger, talking to both and having just a great time. The Berlin wall was a hedgerow compared to these three. I yelled for them to excuse us. The man in the middle looked behind him, then shouted that there was nowhere for me to go and turned back to his conversation. I yelled that I'd be the judge of that if he didn't mind, and could he move. He stood aside, revealing, ohgod ohgod, two more people pushing their way toward the door, a man and a woman, their faces shining with the frantic glee of the newly coupled who simply have to go home and have immediate sex. For one horrible and claustrophobic minute we all stood there bobbing and pushing, like an egg gagging a snake that is trying hard to swallow it. We began to walk crabwise, passing so close that my sweater was snagged on the woman's belt. We did a brief mambo of disengagement and proceeded on. A few minutes later Sarah and I were pressed up against the vast plate-glass window that made up the far wall. Someone's elbow was in my back.

"Let's go," said Sarah.

"If you shouted that someone was handing out grant proposals in the hall, you'd clear the room in a second."

"I want to sit down."

I thought for a minute, trying to figure out how to get a table. I'd pose as a fire marshal and say the place was over occupancy code, but I lacked the hat. I could have the Johnson party paged; in a Scandinavian town such as this, half the place would empty. Then I spotted Marya.

Figures. This was her sort of place. She was seated in the corner, leaning up against the window, cigarette in one hand and drink in the other, laughing. She looked precious, edible, sweet. She was with something tall and thin and dressed for guerrilla warfare, a camera bag at his feet. She pointed across the bar; he turned, and I saw he was the man who had taken photographs at Carver's grave. *Daily* photog, no doubt. He leaned over and put a hand through her hair; she looked down at the table, eyes smiling at him through a tangle of red curls. I wanted to tie him to horses and whip their flanks. Instead I told Sarah to wait, that I was about to get us a seat, and squirmed my way over to their table.

"Hi, kids," I shouted. The photographer looked up at me with eyes that belonged on a breed of dog renowned for being good with kids; Marya gave God in heaven a look borrowed from Job. "Mind if I join you two?"

"We were leaving," she shouted.

"I saw you in Valhalla," I yelled to the photographer. "You were at that funeral? Great job. Your presence really added to the bereavement." He glanced at me as though I had been speaking Swahili. Marya was looking up at me, with wild, frayed fear in her face. Then it hit me.

It was like watching a film of a jigsaw puzzle being demolished, shown in reverse. Things I had consigned to the general chaos of the back of my mind flew together in a perfect fit. Marya had said she'd sat down the afternoon after our tryst and written the story. That would be what, Wednesday, while I was in Valhalla. The editor had seen it Wednesday evening, run it for Thursday's paper.

If he'd seen it Wednesday night, how would he have had time to assign a photographer when the funeral was in the afternoon?

How, unless someone had told him that morning to send a photog up to Valhalla?

"Oh, my," I said. "Ohhhhh."

"Come on, Joe. Let's go."

"Wait a minute," said Joe. "This guy likes my work. It's not often that I—"

"We have to go."

"Ohhhh. Marya." I was just moaning to myself.

"I'll talk to you. Call me." She was shoving items from the table into her bag. There was enough panic in her gestures to make me wonder if she'd sweep the candle into her purse. She knew just what I knew. "We'll have that drink."

"Hemlock and tonic. Have a double. My treat."

Joe stood up, shook my hand and said it was sure good to meet me. Marya stood and he put an arm around her shoulders. I signaled that they should wait, and then I leaned close into Marya's ear and whispered.

"At first I thought it was just infatuation but now I know: I truly detest you. You used my pain and you ordered photographs of it. You lied to me about lying to me. If this was wartime they would shave your head and stone you in the streets."

Marya pulled away. "We have to talk."

"Just buy me a car. Buy me two. That should make us even." I turned away, then looked back at her. "Have you ceased considering that deposition? Just put it in the glove compartment."

Marya gave me something roughly designed to be a smile. It came out looking like the expression of someone wearing poorly fitted orthodontic equipment. Then they turned and started burrowing through the crowd. I spun around, disgusted, and saw that two people had sat down at their table. "Oh no you don't," I yelled. "Up. Up. Come on, that's right, haul it up, these are mine. Up." They got up and moved away from the table. I slid into where Marya had been sitting and waved Sarah over. She wiggled through the crowd and sat down, looking miserable, lovely, honest, not Marya. I was seething, mad enough to kill.

"I feel awful."

"I got you chairs," I snapped. "What do you want? An ottoman? Or do you want to go?"

Sarah slammed her hand down on the table. "Go? We spend an hour getting to one end of this goddamn bar and then you go off and talk to some child and whisper in her ear while I stand in the corner like the hat rack? Go? We're staying here until it closes. Get me a drink."

"Are you sure?"

"Sure I should drink?" she shouted.

"What are you so angry about?"

"Angry?"

"Pissed. Wrathful. Molto furioso."

"I think I'm pregnant, that's what I'm angry about! Is there any service in this goddamn bar? What do I have to do, distill it myself? Jesus." She scraped her chair back and stood up, plowed her way to the bar with her hands and elbows, returned in five minutes with two scotches and slammed them down on the table.

"Here's to Junior," she said.

"Come on," I shouted. "You can't be serious."

"If there's a God in heaven I'm not, but what if I am? Hmm?"

"We've been through this before. Remember? That time, what was it, January 'eighty-three? You thought you were pregnant then."

"My sister was, though."

"So?"

"So she's not pregnant now, and she didn't suspect a thing then, and now it's my turn."

"What?"

"Figure it out. Point is I don't want to be pregnant because I got saucy with my old boyfriend after breakfast one morning after my other boyfriend had left and I was feeling boring and sexless, all right? How stupid can I get? How predictable"—she banged the table—"and idiotic"—bang—"and trite and stupid"—bang—"can I be?"

Stupid enough to use the rhythm method, I thought. Then I realized I hadn't exactly mentioned jogging over to the corner store for milk and some condoms, and I knew culpability was sitting square on my chest, too.

"What are we going to do?" I yelled. I could feel nodes the size of softballs forming on my vocal cords.

"I'll jump off that bridge when I come to it."

"You? What do you mean, you? Don't I have any say in this?"

"I'm not pregnant, I'm just not. This is ridiculous. Oh, if there'd just been a movie the night you came over. We should have watched a movie and then I wouldn't be worrying about being pregnant, which I am not, but if I were I'm not"—she banged the table again—"having an abortion this time."

"This time? What do you mean?"

Sarah looked me straight in the eye. I had no choice but to hold the glance and not blink.

"Never mind." She looked out the window. Then her eyes got wide and she put her hand over her mouth. She pointed.

It wasn't the best picture, but press pictures rarely are. If advertising had asked me for a portrait I'd have given them one, and then told them the whole thing was a bad idea. But there it was.

Half the billboard had a picture of an old-style radical—wire glasses on his nose, headband around his hair, cackling over a newspaper. WHAT'S BLACK AND WHITE AND RED ALL OVER? it said above. THE DAILY WORKER. On the other side was a well-dressed young man reading a copy of the *Metropole*—with my photo on the cover. WHAT'S BLACK AND WHITE AND EVERY SHADE IN BETWEEN? THE NEW METROPOLE.

Below was written: READ JONATHAN SIMPSON ON FOOD.

Below that, spray-painted: READ OUR MEDIA STOOGE. AIL.

Sarah looked at me.

"That explains the recognition," I sighed.

She threaded an arm through her coat. "I can't take this anymore. Let's get out of here." She stood. "Time to go see if there's a God in heaven."

12

Highways 12 and 100 do not so much merge as collide. Leaving or entering one or the other is a matter wholly subject to the whims of your fellow man. If generous they will let you go where you please; if otherwise disposed they will make you drive miles past your destination, and they will go home and sleep well afterward. I was in no mood to depend on anyone's goodwill, least of all my own, and I drove like any other man whose part-time helpmeet might be carrying a blastocyst with his name on it. When the 100 exit hove into view I merged like a man who already pays too much insurance; honks and screeches sounded behind me. Sarah said not a word. I doubt that she even noticed. We were en route to Byerly's, a vast supermarket open all night, home of endless edibles, live lobsters, flowers, magazines and home pregnancy tests.

Byerly's was empty, but you could take the entire contents of the Room and disperse it among the aisles and the place would still look deserted. It was immense. Soft light and anesthetizing music, carpet, chrome, wood, no smell.

"Want to go look at the lobsters? There's a tank in the back. Live ones like big bugs." My voice was hoarse and scratchy from shouting.

"We'll have time for that. The test takes half an hour. Come on." Sarah headed back to the pharmacy area. The pregnancy tests were next to the tampons. A cruel note, that. Like putting hair restorers next to combs.

"Here. This one." She picked up a box and read it. "Reply. I've heard it recommended."

Probably in the product review section of *Rhythm Method Quarterly*.

We went to the register. I picked up a few items to make the purchase less conspicuous—razor blades, dental floss, shampoo, a novel, a bag of charcoal briquettes and a lobster.

After we had made our purchases we stood in the lobby.

"All right, what next?" Sarah said. "Home?"

"Can we do the test now?"

"Yeah." She looked away. "I want to get it over with too."

"What do you have to do?"

"I have to pee into it and shake it and wait. If it turns pink I'm . . . we're safe. If it's clear we got to start a college fund."

"There's a coffeeshop next door. Meet you there?"

She nodded and walked to the rest rooms. I went back into the store and put the lobster back into his tank. Not a word of thanks.

I took a booth in the back of the coffeeshop. A young woman came by and doled out two cups of coffee. Did I want it black? I wanted it pink, lady, I muttered. I was kneading two grooves in my brow when Sarah reappeared. She took something out of her purse and placed it behind a plastic sign on the table that read DESSERTS.

"That it?"

"Uh-huh."

"Does it have to be on the table?"

"I'm not going to have it in my purse. Could leak onto my lipstick." She ran a hand through her hair. "It doesn't say what happens if the solution turns Winter Frost."

"Is that the shade you have on?"

"Like it?"

"Normally I don't like blue lipstick, but yeah, it's okay."

"I'll wear it at our wedding if the bottle's clear."

Pause. Muzak, clattering of dishes. "That would be fine," said someone in my skin.

Sarah smiled. "Are you saying you'd marry me? I don't accept."

"Say again?"

"You don't have to."

"I would."

"I know. That's why you don't have to."

"Wait a minute." I pulled a cigarette out of my pack. The last one. Ten pounds of charcoal briquettes but no cigarettes. "If I wouldn't want to marry you, you'd make me?"

"Mm-hmm. I'd pull out at the last minute but I'd make you go through with it." She grinned, that same old smile I loved. "You're a good man, Jay. Eminently marriageable. You generally do the right thing. You always have. You never notice because you're going over your life with a magnifying glass to find what you did wrong. But you're pretty sweet. You'll make some woman happy."

"Don't I make you happy?"

"If we're sitting here wondering whether or not I'm pregnant, you probably made me happy somewhere down the line." She looked at her watch. "How much time?"

"Twenty minutes. You know, if it's only eighty percent accurate—"

"I know. If it's no, we'll believe it. If it's yes, I'll go buy another one. Do it again. Pee quarts until you're sure I'm not pregnant. I'm glad you ordered coffee. What time do you have there?" She tapped her fingers on the table. "They ought to sell these kits with false nails, you know? Something to bite while you wait."

And we waited. I went to the register for change, bought cigarettes.

When I came back Sarah was slumped against the wall of the booth.

"You look? No fair. I wasn't—"

"I didn't. Just tired. Oh, Jay. I don't want to be pregnant."

"Neither do I. Want you to be pregnant."

"Someday, though."

"What was that you said before about having an abortion?" She didn't reply. "That's all right," I said.

"I had one. With Mac." She looked down. "The condom popped. And we had had a fight that night. Made love just to get back at each other." She shook her head. "Kid would have been born with its hands over its ears."

Sarah looked as though she were about to cry. I got up and sat on her side of the booth and put my arm around her. She put her head on my shoulder.

"It'd be a cute little thing if we had it," she said.

"Don't," I said. I hugged her. "Don't."

"Little toes. Little fingers. Big mouth."

"Please."

"It could have your chin as long as it had my world view."

"Sarah, please."

I bit my tongue. "We're talking about a zygote," I finally said.

"Little Zy."

I waited awhile. Then I leaned to her ear and said, "There's no reason you can't have it, you know."

She shook her head, snuggled closer to me. "No. I have school to finish and you're going to die of additives cancer someday. Neither of us are ready to be parents."

Thanks a lot. I looked at my watch.

"Ten minutes. You want anything else? Pie, something? My treat."

"Yeah. What do they have."

I wasn't thinking. I picked up the plastic Desserts sign to examine the menu; Sarah shrieked. I looked and saw the little vial. It was red. I put the sign back in front of the vial.

"Red!" she said. "Red! What the hell, red! It's supposed to be clear or pink! What am I giving birth to, Lenin?"

"It's red because it's in front of the ketchup bottle."

"So it must be clear. Oh, God, oh, God."

"Maybe it's pink, maybe it's pink. Pink and red are close. It's got ten minutes to turn pinker. Maybe it goes off at the last minute. We'll buy another. Don't worry."

"Don't worry? I can feel this thing subdividing as we speak."

We sat in silence for a while, stirring our coffee, looking at the other patrons in the coffeeshop. There was an old man lunching on his lip at the counter, a young couple reading the paper, their legs twined at the ankles. A middle-aged man, shoulders hunched with perpetual solitude, had bowed his head to say grace over a bagel.

"Nine and a half minutes," I said.

"Don't give me a countdown." Then: "All right, give me a countdown."

I gave reports on the minute. It was all the conversation we had left. It came down to ten seconds; she stopped me at three, then nodded three times.

We looked at the desserts menu.

"Let's have some ice cream first," Sarah said.

"No. Look at it."

Sarah picked up the menu.

She leaned back in her seat and closed her eyes.

Clear, clear as a brook. Clear as a brook in which salmon struggle upstream to spawn.

"Two out of three?" I said.

She shook her head.

I took her hand. "Want to go back to the manor?"

She shook her head and pulled her hand out of mine. "Just want to go home."

We paid, left. On Highway 12 when I finally turned to look at her, I saw her cheeks shining, the light of streetlamps caught in her eyes, the streaks down her face, the tears that had fallen into her mouth as though heading home.

13

I wore a hair shirt and walked the streets crying, "Yea, I have got with child a woman to whom I am not wed." I beat my breast and rent my garments, locked myself in the stocks and implored passersby to bedeck me with spit.

Actually, I just left town. I rented a moving van and drove up to Valhalla to collect the remaining possessions from the house. The lease was up and there was no point in keeping the place. I finished hauling by noon and went to the Hilltop, my old bar. They treated me as if I'd never left, meaning they hadn't acknowledged my presence while I was living in Valhalla, either.

I got into town around five and drove straight back to Sarah's. I had felt guilty all the way back for being absent; perhaps she had needed me. I still couldn't imagine that she was really, truly pregnant; maybe this was an hysterical pregnancy. But Sarah was never hysterical. Enthusiastic, yes, ironic on occasion. I couldn't imagine a doctor saying, "No, it's just an ironic pregnancy."

Actually, when I thought about it, I could imagine him saying that all too well.

I was pulling the van up behind her building when a car roared up the drive into the lot and skidded to a stop in Sarah's spot. It was a sports car with plates that read MY TOY. The door opened and Mac got out, wearing sunglasses. He adjusted his tie, looked right and left, squared his shoulders, buttoned his coat and entered the building. He used keys.

Well. Well, well, well.

I parked the van on the street and walked back to the apartment. I crunched through the thin snow along the building and stood under the bedroom window, a clothes-dryer exhaust vent blowing billows of steam between my legs. There was no light on in the bedroom, no sound; I moved on. No sound from the bathroom. I inched along the building until I was under the living room. I heard the TV. I stood back a few paces, stood at the edge of the pool of light from the next building and looked in the window. Mac was sitting in front of the television with his feet up, eating something.

Years ago I had confronted Sarah about Trotsky's appearances at her house; she'd denied everything. Not this time. I went to the front door and rang the bell. The door buzzed and I went in. I heard the door open and Mac, from inside, say, "Forget your keys again?"

I stepped into the apartment.

"Never had them to be able to forget them," I said. He turned, looked at me with as much incredulity as his features would allow, and then he laughed.

" 'Lo, bro. What's hanging?"

"What are you doing here?"

"Chowing. Here." He held up a cellophane wrapper with a dull and shiny brownish confection inside. "I'm porked. Did a slider and a box of nails on the way over. You want to do this Bettycake? Absolute top choice."

"What does she see in you?"

Mac smiled. "I make a pile of money and I don't try to sing because she knows I can't, and I'm like Hurricane Mac in bed. That about covers it."

"How do you make money? You'd flunk a piano mover's exam."

Mac laughed. "Passed the broker's exam, though."

"Sarah loves a broker. Jesus."

"Don't get bent, bro. I'm not here to come back. She called me, said she had to talk. I still got keys so I let myself in."

"Talk? About what?"

Mac poked a fist into his stomach, paused as if expecting another belch, and, when none was forthcoming, cocked his head in resignation. "I don't know. She called me at work today, told me *urp!* ah, there it is. Pardon me. She told me she'd been to the doctor, had some news."

"Like?" It was hot in there. It was probably just me.

"Like, I don't know. But she's either dying or preggo and neither is cool. You want something to read?" Mac tossed a magazine at me—one of the political journals on the coffee table. "Here, you take it. I don't need it anymore. You'll be quizzed later."

"Yeah." I grimaced and looked at the magazine. THOUSANDS DEMAND END TO U.S. WAR MACHINE, read the headline. Surely impartial and reasoned thought lay within. "So. When was the last time you two, ah, you know?"

"Hey. I take the fifth."

The front door banged open; there was a rustle of packages, jingling keys. "Hello?" Sarah said from the door, and she pushed it open. She saw Mac standing in the middle of the room, and she smiled; he tipped his head down to me.

"Round two," he said.

Her eyes widened. "Oh," she said. "Oh, my."

" 'S all right," I said. "I'm going. I was in the neighborhood. Stopped by to check up on you and little Zy and saw Funboy here let himself in."

"I'm fine."

"What is he doing here, Sarah?"

"That's private, Jay."

"Oh, wonderful. Something with my chin and nose is taking form in your womb and you have secrets from me."

"Holy shit," said Mac. "Don't tell me you're—"

"You tell me what she tells you," I said to Mac. I stood up and walked to the door.

"Wait!" said Sarah. "I'll call you. Where are you going to be?"

"Afghanistan. Call collect."

I slammed the door, stomped off down the hall, tiptoed back and listened. I heard nothing, thanks to a neighbor's stereo. I went back to the truck. I drove home, showered, crawled into bed, lay there staring at the ceiling. Around eight I put my clothes on, climbed in the Pacer and pointed it at the one place in the world where I finally belonged.

"I don't get it. She's pregnant by both of you? She's going to have twins?"

"You're not paying attention," I said. "And will you pass the ashtray?"

"I already did. It's right there in front of you." I looked down. So it was.

"I am aware of that," I said. "Bartender? Will you give me another whiskey on the doubles."

"You sure?" said my best friend in the world, whose name had escaped me. "You've had—"

"I am not sure," I said. "Hence another will convince me one way or the other."

"You talk like you're an actor or something."

"I am neither." I drained my drink. "I'm just cleaning my plate, verbally speaking. Eating my vegetables." Vegetables. Fresh fruit, juices. "Eat vegetables," I said, one finger up to indicate sage advice.

"You speak any other lingos?"

"Yes." I closed my eyes. "Elanay ezzomay eladay ammincay eladay ostranay itavay."

"Sounds Chinese."

"It is the opening verse of Dante's *Inferno* in pig latin." Another drink was set before me on a small pink napkin with the Jolly's logo. "Is this for me?" The bartender nodded and I thanked him. "Have you read Dante?" I said to my friend.

"No."

"It's about a man who gets a tour of hell and finds it is comprised almost entirely of Italians of the wrong political party. Follow me so far?"

"You lost me back when your girl was pregnant in two different directions."

"No, no. I seemed to have gotten her pregnant, but she called her old boyfriend over to tell him about it, and I ask why. Did he have a hand in this?"

"I'd say he had more than a hand."

"Can I ask you guys something?" said the bartender. "It's none of my business, but why come in here, pay a cover and drink at these prices when you don't watch the strippers?"

"I was looking for someone," I said.

"And he has found him." My friend smiled.

But this man was not the one for whom I was looking. That was the little man with the trunk. I felt fear surge in my body, trying to pare the gristle of the liquor off my brain.

"You're Jared, aren't you."

"Jared? My name is Mike."

"You don't poison people, I suppose, do you?"

"What are you talking about?"

"What was that about finding someone, about me . . . being . . . found?"

"Would you like to go to another bar and forget all this pregnancy stuff?"

Now I looked at him with suspicion. "This wouldn't be a bar without . . . without . . . women."

He smiled. "There are some who come close, depending on the lighting."

I was aghast. "Are you trying to pick me up?" He nodded, shrugged, smiled. "Well, no. No, sir. No. What the hell are you doing, trying to pick up men of your . . . your ilk . . . here?"

"I like to be turned down." He was silent for a while. "I used to pay prostitutes to refuse to have sex with me."

"I think you'd better leave."

"But we're having a nice time."

"Leave or I take you up on your offer." He put his palms out, backed off his stool and took a spot farther down the bar.

I spent the next half hour sipping my drink and watching to make sure my friend did not return. He was trying to make conversation with a burly man with a T-shirt that read League of Doom.

"Got a light there, son?" said a voice to my right. I pushed my matches over.

"Hey, Manny," said the bartender. "Who's home tonight?"

"It's just old Manny himself," said the voice to my right. "About time, too." I looked.

The man at the bar may or may not have sold shoes. There was a trunk at his feet. His round eyes, set behind heavy black glasses, stared with awe at the stripper on the runway behind us. He turned to the bartender and said, "Wonder if she washes that money off before she spends it."

"Sold any shoes lately?" I said.

He looked at me as though trying to recall my face. "You have the wrong man."

"Things turn out all right with that woman who kicked you out?"

His face softened. "No, you got the right guy." He sighed. "So tell me. How much do I owe you?"

"You don't owe me a penny."

"I don't? You met two of me and neither of us hit you up for scratch? Shoes, huh. That'd have been Billy. He'd sell coasters to an amputee, that one. You're lucky."

"I'm confused."

"You're confused! I'm a multiple personality, son. Think how I feel." He turned back to his drink.

I made an involuntary check of the distance between myself and the door. Then: "Can we go sit and talk? I have to talk to you."

"Buy me a drink?"

I nodded and ordered a cup of coffee and another of whatever he was having. I helped the little man off his stool and watched him drag his trunk over to a table. "So. You want my life story, that it?" he said.

"That's not necessary, no. What I want is—"

" 'Cause I got about seven of 'em. I'm not crazy. I want to say that up front. See, you ever get those *Reader's Digest* Condensed Books? One book, got five stories all shrunk down like?"

"Sure."

"Okay, if someone gave you a book and said there was seven stories in it, you wouldn't think they was crazy, now would you?"

"No. It's called an anthology. Where are we going with this?"

"An anthology? Huh." He smiled. "Medical terms, they all sound alike to me. Whatever it is that I got, I got it bad. Technically I guess I am, what, crazy. Except that I'm always sane. See, there are six more people up here"—he pointed to his head—"plus me. Allow me to introduce ourselves. Manny Perlstein, the original article." We shook. "Now, can I ask maybe why you want to know?"

"That can wait," I said. "You have six more personalities in your brain?"

"That I know of, yeah. See, five years ago, I'm just like any other joe. Then my head, it starts turning into this party line, and I don't recognize any of the voices. I realize I got company up here. I go to the doc. Doctors. Feh." He looked away. "He doesn't know the how or why, he gives me drugs, fine. But the drugs make me sick. I can't drink and I can't get it up on these things either, so I quit. Back come the voices. The more I get to know the freeloaders, the more I kinda like 'em. Some of them."

"Describe them." I wished I were Marya, with her tape-recorder brain.

Manny chuckled. "So far, besides me, there's Billy, who you

met. Good man but no ambition. No sense. This job, that job, never getting serious. I worry. Then there's Irving." He smiled with pride. "Irving's the one with talent. People tell me he plays piano so sweet you should die, so you never hear worse. There's Esther—"

"You have a woman in there with you?"

"As God is my witness, I swear. Esther." He sighed. "One of those people with just a grudge against life. She'll never be happy. Thinks everyone is out to get her, too. Paranoid, they call it. If there's someone who needs treatment, it's her, not me. She's jealous nowadays, too."

"Of what?"

"Of nothing. There's this TV newswoman. Did a story on me awhile ago. Bobbi Parker. You seen her? Yeah, well, a looker, that kid. I watch her every night. Face like an angel. Irving is sort of sweet on her too."

"So Esther is jealous because, what, she's not as pretty as—"

"Esther is in love with Irving. Absolutely mad with jealousy. In dread I live of waking up and finding she took a penknife to the old shwanz." He shuddered. "Then there's Ken. Goyim. Doesn't come around much. We're lucky if we hear from him on holidays." He shook his head, then scowled. "There's Jacky, you met him too, ladies' man. Shallow but always a day brightener, that boy. And last there is Saul. The worst. Meshugge. Real JDL material. Always with the 'imperialist' this, the 'borschwah' that. All of us live in fear we should find ourselves in a jail cell or dead because of him. Be thankful him you never met."

I didn't say anything. I just looked at Manny. He shrugged, picked up his drink and spanked an ice cube into his mouth.

"You're kidding me, aren't you."

"No!" He bent down and picked up his trunk, placed it on a nearby chair. "Lookit." He opened the case to reveal a jumble of personal belongings, looking as though they had been collected at random from the wreck of a plane. Makeup cases, wigs, toilet bags, books, glasses, vials of pills. "Would I shlep this around if I didn't have to?" He held up a bag containing syringes and a bottle. "I hate needles. But Jacky is a diabetic, so, waddya going to do? These glasses here are Irving's, him and me we got different corrections. Esther wears contacts, 'cause she thinks glasses make her fat. This . . ." He held up a sketchbook, opened it to reveal landscapes and portraits done in a fairly accomplished hand. "Irving's. I can't draw a straight line. Not bad, eh?"

"Why don't you get help? You like living this way?"

He shrugged. "We get along. Sure, some fights, but what family doesn't? And I'm never alone on holidays." He paused. "Now can I ask you why you want to know? Not like I don't like talking, as you can maybe tell. But you and I are mixed up somehow. I can feel it."

"Billy—that's the shoe salesman? Right. Billy was here the night a friend of mine died."

"I'm sorry to hear it. Billy didn't tell me. Nobody tells me anything sometimes."

"Well, Billy said that—" I stopped. God, I was stupid. Saul is the crazy one, JDL, "imperialist" this. It fit, just rough enough to be convincing. "Manny, this is important. Real important. Billy looked at my friend and said this is Jared's work. Does that name sound familiar?"

"Sure it does. Jared's my brother."

I drew in my breath. I felt my knees start to bang together. "He's your brother? Why haven't you gone to the police and told them?"

"Tell them what? That I have a brother in Topeka who's an undertaker? Why should they care?"

"He's a what?"

"Mortician. Dresses stiffs, no disrespect to your friend intended."

"Different Jared." Or so I hoped. I felt the promise start to seep out of the interview. "There's a guy in this town who heads a ring of food terrorists and his name is Jared. Haven't you read the papers?"

"Who needs 'em? Listen, if Billy looks at a dead guy, no disrepect intended, and he says it's Jared's work, he's probably thinking he should get into a line with steady work." He looked at his watch. "It's getting late. Almost time for the news. Bobbi is doing the, what, anchor this week."

"Manny, listen. Saul. The crazy one. Is he up to something you don't want to talk about it? Does everyone up there know what everyone else is doing?"

"They all know except me. From me they keep secrets. And if Saul is in trouble I don't want to know. If I know about it I worry, and when I worry I lose my place. See, we take turns, nice and orderly, but when I lose my cool, it's anything goes. Let me tell you a story. Awhile back I was having problems with the old bladder. Thought

I was going to have to have it taken out. Worried all the time. Irving, who's a hypochondriac—"

"Did he go to the hospital after Thanksgiving because he thought he'd eaten bleach?"

Manny stared at me. "Yeah. Yeah, he did. How'd you know that?"

"Never mind. Go on."

"Yeah. Well. I was thinking so much about the bladder business that Saul just took over, 'cause he's the strongest of the bunch. I come to and I'm in this basement with three other guys, and they're all looking at me. And I look in my hands and what do I see? A bomb I see. I'm no expert but I see a clock with wires going into this putty stuff and I know these ain't Santa's elves I'm sitting around with. I don't know if I'm supposed to be takin' it apart or puttin' it together. So I close my eyes and pray to God. I mean, He in His wisdom gave me this case of anthology. I pray for Saul to come back. He does. Next thing I know I'm sittin' in a plane. I got a ticket in my pocket with Esther's name on it. I got a wig and I got eyeshadow on, blue. Not to be cruel, but the girl don't know from subtle. And I got five o'clock shadow. There's a paper on the seat next to me, says a bomb went off in some airline office. So I know, trouble. Look, friend, it's all I can do to keep a tight leash on Saul. He's showing up more often than we'd like as it is. Don't tell me anything that's going to make us worry."

"Manny, come on. This is serious. Billy meant a different Jared and you know it. I doubt you even have a brother in Topeka." I paused. "Can you let me talk to Billy?"

"Yeah."

"You can do that? Just let the others come in?"

"Takes practice. But if I can't get cooperation from my own head, where'm I going to get it? The others, they respect me. They know it's my name on the lease. They get too outta line, I go downtown, get some of those tranquilizers that make you stare at the floor for a week and poof, everybody outta the pool. Esther in particular is terrified of this, 'cause she watches a soap. Scared I'll go in for treatment and she'll miss her show. But Saul." He made fists. "Hogs the stage. Wants everyone out. Oh, the arguments." He put his hands to his head. "There's enough voices in my head sometimes to really drive me crazy."

"You have to let me talk to Billy."

"I can't."

"You said you could."

"I can, but I won't. Listen, friend. You're a good boy. I don't want to get you mixed up in anything. Not that I know if there's anything for you to get mixed up in. But just in case. Stay out."

"I'm already in pretty damn deep, Manny. If Saul is one of these bastards he's already made threats on my life. Let me talk to Billy."

"I don't know. I just don't—oh. Oh. Oh." Manny put his hands on his temples. "Oh. Oh. Oh. No. Not now. Not now." He stood, staggering back, knocking over his chair. "Saul," he gasped. "All this talk. He's on the way."

"Saul? Coming now? I got to talk to him."

"Get lost," he gasped. "I have a gun in the trunk there and I swear to God he'll use it."

I grabbed the napkin on the table and scrawled my phone number. "Manny. Here. Remember this. Call me. You've got to call me."

"We'll *ah!* have a coffee someday. *Ah!* Go. Get outta here. *Ah!*" His shoulders were hunched against some private wind, his face wrinkled, his eyes crinkled with effort—then his shoulders relaxed and his head lolled back and rolled left and right. His hands went slowly to his face and took off his glasses. He looked ten years younger; his eyes were bright and sharp. I sat wordless in my chair, unable to move.

"Manny?"

He shook his head, slowly, grinning. "Manny can't come to the phone right now, but if you'd like to leave a message?"

"Billy?"

His brow darkened. One hand went beneath the table. "I am Saul. I don't think we've met in person. Mr. Simpson."

I stood, knocked my chair over and backed away.

"I know what you're thinking. Go ahead. Call the police." He smiled. "I'll sit here and wait. I can't guarantee they won't find Esther here when they arrive, though. But go ahead, call them. You want to."

"You're AIL. You're probably Jared."

He shook his head.

"A close personal friend of his, yes, but no, I'm not Jared. As that impostor Manny might say, what's the point of your multiple personalities taking assumed identities?"

"Impostor?"

"I was here first. And I'll be here last."

"You son of a bitch. You put the poison in the brownies."

"As I said. Call the cops. It's what you want to do." He smiled.

Sure. They would find Esther or Irving or someone, Saul hiding deep behind the others. But I had this bastard right in front of me, grinning, sitting right where Lou had gotten it. This was too much. I stood and raised my fist, cocked it back. Saul's eyes grew wide and I let it fly—

A hand wrapped around my wrist and checked my swing. I turned.

"You." The bartender. "Out."

"What, me?"

"You. I remember you. You were with the guy who bought it that night from the brownie. And now you're playing with poor Manny, and he's three of our best customers. Out. And I don't ever want to see you in here again. Get out before I call the cops."

"I'll be back," I said, "and back with the cops. That man—" I pointed to Saul, who now had opened the trunk and was fitting a wig over his—hers?—head. "That man is one of the people who poisoned my—"

"*Get out!*" There was a hand on my shoulder. And another on the nape of my neck. I craned my head around to see a bouncer with a brow you could set a row of books on. He pulled me backward and deposited me outside, shook his finger at me. I lunged back for the door; he put a hand in my chest and it felt like a log fired from a bazooka. I coughed and screamed, "Saul! I'll find you, you bastard! I'll be back! I'll be—" The bouncer gave me a shove and I fell backward, right onto my tailbone. Just like old times.

When the pain had diminished I stood and hobbled, bent over, both hands on the small of my back, to my car. On the way I passed the man who had been my friend, standing on the corner in front of one of the adult book stores.

"Want some company?" he said, his voice tight.

"Go to hell and stay there."

"Thank you," he said, smiling with relief. "You remembered."

14

Grue gave me a stern look when I dropped into my chair.

"You did too much drinking last night, eh?"

It was the most grammatically precise construction I had ever heard flow from her mouth. I was hung over; I was hearing things.

"Mm-hmm. Give me some orange juice and some coffee and toast and eggs. And then more coffee." I dragged the paper across the table. MARYA GETS A BETTER STORY THAN YOU DO, read one headline. MAC TO RAISE YOUR CHILD, said another. No, no. Not that it would even have been news. The front page was full of death in strange places, gun battles disturbing fragile truces, downed jets in troubled regions, an earthquake in a country heretofore ignored but now famous for its death toll. It all made me feel a little better, and I turned to the metro section.

POISON THREATS MAKE MUNCO STOCK TAKE STEEP DIVE, said a head. I read on. The gist of the article was that the stock of Munco, or the Munson Grain Company, was taking a steep dive due to poison threats. The stock had dropped thirty points in the last two weeks, about 50 percent of its value; people were selling as though the shares themselves were dusted with toxins. The company had acted like a normal company and issued the standard assurances; naturally the shareholders were spooked. Heavier trading was expected today.

Breakfast was delicious, sent straight from heaven. Grue's eggs, as usual, contained liberal amounts of shells, but the juice was ambrosia and the coffee pure hot medicine. I felt so good I had a cigarette. That set off the artillery in my head again and I went upstairs to eat a handful of aspirin. Then, squinting from the noise, I picked up a fresh razor and dragged it with shaking hand over several major arteries.

"Your face," Grue said when I came downstairs. I was wearing a roll of toilet paper, torn into scraps, stuck on various wounds.

"I know," I said. "And I use an electric." I steadied myself on the banister. "Listen. The exterminators are coming today."

"So yesterday you said. Time is high that they should come."

I smiled. "I love it when you use idioms."

"Two days ago a rat this big I hear." She gripped her forearm.

"You heard it? Didn't you see it?"

"No. But to make as much noise this big it would have to be."

"Right. Well, have them do the attic. That's where I hear them at night. Right over the bed."

"I will. Aren't you going to be here?"

I rubbed my temples. "To do I have things."

Grue looked at me as though I were speaking a strange tongue.

I went up to the office, just to see if anything was happening. It was not. Fikes ambled past me in the hall on the way to lunch; he had on gray silk trousers, a gray broadcloth shirt with a black linen tie—and sneakers, laces trailing. He gave me a dreamy hello and floated down to the elevator, whistling a melody that would have sounded at home in a calliope.

Daphne looked up as I entered and looked back down again.

"Lawyers looking for you this morning."

"What kind?"

"White-males-with-briefcase kind. Only kind they make in this town." She reached over and drew a sheet of paper from my box, read it. "The firm of blahblahblah, representing—there's a whole bunch of names here—from Valhalla. This mean anything?" She handed me the paper. I read it. Gunderwein, Salmon, Marston, all the old familiar names.

"I wondered when they were going to get around to naming me." I looked at the paper again; it was from the firm representing the *Lacs Standard*. Lou Carver was named as one of the defendants.

"What does it mean?" Daphne said.

"Ruination and shame, that's all."

"Oh." She looked back to her newspaper.

I headed down the hall to the newsroom, to the small and empty cubicle I had been allotted. I sat down and rolled my head back, mouth open to let the evil spirits out. Then I called the police and asked for Bishop.

"Bishop," he said.

"I met a little man from the AIL," I said.

Silence. "Sounds like the first line of a bad limerick," he finally said. "This man wouldn't happen to have a name."

"Many of them, but there's only one you need to know."

"Now hold on here. You got me interested. Let me take this down. You met this guy how, now?"

"At a strip joint downtown. It's a long story. The only thing you need to know about it is the name Saul Perlstein."

"Little guy? Can't tell how old he is by looking? Sort of stooped over?"

"That's him! You already on him?"

Bishop laughed. "You could say that, yeah. Saul, or Bart as we call him around here, is one of those perpetual confessors. Everytime someone whacks someone or knocks over a bank, Bart shows up and spills. Harmless guy, but Christ, kid, he's nuts. Came in here the other day with a wig on and blue eye makeup, told us there was a guy in his head named Saul who was mixed up in this poison stuff. We just listen and nod and send him on his way. That what you called to tell me?"

"Uh, yeah." I had an unlit cigarette in one hand and was shredding it into paper and crumbs. "Thought you'd, ah, get a laugh."

"Oh, yeah, I'm just beside myself here."

"Sorry to bother you."

"Apology accepted." The line went dead.

Manny hadn't said anything about Bart. He'd said there were six people in his head. Saul, Esther, Irving, Ken, Jacky, Billy. He'd left out Bart. Why?

Of course Bishop didn't believe me. He'd never met Manny.

I had to check this out. Perhaps the Public Health Department would know something. I put my coat on and left the office; Daphne was still reading her paper when I passed.

"You look like you're having a rough day," she said.

"How can you tell?"

"You have a face full of toilet paper." She looked up at me. "And besides, lawyers and all. You know."

"Well, you're right."

"I think you ought to come out with me tonight."

"You do. You do?"

"Yeah." Her eyes narrowed and she smiled a little. "Dance."

I felt my shoulders relax and the muscles around my brain unclench. "Sounds fun," I said. "Daphne, I'd love to go out with you tonight."

"Good." She nodded and went back to her paper.

"First, I want to go back to my place," Daphne said. "Take a bath. Scrub off the fake air and fake light."

"That's fine." We were taking her car. It was a foreign number imported from the Eastern bloc, small enough so that if parking was a problem you could just attach it to your charm bracelet and wear it. Riding in it I realized why none of the people in Eastern Europe ever get up the speed to crash through the border posts. Daphne handled the car with expert ability, her long, slim body cupped in the seat, feet performing intricate choreography on the pedals, one hand wrestling the wheel, the other persuading a balky gearbox to do just what she wanted. I watched her, wishing she had more hair. But she was pretty cute without it.

"So how did you*aaaaa*!" A truck had poked its nose into the intersection, and Daphne shifted, slammed down a pedal and squirted the car into the next lane, around the truck.

"How did I what?"

"Come to work at the *Metropole*. I mean, why are you working there?"

She shrugged. "Money. Pays some bills. I go to night school. Only day jobs are waitressing or"—she gave a humorless smile—"being a receptionista. And since I got"—she yanked back the shift stick, brought the car screeching to the stoplight—"fired from my last waitress job, I took that as a sign."

"What, that you shouldn't waitress?"

"That I shouldn't pour coffee in the laps of people who harass me."

"You didn't."

"I did, and more. There was this one guy. Utterly gross, a local slumlord. Gave capitalism a bad name."

"You like capitalism?"

"Don't you?"

"No, I love it. Fits my life-style. But I thought with your haircut you'd, ah, hate capitalism."

Daphne gave me the first honest grin I'd ever seen her make. "Lot of people think so. I own too many stocks to hate capitalism."

She swung down Franklin toward Lake of the Isles. "Anyway, this landlord. Nothing was ever good enough. Used to ask for his pie hot. He'd stick a finger in it to see if it was hot enough. Sent it back every time. One day I put it in the microwave for a good ten minutes. Thing was like a nuclear fuel rod."

"And?"

"And he stuck his finger in it and screamed and howled like he'd been burned. Which, I guess, he was."

"And?"

"And when he started yelling at me, saying I was a careless broad, I poured coffee in his lap."

"And they fired you."

"Yes. With regret."

"So how did you end up at the *Metropole*?"

"Job was open and I took it." She smiled. "I like to be out in the world. I'm a people person."

Daphne lived in an apartment building up the street from the lakes, an old building, vaguely Moorish in ornamentation. A lobby smelling of mothballs—"Keeps out the bats," Daphne explained—led into a hallway paved with flagstones, lined with faded terra-cotta friezes. Two fluted columns faced her door. She unlocked the door, waved me in.

Her apartment was roughly the size of Delaware. The living room was sparsely furnished—a low gray sofa covered in leather, bowl lamps in each corner, a vase on a heavy marble pedestal. One wall was given over to books. I followed her into the dining room. She threw her keys on a table consisting of a thick sheet of glass sitting on two black marble cylinders. "Something to drink?" she said. "It's all in the fridge." She vanished down a hallway the length of a bowling alley, humming. I opened the refrigerator to find half a dozen bottles of champagne, dozens of tins of various comestibles with foreign labels, a bin full of fresh vegetables, five bottles of French spring water.

"Get me a beer, will you?" she called from the next room.

There was a six-pack in the back. I took two and popped them open.

She came out of the bedroom in a towel. Not a large towel, either. She leaned against the doorframe, one hand on her breastbone, holding up the towel, the other outstretched for the beer. I gave it to her, raised mine in a toast and leaned back against the refrigerator.

"Why don't you take your shower? I'll just read a magazine or something."

"Want to take one with me?"

"Sure. I'll just be here— What did you say?"

"Want to take a shower with me?"

"Yes."

Well, I did. Daphne on close examination was pretty, in a somewhat severe and terrifyingly grave way; she also had wonderful legs and a figure as lithe as a bullwhip, and this, this was not bad, not bad at all. A check in the mail from a contest I didn't even recall entering.

"Okay. Come on."

We went into the bathroom. The shower was a circular stall in the corner; a claw-footed bath sat along the wall. Daphne adjusted the water, talking from inside the shower. "I figure we might as well do this first, right? I mean we go out, drink, dance. Get all beat and sloppy. More fun when you're fresh. Why aren't you taking your clothes off?"

I obeyed. She peeled the towel from her body and laid it over the top of the stall, stood under the stream and turned her face to the water. I stepped into the shower, my self-consciousness feeling like a fat red horn sticking from my forehead. Here I was, naked with a tall wet woman whose last name I didn't know. If there was a bruiser like Mac in her life and he chose this moment to drop by, I wouldn't be able to explain this one away. I'm the plumber. Yes, I'm the plumber, and I'm a nudist.

Daphne took a sponge, poured a ribbon of something blue and fragrant on it and began to scrub my chest. Slow, circular motions. I could feel the horn screw back into my head. She brought the sponge around my neck, my shoulders. Back across my chest. The sponge was scratchy, the suds warm and slippery. She rubbed it across my hipbones, hard, first left, then right.

"Turn around." She pushed me slowly against the wall of the shower, rubbed the sponge under my shoulder blades. I could feel her knuckles driving into my skin, kneading the discs of my spine, all the way down to my tailbone, which could use the friendly attention.

Then a warm hand slipped around my stomach and she pressed her body to my back. Lips nuzzled my neck; a long hot tongue slid up my neck and explored my ear. Teeth bit my earlobe and two hands gripped my hips and pulled me against her, then released me.

"Turn around again."

I hadn't thought about it before, but if you're going to make love in the shower, you can't do better than a circular stall. There's no place to brace yourself in a rectangular shower. Here there was no chance of slipping and dashing out your brain on the edge of the tub. I slid down, legs stiff, and braced my back against the wall; Daphne did the same. She eased herself onto me, eased me into her. Her arms were above me, holding on to a rack in the shower; she rose and fell without touching any more of me than was required. When she started clenching her teeth and taking racking, shallow gasps, she leaned over and put her lips to mine, placed her tongue on mine and shuddered. And relaxed. She rode me until I got a good hold on the brass ring and yanked it in, and then she gave me another kiss, barely grazing my lips.

She stood up, shook her head under the stream of water, drew back the shower curtain and stepped out.

I slid down to the floor, let the hot water pound down on me for a while. Then I got out of the shower and took a towel, wrapped it around my waist. I tamed my hair with a comb and started dressing.

Daphne was standing in the kitchen with her beer, lighting a cigarette. "You didn't have to leave just because I did."

"So I'm a romantic."

She smiled. "You capitalists."

"No. Really." I sat down and took my beer. It was still cold and bubbly. "That was, ah, different. Nice. 'Course, I'm used to touching one another during it all, but I'm spoiled."

"Well, I liked it. I'm going to dress. But keep talking. I can hear from my bedroom." She went down the hall again.

"How do you afford this on a receptionist's salary?"

"Trust fund," she shouted. "Wealthy papa. Pays for rent and school and I pay for living expenses. When I turn twenty-one the really big money kicks in. But who's waiting."

Twenty-one? I thought I outweighed this woman by a year at most.

"He pay for the furniture?"

"That stuff? That's cast-off from home."

She came out in black tights, a black leather skirt and a tight black T-shirt. There was a belt made of spent bullet cartridges slung low on her waist. She looked around the room, grabbed a spray can and ducked into the bathroom. A few seconds later she came out with a purple slash painted across her head, a splash of yellow on one cheek. She had a cosmetic case in one hand, and she regarded her face with no expression, pursing her lips.

I adjusted my tie. "Where, uh, are we going?"

"I don't know. Bowhouse maybe."

"What's it like?"

She smeared another gash of war paint across her cheek.

"Don't worry." She snapped the case shut. "It's different. But you'll have a good time there, too." She leaned on the word *there*, implying I'd had a good time here. And I had.

I stood, a passenger in my own life again, and held the door open for her. She cocked a hip into my groin as she passed, and she winked.

The Bowhouse was located in the warehouse district, around the corner from the Room in a no-man's-land not even the artists dared to colonize. You had to know it was there. The building was old and abandoned; a faded sign on the side said GRIP-R-TITE UNDERWEAR. One got into the Bowhouse by way of a set of wooden steps leading up to a loading dock. There were a few patrons leaning up against the wall, taking in the night air, letting it out mixed with laughter and liberal profanities. Daphne took me by the hand and dragged me protesting across the dock.

She opened the door and a hot, thick wave of noise and smell poured out, the splatter and blast of the band mingling with the acrid tang of alcoholic sweat and spilled liquor. The noise was such that you needed a megaphone to hear yourself think; it sounded as though the guitarist were playing his instrument with a cheese grater. Every hair on my body stood on tiptoe.

We were immediately met by a bouncer, bald, impassive and probably deaf. He stamped our hands with a rubber stamp that read CANCELED and thumbed us inside. He tapped Daphne as she passed, jerked his head toward me and raised an eyebrow. She looked at me, arms akimbo, and nodded. Then she took me by the hand again and hauled me down a hallway to the right, into a room marked FEM.

"No, no, this is the—"

"Yeah, yeah. No one'll care." Inside there was an inert young man slumped against a corner, sleeping or decomposing. The two stalls were occupied, but with many multiples of feet; a hand-lettered sign on the wall read OCCUPANCY OF THESE STALLS BY MORE THAN 6 PEOPLE IS ILLEGAL. There was the usual snorting and giggling from the stalls. Daphne turned me in front of a mirror cracked and spattered with unthinkable substances, phone numbers, slogans and names of bands written around its perimeters. "We have to do something about your look. I don't know what I was thinking."

"Maybe you were blinded by love."

"The hair first." She put her hand under the soap dispenser, squirted out a palmful of pink goo and slapped it on my head. I just groaned; there was nothing to do about it. She spread the stuff around my head and thrashed my hair with great vigor. The result looked as though I had been bathing in an oil slick when a gale came up. "Ace. Now. Shirt. Take it off and put it on backwards."

"Backwards? Forget it."

"You're going to look like an accountant in there if you don't do what I say. Come on. I want you to have fun. Not be so self-conscious like you always are."

God help me, I did as she said, wondering just where in her apartment I had left my will.

Daphne buttoned the shirt up the back, turned the collar up around my neck, regarded me in the mirror, and told me to don my jacket. I shoved the sleeves up, started tucking in the tails of the shirt.

"No. Leave them out." I complied. "God, this is perfect." She shoved my tie in a jacket pocket. "I don't know why no one ever thought of this. Come on. Let's dance."

We left the room, passed a door marked OHMS. "Come on in here," I shouted over the noise, pointing to the door. "I want to dress you in a strapless formal with white gloves."

"Can I still wear the bullets?" She grinned.

"Sure. The Deb with a Beef look."

A young woman dressed in torn fishnet stockings, and a torn black T-shirt, all swaddled with dingy lace, passed us and looked me up and down. "That's a look," she said, and she went into the OHMS room.

"You pass," Daphne said, smiling with pride.

We got a drink at a bar made of a plank of wood placed on two blinking sawhorses appropriated from some construction site with lax security. They had three drinks—beer, gin, and beer and gin, the last going by the name of an Anarchy Cordial. I ordered two and stood sipping mine, looking around. From the bar I had a glimpse of the club beyond, a quick whiff of hell. Most of the patrons had their hair in spikes and whorls and swirls glued stiff; the club was dark as pitch, and paved with it as well, from the way my shoes were adhering to the floor. Lights made erratic stabs onto a sea of bobbing dancers. The band was thrashing away at one end, making a sound like jumbo jets competing for mating rights. Occasionally someone would mount the stage and dive into the crowd, arms spread, mouth agape in blind manic glee. The crowd would absorb him, close around him; once it bore a diver aloft, passing him overhead and depositing him on the floor by the bar. He leaped up, wobbling like a top in its final spins, staggered to the bar and requested a Cordial.

"Wanna dance?" Daphne yelled.

"Dance? I'm not setting foot out there without a suit of mail."

"Come on." She drained her drink, a double Cordial, and gestured for me to do the same. I leaned back and sipped. Then something grabbed my arm and yanked me forward, pulling me into the dancers; I looked and saw the young woman with the fishnet and lace.

"You're new here," she yelled.

"Sort of."

"Don't worry. Everything is going to be fun. What's your name?"

"Jonathan."

"Cool. Mine's Cassandra."

She started bouncing up and down in movements that, in any other context, would have made me look around for a pencil to put in her mouth to keep her from swallowing her tongue. I bounced halfheartedly. Cassandra stuck her arms in the air, brought them down around my neck, looked deep into my eyes and slammed her forehead into mine.

"Jesus!" I screamed. A red scrim punctuated with flashes of yellow fell in front of my eyes, and I staggered back.

"You're cute," she said. "I like you."

"Like me a little less!" I shouted. Something pale and vast with teeth like an old fence hauled me off my feet by my lapels and asked what the hell did I think I was doing with his lady, anyway? "Doing? She hit me in the head!"

"Don't make it worse on yourself," he yelled, and he shoved me into the crowd toward the stage. I was caught in the crowd, claustrophobia bolting up my throat again. I began clawing through the crowd to the high ground of the stage. The crowd opened and closed around me, working me out like something foreign and indigestible. Someone rolled under the stage, buckling my knees; I grabbed the edge of the stage to support myself, and started to climb up, swinging one leg on stage, then two. The singer looked at me with no great affection and swung the mike stand away from him and started shouting at me, banging his chest in challenge. "Jump," cried a dozen. Then more. Then everyone. I looked left and right; there were no exits; the stage ran right to the wall. On the other side of the club I saw something tall, a light picking up the purple and yellow of her face. Daphne crooked her finger. I put my faith in God, not that He hung out in places like this, and leaped into the crowd.

They bore me hand over hand, palms and fingers poking into my stomach. And there was cold cement at the end of this. I felt weightless one second, heavy as iron the next, sinking into the flaccid grasp of a group that let me dip down, bang my head on their shoulders and end up facing the ceiling, my feet being pulled along by the next clump of dancers. It took eight hours to make the journey. I was somehow facedown when I reached the end of the dance floor; someone spun me around and let me roll off his shoulder, and I went facedown into the concrete.

At least, I thought distractedly, I won't ruin the front of my shirt.

"You all right?" said Daphne in my ear. "I—"

Then I was standing, thanks to whoever had picked me up. I heard Daphne say something; I didn't hear what. I saw the floor moving below me, and since my feet had reported in as inert, I gathered I was being dragged somewhere. I went along for the ride. I was being taken for fresh air and restoration. They knew I was new at this. They were going to make sure I was okay. Whoever was dragging me along, I loved them.

The noise receded. Oh, even better. My feet banged on the frame of a door; it felt interesting. I went up stairs somehow. Then cool air hit me straight in the face, as sharp and bracing as falling into a plate-glass window. I was back at the Room. Sarah was pregnant. Then my toes were dragged across metal, down stairs. I heard a car.

"I have to go see Sarah," I said. "She's having the child. Not Marya. Although don't I wish." Something stirred in my viscera, and all of a sudden I felt as though I had swallowed several of those wet napkins that come in little packets. "I have to see Marya and give her a child."

"Oh, no," said a voice, not Daphne's. "You're going elsewhere, friend. You're going to see Jared."

15

Terror makes you sober. I was put in a car, shoved into the backseat. I got one look at the two individuals who had requisitioned me for the evening: both wore nylon stockings over their face; their features looked like melted candles. One of them, I noted abstractedly, had imitation pearls and a diamond pattern sewn into his. Then something heavy and scratchy was pulled over my face, down to my chin, and the car pulled away.

"Sit there and don't try anything," said a voice to my left. I nodded.

I was thinking clearly and hating what I thought. This wasn't good, no. You didn't haul someone out of a bar and obscure their cognitive faculties if you were taking them to a Tupperware party. I suppose I ought to have been excited; if there was not hideous death at the end of this, I would have a hell of a story. If there was hideous death, Marya would have a great story. I SLEPT WITH HIM BEFORE HIS TRAGIC DEATH, SAYS REDHEAD WITH TREMENDOUS FIGURE.

The car accelerated, rose; we were traveling up one of the I-94 ramps in the warehouse district. No other place this close could you go this fast. I sat back and counted the exits. We wouldn't be speeding; no sense in risking a ticket when you have someone shanghaied and muzzled in the backseat. The first exit was Broadway, two miles up. I counted to a hundred and twenty, sixty seconds for each mile. There were only two more exits, Johnson and Fifty-fourth Street. We didn't take either. I felt the road curve off to the left, the swing of 94 meeting the belt line. The first exit was what, Shingle Creek Parkway, four lanes across on the other side of the highway? The car swung to the right and sailed up in a gentle curve. Okay. I tried to remember what came next. The car coasted right again, made a graceful arc down, and, if I was right, was headed south again. This whole thing was to throw me off, then.

We slowed; I heard brakes squeal, then relax as the engine roared again. That would be the driver making the yellow on the light on the ramp back into downtown, right by the Room. Ahead was Hennepin, and all the construction. We'd be slowing soon. One lane was ripped up and the street dipped a good foot and a half. But we weren't slowing down.

"Hey, there's a bump coming up here. You want to ruin your suspension?"

"Aw, Jesus," said a voice from the front seat. "Werther?"

"Right," said the voice to my left. And something hit me in the head. The world narrowed to a point, flickered and disappeared.

I woke up. It had been a bad dream; none of it had happened; I had dozed off while waiting for Daphne to get dressed. But how vivid a dream it had been, right down to the scratchy wool mask that was still over my face. I tried to take it off but something from the dream with pickles on its breath grabbed my hand and put it back in my lap.

"No you don't," he said.

It hurt to nod and I resolved on the spot never to do it again. My brain felt wet and lined with metal shards, and the spot where I had been beaned was one huge pink neon sign pulsing on and off.

"What are you going to do to me?"

"Pick your brains."

"Any particular implement you have in mind?"

I was in a chair. I wasn't tied to it. My feet weren't bound. Through the fibers of the mask I saw light, strong light. My nose was covered but my mouth was free. A car passed outside, and I realized my back was to a window. Certainly narrowed my location down: a room where I had my back to a window.

Scared? A bit. Rather a lot, really. If they had wanted to get rid of me I probably would have been lying facedown in a field, brains caved in, vital organs pureed. And why would they want to do away with me, anyway? Because I had lipped-off in print? I had no monopoly on that honor. Because I had suspected Spanks? Nonsense. Because I had met one of their number in a bar and confronted him? How would they know I hadn't gone to the police?

How would they have known I was at the Bowhouse—unless they were tailing me.

Oh. Oh, oh.

There was a hubbub, muted, sounding as though it came from

behind a door or wall. One voice was furious, the other pleading. Something hit the wall, a fist or a small head. Silence, then shouts again. More silence. A door slammed. Someone coughed. Pickles shook me by the shoulder and told me to pay attention here.

"Comfortable?" said a voice.

Manny's voice? No. "Who are you?"

"Call me Joe. I asked if you were comfortable."

"I have a headache," I said. "Pickles here slugged me en route."

"Pickles?" said Pickles.

"Sorry," Joe yawned. "I suppose you're wondering why we brought you here."

"Can't possibly wonder why," I said.

Another sigh. "Teach him some respect," said Joe. A fist or a canned ham slammed into my stomach.

They let me fall unimpeded to the floor. I fell on my side, hands digging into my stomach to keep it from bolting up my throat. No success. I emptied an Anarchy Cordial onto the floor. Pickles hauled me up by my collar and deposited me back in my chair. I coughed and spat.

"There are many ways you could be killed," Joe said. His voice had all the tone and life of fish eyes. "Many ways."

I felt my guts liquefy.

"I could feed you cyclamates. Remember cyclamates?"

I didn't answer.

"I asked you a question." The back of a hand smacked hard across my cheek. "Do you remember cyclamates?"

"Sweetener," I panted. "Banned by the government."

"That's right. But not before it was put on the market for people to eat. So perhaps I could feed you cyclamates until you get cancer."

"I'm not hungry."

Pickles whacked me in the face again. That was it, that was it. I was scared enough to shed my skin.

"Some BHT, perhaps, to make your liver swell? Maybe some polysorbate 80. The average American eats a hundred and fifty pounds of it in a lifetime. Do you know what happens when you take a life's dose all at once? No? Like to find out?"

I shook my head, bowed against the next blow. This time Pickles kicked me in the shin.

"Answer me."

"I don't want to find out."

"Of course not." Footsteps away from me, the creak of someone dropping into a chair. "Nobody wants to know. And they pay for their willful ignorance with clogged organs and dull eyes and rotten teeth and bad gums and death. Death! Death from tumors! You wonder why we have to resort to violence to tell people their habits are killing them? It's going to take a little indiscriminate terror to get these idiots to eat leafy greens! And you—" The chair creaked, feet hit the floor. "You. You deride us." Joe walked toward me, panting with fury.

"Hey," said Pickles. "Lighten up. I thought this was going to be an interview, huh? If he finds out that you—"

Joe sucked in his breath. Pickles clicked his tongue. Then someone hooked a foot on the leg of my chair and dumped me on the floor. I fell onto my hands and knees and stayed on the floor.

"All right," Joe said. "Interview it is. Go get the tape recorder. I'll get Sinclair."

Pickles walked away, came back and put something heavy on a table. He lifted me by the collar, just enough to let me stand of my own volition, and steered me forward a few feet. He placed the chair under me and patted me on the shoulders. I sat. I heard buttons depressed, and someone sat down across the table. Then a voice said, "Interview with Sinclair, deputy secretary of the Central Committee of the Pure Food League." Sinclair coughed. "All right, ask me questions."

"I thought I was going to talk to Jared."

"He's busy." The voice was quiet, untroubled.

"Busy? All this trouble and I don't get to talk to the head man?"

"No. You don't. Nobody does. I speak for the group in this capacity. Now, ask me questions."

"Aren't you afraid someone will recognize your voice from the tape?"

"It is designed to alter voices. Will you please ask a serious question?" No impatience in his voice.

"What happens if I take off this mask?"

"I'll kill you."

"The mask stays, then. Where are we?"

"Where do you think? An abandoned building in a bad part of town. Don't think of trying to find it. Trust me. You can't."

"What time is it?"

"Time? Ah . . . quarter after eleven."

"What is Jared's real name?"

"I'll do it through charades. Pity you have that mask on."

"Tell me about Jared, then. If he exists."

Sinclair drummed his fingers on the table. "Oh, he exists, all right. He's the head of this cell. And that's all I'll tell you. One of his geniuses is for assembling people who believe in the same thing and motivating them to action. Another is for privacy. Few of us have seen him. That way no one can betray anyone else. Next question."

Lou. Why did you kill Lou.

"How do you feel about causing the deaths of innocent people."

Pause. "There are no innocent people. Everyone is a participant in capitalism, willingly or by tacit compliance. The few who stand outside the system are not at risk from our efforts."

"Capitalism? What's that got to do with this?"

"Capitalism is the dominant mode of oppression in the twentieth century."

"And Joe Stalin was a philanthropist, sure. What's this got to do with whether or not I eat snack cakes or broccoli?"

"Everything. The maximization of profits means the concentration of production in the hands of a few and the manipulation of the masses. If people all ate fresh food that was not processed through corporations, business would lose its share of the market. Individual productivity would threaten monopolistic hegemony."

"Says you. Look, I might get ill after fifty years of eating pork with preservatives in it, but I prefer that risk to not knowing whether or not the meat sold by some individual producer has trichinosis."

"We're not talking about pork. You shouldn't eat meat anyway. Let's talk about vegetables. The corporations—"

"Let's talk about vegetables. You ever seen home-grown produce in this town in winter? This is Minnesota, for God's sake. Where am I going to get produce but from another state? And who's going to bring it to me if not capitalism?"

Sinclair chuckled. "Typical. There are always alternatives to corporations. There are the people."

"People. Right. Anybody you put in a position of power is going to act like the people in power act today. And that means if they have to spray something on the food to make it stay green, then they will."

"You've put your finger on it. We've been conditioned to think that food must be treated to look fresh. In fact, a head of lettuce is just as nutritious slightly wilted."

"That's what you're killing people for? The right to buy wilted produce?"

Pause. Sinclair cracked his knuckles. "If you want to put it that way."

"My God."

"I don't expect you to be sympathetic. Not with what you've written. One can reduce the noblest of notions down to absurdity, eh?"

"Do you care?"

"What?"

"Do you really care about people? Individuals. People who no more care about these issues than a lemur."

"Of course. That's why we're doing this."

"Then let me tell you about Grunewald. My housekeeper. An old woman, oh, sixty-five. You have a grandmother? Yes? Don't nod, I can't see you."

"Yes. Had one."

"Okay. Put her in Grue's shoes. She was making me dessert. Bundt mix. She licked the spoon and ended up in the hospital from poisoning. From your poisoning. For all I know you put the stuff in the mix personally. Nearly killed her. Put her in a coma for a month—a month out of a life that's not got much to go anyway. You might as well have done that to your own grandmother."

Silence. I heard another car pass outside.

"Buntmix?"

"Yeah."

"What's buntmix?"

"Jesus, don't you people keep records? It's cake mix."

"Sales of that item, now that I recall, fell to nothing after our effort. The company has since dropped it, and is experiencing difficulty with the rest of its lines. Think of your Grue as a soldier on the front line of the first battle, laying down her life for future generations. I'm sorry for any grief you may have been caused. But some things transcend the individual."

"You are a pure son of a bitch, Sinclair. Nothing transcends the individual."

Sinclair cracked his knuckles again. "So you'd like to believe."

"So I know."

"The record," Sinclair said quietly, "is not on your side."

"Don't start in with the philosophy," said Joe's voice, behind me.

Apparently he was in charge of the Consequences of Mask Removal Department. "Philosophy is useless, that's my philosophy. Action counts."

"Joe has a point," Sinclair said. "One of the virtues of this organization is that we don't bother with a lot of ideology. Just enough, judiciously applied here and there. We take some from Marxism, some from Leninism. I myself am a Trotskyite." Yeah, you and Sarah's old beau, I thought. ". . . And even a soupçon of Bakuninism, where appropriate. That's the pleasure of living in a century with such a rich political heritage. This great smorgasbord of thought."

"And what does Jared believe in? Macrobiotic neo-Stalinism in a medley of national socialism and Oriental autocracy?"

"He believes in the cause. That is all; that is enough."

"What did you eat as a child?"

"Pardon?"

"I said, what did you eat as a child?"

"Awful things. Blood sausages, fish sticks, cod balls. But—"

"I thought so. I grew up with vegetables and fruit. Couldn't wait to go out on my own and eat salt and starch. Maybe you guys are just rejecting your mothers."

Sinclair laughed. "A different mother. The great fat teat of American commodity fetishism." He couldn't see me roll my eyes behind the mask. "Now. I have one thing to say and then this interview is over. I want you to listen carefully and incorporate this into your article."

"What article."

"The one to be based on this conversation, of course. I don't like using you as our public relations vehicle any more than you do. Jared, however, finds a certain humor in it."

"What do you want me to say?"

"This. Munco is, as you must know, the largest grain producer in this area, and the subject of considerable pressure from us and other organizations. Yet the company remains inflexible; nothing has changed. The grain remains poisoned, and—"

"Could I see your statistics on the number of people who die each year from preservatives, pesticides, and the like? I assume you've statistics."

"Don't be naïve. The medical establishment is hardly free to publicize such findings."

"Oh, you're conspiracy nuts, too. Who else is on this? The Rotarians?"

"As I was saying," he snapped. I grinned. "We are intensifying our campaign against all products that use Munson's grain. That means adulteration of prepared foods, such as breads, english muffins, cookies, et cetera. You will be given a list of the products when you leave. But we are also prepared to attack the grain before it reaches the preparation stages. Munson's is based in Minneapolis, as you know. All grain handled by the company passes through here before shipping. Our organization is able and prepared to poison the grain anywhere from the silos in the small towns to the ships up in Duluth. I can say no more except that there is little that Munson's can do to stop us."

"Poisoned with what?"

"Nasty stuff," said Joe, breathless.

"It doesn't matter with what," Sinclair said. "No reason to tell them what to test for. Enough to say it will be done. People will have to avoid the product."

"And if a few people die?"

"Then a few people die. Joe? Get Werther in here." My ride home. "Ah. Werther. Listen, take this man out and kill him. We can mail the tape to the paper."

All the air fled from my lungs and I couldn't move.

Werther-Pickles clumped in and hauled me out of my chair. "Don't," I said, voice wet with terror. "I'm sorry if I lipped-off, I'm sorry, I'll write the kind of article you want, just don't."

"No," said Sinclair, his face up to mine. I could feel his breath through my mask. "Wouldn't do. No one would believe it if you were suddenly a mouthpiece for us. They read you for outrage."

"I'll be outraged. I'm outraged now. Give me a typewriter. I'll be furious at you. You'll be delighted, so pissed will I be."

"Sorry. Werther? Make it discreet. Robbery gone bad, the usual."

"Godnogodnogod."

I was dragged past the door, hands scratching at the air, sobbing inchoate vowels and consonants. Twice I tried to rip off my mask, to see who my executioners were, but Werther prevented me. I finally fell limp in his arms, my mind tearing in panic through a black maze, fear around each corner. I dragged air into my lungs with great racking thirsty sobs, a man standing on the edge of the desert and drinking in all the water he can see. Then there was a hand on my shoulder.

"Just kidding," said Sinclair.

I babbled something.

"Just kidding," he repeated, his voice flat and tired. "But now that you have known true uncertainty and terror—write about it. Communicate that feeling to the people. And then you'll have done as much of our job as we can expect. Werther? Drive him home."

The car stopped; a hand reached across my lap, opened the door and pushed me out. I tumbled onto ground cold and hard, heard tires screech away and ripped off my mask. I stared around; I was outside of the manor.

I staggered up to the manor and let myself in. There was no one up, of course; it was after midnight. I went to the kitchen and got a beer. It went down in one deep glugging draft, and I took another. There were messages on the refrigerator door, all in Grue's plain blocky handwriting: "Sarah called." "Dafnee called." "Marya called." Then I made my way back to the dining room, pouring the beer down my throat. I turned on the computer and looked at the blank screen, the cursor blinking expectantly in the corner. The world was making mad irregular peregrinations under my eyelids, and my hands were trembling, as though there were wind, not blood, going through my veins. I began.

> It was my luck that when I finally got the chance to stare death in the face, I had a ski mask over my eyes.

No, no.

I laughed. I looked up into the thick velvet darkness of the vaulted ceiling, and I knew I was home, safe, safe. And that I had a story no one else had.

When I woke it was morning. Light lay across the table in neat rectangles from the leaded windows. My head ached and my mouth felt like carpet in a farmhouse. I looked at the screen.

"I didn't want to die" I had written. "Who does?"

16

My interview came out on Wednesday, and the issue sold out—or would have, if the paper hadn't been free.

It took one day for the media to realize that the fact of my getting an interview was perhaps less important than its substance. The threat to poison Munson products, unaccountably run in the eighth graph of the first story in the *Times*, bobbed up, exploded and filled the front page the next day. And the next. The *Dispatch* ran a list of products sold in the Twin Cities area that used Munson grain—half the commercial breads, all of the supermarket brands, all of the breakfast cereals of Consolidated Milling. Children were warned that death could result from eating Frosted Ghosties, Merry Berry, Bits O' Grins, Rocket Balls and Colonel Crackle. Adults were advised to avoid Vitaflak, Multi-Bran 2000, which sounded as though it provided fiber for an entire continent, FiberFit, Aunt Rhea's Old-Fashioned Natural Low-Sodium Oatmeal and Flax 'N' Fiber.

It was stressed that the products currently on the shelf were safe. So people stocked up. Bread disappeared from the shelves of the supermarkets, and the new shipments went unbought. Munco, ill at ease in the spotlight, gave a few press conferences defending their use of pesticides and preservatives. One representative asked angrily if we all wanted to go back to the days of spoiled milk and rotten meat—a rather obvious question, and a strange one coming from a grain company, but people got the meaning. Munco also took reporters around its grain mills to show off its security measures. One of the more enterprising TV stations sent a team around after the tour and discovered that there was no one around after the cameras had left. The team was able to get inside of a silo and make a report standing on top of a catwalk leading over a vast sea of grain. The segment ended with the reporter casting a handful of dust over the grain and telling us it was just flour. But what if it was cyanide?

In the meantime, people who didn't read the papers and didn't watch the news bought food. And some of those people died.

We were wrong, you see, in thinking that the AIL would hit the grain silos. They didn't. Instead they spread out among the hundreds of supermarkets in the Twin Cities; they purchased a popular breakfast item called Ooh La La Croissants. It came in four varieties: butter, raspberry, strawberry and almond. Ooh La La was made by a small company, Tricia's Treats. Tricia was living on a private lake somewhere, for she'd made a lot of money when she sold out to Consolidated Milling. ConMill, as they were known, distributed the product elsewhere in the country, and mass production meant hooking up with large suppliers. The wheat came from Munco. It was ConMill's idea to come up with the almond flavor. Almond: the scent of cyanide. If any of the poor souls who popped their Ooh La Las into the oven noticed anything, it was that this batch had more of an almond scent than others. Perhaps it was new and improved.

Twenty-eight died. It could have been more. It would have been more, had not a woman named Janice Hargrove noticed around 3 A.M. that the man with whom she had spent the night was sitting in her kitchen dead. As she told it to the papers, she worked with the man; the day he was laid off they had gone out for a drink to commiserate, and ended up in bed. In the middle of the night he had gotten up, looking for a snack; he had popped an Ooh La La in her toaster oven, eaten it and died, according to the coroner, within thirty seconds. She had woken at three to use the bathroom and had seen a light on in the kitchen; upon investigating, she saw her companion sitting upright at the table with his eyes wide open, looking "as though he had just started being electrocuted." She saw the half-eaten croissant and figured out in a second what had happened. She called the police; while waiting for them to arrive, she phoned the papers. The papers informed the television stations. For the rest of that morning a crawl on the bottom of the TV on every local channel implored the viewer not to eat anything that said Ooh La La.

Munco stock prices evaporated. As soon as it got out that the AIL had simply walked into the stores, purchased the products, poisoned them and returned them to the shelves, nothing was seen as safe. A month before, structural defects had caused the window glass to pop out of Munco's corporate headquarters, and they had roped off the building while replacements were made. It made the entire forty-seven-story structure look like a crime scene.

And Munco gave in. A harried executive held a press conference and announced that the company was rethinking its policy toward pesticides—not that the policy was ever wrong, no, Munco had the public safety first and foremost in mind, but that there were alternatives that might, in light of recent, ah, developments, be explored.

Munco stock fluttered, rose, sat back down. Nothing would help it now, for while their name was on everyone's lips, the product did not have that honor. Within days stores were running ads to proclaim that their bread was Munco-free. Speculation arose that perhaps the AIL were former employees with a grudge, masking a vengeance with this terrorist routine. The police began interviewing disgruntled and eccentric employees.

Bishop showed up on the news to announce an arrest—a former key-punch operator. He had claimed that typing the number six more than three times in a sentence violated his religious beliefs and had been substituting other numbers for over a year before Munco found out and fired him. He had filed suit claiming religious discrimination. When the suit was dismissed—around the time of the latest Munco poisoning—he denounced the judge in the courtroom, saying he would burn in hell; to give him a temporal foretaste the man left a pipe bomb under the judge's car. Police searched his apartment and found a variety of self-penned tracts on the evils of corporations and how fluoride was prophesied in Revelation. But no AIL connections were discovered.

Marya wrote a story in the *Daily* about the people who were claiming to be part of the AIL. The hardy perennials who turned up after every crime to confess. Honors for most inventive confession went to one Bart Perlstein, who claimed that one of his alternative personalities did it.

I didn't know what to think about that. At least I knew why Bishop had laughed at me. But I still believed Manny; there was just nothing I could do about it.

Christmas was almost a week away, and AIL or no, the city was going through the standard motions with varying degrees of sincerity. The buildings downtown sported holly and wreaths, and the trees that ran the length of the Nicollet Mall were draped in lights, block after block of bright white fire. Most of the mansions on Park sported elaborate displays of lights as well, and I had found a few strands in the basement and wound them around the pillars by the front door. Tryg and I had gone out for a tree, wrestled it into the Pacer and brought it home. Grue had screamed when we brought it in—needles everywhere were we dropping—but I caught her smiling as she turned to get the broom. It had been many years since there had been a tree in the manor.

I was wondering if Oscar would play on familial sympathies again and show up, tinsel in hand, when he answered the question ahead of time.

It was a week after the interview. I was in the den with Trygve, watching cartoons. The doorbell rang.

"Would you get that?" said my butler. "I'll tell you what happens."

I opened the door and saw Oscar, and groaned.

"Season's greetings, cousin," he said, smiling, small black eyes shining. "Thought I'd come over the river and through the old woods to pay a holiday call."

I shut the door but his foot was there. "What, no room at the inn?"

"What do you want, Oscar?"

"Let me in. It's cold out here. I'll be good. I was good last time. Besides, I left my gloves here on Thanksgiving."

"And you're coming for them now?"

"I've come before. But Grunewald could not see her way to admitting me."

I sighed and opened the door. Oscar strolled in.

"What did the gloves look like?"

"Kidskin. Brownish. Sink me if they didn't stand out."

"I'll ask Trygve."

"Well, you might as well ask the wall, cousin. Where would the gloves be? I'll look."

"We don't have a lost and found, Oscar. Look in the hall closet. If they're not there I don't know where they can be."

Oscar came into the den after a few minutes, said he couldn't find the gloves—at least we knew what to get him for Christmas this year. He was invited, wasn't he?

"They don't celebrate Christmas where I stay, you know. Buddhists."

"You're still at that restaurant?"

He opened his mouth to reply, but the phone rang. Oscar bowed and waved toward the phone. I took the call in the dining room.

"Hello?" said a small, jumpy voice. "This the guy I was talking to at that bar, what's the name, Jolly's? This him? I mean, did you give me this number?"

"Manny?"

"At the moment, yeah."

"Manny. You've got to go to the police and explain all this. Tell them about Saul. You have to let me help you."

"No police. They'll put me on drugs. Besides, Bart was there already, the shlemiel."

"I know. And they won't believe *me* because of him. You didn't tell me about that one."

"I'm ashamed to. A pervert, that Bart. Feels guilty about everything. Always has to confess. Less said the better, all right?"

"Fine, fine. Tell me where you are, Manny. I'll come and get you and we'll find a safe place. You have to stop Saul. You have to let them stop him, Manny."

"Look, they beat it outta him with the rubber hoses, it's me who wakes up with the bruises. Forget it. Listen. I called to tell you they're up to something. Last night, laying in bed, I hear people talking in the upstairs department. Saul and Esther. He was bragging. They're planning something big."

"The AIL? Don't you read the papers? They've already done something big."

"Bigger. Don't know what, but it has to do with radioactive stuff. Listen, I gotta go. Just watch out."

"Don't hang up! You—"

The line went dead. I slammed the phone down and swore.

"Cousin," called Oscar from the doorway of the study. "About Christmas, then."

"Not now." I picked up the phone again and called the *Metropole*, got Fikes on the line.

"Fikes. Simpson. I have something, and it has to go this week. Open letter to someone. Too long to explain. It has to do with the—" There was a beep on the phone, the signal of another call on the line. "Hold the line, will you? Can you hold?"

"Mrrgh," he said.

I depressed the hook and said, "What."

"Who. When. Where. Why," said Marya. "At least you're one fifth a journalist. Can we have a drink if you promise not to throw it in my face?"

17

“Hate me?” Marya said.

“That’s a strong word, ‘hate,’ ” I said. “Not all that inaccurate, but strong.”

We were at a bar called the Madison’s. I was watching the usual ragged Uptown milieu flow by, punks bristling with leather bumping into lacquered young suburbanites en route to queue at the dance hall next door, everyone shivering in the December cold. Marya was talking with Judith, our waitress, a reporter from the *Daily* picking up extra money, and an old roommate of Marya’s.

When Judith brought our scotches we lifted them in a toast, neither of us sure what we were toasting. Marya took my matches, lit her cigarette and took a quick drag. I folded my hands and waited.

“You’re looking better,” she said. “You’re looking good.”

“My face healed.”

“I knew it was something.”

“You’re looking all right,” I said, aiming for a tone of voice of someone admiring the qualities of a painting from a period about which he is indifferent. “Did you change your hair?”

“This?” She pointed to her hair, swept up and gathered in a kerchief. “God. I didn’t have time to wash it so I just stuck it up. I almost forgot we were meeting. I was at aerobics when the instructor started making these, like, punching motions?” She jabbed the air. “And I thought of you.” She put a hand over her mouth and grinned. “I know that’s awful. But I thought you were going to chew me out something bad.”

“I am.”

“Oh.” Pause. “When?”

“I’ll let you know.”

“God, that’s just what Daddy used to say.” I raised my eyebrows. “He used to give me spankings? And he—”

"You got spanked? I can't imagine why."

"Oh, I was just a lippy little brat, I told you that. I spent half my childhood sitting on Daddy's knee and the other half lying across it. But he couldn't, like, paddle me every time I mouthed off; the man would have had calluses on his palms. I always knew when I had said something that was maybe, like, an inch over the line, and I would look at him and say, 'Are you mad?' And he'd look down and say, 'I'll let you know when I'm angry, young lady.' Which meant I was safe. If he didn't say anything I knew he was critical mass and I was going to get it." She laughed. "Mother told me he would say that this was going to hurt me more than it hurt him but that the difference would be negligible. I never knew what 'negligible' meant. One day I dressed up in some of Mom's clothes when she was at the store? I put on her negligee. And when she came home she said, 'Oh, my best negligee.' I thought it was what Mom wore when Dad spanked her. That was the difference Dad was talking about. So the next time he told me I was going to get a spanking, young lady, I went and put on Mom's negligee. I come out of the bedroom, this little twit in this big pink frilly thing, and Daddy says, 'What are you doing in that?' and I say, 'Isn't this what Mommy wears when you spank her?' "

"What did they say?"

"No-thing. They looked at each other and didn't say anything. And I didn't get a spanking that night."

"Did Mom?"

"Probably."

"Ever catch your parents making love?"

"Uh-huh. There was one day when Daddy sat me down and explained that Mommy sleepwalked."

"So?"

"That was to explain why I had walked in and found him, like, lashing her to the bedpost." Marya shook her head, smiling. "Twenty-six years ago they tied the knot, and they still tie four more every Saturday night, probably. And they're happy as clams."

"I don't think so." I lit a cigarette. "Clams have no arms. Hard to be into bondage when you have no arms."

"Happy as centipedes, then." She looked out the window.

"It was right over there I got taken apart." I pointed to the library across the street.

"Do you know who?"

"No." I stared out the window until my focus wavered, and I saw my reflection in the window. "I thought I did. I thought it was Jared, but that made no sense, when I thought about it. He hardly shows himself to his staff. No reason to risk an assault charge kicking the kidneys out of me.

"And there was Spanks, whom I was following around. Her I still wonder about."

"Spanks." Marya took another quick drag.

"Mm-hmm." I grinned. I decided to lie a little. "That's my lead, sweetheart. Don't expect me to tell you any more."

"Oh, I won't, I won't." She ground out the cigarette, half finished, then smiled, head down, looking through a mess of red hair. "So, who was it?"

"Fellow name of Bart Perlstein," I said. Lie number two.

"What? Come on, silly."

"You don't know about Bart?" I smiled. "You just took the cops' line on him and let it go at that?"

She stared. "You're teasing. You read my piece and you're teasing me."

"I read your piece and I'm telling you the truth. You'll have to read my piece next week to figure it out and that, Marya, is all I'm going to say."

"I can't worm it out of you? An advance preview?"

"We're here to talk about how you swiped pertinent aspects of my recent life for a story. What I have since uncovered is none of your business."

"Maybe we can trade. Pool resources?"

I shook my head.

"All right." Marya leaned forward, her breasts cupped between her elbows. She sipped her scotch through a straw, I noticed. "Shouldn't we be apologizing here? Isn't that the point of this?"

"We? What have I got to apologize for?"

"For not forgiving me after I tell you I'm sorry." She smiled; I saw the candlelight flicker in her eyes.

"Maybe. Start."

"Okay." She leaned back, squared her shoulders. "I was wrong. And, I'm sorry."

I waited. "That's it?"

"Doesn't that cover it?"

"Cover it? That's like hiding a battle cruiser behind a napkin. Keep going."

"Well, if you, like, hold a napkin up in front of your eyes it pretty much covers everything."

"Knock if off, Marya."

"I suppose you want the truth or something."

"For pure novelty value, sure."

"Okay. Here it comes, and it's going to sound real stupid. But." She took a deep breath. "I had too nice a time with you. That's why I stole your story."

I waited. "Too nice a time."

She gave a brisk nod. "That night we had was so sweet I could've died. That kind of stuff makes me want to stick around, so I had to ruin it."

"Naturally."

"Look, I know it's stupid, but I was doing us both a favor. I'm real bad with fidelity. And I have no business being with someone I really like, because I'm just going to mess them up. And me in the process too. So I stole the story. Plus, let's be honest, I got some serious professional mileage out of it."

"If I'd slapped you around you wouldn't have stolen my story. That it?"

"Not slapped, I hate that stuff. Just been, oh, like emotionally . . . unshaven, if that makes sense."

"I think I understand. Excuse me." I stood and walked off to the bathroom, where I smoked a cigarette and shook my head some more. Let's see if I had this right. Jane had left because it wasn't good anymore. Marya strangled it in the cradle because it was going to be too good. Sure, I understood life. I even respected it. It had a good jab and a long reach and it was going to win the title this year. Meanwhile, I was due back in the ring again. I washed my hands and went back to the table. Judith was there, setting down fresh drinks. "Say hello to Kate when you see her," she said to Marya. She smiled at me and departed.

"Kate?"

"Old roommate. There were three of us back at Pioneer Hall. Me and Judy and Kate. So—"

"Kate Carver," I said. A wild shot. "Goes by Spanks." Marya blinked.

"I don't remember her last name. So as I was say—"

"I think you do."

Silence.

"There goes my bargaining chip," she said.

I waited.

Marya leaned close and looked me straight in the eyes. She appeared five years older now; there was no nonsense in that face. "All right. From the top. It's like this. I'm sorry I took your story. That was a bad thing and I paid for it. I did what I did because I was being uncaring and pretty much unthinking, but I knew I wanted you mad at me. I was breaking up with my boyfriend and the last thing I thought I needed was someone else right away, and this was a gutless way of driving you off. Believe me when I say we shouldn't have gone on. You're too nice a guy and I am not what you want. You want someone who isn't going to take off, and all your talk about Jean—"

"She doesn't matter. And it's Jane."

"Jean, Jane, she meant everything because she was supposed to be the last woman in your life? Right? You're looking for someone to be the last woman in your life. And it isn't me. I probably would've demonstrated that one way or the other, and—"

"Marya, this is the biggest bunch of hornswaggle I've ever heard in my life. I think you took that story because it was a good one and you didn't give a damn for the consequences. And if you're sorry now—not that you're exactly the picture of contrition—where, I want to know, was this repentance before I found you out?"

"I felt bad. I didn't know how to—"

"You slept with me to get the story, didn't you?"

"I did not."

"Right." I looked away. "You just fell into it somehow, had a rapturous time, which, of course, meant you had to end it, understandable, of course. Why didn't you just dash my brains out with a poker while I was asleep?"

"Stop it." I looked back at her. Her eyes were wet and her jaw had a small quiver. "You don't have to believe me."

"Good, because I don't. If you were telling the truth and you had had as good a time as you say you did, we'd have been crawling all over each other thrice daily for the last two weeks."

We sat in silence for a while. Finally Marya cleared her throat. "How do I make up?"

"What do you have in mind?"

"I can give you something on the story. And make you a bargain."

"Such as."

"Such as we do this story together from now on."

I shook my head. "You're out of your skull. I've been reading your stuff. It's good but it's standard wisdom, recycled police handouts. I probably know more about the AIL than anyone in town and you want to hook up with me so I can profit?"

"Spanks is sleeping with one of them."

I coughed.

"I think," she said. "A year ago the *Daily* decided to do a story on the Progressive Students Front, because they were getting really funky. Allegations of funding from off campus, all sorts of stuff. We planted Kate—that's Spanks to you—in the organization and she's been there ever since. All that hair and attitude is fake.

"Awhile ago she met someone in the organization she likes. He's like a charmer but *real* gone on the left. Charismatic but doesn't take leadership positions, just hangs out. The weird thing is that he strikes up these friendships with people and they get all tight and everything and then the people drop out of the PSF. So."

"So, what."

"So she thinks, and I think, that this guy is your Jared."

"Oh, my God."

"You're telling me. Imagine what's going through her brain. Although it's not like I'd know. I haven't heard from her in weeks. And I am worried and I want your help."

"Help? Cooperation? Forgiveness? Which is it here?"

"Jonathan." She took my hand, squeezed it. "Please. I'll give you that deposition and I'll help you write anything you want. Just do two things. Don't want to sleep with me and help me find Kate. You know Valhalla and where she might go. Please?"

I wanted nothing more, fool that I am, than to ignore the former and do my damnedest to fufill the latter.

"You'll help?"

"Sure."

"And you won't want to . . . to . . . you know."

"Scout's honor," I lied. That made three.

18

So Marya and I were going to be buddies. She took the lead with some locker-room talk about her photographer paramour. I listened and laughed and smoked my cigarettes past the filter and laughed in the wrong places. When we parted around three in the morning she gave me a kiss on the lips. I went back for a second sampling, and she drew back and said, "Friends. Remember?"

I couldn't forget at all, that was the problem. And so I told her before she left that I was, all things considered, still fond of her. In fact, I was about an inch from falling in—

"Stop that." She put her hands on my lips. "Don't tell me. Convert it to metric. That'll take your mind off it." And she left.

The next morning I walked to the office, caroming off the walls of the narrow hallways in exhaustion.

"Hey," said Daphne. "Dressing for me?"

"Mrg?" I looked down and saw that my shirt was on backward and inside out. A cotton-poly-blend wearer and proud of it. "Mmm," I said and waved. Back to the newsroom.

Fikes was standing in the middle of the room. His pants wore a crease sharp enough to make the air bleed and his coat was thick black wool flecked with gray. He handed me a package.

"Whassis? The tape?

"Yes. You saw it on the news last night, mrrgh?"

"Mmzm."

"Christ, wake up, man." He grabbed me by the shoulders. "You look awful. You need some coffee. You want it black?"

"Yes. With cream."

He stomped off around the corner, returned with a cup and stuck it in my hand. We retired to the conference room, where, God be praised, more coffee was brewing. Solly drifted by, gave me a narrow stare, then took a chair at the back of the room and folded his arms. Daphne had probably told him everything.

Fikes put the tape in and sat on the edge of the table, arms akimbo. The picture went from a hissing haze of static to black, then there was the same image we'd seen before. A figure in a ski mask sitting at a desk, the banner Eat Right or Die behind him. To the left, a door.

"I know that door. I begged for my life there."

"This where you were?" said Fikes. I nodded.

"Has to be."

"Sshh," said Solly.

"—am Sinclair," said the figure in the mask, "of the Central Committee of the Pure Food League, speaking at the request of Jared. Greetings to representatives of the media, tools of capitalism though you may be, and to the dietarily repressed people of the Twin Cities. We contact you today with news of success and information about our final proposal for cleansing the town of pernicious poisons."

"Better production values," I said. "Notice how steady the camera is?"

"Shut up," said Solly.

"And the voice is different."

"Would you—"

"But it is. That's the guy I talked to. There's nothing to disguise his voice this time. Listen."

"I can't listen if you're talking."

"Be still!" cried Fikes.

"First, we proclaim a victory of the people over Munco. In agreeing to reexamine its policy of lacing the fruits of the earth with chemical agents, Munco has fulfilled the purpose of the initial action. All action against Munco products is hereby ceased. I repeat: the Munco boycott is ended, contingent on Munco's presentation to the general public of its plan to remove chemicals from its food.

"In the meantime," Sinclair continued, "we have another warning for the people of the Twin Cities. Our victory has emboldened and empowered our cause so that we now address an issue of equal import to the first."

He looked behind him. Someone just beyond camera range tugged at the banner and it fell away, revealing another. It too said Eat Right or Die but now the AIL logo was written inside three inverted yellow and black triangles. The symbol for radioactivity.

"Oh-oh," I said.

"Food is poisoned from many sources," Sinclair said, sounding for a moment like a home-ec teacher. "It can be poisoned by man through chemicals in the fertilizers. It can harbor bacteria that have grown resistant to the antibiotics man shoves into his cows. It can have additives added to keep it fresh. But none of these is as pernicious as *this*!" He pointed back to the radioactivity logo. "The food industry in its never-ceasing rapacity for profit has begun the irradiation of food—lettuces, grains, fowl. All in the name of freshness.

"This can stop," said Sinclair. "This must stop. Action by the AIL will make certain it does stop. Enclosed with this tape is a list of stores known to carry irradiated food. We demand its publication. We also demand the cessation of irradiation, but realize that this takes time; the stores therefore have three days. Three days to assure the consumer that irradiation will cease. By the end of that period we also demand that all irradiated foods still on the shelves be marked as such. If not, we are prepared to make our point by the same means. In other words"—Sinclair put down his text—"we will fight radioactivity with radioactivity."

I sat up.

"We have secured a quantity of plutonium from the Meadowglade facility and will introduce it into the water supply of the Twin Cities in approximately seventy-two hours if our demands are not satisfied. That is all. This is the AIL. Eat right or die. Do not drink the water."

The screen went white.

"What is this Meadowglade facility?" said Fikes. "They explained it on the news last evening but I missed that portion."

I was staring at the white snow of the screen, thinking, No they can't. Oh, yes, they can.

"Jonathan?"

"When," I said slowly, "did you guys come to this state?"

"Last year," said Fikes. "Why?"

"Meadowglade. A power plant they were building up north in the early seventies to supply energy for the mining region. They built it, went through licensing, testing, the whole thing. It even went on line. Then the mining industry went under, and they cut back on staff, shut down all but one reactor. They wrote off the investment and raised everyone's rates, but that thing is still there."

"So?"

"So it's a nuclear power plant. Powered by uranium. The by-product of which is plutonium."

No one spoke.

"You're not saying that they actually—" said Solly.

"They're saying it. What they just said was that they have plutonium. And they're going to put it into the water."

Silence again.

"Can't be." Fikes banged his palms on the table and stood up. "Just can't be. They don't let plutonium out of their sight." He ran a hand through his hair, messing it. There were dark stains under the arms of his shirt.

I sighed. "Well, it's not like you can walk up and say, 'Hello, I'm your neighbor, mind if I borrow a cup of U-238 derivative?' But they don't pay a hell of a lot of attention up there, and I know that for a damn fact. That plant is about thirty miles from my old house in Valhalla. My girl friend at the time worked on the local paper, and she did a story on the plant, its security measures. They had no security. She got a job there without a background check, had free run of the place. Wrote this big exposé article about it, but still they didn't change a thing. They're sloppy up there, real sloppy."

"So," Fikes said. "Mrgh. The water's next."

"Maybe. Who's to know? You want to take the chance? It's a big river, Fikes. You could dump something into it at any point from here to Itasca. They could hit the wells. The filtration units. There's no way the entire river can be defended. It used to be a border between French and British territory. But defenses have lapsed in the last couple centuries."

"Granted. But I'm certain the dailies are already sending someone up to Meadow, what, Meadowglade. They'll find out if there's plutonium missing."

"And if there is?"

"There's no proof they have it. It may be a bluff."

"These guys don't bluff. They're the kind of poker players who'd rather shoot you than ante."

"Then we have two alternatives. Give in. Or find out who they are." Fikes looked up at me. "And the latter is your job."

"I don't know who they are." I stood up. "I don't have anything. Anything. No one does. No one has seen these guys. No one knows if there even is a Jared. No one's heard from this Jared since the letters stopped and the tapes started. All I know about them is that they like black ski masks, killing strangers, and that they mix and match ideology according to their purposes. Sinclair is a Trotskyite, for God's sake. What sort of rational action do you expect from a man who follows a dead Russian who left this earth with an ice pick in his head?"

I stopped, hand frozen in midgesture.

How many Trotskyites were there in this world?

"I know who he is," I said slowly. I felt cold and I began to feel sick. "I know who he is."

I walked out of the room, Fikes shouting behind me. I took the elevator down and stalked across the parking lot to my car, my stomach burning. I rummaged in my satchel for the tapes of the interview, put the cassette in the tape player and fast-forwarded it. "I, myself, am a Trotskyite," Sinclair said. "He's a Trotskyite," Sarah had giggled about Mark, years ago. "I think that's cute."

So had Spanks. She even gave him a rose, to make his day at We-B-People go a little easier. Now I knew where I'd met the bastard before.

19

Sarah smiled when I sat down at the counter.

"Tell me about the guy you dumped me for."

Now her face looked like a hastily erased chalkboard. "Don't waste time on pleasantries, Jay. Come right out and tell me what's on your mind."

"Okay, hi. How are you. I'm fine. Tell me about the guy you dumped me for."

Sarah looked at the floor. "Come on, Jay," she said in a soft, low voice. "This isn't necessary."

"Come on. Spill."

"Well, you and I weren't going anywhere, you know that."

"That wasn't my impression."

She looked up, frowned, shrugged. "Well, it was mine. What was I suppposed to do? I loved him. Love him. So he's a jerk on occasion. He's a known quantity. And he wanted to come back. And he's certainly in a better position to take care of me."

I stared at Sarah. "We're talking about two utterly different things here," I said. "I'm not talking about Mac, I'm talking about that Trotsky sod you canned me for five years ago and do you mean to tell me you got back together with Mac?" She nodded. "Are you crazy? He's a dunce. He's got the IQ of a snowflake."

"Every snowflake is unique," she smiled.

"So is every bullet that comes out of a rifle barrel. This guy is going to be papa to our Zy? I can't believe this. I can't."

"And where have you been? If you've been so concerned about what you may or may not have planted in the back forty, then why no calls?"

"What do you mean, 'may or may not'? Did I get you pregnant or not? You telling me you don't know if it's me or Mac?"

She nodded. "I'm still not sure I'm really pregnant, either. You know me, Jay. I always tend to overlap my boyfriends."

That she certainly did. I gave her a weary stare. "Maybe you ought to color-code your sheets. Blue for Mac. Red for me. Help you keep track."

Sarah glanced back to the kitchen, then picked up her coffeepot. "I have an order up." She turned around and walked away. I called her name, and she stopped, her back still facing me.

"Speaking of overlaps. Five years ago. Trotsky. What was his last name."

"Why?"

"Because I want it. What's his name?"

"Mark. Mark, ah, Lewis. God, I haven't thought of him in—"

"Fine." Lewis. That was the name he'd given me at the employment agency; I never considered it might be his last. I started to dig in my pockets for change.

"What does it matter?"

"He's AIL."

She sucked in her breath. "Come on."

"Do you know where he lives?"

"Come on, Jay. It was so long—"

"Where, Sarah? Please."

"He was on, mmm, Upton. I think. His parents had a house there and they were killed and he inherited it."

"Is there a phone book here?"

She pointed back to the rest rooms. I found the phone book and plowed through the *L*'s. There was an *M.* Lewis on Upton Avenue. I took down the address, and as I wrote "Upton" I started to laugh. These guys are idiots, I thought.

I went back to the counter; Sarah was still standing there, looking at me with a worried expression.

"Look, Jay. I don't know what you suspect, but don't—"

"Remember that American studies class we took? Activist literature?"

"I made you take it." She smiled.

"Remember one of the texts? *The Jungle?* All about unsanitary conditions in the meat-packing industry?"

"Was that the book where the man died from a cut on his finger, because there was so much bacteria in the factory?"

"The very one. The book that launched the FDA. Now, one of the guys in the AIL—the one who interviewed me—was named Sinclair. Called himself a Trotskyite. Think of your Trotsky friend Mark. Where does he live? And who wrote *The Jungle*?"

"That was Sinclair Lewis. No—that was *Main Street.* Who was the—Sinclair, Upton Sinclair!" Pause. "Oh."

"Right. See? These guys are so goddamn smug. Don't think anyone's read a book." I grinned. "We got them now. We have them, period."

"Mark? AIL?" Sarah put a hand to her throat. "What are you going to do?"

Good question.

"I'm going to call the police," I said, and went back to the phone. I asked for Detective Bishop. They put me right through.

"Bishop. It's Simpson."

"Well. Well, well. More information on Mr. Perlstein? He tell you all about Judge Crater? He did that one too."

"Listen carefully. I know who one of the AIL is and where he lives."

Pause. "And I suppose it's just plain old public-mindedness that's making you call me here."

"Well, yes."

"I don't suppose you'd want to be in on the bust."

"Of course I would. I—"

"How do you happen to know this fellow, eh?"

"Long story. The guy who interviewed me said something that reminded me of someone I used to know, all right? I checked it out. I've got one of them. Got one."

"Based on what, or can I ask?"

On a book I never finished. "Never mind. Trust me. Trust me. You have to—"

"Gimme the name and address." I did. He laughed.

"What's funny now?"

"You're the third person to give me that name today. We already got the place staked out. They're waiting for me to come down and have a look. Feel free to drop by."

"Who else called?"

"Old associates who recognized the voice, I guess. His mother, maybe. I don't care at this point, son."

"I'll see you there."

"Imagine I will." Click.

I hung up. Sarah was still standing at the counter.

"I don't know what you're doing," she said, "but be careful."

"I could tell you the same thing," I said. "I'll be by. Soon."

"Call first," she said, and she went back into the kitchen.

There were six squad cars, two unmarked vehicles and three TV vans pulled up in front of Mark Lewis's house. Bishop was crouched in back of a plain white car; he had a walkie-talkie in one hand, a shotgun in the other. It was a standard lakes-area house, immense, a relic of the days when four generations shared the same roof. It looked as though the police were smoking out the last nuclear family in town.

I parked down the block, made my way along a row of parked cars until I spotted Bishop, barking into his walkie-talkie. No one stopped me; one policeman put out a hand but I flashed my *Metropole* ID and kept moving. He took off after me but I was by Bishop's side before he collared me. Bishop looked at me with no love.

"I said you could watch, not hang around in my goddamn back pocket. Get back, son."

I stepped back a few feet, crouched next to a tree. Bishop reached into the front seat and came out with a walkie-talkie. He fumbled with the switch, coughed once into the mouthpiece.

"What is this?" I said. "How about going to the door and asking if he's home?"

"This is our boy all right," Bishop said. "No sense taking chances." He turned around and gave me a wide grin. "Might please you to know we've been watching this one for a month now. Then they got dumb enough to not disguise their voice on that tape, and bingo, we got 'em. Voice print matched the voice on a tap on his line and everything. Nice of you to call and second the motion, though."

"You've known about him?"

"Oh, we know lots of things." He turned on his walkie-talkie. "Everyone ready?"

His walkie-talkie crackled with signals from officers behind the house, the policemen hugging the wall by the front door, the sharpshooters on the roof across the street.

"Everybody go ahead now."

I watched the porch. One policeman bent down, grabbed the latch on the screen door, nodded to his partner; his partner nodded back. He pulled open the screen door. The other policeman wheeled around, put a foot into the lock and smashed the front door open. As they ducked back to paper themselves against the wall, Bishop stuck a hand on my head and pushed me to the ground. No lead came flying out. No sound. "Move in," said Bishop to the walkie-talkie. I leaned around the bumper of the car and saw the two policemen dart into the house, guns held out by arms stiff as rails. Bishop motioned two more from an adjacent car to join them, and they ran, crouched, to the house. We waited for a year or two. Then Bishop's walkie-talkie crackled. "Nothing," said a voice. "No one here. Come on in."

Bishop swore, hitched up his pants and spat something brown and substantial into the snow. He started walking toward the house, and I followed behind, hunching my shoulders, trying to look as though I belonged. Bishop turned around.

"Simpson? Stay."

"There might be something in there I recognize."

"Recognize? You had a goddamn hood on your face when you met this asshole."

"So maybe I'll see the hood. Come on. You don't know just how much I know. Do you?"

He gave me a look, turned away. I took that as consent.

Sinclair's house smelled like the home of someone's spinster aunt. It was the smell of old yarn and mildewed pillows and newspapers saved because you never knew when you'd need them again. The air felt like an old book so long on the shelf that it stuck to its neighbors when you pulled it down. The light played on the dust and gave the room the cast of amber, of old gilt. Sheets covered the furniture. Walking on the carpet raised wraiths of dust. No one had lived here for a very long time.

"Hey! Bishop!" called a voice from upstairs. "Up here!"

Bishop huffed his way up the stairs; I stayed in the living room. Two policemen were looking around, one peering in objects on the mantelpiece, another sifting through the ashes in the fireplace with a poker, looking up the flue with a flashlight. I wandered back to the kitchen. Here things got a little more modern. It was clean, dust-free, with appliances: a coffee maker, a food processor. There were a few dishes in the sink. A small garbage pail by the door was filled with green leaves, as from a head of lettuce; they were fresh, unwilted. There were two cigarette butts and ashes dumped on top of the leaves. I picked up one of the butts. Unfiltered, purple lettering on the end. Sniffed it. Clove. Spanks had smoked clove cigarettes during our interview in Valhalla.

"Hey!" I dropped the cigarette and turned to find a policeman frowning at me. "Put that down! What the hell you doing here?" I raised my hands in surrender and said I was media, Bishop said it was okay; he told me to go back outside and I left. While he was poking through the trash I slipped up the stairs.

I heard Bishop's voice and headed for it. He was standing in a bedroom, talking into his walkie-talkie, another policeman examining items on a desk. The room was decorated in Late Bolshevik. A poster of Lenin leading the masses into a future devoid of civil liberties adorned one wall; someone had drawn a mohawk on Lenin, and painted a red A for "anarchy" on his chest. There was a rumpled bed in the middle of the room, clothes thrown on chairs, heaped in a pile in the corner.

I trod on a board that gave a creak, and Bishop turned. "Don't touch," he said. "Look around. Tell me if you see anything that looks familiar."

I nodded, took out a note pad and started to jot down descriptions of the room. I had no more than two words down when the nib of the pen went dry. I swore to myself and hoped I had another ink cartridge in my pocket. Usually after doing laundry I apportioned cartridges in the pockets of all my pants in case this should happen. I had evidently not worn these pants since washday—they were stiff and tight, and I had to shove my hand into my pocket. But I found a cartridge, and I pulled it out. I also dumped the contents of my pocket onto the floor. Several coins made a break for the bed and rolled out of sight. I got down on all fours and stuck a hand under the bed. I felt dust, a magazine coated with dust, a coin, dust, something long and metallic . . .

I drew the last item out into the light. A crucifix. Silver, a silver chain. Plain. I turned it over.

TO KATHERINE ON HER CONFIRMATION, MARCH 30, 1980. FIRST LUTHERAN CHURCH OF VALHALLA. LOVE MOM AND DAD

I put the crucifix in my pocket.

I stood up.

"Nothing looks familiar as far as I can see," I said to Bishop, my voice quavering with the effort of sounding casual. He waved a hand at me, not bothering to turn around, and continued consulting with the officer. I walked down the stairs and out of the house, past the squad cars, past the porches of the neighbors' houses, past the TV vans, wondering just what I had done and why.

Katherine. The last person to call her that had probably been her father.

I didn't want her paying for this, too.

I got in the Pacer and drove until I found a phone booth. PHONE FROM YOUR CAR, said the sign. The Pacer was so low that I had to get out, dial the number and get back into the car, defeating the whole purpose.

I called Marya at the *Daily*.

"Jonathan!" she said when she heard my voice. "I've been trying to reach you. I heard from Spanks. Something bad has happened. I mean, major big-time hysteria. She wouldn't even tell me where she was. I'm kinda nervous."

"I know why she's scared," I said. "And I know where she is."

20

"Valhalla is where we're going."

Marya looked out the window of the Pacer at the flat white countryside. She was smoking a cigarette, her expression that of one expecting irony. "Why don't you just go up there and see her yourself?"

"Because she has not been overly disposed to talking to me. She's been nothing but hostile from the start. Even before she had a reason. How much of that was an act, I don't know, but—"

"Probably an act. She's been real cool about playing this whole radical bit."

"I don't know. I was with her father when he died, remember. I think she blames me somehow. Either that or she is an incredible actress."

"She loved her dad," said Marya. "She thought he was the neatest thing. This whole undercover bit was something to get his attention. And respect."

"Why didn't she tell him?"

"She was trying. After he bailed her out, she called me up, in tears, said she couldn't do this anymore, her dad thought she was a total spaz. I told her to tell him—what was the harm?—but stay with the story. So she was going to tell him. Tried all night to get ahold of him. But."

"But what?"

"But he was out with you." She popped her gum.

We drove in silence for a few miles.

"How far is Valhalla?"

"Two hours. We can stop somewhere."

"Make it a motel." Marya curled up in her seat and yawned. "I'm sleepy."

"Didn't get to bed last night?"

"Oh, I got to bed."

I sped up and ground my molars until a high C sang in my ears. "With the photographer?" I said.

"Mm-hmm."

"What do you see in him?"

"It's usually too dark to see anything."

I ground my teeth down to nerve and pulp.

"You're not saying anything," she said after a few miles. "Is that jealousy I hear?"

"Let's not talk about it," I said.

She slid down in her seat, put her feet up on the dashboard. "But if we were talking about it, what would you say? About what you think of me."

I drove about five miles, deciding how much of the store I wanted to give away. "I think you're obnoxious. And charming. You're cute and in ten years you'll not only be cute, you're going to be beautiful. You have moxie and spunk and you make me laugh. I want to kiss you. I want to sleep with you. I want to change you."

That last one fell out of my mouth without permission, dropped with a thud onto the floor of the car and started to smoke.

"What is this 'change me' stuff."

"Never mind."

"You want me to wear heels and lingerie, that stuff?"

"I mean change all the stuff that is going to bring you grief. Look. It's no mark of distinction on my part to want to sleep with you. Any breathing member of the male species is going to want to sleep with you. But there's heartbreak and nonsense that passes as love that you are going to have to go through before you wise up, and I want to—" I saw the words coming, and did nothing about them. "I want to save you from all that."

All she said was "Why?"

Because I want to sleep with you! Aren't you paying attention? "Because I do, that's all. Look. You're going to spend your twenties bouncing around in a dozen relationships of differing intensities, each ending up on the same slag heap, right?"

"If you insist."

"I do. You'll have a parade of men, from vacuous buccaneers like that goddamn basset-eyed photographer, and you'll end up with nothing." Or you'll end up like Jane, with everything. Or like Daphne, with just what you need. I realized the gist of this philippic: choose me, so you don't end up like me.

Marya looked out the window. "Well," she said. "I don't suppose you couldn't want to sleep with me without wanting to change me."

I shook my head no.

"We're in trouble," she said.

"I'll settle for minor alterations," I said.

"Why should you settle for anything?"

"I'm an idiot. And I'm in love with you."

Well, there it was. Nothing like laying down the royal flush while everyone else is deciding whether to meet the first raise.

"Stop the car. Pull over."

I did. We sat on the shoulder, engine idling. Polka drifted from the radio.

Marya turned in her seat to face me. "Listen to me. When you called me to go up here and do this I said only if we were partners, right?" Right. I had agreed to let her cowrite the story for the *Metropole*. "If we're going to be partners we have to get along. Talk. Share. Communicate. Be honest. And maybe that means no sleeping together."

"Marya, we have a different understanding of some very basic human fundamentals."

"Sshh." She put a finger to my lips. "Listen. I love you too," she said.

"Don't say what I think you're going to—"

"As a friend."

"Aw, you had to say it."

"I had this teddy bear," she finally said. "He was my best friend when I was a little girl." She took a deep breath. "I slept with him every night."

Then Marya leaned forward and kissed me. It was a good kiss. Not a bon voyage kiss but a meeting-the-ship kiss.

I pulled onto the road again, earning me the honks of a driver who simply did not understand that I had kissed Marya and could now drive where I damn well pleased, and we drove north without a word. After a while she started yawning again, and she curled up in the seat, put her head in the crook of my shoulder and fell asleep. I smiled all the way up.

I stopped for gas outside of town. An old familiar face, one with a wen on its nose, was at the other pump, filling up a truck with *Zeke* written on the side. He gave me a look as though he were trying to place me, and I smiled. Just being one of the locals. He frowned and squinted at me, shrugged, got in his truck and drove off without looking back.

I took a long route to Carver's house, avoiding most of metropolitan Valhalla, thudding and bouncing down county roads. Carver had a house on Lake Lelac, a modest bungalow appropriate to a widower whose daughter lives away. It was covered with knotty pine, shingled with rough slabs of bark. The driveway was unpaved and the mailbox on the edge of the road was a hollowed-out trunk of a small tree. There was a satellite dish in the front yard.

"I'll go up," Marya said. "Anybody else and she'll freak. You're sure she's here?"

"No, I'm not. But it's likely." She nodded and got out, stamping up the drive with her usual into-the-wind posture.

I saw someone peek through a curtain in a room at the end of the house. Marya rang the doorbell, put her face up to the glass and said something. A few minutes later the door opened; Marya was yanked inside.

I got out of the car and ran up to the door. I listened. Nothing. Dammit. Now what? Knock? Drive the Pacer through the picture window? Then the door opened—I stepped back, ready to run, but it was Marya. She waved me inside.

I'd never been inside Lou's house. It was what I would have expected. There was a big fish on the wall, mouth agape in surprise, the head of a deer mounted on the opposite wall. A Western painting hung above the sofa, yee-hahing men roping cattle. Here and there were cenotaphs of Mrs. Carver—a fragile and ornate vase, a frilly valance above sheer curtains doubtlessly imported from their previous house; they clashed with everything in the room. Carver hadn't noticed. Or cared.

Spanks sat on the edge of the sofa, smoking a clove cigarette. Her hair was unspiked now, but still answering the dictates of the styling gel, hanging in loose spirals like ice cream cones subjected to great heat. She glared up at me.

"What is he doing here, Mar?"

"He drove. He's okay, Kate. Really."

"Your boyfriend," I said. "He's Sinclair, isn't he?"

She nodded.

"The police know about him." I said. "They'll be picking him up soon. You don't have to worry about retribution or anything. No one knows where you are. No one would think of coming up here."

"What happened?" said Marya. She was sitting next to Spanks now, her arm around her shoulders. "Hmm? What made you jump ship, kid?"

"He hit me," she said in a small, angry voice. "He came home and just started whapping me."

"Why?"

Spanks swallowed. "He had asked for video equipment again. So I—"

"Hold on," I said. "Back up."

"How far?"

Childhood. What was Lou like as a father? "When you started hanging out with him."

"September or something. A couple of months ago Mark asks for video cameras, said he was doing a documentary for local access cable. About drug use or something. I didn't think anything of it, see, because I was supposed to find out if he was—" She laughed, a laugh with no pleasure. "I was trying to see if he was from the campus Republicans, convincing people to drop out of the Progressive Students Front."

"That's what our editor thought," Marya said to me.

"So the first time he gave me the camera back, I noticed the mike was all screwed up. Had this weird foil stuff inside the windguard. So later he asks for a camera again, and I go, sure. The next day I'm at his house. He was downstairs making dinner, I was upstairs in bed. I saw the camera in the corner of the room. I don't know why but I looked at the mike, took off the windguard. And there was that foil. I took it off—why I don't know."

"Maybe you knew," Marya said.

"I showed it to one of the guys at school the next day, and he goes, well, it would disguise the voice of anyone talking. Make it hard to hear and hard to recognize. That scared me. That really scared me. 'Cause I was already starting to put stuff together. The way he talked about the AIL, all these late-night meetings, weird phone calls. The foil just clinched it. So I went back to his place to get my things." She paused. "That was stupid."

"Were you . . . involved with him?" I said.

"Well, yeah." She put a knuckle to the corner of her eye. "As soon as I got to know him, I didn't think he was what we thought he was at all. I mean, a Republican. He was pretty serious but he seemed all right. So I was getting my stuff and he came home. This was . . . this was the day the AIL sent the last tape. I hadn't seen it but I knew it was out. He comes home and accuses me of messing up the videocamera, and he hit me." Her jaw tightened. "Started grabbing at me. I ran. He came down the stairs after me but he fell, and he was lying there on the steps yelling and swearing and I ran. I got home and got my car and came here." She leaned her head against Marya's shoulder.

"Does he have plutonium," I said.

"What?"

"Plutonium. There wouldn't have been any canisters around the house that gave off a certain unnatural glow?"

"No, none of those. But I know he took a trip up north a few weeks back. Said he was going to visit relatives in Hibbing or something. When I heard about the Meadowglade part, about that reactor, I freaked again. If he says he has it, I'll bet he does." She paused. "Not that I turned out to be a great expert on the guy."

"Come on," Marya said. "How were you to know he was a food terrorist, huh? It's not something you suspect of your dates, kid."

"I should have known, Mar. What's your story going to be about? How I slept with the guy who killed my dad?" Tears began to roll down her cheek. "I mean, he killed Dad. My dad."

I walked to the front door, taking in as much of Lou's abode as I would be able to remember, then went over to Spanks and sat down next to her. I took the crucifix out of my pocket and placed it in her hand. She looked at it, then looked up at me, face wet with tears; her eyes bore all the forgiveness I would ever need.

I went back out to the car.

Half an hour later the Pacer was starting to warm up. I was listening to the local polka-free station. At the top of the hour the announcer read the news. Nothing new overseas or across the nation. But when they got to state news there was something unusual. "Authorities in Minneapolis are bracing for the biggest civil disturbances since the Northside riots of the sixties," the announcer said. "Threats by a group calling itself the Alimentary Instruction League to poison the water supply have prompted near-riots in several stores around the Twin Cities, as people attempt to stockpile bottled water. Police report fights breaking out in at least a dozen stores across the cities, and they are emphasizing that no evidence exists to confirm any danger to the water supply. There has been no further word from the AIL on the matter, and—"

I went back to the house, walked right in. Marya and Spanks were still on the sofa, talking.

"Marya," I said. "Minneapolis. Water riots. The police are saying there's no cause for panic."

She ran her tongue along the inside of her lip. "It's that bad?" she said.

"It's going to be. Let's go."

21

I was not about to be caught in the middle of a water riot with none of the stuff on hand. The only liquids at home were orange juice and scotch, and I did not fancy performing morning hygiene with either. I stopped at a suburban convenience store and bought twenty gallons of distilled water, desalinated and decalcified, several six-packs of water in various flavors and two bottles of imported French water, for any special occasions that might arise. I put the bottles in the trunk and set off for the riots.

It was as bad as they had said on the radio, perhaps worse. Half the convenience stores we passed en route to town had signs in the windows reading NO WATER; a few were closed prematurely. "Look," Marya said. "That store there with the cop car. Come on. Let's check it out." I turned into the parking lot and we went over to investigate. There was a crowd of perhaps fifteen people, hands in coats, all silent, long silent plumes of smoke coming from their nostrils. Glass from a broken window lay on the ground, along with the letters R, Y, C and H. The intact windows read MER RISTMAS. A clerk was giving a statement to the policeman; inside the squad car sat a sullen young man, hating the world in general and the backseat of the car in particular.

"Water?" I said to one of the onlookers. He turned away from the scene and said, "Yeah. How much you want?"

"No. I have some. Was that what this was about?"

"Of course."

"There's nothing left here," Marya said, tugging on my sleeve. "Let's go somewhere where it's happening."

"Wait. I want to call home and tell them to stay put. I don't want Trygve going out for Popsicles and getting nailed."

There was a phone at the side of the building; I called the manor. No answer.

"No one home," I said to Marya when we got in the car. "They're either asleep or out. And the only place they ever go is shopping."

"Don't worry." She patted my hand. "They'll be fine. It's not like a major breakdown of civilization or anything."

A reasonable assumption, and a wrong one. Within a few minutes we were at the the Red Rover Food Market, a warehouse store near the manor, the place where Trygve made his weekly pilgrimages for food. A block away we were stopped by a barricade; a policewoman in a jacket with reflective stripes waved a flashlight at us and directed us to turn right. Flashing lights from police cars blinked beyond, and a dull red glow throbbed in the sky. "This has got to be bad," Marya said. "Bad. Park anywhere you can. I got to get to a phone."

"For what?"

"Call the paper. We need a photographer down here. There's going to be blood and everything. It'll be choice. This is, like, primary stuff."

"No you don't. Remember? We share everything from here on in."

"You can help me write it for the *Daily*. Come on. Please."

"If I wrote so much as a letter to the editor about this subject for anyone but the *Metropole*, I would be canned in a second. No *Daily*, Marya."

"But someone else will get the story before I do."

"Welcome to the world of weekly papers," I said. I saw a spot and started backing the Pacer into it. "What we lose in immediacy we gain in time, to make the long-term appraisals. And so help me God I'll spank you if you don't play along."

We got out of the Pacer and cut through an alley, emerging at midblock with the store on the other side of the street. We stopped. And looked.

And listened: there was the steady cry of voices in contention—angry shouts, screams, curses, threats, burrs and thorny vines stuck to the cold sharp air of the night, rising and roiling from the crowd around the entrance. Police were trying to hold the crowd back, pull people from the store, but they were losing, hesitant to really unleash the goods on the taxpaying citizenry. There were five, six ambulances, all with doors open, attendants loading the wounded. A dozen police cars ringed the entrance to the store; officers stood guard at side doors, watching the melee at the front. Every TV station in town had a truck on the scene, and I watched with satisfaction as a reporter, doing a stand-up by a truck marked KJGO, was flattened by a man thrown back from the crowd.

"Boy," said Marya. "This is your thin veneer of civilization here. Was this what it was like in the sixties?" I glared at her. "Let's go." She took my hand and pulled me forward.

"Go? Into that? Are you nuts?"

"It'll look good on the résumé. Come on." Her hand was tight around mine.

We ran across the street and plunged into the crowd, threading smoothly through the onlookers until we hit those directly participating in the mob scene. They did not budge. "Journalists," she shouted. "Hey. Journalists. Make room." New recruits to the crowd closed behind us. I thought of the Room, the Bowhouse, and wondered why, why in a nation as vast as this one, I kept ending up in crowds. But I wasn't going to panic, I wasn't going to panic.

Christ, how I was going to panic.

I spun around; Marya's hand slipped from mine. I charged south for an exit and smacked skulls with someone; he sent me spinning around back toward the store. I saw Marya's face, turned to mine, shining in excitement and fear. "Saying we're journalists doesn't work!" she shouted. "These are the people in the surveys who hate the media! We got to be hairdressers or actors or something!" Right, right, fine, get me out of here, now, *now*. I started plowing through the crowd; something grabbed at my coat. I put my fists into the back of whatever body appeared before me and I made amazing progress. I saw light, more confusion, heard shouts from inside the store. I kept hammering my way through the crowd, leaving a depression in the crowd behind me, like earth that has sunk over a fault. Then there was no one in front of me and I stumbled out of the crowd and sprawled on the ground, something still hanging on to me. I looked up to see Marya getting to her feet and a policeman, arms laced with his brethren, looking over his shoulder at me. "Get back!" he bellowed. "Get the fuck back!"

"Journalist!" I shouted from the ground.

"Hairdresser!" I yelled, but Marya was pulling me up. We dashed into the store.

There was a no-man's-zone between the cordon and the store. The front windows were entirely blown out; glass lay smashed all around. Yet we still entered through the doors, neither of which had any glass either. The store looked empty, but there were shouts and voices from the far end of the warehouse. A banner proclaiming We're Glad You're Here! fluttered from the roof.

"Soak this up," I said to Marya, panting. "Start memorizing."

"Way to show initiative back there, man," she said. "Hey. You okay?" I was bent over, dragging air into my lungs, which felt paved with fiber glass. I smacked my hands together to get the feeling back but the panic would not subside. I saw the lights and crowd and noise behind me, heard the fury ahead; the world seemed to wheel, and everything looked utterly unreal, as though my eyes were huge telescopes sucking up the world and ramming it sideways down my optic nerves. "Oh," I said. "Oh. Oh."

"Jonathan." She put her arms around me and held me tight. Then something grabbed my collar and ripped me from her.

A policeman. He had me, and he was motioning for Marya to follow.

"Journalists," I said. "Please. A break, please. I'm with the *Metropole*. I have to get this story."

The policeman held me at arm's length and examined me. "Yeah. You were at that house we raided."

"Right. Right." The house from which I took evidence. "Right."

"What about her?"

"*Daily*," I said.

"Really?" He cast an approving glance at Marya. "I don't blame you."

Stupid sexist lout! I thought. And don't I wish! "*Minnesota Daily!* The newspaper! Is Bishop here? I have to see him."

He thought a second, shrugged. "Okay. Go on. The fun's at the end of the store. But be careful and stay outta the way." He let me go, strolled back to the cordon, casually cuffed someone back into place and resumed his position in the chain.

We walked back down an aisle marked BREAKFAST CEREAL; the shelves were empty, the suspect items having been pulled weeks before and the rest of the stock bought up. At the end of the aisle we saw a sign—SODA. JUICE. WATER—and we peeked around the corner.

The aisle was demolished. The shelves were empty, stripped of their contents; broken glass was strewn everywhere, water resting in pools on the linoleum floor. There were half a dozen people sitting around, a few in handcuffs, one in a smock talking to an officer; paramedics were attending to a woman laid out on the ground and moaning. I recognized the broad, hard back of Detective Bishop. I called his name. He turned around, looked up to the heavens and back at me.

"What the hell are you doing here?"

"They let us in. What's going on here?"

"Little riot of sorts. 'S under control." Bishop looked rattled, pale. "I don't know what gets into folk," he said. "We've been takin' sticks to people who feel like a felon if their parking meter runs overtime. You saw that stuff out there."

"Confrontation with early mortality," Marya said.

"How many injured?"

"Say two dozen. Scrapes, cuts, few bonks on the head. This was over pretty quick in here. It's those lunatics out there I gotta worry about. 'S about time for a little gas if they don't settle down. I'd recommend that you leave by the back. And I'd recommend that you leave." He put a hand on my shoulder and started pushing me toward the door.

"Wait. When did this start here?"

"Hour ago. Now, come on. I don't mind you much, boy, but you do rub my patience raw. Come on, now. Grant?" he shouted to an officer by the back door. "Let these here two kids out. Escort them down the block until they get safe outta here. We're going to start gassin'." Grant nodded and motioned for us to come. We walked, silent, to the door. There were a few more people back here, being bandaged, getting the glass out of wounds. One of them could have passed for—

Oh, my God.

"Trygve." I stopped. He was sitting on the floor, a bandage across his head. His face looked like an old piece of gray leather, and his hair was spun into peaks and whorls of disarray. "Trygve."

"This man belong to you?" the officer said. I nodded. "He's my butler."

I bent over Tryg, shook his shoulder. Marya crouched down beside him. His eyes were red and his face was wet; he looked at me, his memory floundering, trying hard to put a name to my face, but the graft wouldn't take. "We've got to get him out of here," I said. "Help me get him up."

"Should we move him? There's something wrong with him, Jonathan. Maybe he has a concussion." I heard a *boomph!* outside, probably the gas; we looked toward the door.

"He's always this way before his bedtime. If he was standing around discussing Newton's laws, that's when I'd worry. Lift." We got him to his feet, where he swayed like the Tin Woodman. But he was an old man, all string and straw, and we were able to keep him from crashing back to the floor. With the officer's help we got him out of the store. "Walk him to that barricade," I said. "I'll get the car." And I sprinted around the corner of the building, breathing the clean cold air.

I ran straight into the tear gas. I felt the stab in my nose and eyes, and I instantly turned away, covering my face with my collar, and headed across the street, coughing and spitting. I hadn't inhaled much, just enough to get the point. I stopped to look behind me: the gas was blooming in the air, sick yellow billows; the crowd was falling back. I had to get to the car. I ran down the alley, still hacking out sputum with coughs that began in my ankles. I stopped at the Pacer; someone fleeing the gas knocked into me, knocked the keys from my hands. I bent down, eyes smarting, patting the ground for the keys; someone else slammed a foot into my thigh and tripped over me, sprawling onto the street. He got up, limped away, weeping. I found the keys, got in the car and started the motor. I pulled out heedless of who was running in my path—I couldn't see much, just the thin slit of the world that came in through my narrowed eyes. As though I were driving a tank. I turned left into the alley, honking my horn; people dove off the road in front of me, and twice I swerved to avoid them and ended up demolishing unfortunate trash cans. At the end of the alley I turned left again and headed for the barricade by the back of the store. Fewer people here, but I could see the gas wafting its way toward me through the still air, headed this way. I pulled up to the barricade, unlocked the doors. Marya folded Trygve into the front seat, then squeezed into the back. "You all right?" I shouted. "Get any gas?"

"Not as much as I'll tell my friends I got," she said, coughing. Tryg stared straight ahead, eyes blinking normally. Then he turned to me.

"It's been a long time since we've made popcorn, hasn't it?"

"What?"

"I went to the store to buy popcorn. To string on the tree. And then I was hit on the head." He sighed, then slumped down in his seat and closed his eyes. "Ah well," he murmured. "Christmas is really for the children, anyway."

22

We arrived at the manor around eleven. There was a light on in the study, frost on the windows; snow hung in beards from the chins of the gargoyles. We let ourselves in, propped Trygve against the wall and hung up our coats.

Grue was sitting asleep in an easy chair in the study, feet up, a book propped against the eave of her bosom. Her eyes fluttered open; she looked up and started to struggle to her feet.

"What time it is being," she muttered.

"Late," I said. "Grue, we need help. It's Tryg. He needs attention."

Her eyes snapped open. I took her arm and guided her to the hall. She drew in her breath when she saw Trygve.

"What happened to my dear idiot? Oh, Gott, Gott."

"He's okay. Shaken up. Riot at the grocery store."

"Popcorn he goes for and this happens? America." She helped us steer Tryg, smiling in some private dream, to a chair. She peeled off his bandage, revealing a slight scrape.

"No trouble. Just a head wound. A clean bandage and iodine he needs." Grue went for the medical kit. She came back, clucking concern, and daubed something red and metallic into Trygve's wound. He winced and smiled, eyes closed. Grue pulled a clean strip of cloth from a bolt of gauze and wound it around his head. Tryg looked as though he should be playing the fife in a Revolutionary tàbleau.

"For now leave him there to sleep," Grue said. She patted him on the head. "My idiot." She walked back to the kitchen, shaking her head.

"Shouldn't we get to work?" Marya said. Her hair fell over one eye. Daily? I don't blame you.

"Yeah. Let's get this done."

"Can we have hot chocolate?"

I nodded and went into the kitchen. Grue was putting away pots and pans I didn't know we even owned. "Grue? How about some of your famous hot chocolate?"

She frowned. "Famous my cocoa is?" Her lips formed a thin line. "Oscar. He sells my recipe. Oh, that man."

I walked back to the living room. Marya was running a hand along the computer on the dining-room table.

"You type. I'll dictate. Okay?"

"You'll wha—?" Marya tapped her head, and I remembered. The old photographic memory. The one that had done me so much good before.

"What software do you have?"

"Writeplus."

"Really. That's what we use at the *Daily*."

"Standard newspaper program. The *Metropole* gave it to me. And this." I patted the modem for the phone. "But I don't like it. It's wrong." I turned the computer on. "I believe in hard copy. Something I can hold in my hands."

"That's no surprise," she said. The cursor appeared and the computer beeped. "I want to call the *Daily* computer, get my notes on Spanks. Can you get this thing to print?" I turned on the printer, handed Marya the phone. I sat down and lit a cigarette. She called a number, punched in a series of tones, placed the phone into the modem and waited. After a while the printer coughed and brred, and began to race back and forth across the page.

"This is the spooky part," she said. "I always think, what if someone had typed this, and then they died, and here are their hands typing again."

"At sixty characters per second."

"Maybe there's a lot of coffee in heaven." She watched the printer for a few seconds. It stopped, beeped once and fed the paper to the end of the page. "Ready," she said. "Shall we—"

"Cocoa!" called Grue from the kitchen. She came into the dining room with two mugs. "Famous cocoa. In health that is good you drink." She leaned over and whispered into my ear. "Cute. That she is." Then she straightened and wrestled the chair with Trygve in it across the floor. She paused at the landing of the stairs, and summoned the chair. It floated down at the usual leisurely pace. She manhandled Trygve into the seat, pushed the button and sent him floating upstairs into the gloom. She waved good night and began to trudge up the stairs.

I sat down. "Ready."

Marya cleared her throat. "I know," she said in a muffled voice.

I turned. She had taken off her sweater and was wearing just a T-shirt that read *Minnesota Daily*. It was a size too small.

"Memory fail?"

"No." She sipped some cocoa. "I'm just tired. Of this."

"Me too."

"You have chocolate around your mouth."

"So do you. Should we try this anyway?"

"I think"—and she leaned closer—"we should definitely try it." She leaned forward and kissed me. She drew back and let her tongue play along my lips, gathering the cocoa. "Mmmm," she said.

I put my arms around her and held her again, not out of panic this time, not even out of the odd mixture of lust and fascination that had characterized the last time, the only time. I just wanted to hold her. A dozen caveats were queuing up in my mind, waiting to present their case, but I really didn't care. Perhaps she, too, hated yams. We started kissing and didn't leave off for a while.

"I want to say something to you," she said.

"What."

"After. Wait until after."

"After what?"

"After we write this and we take a ride in that chair? Can we?"

"Sure. As much as you like of whatever you want." I kissed her again but broke off early.

"That's all I get?" she murmured.

"I don't want this to be too good," I said. "I want you to stick around."

She was sitting cross-legged in bed, hair more of a mess than ever. It was cold; I hadn't made a fire. She had put her *Daily* T-shirt back on. She looked a mess. Lovely, too.

"I meant everything I said before," she said. "About fidelity."

"So you need lessons."

"Maybe I need something good enough to stay around for."

"You expect that out of me?" I smiled. "That's a big responsibility."

"You're doing fine so far," she said.

She'd have to leave the country after this one, I thought. There had been no hesitation or reservation; this time there was as much emotion as passion. Now I felt full of sweet narcotics, and wide awake; there was a loose, untroubled strength in my body. There were things I wanted to tell her and this time I knew they would not make the morning paper. I hadn't a worry.

That was the problem. Nothing that had happened had really left a mark on me at all. Valhalla got libeled. Tryg got knocked out. Oscar, damn him to eternal flame, slept in a restaurant. Sarah got pregnant. The whole city spent a month and a half fearing, choking, rioting, dying. Dying: there was Lou to think about too, a shade too kind to point a finger at me, but still. All this happened to others. And me? I was living in a twenty-room house with a butler and a cook, and I had the bright sparkling eyes of a beautiful little redhead fastened on me as she told stories.

Marya paused, turned around and asked if I'd mind scratching her back, please? Thereohthere. Then she sat up and went on with her story. I listened to a few bars; it was about how she had showed up this, like, absolute goof in her European history class who confused, get this, Robespierre with Rochefoucauld.

Smitten? Taken? In love, as much as you should be at that point, and a little more as well. I watched her, hands drawing circles in the air, her soft pliable mouth contorting to fit the voices of the characters she was demolishing. But there was no malice in that face. Something devious, maybe. Something selfish and unselfconscious. You didn't know if it was good or bad but you wanted to be around it.

And this, I thought with a start, is where I get paid back for the punishments deferred. I'm going to fall in love here, and it looks like she's going to do the same, for a while. But this one will not stay. She's young and fickle and maybe what we have done here is paper over a hole in the wall, not brick it up.

I took one of her hands in mine; the other gestured with twice the animation. I squeezed her hand and she squeezed back. I felt good about knowing what was going to happen.

Mainly because I really didn't believe a word of it.

I woke up somewhere around three, the real bad neighborhood of night. I lay there waiting for an explanation. I had a brackish taste in my mouth, but who didn't at three; my bladder was quiescent, and I had not fallen asleep on my hand. But I had not been drinking; I was with Marya. Ah. Marya.

The door was open a few inches, and I saw a light from downstairs. I got out of bed, slipped through the door, the hinges for once not making a sound like the days before painless dentistry, and made my way along the wall. The bathroom was empty; the rest of the doors—the children's room, Grue's, Tryg's—were closed; a long and satisfied snore came from Trygve's. Nothing like a subdural hematoma for a good night's rest.

There was a voice downstairs. I looked down the balustrade and saw Marya at the computer, phone cradled in her ear. A cigarette was tucked in her mouth, and she was drumming her fingers on the table.

I stepped back, got down on hands and knees and looked out through the pillars of the balustrade. The acoustics I deplored were now to my advantage; the vaulted ceiling picked up her words and handed them right to me with hardly any loss of volume.

"Finally, God. Don't you people answer the phones? It's Thompson. . . . I know it's three o'clock. I told you I'd call. . . . I know when the paper goes to bed, don't tell me— Look, I . . . Look, Slothower, you knew I had this story coming in and you knew it would be late; they laid out around it, didn't they? Isn't there a, like, twenty-inch hole for this? Okay, then. I'm sorry I'm late. It's worth it. Trust me. Now. I'm going to be sending it in slow, this is an old computer I have here— What? No, I don't have a computer. Hmm? . . . Never you mind where I am. Have someone there start proofing it as soon as it comes off the wires, 'cause it's rough. Okay? Get ready. And thanks for holding the paper for me. . . . Well, let them read it at lunch, then. Okay. Here goes."

She put the phone in the modem, typed in a few commands, sat back and lit her cigarette.

I rolled over and lay, facedown, on the old dusty carpet. She was down there writing the story, sending it in, and tomorrow the *Daily* would scoop everyone in town. It'll look great on her résumé, I thought.

What was I going to do? Stomp down and yank the phone off the modem? There'd be an argument, and I felt too horrible already for that. The sight of those lips pouting in feigned contrition would be murder, murder. Wait until the piece was printed, then haul my sorry self down to the *Daily* and rerun the previous scene? Obviously, here's a man who learns his lessons.

Then I knew the right thing to do. I went back into the bedroom and picked up the extension phone. It was full of whirs and beeps. Just picking it up ought to have put a wrench in it all, but just to make sure I hummed into the mouthpiece, made low whistling sounds and banged the receiver against a pipe a few times. I whistled a few bars of Beethoven's "Ode to Joy" in the receiver and hung up. That ought to make gibberish of the story.

I crawled back into bed feeling like stone—worse, a stone that does not want to be stone.

After a while I heard her come up—she used the chair. Marya used to love that chair, I heard myself saying, an old gray man talking to the walls. Downright plum loved it. 'Course, that was before I killed her.

She came into the bedroom and got into bed. I feigned a thick, impenetrable sleep. She fitted herself around me; her hands and feet were ice, the rest of her warm and soft. She slid a hand down my stomach to my groin and cupped my genitals. I stiffened and turned.

"Sorry," she whispered. "My hands are cold."

"Mmrr," I said. "Whaddime izzt."

"After three. Go back to sleep."

This was the last time I'd really be able to ask. "What," I mumbled, "did you want to tell me."

"Ssshh," she said. "Later. It'll keep. There's plenty of time. Go back to sleep, sweet man."

She fell asleep quickly. I lay awake for a long time, almost until sunrise, her arms around me, not wanting to move, staring at the window.

"You're quiet this morning." She was toweling off from her shower. There was no time for breakfast, she'd said when she got up; she had to take the train to her parents' home that night, and had lots to do until then.

"I didn't sleep a whole lot."

"*Pourquoi?*"

On account of your boundless duplicity. But I said nothing.

She dropped the towel, looked at me and grinned, then plunged naked where I lay and shook her head, scattering a shower of water. She straddled me; I put my hands on her hips. Instinct. She bent down, kissed me, laughed and began to tickle me. I was a second from standing and throwing her out the window; instead, I caught her hands in mine, said, "Don't."

"You always this grouchy? You weren't the last time."

"Depends."

"Well, if you are, no more sleepovers. Not that I'm a morning person." She struggled off of me, stood up. "I work best at night."

"So I noticed."

She laughed again. "That wasn't work," she said. "That was anything but." She started to dress.

"You want me to see you off at the train tonight?"

"Oh, that's hardly necessary, Jonathan. I don't know if we should be seen together. Ruin my image." She fastened her bra and fought her way back into her *Daily* T-shirt. "Hello? You listening? I was just kidding."

"Will you bring a copy of the paper with you?"

"Why? The most exciting thing will probably be an interview with the vice-president for undergraduate affairs about admission standards."

"I'd still like to come. We'll critique your piece."

"Don't come." She hopped into her jeans, then climbed back onto the bed. "The train station is boring. Full of fluorescent light and screaming snotty kids. I'd rather leave this as our good-bye." She looked at me, unresponsive me. "Well, last night as our good-bye then, before you turned into such a log." She grinned and kissed me, a swift buss. "I gotta go. Have a merry Christmas, okay?"

I looked at her, all energy and cheer; I put out my arms and she slid into them. We hugged and held one another tight, and I didn't want to let her go: this would be the last unclouded moment between us, murky as it already was.

"Merry Christmas," I said.

Marya smiled and left.

I heard the door downstairs slam shut.

After a while I got up, fumbled into a robe and went downstairs.

No one was up yet; my God, it was seven in the morning. I made some coffee, went out for the paper and read about the water riots. The accounts were thin, based mainly on police reports; no style, no language. Nothing like the piece I would have written, nothing like the piece that would be in the *Daily* today, nothing like the piece I would, dammit, write anyway.

I went in and got my coffee. Sat at the dining-room table in front of the computer. I lit a cigarette.

There was still a disk in the computer. I took it out: a blank disk marked MISC, not the word-processing disk. I turned on the computer, booted up the word-processing software and waited. The computer clicked and whirred and presented me with the menu. I inserted the Misc disk and asked it to give an inventory. All the names of the files were familiar, except for one: ENROLL. I called it up.

> Thompson
> slug: enroll
> sug head: Sloane Suggests Limiting Enrollment
> There are too many students at the U, says Vice-President for Undergraduate Studies Victor Sloane, and it's time the university stopped trying to start accommodating all who come—and start to keep some from coming at all

I stared at the story. I read it all through to the end. Nothing about anything but the VP. Just a story about a policy decision that represented a complete turnaround on the U's previous policy. Nothing major. Nothing they couldn't put in tomorrow's paper, except that there wouldn't be a tomorrow's paper; the *Daily*, as a note at the bottom said, ceased publication until the following Monday, and Merry Christmas!

She hadn't stolen our story. She'd been sending one of her own. There was nothing in the local paper about the VP's decision. Figured. They were never up on the U. The *Daily* always scooped them there, mostly because of bright, resourceful people, like Marya.

Whose story I had destroyed.

The phone rang. I ignored it. I went into the kitchen and got another cup of coffee. The phone continued to ring, and I finally picked it up.

"Jonathan? Hi. Me. I'm at the bus shelter. The bus is late."

"I can—"

"No, don't come get me, it'll come. I just wanted to tell you how much I loved what we did, and that . . . that . . . I want you to meet me at the train station tonight and say good-bye."

"You do?"

"I do. It leaves at eleven. My roommates are dropping me off at ten or so, 'cause sometimes it's early. But you can come at ten too. There's a balcony upstairs where no one goes and we can go up there and neck."

"Okay."

"I'll be waiting. G'bye, love."

"I love you."

There was the sound of breath let out, slowly.

"I just wanted you to know that," I said.

"You did."

"This seemed like the best time."

"Well." She laughed. "You beat me to it, then. See you tonight, sweet man."

I hung up the phone and stared at it. Then I went into the kitchen and drank a glass of tap water. I neither glowed nor doubled over. And I was disappointed.

23

Fifty years from now, when I am an old man, I will set my grandchildren at my feet and tell them about the year of the blizzard. I'll tell them how the snow came so thick, so fast, that the city had no time to hide. How stores closed at three in the afternoon, buses ceased to run, offices emptied and the highways filled with long bright rivers of cars creeping down the road at five miles per hour. How by five the city was in hiding, the winds hammering at every window, drifts sealing the doors. How your grampa was the only man on the streets that night. The children will ask why grampa was so stupid as to go out on a night when common sense clearly dictated staying indoors, and I will have the choice of telling them about love and lust, or shutting up.

It was different the night I was fool enough to be out, driving around in the blizzard. Then I felt the odds of ever having breakfast, let alone grandchildren, to be slim. The car would not stay on the road, possibly because there was no road for it to stay on, and every time I touched the brakes the car did the rumba all over the road.

At least there was now water for everyone. Take it in and melt it.

The train station was miles away from the manor. I crossed the Mississippi onto University and pointed the Pacer toward St. Paul, the tires making the sound of someone gagging on wet cotton balls. I drove hunched over the wheel, heart yammering in terror. The Pacer would not stay warm for long if I ran into a ditch or an insurmountable drift. At least in Jack London's day they could kill their form of transportation and stick their hands in it.

But I made it. I pulled into the train station at midnight. When I had called the train station they'd said yes, the train was running, just running a little late. Like three hours. I had been calling Marya all day but had gotten no response. Which could have meant anything. But there was no way she could think I was responsible for her story not getting in the paper (and it hadn't: I had driven to the U that morning and gotten a copy of the *Daily*). I'd tell her what I did, all right, but later. On our fiftieth wedding anniversary, maybe, by which time she would be deaf. I got out of my car, drew my scarf around my face; far away, miles away, I heard the whistle of the train, hanging in the wind. I ran into the station.

It was not a happy place. A glum torpor hung over the room, and by looking at the faces of some, I guessed that the only way to find out how long they had been waiting would be to use carbon dating.

Marya was sitting in a corner. A book lay in her lap; she stared straight ahead. I made my way over suitcases and babies to her chair. I cleared my throat, mostly to shove my heart back down, and said hello.

She whistled the "Ode to Joy."

"Yeah, well, uh," I said.

She picked up her book.

"I want to talk about this," I said. "We need to talk about this."

Marya put her hands over her ears and said, "*Mmmmmmmmmmmmmmm.*"

There was a vibration in the room, a low hum from outside. Everyone turned to look out the window for the train but it hadn't yet pulled into view.

"Marya." I crouched down. "Listen. I drove through fifteen miles of blizzard to get here and talk to you."

"*Mmmmmmmmmmmm* I can't hear you *mmmmmmm.*"

The sound of great panting diesels came from the west. People started to shift in their chairs, look at their suitcases, finish their cigarettes. Marya looked up, gazed out the window, waiting, patient. The train rolled slowly into the station and stopped, hissing steam, blind with exhaustion. Marya put her book in her backpack, stood up and walked to the gate.

I followed, of course. If I was the villain here, that made us about even, so there really should be no cause for disputation. I caught up to her in the line.

"Will you at least listen? Don't start in with the Beethoven, for Chrissakes. Tell me at least how you know I did it."

She gave me a look that, in another setting, would have made me check my back for the existence of a hump. "Everyone at production heard it. They had the modem on a speaker phone or something, and they heard someone start whistling stuff, not to mention banging the receiver around and doing everything he could to screw up my story. They didn't know where I was, so they couldn't call back for me to transmit it again. And me, stupid me, forgot to pick up the phone and say, 'Get that? Anyone whistling Beethoven's Fifth while I transmitted?' "

"*Now boarding for: St. Cloud. Staples. Detroit Lakes. Fargo. All passengers holding tickets to these destinations please proceed to the gate.*"

"That's me," she said. "Bye. Nice of you to come. Have a merry Christmas. I'll call when I get back. Just what I am going to call you I don't know, but I have five whole days to come up with something good." She turned and walked through the gate.

I felt in my pocket for my checkbook: it was there. That was all the spur I needed. I followed Marya through the gate, onto the platform. She was striding along, head held high in disdain for any part of the earth on which I might conceivably tread. I followed her to the car five away from the engine, hung back a second while a porter helped her step aboard, then advanced.

"Fargo?" I said.

"Fine. Watch the steps. Smoking is in the rear of the car."

I turned left and headed into a bathroom; I bolted the door and sat, waiting for the train to move. I had no agenda here; there were three stops before Fargo, and I could get off at any one and take the train back in the morning. I just had to get her to listen.

The train lurched and swayed; there were some hideous scrapings of raw unhappy metal, then the regular clacking slap of the wheels on the track. A voice came over the intercom and announced that due to the lateness of the train the bar car would remain open for another half hour. I passed the time glancing through the half-score magazines stowed in my satchel, too nervous to pay attention. After ten minutes I was certain they had collected the tickets, and I could go. I sat up, combed my hair, washed my face in cold water smelling of rust and left the bathroom.

I headed for the rear of the Fargo car, where Marya would be smoking and detesting me. I didn't find her. But her coat was laid across a seat. She'd be back in the bar car.

I spent a harrowing interval between cars, shivering in the cold air, waiting for the door to the next car to open, nearly driven deaf by the roar of the wheels; eventually the door opened into the moist, doughy air of the next car. It was full of sleeping people, their legs jutting into the aisle, mouths open as if expecting fruits to drop from heaven in the night. There was a man hacking in the back and a baby sniffling for its feeding. I tiptoed through the car, got another sample of loud purgatory before passing into the next car. It was a duplicate of the last, down to the coughing man and the testy infant. In this car I encountered the conductor, who asked for my ticket. I checked my wallet. Not a sou. I pulled out my checkbook and found, of course, only deposit stubs. I did some quick lying—thought the tickets were in here, wife must have 'em. She's in the bar car; back in a second. He nodded, and I headed back to the bar.

Empty, or nearly so. The promise of extended hours had not meant much to this train. Marya was sitting at the end of the car, talking to a man. We'd been moving all of fifteen minutes and she'd already found a man, or had been found. I stood behind her and said hello.

She turned around, and her eyes closed. "No. No. Absolutely no, you didn't."

"I did." I looked at the man with whom she was sitting, a good-looking number in a thick wool sweater. "Leave," I said. He looked at her. "Leave," I repeated, "or I'll kill you. I'll kill you and then I'll sue you." He got up and left. I sat down.

"You," I said, "are going to listen to me apologize if I have to make you watch me crawl on my hands and knees."

She stared out the window, pouting.

"Marya, I am sorry. Honest to God. But how was I to know you were sending one of your pieces? All day you're talking about putting this all in the *Daily*, getting a photog, and when I wake up and see you down there talking to the *Daily*, what am I supposed to think? That doesn't excuse it, I know, but you have to understand."

"That's what you thought?"

"Of course. What else?"

"Well, I thought you were maybe trying to get back at me by screwing up this VP piece."

"Marya. I didn't do that to get back at you. And don't tell me it didn't cross your mind that I thought you were sending our story."

"Our story. You make it sound like it was our kid or something."

"It was. It was like waking up and seeing you sell our child to black marketeers."

"Some father you are. Do you stop me? No. You whistle. Why didn't you just come downstairs and ask what I was up to?"

"I didn't want to spoil our evening."

"So you just spoiled my piece." She spun around in her chair and glared at me. "Nothing big. Just an interview with the veep on a big huge change in the way the university conducts its admission policy. You probably want to write the story for the *Metropole*."

"Me? What do I care about admission policies? I have my degree! I don't care if they ban admission to all but ambidextrous Bantu warriors! And tell me why if this story is so goddamn important you wait until three A.M. to get the thing in."

"I forgot about it," she said in a small voice.

"Great. The biggest story of the U, you say, and you forget to write it."

"I didn't say I forgot to write it. I said I forgot to send it in."

"So you— Wait. You had it written?" She nodded. "Why didn't they take it off the computer?"

"I had it hidden."

"Oh."

She nodded. "Filed it away in a weird part of the computer under a cover name. I didn't want anyone jumping on the story at the paper.

They couldn't find it in the computer after the transmission was garbled. They aren't too happy with me. I caught some hell today."

"So you're mad because I screwed up your attempt to cover your screwup, is that it?" She nodded.

She rolled her eyes. "I don't know what to think. I'm tired. I want to go home, which is why I'm on this train. I don't want to think about you or see you for a while. Could you go? Please." She hunched down in her seat.

"I can take a hint." I stood. "You want me to go fetch that moody side of beef in the sweater? No? Fine."

"Jonathan." I turned, paused. "You didn't trust me."

I thought for a second. "You're right. I didn't. Think about maybe why."

I opened the door and headed into the dining car, wondering how a man so bad with tools was such an expert at throwing wrenches into things. The porter looked up from his paper. "Taking her all the way to Fargo tonight?"

I stopped, swore, headed back to the bar car.

Marya was looking out the window. I sat down.

"I need fifty dollars," I said.

She pursed her lips.

"We're doing bad enough," she said. "No need to drag money into this too."

"Think of me as a stranger in need."

"Give me five minutes and I won't have to imagine the stranger part."

"I got on without a ticket. I thought I had checks. I don't. I need to get off at St. Cloud and get home. Fifty ought to do it."

She let me twist for a minute, then she reached down to her backpack and got out her checkbook. She wrote out a check to Amtrak, writing it with excruciating concentration. She ripped it off, waved it in the air for the ink to dry and for all to see, and handed it to me.

"Thank you."

"Interest-free loan. My Christmas present to you. You can mail a check to me at the *Daily*."

I backed away and went back to the Fargo car. I ran into the conductor en route; he looked at me, smiled and rubbed his fingers together, eyebrows cocked in inquisition. I waved the check. He got out a pad and wrote me a ticket, round trip, to St. Cloud.

The train pulled into St. Cloud around one thirty in the morning. I got out and stood on the platform, watching it pull out. When the bar car came by I looked for Marya. There she was. The guy in the sweater was back, too. Their heads were tilted back into the reading lights that shone from the ceiling, and both were laughing at something or someone.

24

The train station at St. Cloud had been beautiful before the twentieth century got its hands on it; now it had the drab, outdated look that follows ten years after something is modernized. The walls were painted the color of skin in a Victor Mature movie, and the ticket counter, which had probably been something writhing with filigrees of brass, had been replaced with a tan Formica slab that looked like an altar for a sect of accountants. There was one clerk on duty. He looked up at me and said the train wouldn't be in for four hours. I told him that was fine.

"You going to wait here four hours?"

I nodded.

"There's a café down the road. Open twenty-four hours a day."

"This is fine."

"Train might be late."

"Might be early."

"Most likely late. You're sure you want to wait all that time."

"Look, am I bothering you? I can go stand outside. I can spend my last quarter here to climb in a locker. I'll give you the key. Let me out when the train pulls in."

"Don't get exercised." He went back to his magazine. After a while he stood, walked back into an office and shut the door.

I sat for a while, nodding, finally sleeping.

I woke with a jolt, sat up and stared around; the room was still empty. I rubbed my eyes. No sense in buying coffee now, I thought; save that for a special treat. According to the clock I had only been asleep for an hour. But if I slept again I would sleep through the train; I didn't trust anyone to wake me. I bought a cup of coffee and sipped it, slowly.

I tried reading to keep me awake. My satchel had the usual magazines, political journals I had carried around so long that none of the issues in them mattered anymore, and literary journals that would have put me back to sleep as surely as a blow from a hammer. There was one I didn't recognize; I gave it a closer examination. *Vox Populi.* Now, where the hell had I picked this up?

Here, you take it. I don't need it anymore.

Mac had said that. And I had taken it.

I looked through it. The usual mix of far-left, over-the-edge-of-the-world-and-hanging-on-to-the-horizon cant and paranoia. What had someone said, "The unknowing right and the unseeing left"? This magazine should have offered white canes with a year's subscription. About the only accurate thing in the entire publication was the subscription label. James Robert Edward MacAdam, 719 4th St. SE, Mpls Mn 55414. The address—my old address—loosed a dark, sad wave of nostalgia. My home. Her home. And now Mac was there patting her stomach saying, "Deec, man, a babe, hope it's a chick." I stared at his name, hating it. All those syllables for so small a cerebellum.

Then I saw it.

I put down the magazine. My hands were trembling. I went to the washroom, dashed my face with cold water and went back to my seat and picked up the magazine again. I saw it again.

James Robert Edward MacAdam.

James Robert Edward.

Ja, R, Ed.

Jared.

No.

Yes.

It had to be. Nothing fit together but it would, it would. No, no. This was ridiculous. Mac, Jared? Come on. Why? He hardly was the type. All Mac wanted to do was make money. The only money involved here was the money lost by those poor folks who had invested in stock in the companies the AIL had targeted. Munson had gone from what, fifty a share to a buck. It would rise, now that the AIL were after irradiated—

I closed my eyes. The stock would rise. And everyone who had bought in at a dollar would make a fortune.

He couldn't. He wasn't that cold.

Oh, what did I know. I had met the man three, four times; he had known just what sort of persona to don for my benefit. He had been the loving leftist to Sarah, the playboy to his friends, the professional at work—where did he work? I passed the broker test, he had said. A commodities broker? Gold? Silver? Aluminum?

This was Minneapolis, the Mill City. Home of King Flour. The bastard probably traded grain for a living.

I went to the desk and shouted, "Hey." The clerk came out, asked what he could do.

"I need to make a phone call. I haven't any coins."

"Need change? We can do you that."

"No, no, I don't have any money. Any. I want to use your phone."

"Sure. If it's a local call."

"Sort of."

"It is or it isn't, kid."

"Minneapolis?"

"Sorry. That's long-distance."

"It's important. Please. You don't know how important this is. Too long to explain."

"Can't," said the clerk. "With cutbacks and whatall I'd have a helluva time explaining what a long-distance call was doing on the bill. Doesn't take any coins to call collect, though, if you want to try that phone there."

Call the police collect from St. Cloud? "I don't think so. How far out is the train?"

"Ought to be in in an hour. They're making good time."

That would put me in the city around eight. Arrest him while he's still in bed. With the TV cameras around and one reporter, me, there to claim it. No, no, couldn't be.

No. It was. Suddenly I felt an extraordinary pleasure, a broad crackling sensation of happiness. Everything was about to come together. Mac's comeuppance. Marya sees it on TV and curses herself for not being there. The city is saved, or at least shown it needn't worry. This, this was going to be wonderful.

And if I was wrong?

25

The train pulled into Minneapolis around eight in the morning. I had called Fikes collect from St. Cloud, praying he wasn't over at Betty's. The phone rang twenty-three times. Fikes answered in a voice clogged with sleep, growled a mrrgh, accepted the charges and listened to what I had to tell him. He said this was wonderful, his voice numb with fatigue, and promised to meet the train.

Indeed, he was standing at the gate. He had on a trench coat, with a long black silk scarf wrapped around his neck, black leather gloves. The final touch today was a red cotton ski cap with the motto A-1 E-Z Auto Repair. "Car's outside," he said. "What's this about?"

"Don't you remember what we talked about on the phone?"

"Not a word."

"This is about Jared."

"Well, yes. Go on."

"I know who he is."

He snorted. "So?"

"What do you mean, so?"

"So you read the papers."

"No, no. I read a magazine. It was the address label that—what do you mean, the papers?"

"You don't know, do you?" He shook his head. "Here." He took me by the arm and led me across the station to the rack of newspapers by the door.

AIL HEAD ARRESTED, read the headline.

"No!" I shouted.

"Quite a Christmas present, mrrgh?"

"They got the wrong man! They had to!"

"Gent by the name of MacAdam, or something," Fikes said. "Can you keep your voice down? People are looking."

I stuck my hands in my pockets to get change for the paper—but no, I'd wasted it all on train-station coffee, high-living fool that I was. "Buy one," I commanded, pointing at the rack.

"I've a copy in the car."

I knelt down and attempted to read the story through the scratched and stained plastic. "When the police arrived early this morning, James MacAdam, the man police suspect as being the ringleader of the AIL, was sitting at home, having a beer. His T-shirt read—"

The rest of the story was below the fold, out of sight. I stood and grabbed Fikes by the lapels.

"What did his T-shirt say?"

"Calm down, Simpson. I have the paper in the car. You can read it on the way to the office." He led me outside.

"*Aaaaaaaaaaaaaaaaaaaaaaaaaa*," I said. I sucked in a chestful of the air, panting. "*GOD DAMN IT!*" I looked up and addressed the empty sky. "I'm talking to You! What have I done to deserve this? What? Can You put it in writing and send me a copy?"

Fikes was laughing.

"What's so goddamn funny?"

"You. You have a bit of a gift for spontaneous invective."

"Go to hell." I stomped over to a parked car and leaned against it. I took deep breaths; my lungs hurt. My head hurt. My career hurt.

"I had this figured out," I finally said. "I was going to take the police to Mac. I should have been there when they picked him up."

"You would've been, if you'd, mrrgh, been here."

"What?"

"We got a call last night. Our friend Detective Bishop. All your cooperation apparently bought you some goodwill. They were getting ready to move on Mr. MacAdam and wanted to know if you wanted to be in on it. We tried like mad to find you yesterday, to no end." He looked at his fingernails. "We were going to send Solly, but Bishop said you or nobody—that he owed you, but not the *Metropole*."

"How did they know? How the hell did they know?"

"Ah." Fikes coughed. "I gather they'd known for a month or so. They were just confirming, building the case. The news reports have said that the tip-off came from Chicago. Brokers at the Board of Trade were noticing unusual stock trading on Munco stock, among others. It took them two weeks to trace it here, and then to MacAdam. They began to investigate him, and they made the case. Really as simple as that. This has all been about stock manipulation. The ideology and all was a batch of smoke Mr. MacAdam concocted to confuse the issue." He shook his head. "Apparently he's been the only suspect, and he's been under observation throughout this entire affair."

"That's why Bishop used to think I was in on this. Never mind that I seemed to be poisoning everyone around me. He saw me arriving and leaving the apartment where Mac was living half the time." I stopped, thought. "Then how did he know I wasn't in on it? Unless he had the place bugged." I grimaced. Of course he had. The things he had heard.

"I don't know what you're talking about. What do you mean, you were at the apartment?"

I rubbed my eyes. "I used to go out with Mac's girlfriend. We sort of picked it up again awhile ago. She's pregnant with either my child or Mac's." I turned my face to God again and mouthed *Why*.

Fikes stood there, mouth agape. "What?"

"Uh-huh. That's how stupid I am. I've know this guy for a couple of months. Lunched with him, slept with his girlfriend, bathed in his tub, napped on his sofa, everything. And did I know what was going on? Nah." I shook my head. Fikes still stared. I explained about my revelation in St. Cloud.

He began to laugh. It sounded like a porpoise having an orgasm. Then he grabbed me by the shoulders and shook them and hugged me and took off his cap and threw it in the air.

"Oh!" he said. "Oh!" He picked up his cap, slapped it on his knee and crammed it on his head. "Don't you see? You don't. Oh. Oh, this is even better. I couldn't have dreamed it. MacAdam is being held incommunicado, no one can see him, no one can talk to him. All the other papers have is the facts of the arrest. They'll be scrambling for details, background. They won't get anything for days. But you. You can write the story no one else has. You actually knew the man. Oh, happiness. Happiness!"

"But we won't publish for a week."

"We'll publish Friday. The entire next issue is laid out and ready to go, except for the piece you were going to do about that woman—Sparks, Spanky? Forget about that. Look. We have to get going. You have to write the piece, today. It's Christmas Eve, I know, I'm sorry. I'm going to call the typesetter and get someone in tonight. I'll do it myself if we have to. This is going to be perfect, perfect. Don't you see? I SLEPT IN JARED'S BED. Oh, we can actually charge for this issue. Oh. This is simply too fine. Do you know how lucky you are?"

I looked at him for a while, then I nodded. "I know exactly how lucky I am. That's why I'm nervous."

I was feeling better when I reached the manor.

"Merrrrrry Christmas," I shouted. "God bless us everyone! Grue? Tryg? Got the wassail on yet?"

The door slammed behind me, and I turned. A figure stood against the door, only its silhouette visible. It locked the door and stepped forward, into the light.

"Merry Christmas to you, too," he said. "We've been waiting for you." He pointed into the main hall. "It's party time."

"Mark." Mark Lewis. Trotsky.

"Call me Sinclair." He wore no expression. "Ho, ho, ho."

26

I would have told them they would never get away with this if I had known what "this" was. As it stood I was playing host to the grimmest lot of professional lunatics this side of my mother's family. The AIL all wore fatigues or basic black, combat boots, a beret here and there. Oh: and guns. They all carried guns.

I wasn't scared. That was the odd thing. I was angry. I felt furious enough to thrash them all if opportunity arose. I knew I was going to come out of this alive. I just knew it.

I also had known that Jane was going to spend the rest of her life with me; that I was going to be a famous writer; that Mac was just a glad-handing idiot.

Perhaps I was too stupid to be scared.

I had tried to bolt out the door, but Sinclair would have none of that. He put a friendly hand around my neck and propelled me into the main hall. My requests as to the whereabouts of Tryg and Grue earned me a thumb on my common carotid, so I dropped the matter for the moment. He said I should be introduced to tonight's company. He shoved me toward a young woman standing by the window, peering through a curtain. "Say hello to Greta."

"Hlo." Greta gave me a dull hard look of indifference, with hatred waiting in the wings should she decide to get emotional about me. She was short and broad and looked as though she came from a family where the menfolk liked to twist off the ears of the family pets. She looked as though she twisted the ears of the menfolk. "Greta's watching for our friends," said Sinclair.

"There's more of you coming?" I said. "I don't know how many we can seat at the—"

"The police are coming. But don't get your hopes up. Now here. . . ." He steered me into the study, where a tall young man sat under the window. There was a rifle at his side and far too much ammunition at his feet. He had the same dead look in his eyes as Greta, but there was an intelligence to his face. He looked as though he could be reasoned with, provided you shot him first. "This is Gunther."

"Hello," I said.

"Pig."

"No, turkey. We have turkey on Christmas around here."

"You're a funny man," said Sinclair. He was holding me at arm's length, studying me like an insect on a pin.

"Reflex," I said. "I talk without thinking. Like a chicken with its head cut off." Oh, good. Give them ideas.

"Now . . ." He pushed me backward into the dining hall. A disheveled young man who apparently saw a fresh, sharp razor blade as the embodiment of decadent bourgeois luxury was working on the cord for the drapes.

"This is Werther," said Sinclair.

"Where do you do your hiring? Spandau?"

"Some of us have taken our revolutionary names from those slain in the 1848 uprisings. When the Austrian parliament was dissolved," he added.

"I thought it was a bad idea," I said.

"You will fix these drapes," Sinclair said. He tightened his grasp on my throat. "They are stuck."

"I know. They've been stuck since I got here. Don't worry. That's the intensive care ward up there. They don't notice anything. They're too busy dy—" Don't give them any ideas.

Werther was tugging on the drapes, exposing himself to the window. He spied the hook that would not give, took out an automatic pistol and fired—*tumph!*—and the hook exploded. "It's all right!" Sinclair shouted. "Werther is just fixing the drapes." Werther yanked on the drapes and they slid along the runners, blocking out the precious world.

"Good shot," I said. My knees were pudding. "I wonder if you could do something about a door I have upstairs. It sticks." Sinclair was leading me back to the kitchen. A young man was guarding the back door. "This is Joe."

"Joe? They had Joes in 1848?"

"Joe disagrees with the action of 1848. Don't you, Joe."

"Premature," Joe grunted. He turned to Sinclair. "Let's kill him now instead."

"Premature." I held up my hands. "What's this 'now instead' stuff? Would you please tell me what is going on here? Where's Grue? Where's Tryg?"

"If you mean your own personal servant class—"

"I mean my friends," I said. "My family."

"Family." He smiled. "Which you hold in servitude."

"Servitude? Who do you think pays the mortgage on this heap? You think I have that kind of scratch? The butler inherited all the money, friend. He gives me money."

"Parasitism," said Joe. "Living off the fruits of the lower class."

"Your friends are upstairs," said Sinclair. "Saul is looking after them."

Saul, ergo Manny. My heart quickened. Maybe I could bring him around.

"Can I see them?"

"Eventually." He led me out of the kitchen. "You have not exactly made a friend in Joe."

"He's broken into my house and is standing at my back door with a rifle and you say I'm on his bad side?"

Sinclair let go of my throat. He pointed to a chair. I sat.

"You are the medium here. The bait, if you like."

"For what? You guys are finished. Mac—excuse me, Herr Jared—is in jail. This whole thing has been a scam and everyone knows it. What's the point?"

"It hasn't been a scam." He began to pace, slowly, hands behind his back. "Jared deceived us, yes. His objectives were—how should I put this—disheartening. But that does not discredit the validity of what we seek. And that is what we have to prove."

"So what's this all about? Why not make another tape, disassociate yourself from him?"

He sighed. "Jared knows who we are. A matter of time before he tells the police. He probably has already. So individually we are no longer safe. Collectively we have one last statement to make. Which is this."

"You're all going to jail."

He nodded. "Those who survive, yes."

"What do you mean, 'survive'?"

"I mean that this situation has several possible outcomes, the death of us all being but one."

"Go get killed somewhere else. I want to have Christmas."

Sinclair smiled, almost sad. "No. Not this year. You see, there is only one way to reclaim credibility. Prove to the people that some of us were sincere."

"Okay, how."

"By killing Jared."

"He'll never come here. They'd never let him."

"Perhaps they will when we tell them that we have hostages. And that we will kill them if they don't deliver. And that's the difficult part, you see. Once you start to kill hostages the police react in strange ways."

Well, well, well, well, well, well, well, well, well.

"But he'll come," he said, "and we will kill him."

"And after that?"

He shrugged. "Improvisation."

And now, finally, I was truly afraid.

The police arrived after five. Fashionably late. Sinclair had called them up, asked for Bishop (my suggestion), laid out the details of the situation and told them to drop round. What he actually said was "I'll kill them, I swear to God I'll kill them," in an uncharacteristically agitated voice, and hung up. "They don't believe you unless you sound crazy," he explained. He proceeded to call the TV stations and told them there was a hostage drama scheduled tonight at the following address.

"They should be here soon," Sinclair said. "Everyone in position. Stay loose for now."

"We got company," shouted Gunther a few minutes later. "Three squads."

"Up," said Sinclair. He grabbed me by the lapels and held me by the collar, one hand digging into his coat. "Is there TV yet?" he yelled. He pulled a gun from his pocket.

"No. Wait a minute—okay, the truck just arrived. Channel twelve."

"Channel four has better ratings. We'll wait for them."

"I'll watch from the set upstairs," I said.

"You're coming with."

"Four is here," Greta bawled.

"We'll give them a few minutes to set up," Sinclair said to me. "Sound checks, lighting." To Gunther: "Tell me when it looks like they're rolling."

"They already are."

"Let's go." I felt the barrel of the gun in my back. Sinclair shoved me toward the front door. "Open it. Foolish things will occur to you, such as running away, but I will kill you if you do. Remember that we have your friends upstairs. We can do without you if we have to."

"I'll be good."

"Fine. Now, open the door."

I did. I took one step outside, Sinclair's gun grazing my temple. I took a look at what might possibly be the last view of the outside world I would ever be allowed. I realized I had never had the fence fixed. It still wore a dent the size of car. Then I looked out over the world.

There were three squad cars outside, with more arriving, from the sound of the sirens. Policemen were crouched behind the hoods of the cars, guns drawn. Barricades were being set up at the end of the block, and there were people in every window in the buildings across the street. On the porch of the house down the street I saw a small hunched figure in plaid behind a brass walker, the old woman who had cursed my arrival here. Above it all, pink and purple clouds basking in the sunset.

At the sight of Sinclair shoving me out the door, bolts clicked and triggers were cocked back. My guts turned liquid again. I backed into Sinclair, but he shoved me forward and jammed the gun into my temple.

"Hold your fire!" a voice from the cars shouted.

"Nobody shoot anybody!" I screamed. "Not at all! Not never!"

"No moves!" Sinclair shouted. "I speak on behalf of the AIL. We want to talk to Jared. Now."

There was a pause, then the crackle of static. A voice came over a bullhorn. "This is Detective Bishop here. Identify yourself."

"Sinclair. AIL Central Committee."

"This is pretty pointless, son. We got your boss in irons and he just about got laryngitis trying to tell everything he knew. There's no way out of this. Why don't you just put down your—"

"We seek not freedom but justice. I demand to have Jared brought here. Don't force me to kill to get what we are owed."

"All right, all right, now, nobody wants any trouble. We'll set up a phone link with Jared. Just hold on and be patient."

"In person. We want him here in person."

"Can't be done."

"In person, or the hostages die. We have three."

"Is that Simpson you got there?"

"Present," I said.

"Aw, Christ. Can't we do *anything* without you?"

"Just do what he says!" I yelled.

"Half an hour!" called Sinclair. "If he's not here in half an hour we start to kill the hostages. One every five minutes."

"How many you got in there?"

"Three. And there are ten of us."

"Ten?" I said. I flashed "five" with my right hand.

"So we got, what, forty-five minutes."

"Bishop!" I yelled.

"Half an hour or people start to die," Sinclair cried.

He pulled me back into the house, bolted the door. "Gunther! Greta! Report!"

"No motion," called Greta. "Nobody on the roofs yet."

"The fat cop is talking into a mike," said Gunther. "The TV person is talking into a camera . . . Two more cars arriving. And a fire truck."

Sinclair beamed. "Well. I think that went well, didn't you? Damn." He smacked his hands together. "That went perfect."

"You. Won't. Kill. Us," I gasped.

"What?"

"You won't kill us." I swallowed, found my voice. "If Jared isn't here in half an hour you won't kill us every five minutes."

"What do you think I am, a maniac?"

"Jesus," I panted. "You're not my choice to lead a pack of Cub Scouts."

"There's no point in killing you if they don't come through right away." He looked out the window of the door, bit his lip. "It's not as if we've an infinite supply of hostages. We have to ration."

I nodded. Set my mind at rest. "Can I see Tryg and Grue now?"

"Yes." Sinclair put the gun back in his holster and drew the zipper of his jacket halfway up so that he could get at the gun but I'd have trouble grabbing for it. "Yes. Let's go."

Tryg and Grue were in the children's room, guarded by a man who had one foot up on a samples case the size of a steamer trunk. Manny/Saul was leaning against the closet door, rubbing the barrel of a pistol up and down his thigh.

Trygve was sitting in a chair, unbound, hands folded in his lap; Grue was tied to her chair, shoulders working back and forth. When she saw me she stopped struggling and let her eyes go wide with alarm.

"Master Jonathan! Go! Men in the house with guns there are all over!"

Sinclair stepped from the hallway behind me, and Grue's face darkened.

"You." She spat. "For an old woman no respect he has. Of all the rooms to be choosing, this one he chooses. I have not in months here vacuumed. Put me in a clean room, I ask of him, but for an old woman no honor he pays."

"I know, Grue." I bent down and mopped her forehead with the sleeve of my jacket. "It's going to be okay. What they want has nothing to do with us. There are already police outside. We'll be fine. How's Tryg?"

"Scared," said Trygve in a small voice.

"Are you all right? Can you look at me, Tryg?"

He shook his head.

"Why not?"

"If I raise my head they will still be there."

"All right. Do you want something to read, as long as you're looking down?" He nodded yes. "I'll get you a book or a magazine." I looked up at Saul.

"Hello, Manny."

He grinned. "Manny hasn't been around. Haven't seen him in some time."

"Manny?" said Sinclair.

"Private joke," Saul said.

"You two know each other?"

"Mutual acquaintances," I said. "You in there, Manny? Bobbi Parker's outside with channel twelve, Manny. Bobbi Parker."

"Shut up." Saul brought his gun up.

"She's looking good, Manny. Got a floppy tie on, just like you like it."

"Shut up." He slapped his pistol and cocked it.

"Hey. She asked about you. Just relaying the message."

"Shut up!" He pointed his pistol at me, hands shaking, but lowered it immediately.

"Come on," said Sinclair. "We don't need this. There's only fifteen minutes left. Back downstairs. Come on." He took me by the collar again. He was going to ruin this sweater.

"What was that about Bobbi Parker?"

"You don't know about Saul?" I whistled.

"Tell me."

"Not until you tell me some things. And don't say I'm in no position to bargain, because you don't have an infinite supply of hostages."

He blew a gust of exasperation, looked at his watch and said, "All right. What? Ask."

"Was Sarah in on this?"

"Sarah? I don't know any Sarah."

"The hell you don't. You dated her in college. Tall, dark, nervous, brainy, gorgeous? Come on. She's not exactly forgettable. She dumped me for you. That Sarah."

"Sarah? My God! That was five years ago. What would she have to do with this?"

I laughed. "Sarah was living with your Jared. Has been for four years." I shook my head. "She dumped me for you. I wanted to kill you."

"I surmise you still do." Sinclair scowled, looked away. He did not like that Sarah had been with Jared; he had the look of a man finding out the extent of his ignorance.

"Spanks," I said. "What about her?"

"She . . . was smarter than I thought. I don't like being fooled and I let her fool me. I was using her, for the video equipment. I thought she had no idea what it was for, either. I said I needed something to alter the voices, so—"

"I know. She told me."

He stared at me.

"I know her. I've talked to her. I also talked to the police and they, in case you haven't read the papers, were on to you long before Spanks put your voice into general circulation. So don't blame her. Blame yourself for being such a loudmouth about your convictions."

Sinclair's jaw tightened.

"You killed Spanks's father, you know," I said.

"I know." The same dead-fish voice.

I stood up. "That's all you have to say, 'I know'? You slept with the woman and you don't care that you killed her—" He put one hand into his jacket, gestured for me to sit with the other. I sat.

"All right. The plutonium. Do you have it?"

He shrugged, shook his head. "Didn't have to have any. You observed the effect the suggestion had on the city."

"If you didn't have it, why say you did? They'd test the water—"

"And they'd find plutonium. There are trace amounts in most rivers. A few years ago in New York, you might recall, there were stories about the amounts of plutonium in the water; people went berserk, as you might expect. It exists in most water supplies. Too diluted to do harm. But once the papers printed the story that plutonium was found in the Mississippi, that was all the people would need. You would have seen the end of irradiated food."

"One more question. Who beat me up on Thanksgiving?"

"Beat you?" He looked away. "It wasn't us."

"Sinclair!" Gunther cried. "Someone's coming up the front walk. A cop. It's . . . it's the same one who was talking on the bullhorn."

"Is he armed?"

"Not that I can see. Has his hands up."

"Let's go," Sinclair said, motioning me up. Back down the hall to the front door. I opened it and the gun was at my head again. I looked out, saw police, TV cameras, Bishop standing on the walk, arms up in peace and goodwill. It was dark; there were floodlights from the police cars, the TV trucks and the fire truck, all pointed at the manor.

"Trade," he said. "Me for him. We're working on getting Jared here. It's not as simple as you think."

"You've got him in jail!" I shouted. "It's not like you have to back order him from the stock room!"

"Calm down, Simpson," Bishop said.

"No trade," said Sinclair, then his arm tightened around my neck. "Stay there," he said to Bishop. We backed into the house, and Sinclair shut the door with a foot. He turned around and said, "Saul. Explain."

"Nothing to explain. I knew him at school. Had a friend named Manny. That's all."

Sinclair jammed the gun into my neck. "You called him Manny. Explain."

"Saul, or Manny, one and the same. Or seven and the same. He's a lunatic, which apparently goes unnoticed in your circles. He has a multiple personality. Saul happens to be the strongest of the gang right now."

"Why did you call for Manny?" The gun dug a little deeper.

"Because because because Jesus! Put the goddamn gun down I'm telling you already!" The gun stayed where it was. "All right! I was trying to bring him out, even the odds, that's all!"

Sinclair pulled me back, opened the door again and reassumed the familiar posture. Bishop was still standing there.

"I'll trade," Sinclair said. "You for this one."

"*No!*" I cried. Bishop looked at me with alarm. "I'm not going! He's got my friends in there! I'm not leaving! Manny!" I screamed over my shoulder. "Manny! I'm out here with Bobbi Parker! She's been asking about you! I think she likes you!"

"Take off your shirt," Sinclair told Bishop. "I want to make sure you're not wired." Bishop peeled off his jacket, put it on the ground and took off his shirt. He stood shivering, arms raised. "Now turn around. Fine. Now the pants." Bishop looked back toward the cameras; they didn't move. Bishop swore, then started pulling off his pants. There was a snicker from the squad cars, followed by a slap, and silence. When he was reduced to socks and boxer shorts, holding himself against the cold, Sinclair pronounced him admissible and told him to dress again. When Bishop was back in mufti he was waved closer and told to stand in front of me. With one motion Sinclair let go of my neck, smacked the butt of the gun into the back of my head and kicked me forward, wrapping his arm around Bishop. I fell, grabbing the back of my head by reflex, and flung myself back at the door—just in time to bang my forehead on the grille over the window.

I stumbled backwards and started kicking at the door, yelling for Sinclair to let me in you goddamn maniac, let me in let me in—

Someone grabbed me by the waist and pulled me away. I struggled, but another pair of arms joined the effort and hauled me down the sidewalk. "Don't you dare frighten that butler!" I yelled. "Don't you dare!" And then I was shoved along until I reached the open door of an unmarked car at the end of the block. They pushed me in and slammed the door shut; I fell into another body, turned to start complaining.

Mac smiled. "Hey, dude," he said. "Guess we travel in the same circles."

I hit him very, very hard. Three months of unending sturm and drang went into the punch. His sunglasses flew off and his jaw cracked and he flew back into the seat. They pulled me off of him before I got a chance to really tell him what I'd been thinking.

"I'm Lieutenant Nashua," the man said. We were in another car. He was smoking a pipe tobacco cured in a sty. I was sitting in the backseat.

"How do you do."

"You know, it's not smart to attack someone in the backseat of a police car." He chuckled. "I think we'll be too busy to press charges."

"Forever in your debt."

Nashua handed me a cup of coffee and explained the situation. Bishop had not expected to trade places with me. They were trying to gain time, not appear to be too acquiescent. No one had expected Sinclair to throw me out. I explained why that happened, and Nashua winced; he didn't like the idea of Manny/Saul. Another wild card. I explained where the sentries were, described the weaponry.

"Two doors, both guarded. I wouldn't suggest the chimney. And forget about going through the windows."

"The ones facing the hospital? Why?"

"Why? Do you know what those things are worth?" And I could still see that angel laid over Marya's face.

"Well, there's no sense charging through there. We'd be going in blind."

"What are you going to do?"

"We're going to give them Jared."

"They want to kill him."

Nashua nodded. "We know."

There was a pause.

"Court docket overloaded, is that it?" I finally said.

"No, we don't intend to let them kill him." He tamped down his pipe with the end of his lighter. "Your house is bugged. It has been for a while now. Sorry about that. But we thought at the beginning you were part of this whole thing, you know, least Bishop did, and once he gets a bee in his bonnet—" He smiled, puffed. "Well, we got a bug in there, and somehow never got around to taking it out. So when we hear Bishop shout 'gosh,' that's the cue, and we're going to go in, storm the place proper." He sighed. "I should be home. This is one of those peace-on-earth days, for Christ's sake. At most a knife fight on the Northside."

" 'Gosh'?"

"Bishop never says 'gosh.' Sort of out of character. When we hear that we know something's wrong."

"What are you going to do when you storm the place?" I asked.

He shrugged. "We'll wing it."

"Improvise."

"Don't worry. Your friends'll be all right. You see, we've got a—"

There was a knock on the window. We looked up and saw Bobbi Parker. She mouthed a few words; Nashua rolled down the window.

"Sorry to interrupt you guys, but can I get a few words with Mr. Simpson there?"

"In a minute," I said. I turned to Nashua. "I have to get back in the house."

He shook his head. "Absolutely not."

"Look, I'm not going to stand out here and wait. I have friends in there. Tell me what you plan to do and I can help."

"Sorry. Don't worry about your friends. We've—"

"Then let me talk to Jared."

He thought for a second, shrugged. "No harm there, I suppose. Just don't hit him. We need him."

"Promise."

"Why?"

Mac looked away. He was cuffed at the wrist, and cuffed again to the handle of the car door. It really hadn't been fair to hit him before. And it was all too tempting to hit him again. I was the one who needed handcuffs. I was sitting in the front seat of the police car just to keep a safe distance. "Come on, Mac. Why?"

"I already told the police," he said. He spoke in a soft, well-modulated voice, with no trace of slang. "You can read their report."

"I'd rather hear it from your lips. Before I split them open."

Mac looked at me. I waited. "I didn't mean for it all to get this . . . bad," he said. "Not at the beginning. I just got the idea of setting up this group, going after a company and knocking down the stock price. I didn't intend for anyone to be killed. You have to believe me."

"That wasn't soy sauce you were sticking in the food."

He chewed on his lower lip. His eyes drifted closed. "It just got out of my hands. Sinclair, Lewis—he's the one. He actually believes in all this stuff. A fanatic about what he eats. I went along with putting the poison in the cake mix—"

"Bundt mix."

"Yeah, bundt mix. I insisted on the warnings we put in the box. And when we sent the brownies to the papers I demanded warnings accompany those too, but Sinclair went behind my back. Removed the letters and sent them separately. When that man died—"

"Louis Aloysius Carver," I said. "Aged fifty-six, liked to drink, big heart, one daughter named Katherine—"

"Stop. Don't."

"No, I'd like to go on. I want to tell you everything about him. I want you to know who you killed."

"I didn't want to kill—" He stopped, his voice choking. "I—didn't—want—them—to—die. When the first one died I panicked. I backed out. Left it all to Sinclair. I tried to find some way out of it. But I couldn't. I couldn't go to the police. I couldn't stop them without exposing myself. And I wasn't ready to go to jail."

"So you let them do the work in order to buy off your conscience, while you sat back and screwed around with the market, right?"

I leaned back in my seat, looked out the window. Nothing was happening. No motion anywhere, everyone frozen, waiting.

"I think I'd prefer that you'd believed in this stuff," I said. "But you don't believe in anything. Just greed and cowardice." Mac stared out the window. "What does Sarah know?" I said.

"Nothing. She never suspected." He closed his eyes. "I was going to try and make it work with her again. All that garbage I fed you at the bar was designed to try and figure out where you and her were at. I didn't want you anywhere around." He smiled, sighed. "I called you on Thanksgiving, you know. To meet me at the Uptown. I was going to give you a lesson and scare you off Sarah."

Tell me about it. "Is she pregnant?"

"I don't know. She wouldn't tell me one way or the other. I hope she isn't. If it's mine I'll never see it, and if it's yours that'll just rip me up." I must have looked surprised, for he shrugged and said, "Hey. I'm human too."

"I know. That gives me consolation." Mac looked up at me, quizzical.

"It means you're going to die someday."

We sat in silence for five minutes. I never took my eyes off of him, and he never looked at me.

I ran to KJGO's truck. Bobbi Parker was sitting in the doorway of the van, microphone in her lap. She saw me and stood, eyes darting to see if I had come from any of the other TV trucks. She gave me a smile of astonishing insincerity and motioned for a cameraman, sitting next to her in the van, to stand and get busy.

I got into the van. "Ms. Parker," I said. "You can either get an exclusive interview here or perform a public service. I hate to give you a dilemma like that but that's what it comes down to."

"What are you talking about?"

"One of the men in there has a crush on you. He's crazy. I don't mean to imply that his insanity has anything to do with being attracted to you. You're very lovely. Thing is, if you make an appeal to him, it might tip the balance of power up there. Trust me. What you have to do is have someone else, preferably male, say that he has a message for Saul. Got that?"

"Saul."

"Correct. Wait a few minutes for him to go to the television set. There's one in the study where one of them is and I'm sure it's on. Then you step in and say something along the lines of this: 'Hello, Manny. I know you're in there. I haven't been able to stop thinking about you since we met. I'd like to go out for dinner with you. Maybe Chinese. You like Chinese, Manny?' " I stopped. She was staring at me. "Something like that, all right?"

"Manny Perlstein? The guy with the people in his head?"

"You got it. He's one of them. Can you do that?"

Bobbi Parker grinned. "We're in sweeps right now. You bet I can do it."

"Good."

"Wait a minute," Bobbi said. "How are you sure they'll be watching channel twelve?"

"I'm not. I have to go around to the rest of the TV crews and convince them to tell the guys inside the house to tune to twelve." And I sprinted over to the nearest TV truck.

"Let me get this straight," said the newscaster when I had finished my request. "You want me to interrupt my show to tell the AIL to turn to channel twelve."

"That's right."

"You're outta your head."

"Look, I'm sorry, but it could save lives in there. It's too long to explain. You've got to trust me. You have to cut in and tell them to switch the channel for a special message. There's no time to set up a common feed, and anyway it's Bobbi Parker who has to talk to them."

"Her?" the man said. "Did you see the last Arbitrons? Nobody watches her. Look, we're the station with credibility. Something happens, people turn to us."

"Just *do it!*" I shouted. "When this is over I'll give you an exclusive interview, all right?"

It was the same at both of the other stations, adamant newscasters swayed by the promise of an exclusive interview. I was as exclusive as a gumball machine by the time my route was finished, but everyone agreed. I stood and watched nearby while Bobbi Parker asked Manny to go out and see a movie, dinner, her treat. When it was over I wandered across the street, just to get away from the mess of cables and cars and vans. I wanted to be somewhere where they weren't waiting for the worst to happen, but that category comprised most of the known world and I had to settle for a porch. People were eight deep at the barricades on either side of the street. Patients from the hospital had made it from their dying beds to stumble to the window and behold the scene.

Everything was still, silent. There were a few snowflakes in the air. Christmas.

I heard a door creak open behind me, and then the occupant of the house came out, stamped her brass walker on the porch and demanded, "Ye get off my parch afare I called the polis." It was the same old musty beldam who had bewailed my presence on the block months ago.

"Ye braught it on yer own self!" She howled. "Fair and peaceful it was, and now look! Your grandmither and servant, captive to agents of death and ruin!"

She stopped, looked across the street. Something was happening. There was a policeman walking up to the sidewalk, one arm steering Mac alongside. The headlights of the cars facing the house were being turned off, one by one, and now an alley of black led to the front door, with light from the house spilling out on either side.

The pair moved up the dark lane of the walk.

They paused at the door. I saw the officer knock.

Please come home, Master Jonathan, Trygve had said that morning in Valhalla; please come home and save us.

What else could I do? I sprinted across the street, leaped over the cables from the TV vans, flattened one policeman who stood in my path and bolted up the walk. I tucked my head down and prayed, heard the door creak open; I looked up and saw it open an inch, a foot—the officer stepped aside. I put my weight into Mac's back and blew us both into the hallway, smacking my head on his, tasting red, sliding onto the tile hall floor. "Just me!" I shouted. "Don't shoot! Don't shoot!"

This was an awful idea; this was wrong, wrong. Sinclair fell back against the wall, kicked the door shut and dropped to his haunches. Mac was crumpled against the closet, holding his head; I scrambled up the hallway into the dining room. Sinclair pointed the gun at my groin. "Gosh!" I yelled. "Gosh, gosh, gosh!" Sinclair grabbed Mac by the collar and slid him along the floor into the dining room, where Werther stood holding a gun on Bishop, who sat in a chair in the middle of the room, eyes wide at the sight of me. I kept crawling backward until I struck Werther's legs; he put a boot on my chest. "What the fuck is going on?" he yelled.

"Simple," Sinclair said. "They've introduced some complications." He put his foot in Mac's groin and stood on it; Mac snapped to attention and began to howl.

"First things first," Sinclair hissed, and he leveled his gun at Mac.

"Gosh!" I screamed. "God damn it, gosh!"

"God damn it, Sinclair, don't," Bishop snapped.

"Goshalmighty!" I yelled. "That's gosh, g-o-s-h, gosh!"

"You lied," said Sinclair to Mac, his voice high, almost frantic. "You lied and misled us. You did for money what we did from dedication. No, don't try. I don't want to hear you speak. I. Just. Want. To. See. You. Die."

I closed my eyes.

And opened them when I heard the shot from above.

It was like watching someone plucked from earth by wires. Sinclair rose half a foot in the air, spun around, hit the floor staggering, his legs giving way, one hand clutching his shoulder. Werther spun around, and I rolled onto my stomach; Werther looked madly around the room, then let fly a spray of bullets toward the mezzanine, up where Tryg and Grue— No. I tackled him from behind and drove him hard onto the floor; his head bounced off the tile and his gun went skidding across the room, where Bishop dived for it. In another second Greta, Gunther and Joe were scrambling into the room, guns drawn. I put my head down and wrapped my hands around my brain and prayed that whoever was about to receive my soul would recognize it.

"Don't any of you move," said a voice from the mezzanine. "You cannot see me and I can certainly see you. Be so kind as to put your guns down. Now. Or I shoot. Clear?"

I unwrapped my head, looked up. And cried: "Oscar!"

"Now, stand back from your host. You people really are dreadful guests. That's right. All right, cousin. Up. Up the stairs. Quickly." I stood, backing away from Greta, Gunther and Joe, then dashed toward the stairs and took them three at a time. When I reached the top I saw Oscar laid flat, peering from the darkness into the hall. "Down," he snapped. I rolled along the floor until I was by his side. "Jesus, Oscar, I can't thank you—"

"Thank me when we're alive and you're feeling hideously guilty."

Pooomph! Glass crashed in the study, and a canister came bouncing into the hall. Smoke began to billow.

"It's going to be a bit like hell in here in about five seconds," Oscar shouted. "Come on."

Gunfire at the back of the house. I looked down to see Joe scooping up his weapon and heading back for the kitchen. Gunther and Greta already had theirs and were reassuming positions; Werther was on his hands and knees, still groggy, swaying in the smoke as he hacked and spat. Neither Mac nor Bishop was anywhere to be seen, but I could see floodlights pouring in the door. They'd made it out.

"We have to head for— Christ!" A volley came from the hallway, throwing hundreds of pellets of lead into the hall, clanging off the heraldic shield. More gunfire came from the library, where Gunther stood defending; he probably disagreed with every book in the room. Oscar and I rolled over and scrambled into the children's room as another blast took out a window downstairs; there was a cry, female, a spurt of gunfire from the kitchen. Oscar kicked the door shut and ran for the closet. I looked around the room: two chairs, empty. Oscar was pawing through old dusty clothes left hanging in the closet; then he crawled under a rack of coats and disappeared. I looked and saw a small crawlway in the corner of the closet; I followed him through.

We were in a dark small space, damp stone walls all around. "Watch the steps," Oscar said, and I heard creaking boards. I followed. Faint gunfire sounded from downstairs.

We walked up to a square of light. Oscar put a hand to the ceiling, lifted a door, lifted himself up and into the light. I followed.

The attic. A bed, a table, a chair. Two lamps. Trygve sat on the bed, paging through a men's magazine, brow knit in wonder and alarm; Grue sat in a chair, arms folded; she saw me and called out my name. Manny sat in another chair, shoulders slouched, the usual worried look on his face.

I lay on the floor for a minute or so, not moving.

"The fracas should be over soon," Oscar said. "I'm hungry. I know an excellent caterer." He picked up the phone. "Salmon all right?"

No one spoke.

"All right, then. Pheasant?"

27

I stood outside, watching the scene dissolve, feeling peace and great happiness. Half the squad cars were gone, and the ambulances had borne the damaged goods to the hospitals. Sinclair had been wounded in the shoulder, a lung punctured; serious, expected to recover. Greta had suffered cuts and bruises when a tear-gas canister went through the window by which she stood; she had been treated and sent to the holding tank. Gunther and Werther had both been shot in various appendages. Joe had turned the corner into the kitchen only to greet and provide a resting place for several dozen pieces of ammunition. He was listed in stable condition, which is to say he was dead and likely to remain so. Mac had fled before the real shooting started, run gibbering back to the police. He was also back in jail.

I had lain motionless on the floor of the attic until we heard Bishop calling for us. Oscar had gone down reluctantly—his heroism notwithstanding, there were still a few minor warrants out on him, and there was more police around than anyone was likely to see in their law-abiding life. Outside he tried to stroll away but was cornered by a TV reporter; when he gave his name for the interview, a policeman with a large memory and obstinate sense of duty ran the name through the computer and learned of the many warrants. The folks watching at home saw Oscar yanked from their screen in midboast. He was led away, calling for me to help; I yelled that I'd be down to bail him out.

Manny came out of the house, shaking his head. He stood at my side and sighed, long and wearily.

"What's the matter?" I said. "You're alive. They won't put you in jail. Maybe you'll get treatment, even."

" 'S that Bobbi Parker." He sighed. "Just did an interview with her. She's got a ring on her finger. Such a rock I should be able to afford." He looked up at the sky. "So God makes me a—what was that word?"

"Anthology?"

"Yeah. So He makes me an anthology. Why couldn't any of my sides have any business sense? Not one of them knew how to make money." He sighed again.

"What happened up there? Did you hear Bobbi Parker on TV?"

"Oh. Maybe, I don't know. All of a sudden I take over and I'm holding a gun on two old people. Well, thinks me, this is a sudden turn of events. Last thing I remember I was having apple pie in a restaurant, and I had to, you know, take a leak." He hitched up his belt. "So I was in the can. I got, you know, my little guy in my hand. Then *shazaam*, blackout. Saul musta come in. Then I takes over again and I now have this gun in my hand. And I still have to take a leak.

Confused? I even shook the gun. So I go to the bathroom. I see what's going on downstairs, and I figure maybe I better hold it awhile. I go back in the room and there's this guy, see, and he's taking the ropes offa the old lady. He raises his hands." Manny shrugged. "I gave him the gun. Anybody untying an old lady has got to be on the right side of things. He sent me upstairs."

Bishop came over, smoking a cigar. He put his hands on his hips, grinned, rolled the end of the cigar around his lips and took it out, let a wraith drift from his mouth and pull itself apart in the air. "You're Saul, right?"

"Manny. Manny Perlstein." Manny fingered his throat, shook his head. "I gotta tell you, officer, I didn't know nothing about this. Like I was saying, I was eatin' pie and drinkin' coffee. I drink too much coffee." He looked deep into the sky. "Maybe that's my problem. Drank decaf, I could keep a handle on things."

"We know who you are. There's an officer who'd like to talk to you. Nothing to worry about. You're going to get help."

"No drugs. They make my mouth dry."

"No drugs. Promise. Now, just go over to that man by the car there. That's the ticket." We watched Manny slouch off into the darkness.

"No drugs, my ass," Bishop said. He turned to me. "That was the stupidest butthead thing I've ever seen anyone do. Crashing in like that. You're damn lucky he didn't take your head off the minute you came through."

"You people didn't exactly seem to have a plan."

"Plan? We had a plan all right. That cop you knocked over was going to get inside, take care of Sinclair, and we were going to take everyone else out."

"What about the guy upstairs with Tryg and Grue? You going to leave that to fate?"

Bishop grinned. "We got a call from your friend Oscar early on, telling us that wasn't a problem anymore. If you hadn't run off to gab at that news woman, maybe Nashua might have had the chance to tell you."

"Oh." I felt uncommonly stupid.

"Anyway, probably better this way; only one guy bought it, and the rest will live to face justice." He replaced his cigar. "A lot of justice."

There was the sound of an argument inside, a male voice competing with Grue's. I excused myself and headed indoors.

"It's evidence, lady!" the cop was saying. "We gotta photograph it first."

Grue had a broom. "Nothing but little balls it is!" She saw me, jerked a thumb at the policeman. "With their shooting a mess they have left and now until pictures they have taken sweep I cannot? Evidence is this? Is mess." She started to sweep up the buckshot.

"Grue. Isn't there some blood you can mop up?"

"Oh, all right." And she stomped off.

Bangbang bang bang. The policemen in the room dropped, then relaxed when they recognized the sound. Smiles all around. I went to the kitchen and found Tryg at the stove, making popcorn.

"Tryg. What are you doing?"

"Master Jonathan!" He smiled. "Do you still want to trim the tree?" The paramedics had wanted to take him away for examination; they thought he exhibited signs of trauma. It took a lot of explaining to convince them he was always this way.

"Sure." I stood behind Trygve and gave the old man a hug. "We'll do the tree."

And we did just that.

I had made it through another episode without a scratch. Which, when I think about it, should have warned me.

Everyone had left by ten. I had waved good-bye and shut the door as though saying good-bye to departing relatives. I went back down the hall, looked around. Grue had swept and scrubbed. No indication that anything had happened, except, of course, for the dents in the armor, the phone that had been yanked out of the wall, the blasted windows and the line of automatic-weapon fire stitched in the wall upstairs.

Grue and Tryg were passed out by midnight. I was sitting at the hearth, watching the fire, unwilling to let the day go: I finally had control of it and was in no mood to relinquish it to something as random as sleep. There was a knock at the door—

And I knew who it was. And I didn't want to talk to her at all.

I slouched down the hall, yawning. Opened the door. Nothing prepared to say. Let her do all the apologizing.

There was a man with a wen the size of a medicine ball on his nose. The man who'd given me a ride to work in Valhalla that day when I'd written the famous column. Zeke. At his side was a thin young man with a pockmarked face.

"That's him, Paw," he said. "That's him all right."

"We saw you on TV this evening," said the man with the wen.

"Saw you and came right down," said his son.

I stepped back but the man put a hand on the door. "No you don't," he said. "I owe you something. You called my wife a lesbeen," he said—and his fist shot out and nailed me in the jaw. I staggered back against the door, felt the knob jab into my kidney. "Who—who—" I began. I saw him raise something above his head. I brought my hands above my head in time to absorb the blow and felt all the bones in my hands snap like green twigs. The blow knocked me to the ground, right onto my tailbone. We were playing all the favorites tonight. I tried to crawl backward into the house but the bat came down on me again, right in my stomach. "A lesbeen!" he cried, and whatever he said after that I'll never know: the bat cracked square into my skull. I was a small bug, and unconsciousness was an anvil dropped from a great height with perfect accuracy. I never even had the chance to apologize.

28

I woke on a clean harsh sheet. I turned my head and I saw an angel. I went back to sleep. I saw the angel in my dreams. When I woke, I saw it again. The window of Marvel Manor. I was looking down at it.

I bolted up in bed and screamed: I was in the hospital. Looking down on the angel. I was in the terminal ward.

A nurse bustled in and pushed me down into the bed, murmuring soothing words; there was another person in the room, something *ouch!* in my arm, sleep again, no angels.

Then a hand holding mine. My eyes opened. The world was

made of spun sugar and Vaseline, unreal. A confection with Sarah's features sat at the edge of the bed.

"Mmmrgh," I muttered.

"Don't speak."

"Want to. Lots to say."

"I know. That's why I don't want you to speak."

"Angel," I murmured.

"You're sweet."

"There." I raised a hand toward the manor. "Angel. Means I'm. Dying."

"What? No, no, Jay. You'll be fine, fine. Concussion. Broken arm and ribs. Nothing serious."

"Terminal ward."

"This?" She squeezed my hand. "I wondered about that too. But they're short on beds. There was a vacancy here."

I faded out. When I came back she was still there. I looked up at her.

I was almost grateful for the drugs; they kept me from speaking. But I had to know. I struggled to talk, like a paralyzed hand tapping at a telegraph terminal.

"Baby. Is there."

She looked away. "Yes, then. No, now."

My hand wandered across the sheet until it found hers. I tried to squeeze it. She either didn't notice or didn't care. I started to withdraw my hand but she grabbed it and held it tight.

"As much as I. Care for. You. Let's forget. That we. Met a second. Time."

"Oh, Jesus, Jay." She sat on the edge of the bed, smoothed the sheet. Daubed at her eyes. "I can't believe any of this, I don't want to. I didn't know about him. How could I have thought he'd done that?"

"Don't blame you." Goddamn. This was like trying to fit a dictionary on a business card.

"You have to know this, Jay. I wasn't kidding or fooling whenever we did . . . something. I wasn't. I wasn't trying to get him back through you. It was just all . . . confused."

"Only. Human," I stammered. "I under. Stand."

"Human is no excuse. It's the worst of them all. I feel so awful, so awful." She had one of my hands clasped between hers.

"At least. You. Didn't kill. Anybody."

Silence; Sarah's breathing, mine.

"Tell that," she said softly, "to little Zy."

I opened my eyes to tell her that wasn't how it was, she knew it, the feeling will pass, let me hold you. The room was empty, I was alone in the bed.

So would she be. Not right, not right at all.

I slept again, and if there were dreams I don't recall them.

I woke with a great thirst and rang for the nurse. I asked for water. She brought me a pitcher, poured a glass and told me why I was here. Zeke Gunderwein, now in police custody, had been softening my brainpan with a bat when Oscar returned from the police station. He had saved me again, wrestling me away from my attackers, bolting the door and calling the police. I had apparently been muttering "Zeke the lesbian" or words to that effect, and Oscar told the police to look for a Zeke.

Oscar had been released on his own recognizance just half an hour before, and he needed all the goodwill downtown he could accumulate.

He came to see me in the afternoon. Felt the sheets and made a face.

"Cotton poly blend. And they expect you to recuperate on that. Might as well wrap you in sandpaper." He looked out the window down at the manor, turned back to me. "Mind if I smoke? Thank you. So. How's that precious head of yours?"

"Ask me when the drugs wear off," I said, beaming. I felt slightly awake and, in general, wonderful.

"They tell you how you got here?"

"They did. And I say thank you, Oscar." I giggled. "How can I ever?"

"Well." He coughed. "Perchance you could let me keep living up in the attic."

I grinned. "Oh, that's fine. Happy to."

"After all," he said, "I've been there since you kicked me out. That was Uncle Marvel's catting room. He used to sneak whores in there. Steps go down to the basement. Entrance out back." He laughed. "When I took Grue up there she looked at me and said, 'You! You are the rats!' You must have heard me up there from time to time."

I nodded.

"Anyway. I'm not much trouble. And I did save your life. Do you mind awfully if I stay up there? I have a little jail to do, but when that is over it would be nice to have a home to . . . you know. Come home to."

I smiled. "You can stay." Everyone can stay. It was a big happy soft world and everyone could stay right where they were.

People came and went all day. I swam out of sleep to feel Grue's powdered face on mine, hear the words "Sleep you must and well you shall get." They had the ring of a dictum of Moses. When next I woke, I saw Tryg sitting at bedside, a checkers game set up on the tray. "They say you should keep busy to recover fast," he said. "I've already moved." I faded back to sleep. Three times I woke up and he was still sitting there, waiting.

I heard a mrrrgh once. Cracked my eyes apart to see something in a baggy stained sweatshirt, plaid pants, pacing the room. "It's not as if I expected it," the figure said. "From all indications she truly loved me. But Christmas Eve! What a day to choose to tell me it's over. I'm stunned. A bartender, mrrrgh. What in God's name does a bartender have that I don't? Not that I expect you to tell me. You're unconscious. That's why I'm telling you this. Everyone else will tell me I'm better off without her and that's the last thing I want to hear, by God almighty. Mrrrrrggh."

Later I saw something with short straight black hair. It bent down over me to kiss me on the forehead and I felt something metal hit me in the nose. Then something was laid on my neck. "You wear this for a while," said a voice. "I don't think Dad will mind." A male voice called her Katherine and said it was time to go.

Things swam, turned over, folded into darkness. "He's asleep," I heard another voice say.

"Better wake soon," said Solly. "We got an issue to put out and this is the cover story."

A hand fingered the object around my neck. "Love the cross," said Daphne. "Great accessory."

Day passed into night, thought better of it and retraced its steps to day again. I dreamed Jane was standing at the edge of my bed, talking. ". . . Of course I should've called, written, something, I don't know, I just felt so bad, and I can imagine what you were thinking, but I was so caught up in it all, the city, everything new, and then meeting Peter. . . . Anyway, we're married now, it was a nice ceremony . . . and I'm already bored. I don't think I did the right thing, Jonathan. He used *access* as a verb last night and I looked at him and realized I may have made the worst mistake of my life. But I can't tell you this because you'll hate me even more, I know, and I know it's cowardly, but if you were awake I don't know what I would say to you, I don't . . ."

The dream went on in this vein for some time. I lay there with my eyes closed, swaying in and out of consciousness. When the voice ceased, I opened my eyes; the door to my room was swinging on its hinges.

Sleep again. It was sunset when I woke. My mind felt wet, gray, the edges all unraveled. I felt it latch on to reality like someone pulling himself up a thick, bristling rope, hand over hand. When I felt in full possession of whatever faculties were currently on duty, I realized there was something soft and warm holding me, its face buried in my neck.

"You gotta get well," it was saying. "If you knew the trouble I went through to get here. The planes are all booked the day after Christmas, you know. My folks think I'm nuts, leaving like that. But I saw you on TV and I had to get back." Lips on my neck. "Wake up and apologize again. I'll listen. Promise. And then I'll apologize too. Come on, love. Wake up and let's not be jerks."

I opened my eyes. I was facing the manor. I turned away and faced her, and as proof of the level of chemicals in my blood or bruises on my brain, I looked at Marya and smiled and said: "Angel."

"Me? Angel? What drugs do they have you on?" I tried to answer but sailed back into sleep again. I woke up when the voice of a nurse, irritated as only a nurse can be, told someone that visiting hours were over, and get out of that bed. I snapped awake to find Marya lying on the bed, outside the covers, arms around me, sleeping. I grinned and lay my head back down and saw no need to sleep any more.